DESPERATE DESIRES

He turned her about and found her lips with his, his hands holding her body close.

"Oh, Nate, Nate . . ." Jette yielded to his embrace, her arms encircling him as she laid her head against his shoulder. "He wouldn't approve . . ." She clung to him, her body trembling with the sudden fires his nearness aroused.

"Is there someone else?" he asked. "Is that why he wouldn't approve?"

"No . . . yes . . ." she stammered.

"Which is it, darling?"

She raised her arms about his neck and replied, "Father's promised me to Asa." There was a note of desperation in her voice.

"And is that what you want?" His fingers touched her breast, softly, gently, in a caress she had never before known. "Tell me, Jette, is Asa what you want?"

Jette was aware only of Trasker's face dimly seen in the darkness, his strong arms around her, his mouth on hers, his hands arousing in her a violent physical longing.

"No," she whispered. "No, Asa is not what I want."

MARIA LUISA YEE

KATHALYN KRAUSE

LEISURE BOOKS ∞ **NEW YORK CITY**

Dedicated with love
to
Matilda
and
John Christen

A LEISURE BOOK

Published by

Dorchester Publishing Co., Inc.
6 East 39th Street
New York, NY 10016

Printed in the United States of America

Chapter 1

"One way ticket to San Francisco." Jette Allenby opened her silver-clasped handbag, counted out fare, and
thrust it under the brass grill of the ticket window. Her
black eyes filled with apprehension as a team and wagon
rattled into the graveled railway yard.

Harmon Phillips, the station agent, slapped his palm
over the money and sorted it into a cash drawer beneath
the counter. He allowed his spectacles to slip down his
nose far enough so that he might focus through them on
the ticket—and over them on the young woman. Her
dark auburn hair was piled high and topped by a wide-
brimmed green felt traveling hat. She was still out of
breath, her beautiful face flushed, her breast heaving.

"Intending to stay a good while, eh?" Phillips asked
as he folded and punched the ticket, then rechecked it
before handing it to her.

"You might say so," she replied and extended her
hand under the brass grill, not waiting for him to slide
the ticket across. From the rolling valley south of town
came a faint wail and hoot. Northbound 8:15, the morning freight and passenger train from Los Angeles, was
right on schedule.

"Thank you," the girl said as she turned from the
window and picked up a small brown leather valise from
the waiting room floor. She looked up nervously as a
horsedrawn surrey clattered into the dusty yard outside.
"I'll send for my trunk later," she whispered to the
agent.

"That'll be fine, Miss Allenby. We can ship by freight and arrange for delivery by dray. Send us word when you want it." The station agent glanced uneasily down a narrow road which ran almost parallel to the tracks. Already a low cloud of dust was visible as it steadily neared San Genaro station from the north.

Low hills south of town echoed the rumble of Northbound 8:15 which trailed a pall of smoke and steam as it approached the squat, mustard-yellow station. A frightened Jette Allenby lifted her skirt and petticoats with one hand, valise in the other, and ran down the passenger platform. She intended to board the train the instant it stopped. Once aboard, once the train pulled from the station, she would be safe. Even Elias Allenby could not catch her then. She gripped her valise and small handbag, and held aloof from other travelers who were gathered in a noisy group near the center of the platform. Desperation clutched at her throat—conversation would have been impossible. She waited in an agony of fear, her eyes never leaving the track.

"Hurry! Oh, please hurry," she silently pleaded as the huge engine burst from behind a screen of live oak and with a great hissing of steam thundered to a slow stop.

"San Genaro! San Genaro!" the station agent announced to those arriving, then rushed to assist the boarding passengers. From the corner of his eye he spied a buggy, pulled by a lathered team of sorrels, careen around the turn into the railroad yard. Elias Allenby flogged his horses with a bullwhip, his yells roaring loud in the quiet morning air. As the rancher reined his horses beside the platform, Agent Phillips caught sight of the shotgun.

Almost before his team halted, Allenby leaped from the buggy, the gun in his arms as much a part of him as the grizzled beard and hard, heavy body. In the dining cars, passengers neglected their sausage and eggs and stared from windows as the old man took the steps to the platform in two easy bounds.

"Jette!" Allenby's voice lashed at the girl as if it had been his bullwhip. Waiting passengers and railway men scrambled to safety in the train's vestibule.

The girl started in dismay, ran to the carriage door, grabbed the handrail to board. A metallic click told her the shotgun was cocked and ready; one glance told her it was aimed at her.

"Get down here, girl!" Elias commanded.

"I will not!" she spat with rage.

"I swear I'll shoot you where you stand!" The old man's voice was low, but his face was livid.

"You wouldn't dare!" Jette stared into twin barrels inches from her breast. The rough finger on the trigger tightened. The barrels moved closer. Diners deserted the windows and took cover.

"Go ahead. I might as well be dead anyhow." Jette dared him to commit cold-blooded murder before the horrified witnesses staring from train and station.

"By the Lord, Jette, if you don't get into that buggy, I will." His words were quiet. The whole station held its breath.

Agent Phillips tiptoed from the baggage room to the platform, his eyes flicking between the open loading door and the shotgun-wielding rancher. Should trouble start, he wanted to be well out of the way. When first he saw Elias coming, he should have sent for the sheriff. Without a gun, Elias Allenby was dangerous; armed, he was a menace.

"What the hell's going on over there, Harmon?" The baggage handler slid the compartment door back another foot and peared cautiously around it.

"Rancher north of town come to get his daughter—take her back home." Phillips swung down

7

three crates of cheeping baby chicks and placed them inside the station out of the sun. "Most likely she'll go peaceable. Has before, but one of these days . . ." He flattened himself against the wall and maneuvered to a better view.

Elias Allenby's eyes were of a cold, icy blue, pale in his browned and leathery face. "I'll not have my own daughter disgrace me by behaving like some cheap Hurley Road slut," he growled. "Your mother's behind all this—don't bother denying it. And believe what I say, she'll answer to me for it."

"You wouldn't hurt Mother!" Jette gasped as his meaning became clear. She paled as she confronted his scowl.

"She'll answer to me," he repeated, his eyes narrowing.

For a moment Jette hesitated, her face now white in the golden early morning light, her black eyes clouded with indecision. All too well she recognized the threat. Should she leave, her mother would suffer. She could not abandon her mother—not even for her own freedom.

Reluctantly she descended from the steps of the passenger coach. Twin gun barrels brushed the twisted frogs that closed the jacket of her green silk traveling suit. She was almost desperate enough to wish her father would pull the trigger.

"Get into the buggy," she heard Elias command, but her mother's words kept echoing inside her head: "Go away! Go away now, before it's too late. Your father intends to marry you off to Asa and you'll have no say in it. You'll wind up just like me—a prisoner in a nightmare!" Jette hesitated, valise in hand.

"That's right, Daughter. That's being sensible." Elias Allenby was pleased by his easy victory. Threats of retaliation against Verdie proved useful in handling

Jette. It had worked before; it worked this time. And Elias had already instructed Asa Beemer in the art of intimidation as it applied to the Allenby women.

As Jette climbed into the light phaeton, the station agent threw open the side door of the warehouse and wheeled out a cart to receive crates of summer dimity and lawn consigned to Raizes Department Store.

"That poor girl," Agent Phillips muttered as he watched Jette slump in defeat beside her father.

"From all I hear, she ain't poor," the baggage handler laughed. "Not by no way of figuring. Don't old Allenby own the best land in the county? And I heard over to the cattle auction last week that he's got himself more of them fancy blooded Scotch Angus than any spread west of the Rockies. No sir, I don't see how you can call that girl poor!"

"It's according to what you call poor, Amos," the agent replied.

* * * *

The expensive matched team of sorrels pranced west on Calle Aluin, then turned and headed north on San Genaro Road. No longer goaded by the stinging bullwhip or harrassed by Elias's urging, they picked their way, daintily high-stepping back to the Allenby ranch. Jette and her father rode for a good mile in silence as the buggy jiggled and bumped along the dusty ruts of the highway.

Finally Jette asked, "Why must you treat me as if I were one of your prize heifers? Have I no rights? Are my wishes never to be considered?"

"You have no rights, Daughter. Until you reach twenty-five you'll have no money of your own and you'll do as I say." Elias refused to look at her or to meet her angry black eyes. "Or until you're married."

"To Asa Beemer?" Jette pronounced the name with fury.

"I gave him my word, and you'll not make me a liar." Elias' face was immobile, the deep lines about his eyes and mouth set with rage. "Yes, by damn, to Asa Beemer!" He settled back into the leather-upholstered seat, pulled from his shirt pocket a thin black Mexican cigar which he clamped between his teeth unlighted.

"I loathe the man!" she exploded. "How could you promise him such a thing without even consulting me? Have I no say in my own future? Not even as to whom I shall marry?" Jette eyed the shotgun in her father's lap. If only she had the nerve to use it to settle her dispute with him—just as he had used it in the past to resolve his own quarrels—but she had inherited none of his ruthlessness.

He caught her glance, the chuckle in his throat sounding more like a growl. "Don't consider such an act, Jette. Juries are just as quick to hang a woman as a man." The scathing ridicule made her even more furious.

"If juries were made up of women, we'd see some justice!" Jette retorted.

"And what would you do with it? Hang a few men you couldn't run to suit yourself?" He slapped the reins on the sorrels' rumps and stared across the roadside fence to the top of a low chain of hills in the distance. Silhouettes of sleek Angus cattle, black and square against lush green spring pasture, attested to his own sound judgment and business acumen. "I'm sixty-eight years old. I intend to see that when I go, my estate will be in the hands of someone I trust."

"And you don't trust Mother or me?" she asked.

"I watched what happened twenty years ago—in Texas and Wyoming—when women tried the cattle business," Elias answered. "I don't aim to leave my holdings to be run by females." It was final. There was never discussion with him. His own opinion was all that mattered; his wishes, the only ones worthy of consideration. He had made his own world, and he molded it to his choice.

Dry-eyed, Jette mulled over in her mind events of the morning. How had her father discovered she had fled? At daybreak he had ridden out to the east pasture to check the new heifers with Asa Beemer and some of the Mexican hands. Not even Elvira, their young housemaid, had known of her leaving.

Jette had looked back at the house as she hurried down the graveled driveway and into the main road. She would walk to San Genaro and take the northbound 8:15 train. Later her mother would send along the trunk they had so hopefully packed the day before. Her mother had stood on the veranda steps, one hand raised in farewell. There had been no tears, no hesitation as Jette waved back, then quickly passed out of sight behind the eucalyptus hedge that screened the ranch buildings and rambling, balconied adobe house from the county highway.

"Get away now, while you've got the chance," her mother had said as she took every last coin from her cache behind dusty, shelved volumes of Bronte and Thackery in the back parlor, the once place secure from Elias Allenby's scrutiny. "I'll be happier just knowing you're far away from him, making a life for yourself. Go now, before your father comes back."

Verdie had pushed the money into her hand. "Once you're on the road, keep going as fast as you can. If your father comes back early, I'll make some excuse for you. He won't know the difference until you're halfway to San Francisco." The woman's fear of her husband was less than her determination to see her daughter escape.

They had hugged each other and parted under the somber live oak which shaded the south side of the house. Already the air was redolent of blue gum and pepper trees baking in the hot sun.

"Don't write. At least not for a while," Verdie had said. "No need to have him know where you are and make trouble."

Jette had hurried down the dusty drive toward the main road. Beside her mother a long-legged mongrel and a fat spaniel stood, their tails describing slow arcs as they whined at her departure.

Perspiration had trickled down her face and wilted the high, boned, lace collar of her white silk pongee blouse. More than once she had stumbled in the rough gravel of the roadbed, and her breath had come hard as she raced toward town. No one had passed her going either way.

But someone had seen her leave. And someone had informed her father. It was useless to speculate, for she had been forced to return, humiliated, and face both the anger of Elias and the loathsome presumptuousness of Asa Beemer.

Now as the phaeton turned into the Allenby ranch drive, Jette recognized the slouch of Beemer's figure near the side door of the house. He was awaiting their arrival, his wide-brimmed felt hat pulled low over his eyes against the morning sun. Of course—it had to be Asa who had seen her leave. Hatred and resentment welled within Jette as she saw the man step into the drive as they neared.

"Morning, Miss Jette." Beemer's lean face broke into a wry smile as he came to the side of the buggy and offered to hand her down. She recoiled from him and waited for her father to get out of the carriage, then followed him on the side opposite Beemer.

"You were spoken to, girl," Elias said, his tone implying that for her own good she should answer the man.

Her dark eyes blazed with anger. "Yes, spoken to by a sneak—an unprincipled gossip who can't mind his own business," she shot back.

"You *are* his business, just as anything else on this ranch, and don't you forget it," Elias countered as he grabbed the small leather valise before Jette could take it. He handed it to Asa Beemer and motioned toward the house.

The young woman drew herself up and faced the two men. "I'd rather die than be any business of his!" The venom stung Beemer. His expression hardly changed, but he shifted the valise from one hand to the other and looked away from the girl.

"I'll settle with you directly, Jette." Elias took her arm and brutally turned her into the path which led to the house. "This time I'll teach you a lesson about whose business you are and just how far you can go with me."

She stumbled in the walkway, but Elias gripped her arm in his hard hands and yanked her to her feet. When she started for the side door, he dragged her along the path which led to the rear of the house, then pushed her before him and up the outdoor staircase which led to the upper floor of the adobe.

As they neared the top of the steps Pecky and Buff dashed wildly after them, squirming and yelping excitedly, their barks echoing hollowly down the hall which ran at a right angle to the stairs. The dogs' joyous welcome was short lived.

"Get out of here!" Elias shouted and kicked at the animals, missing them, but sending them to whine and cringe against the wall.

"Leave them alone." Jette bent to comfort the dogs, who pawed and wriggled close to her, their wet tongues licking at her hands and face.

"Into that room, girl!" Elias ordered as he flung open a door on the north side of the upstairs hallway.

"I won't!" she cried as he grabbed her and thrust her into the room. Briefly she struggled with him, wrenching from his grasp only to be struck a sideways blow with the flat of his hand which sent her sprawling to the floor, stunned. Asa Beemer stepped around her and placed the valise on the foot of the bed, the wry smile returning to his dark face.

"We'll see what you will or won't do," Elias said. "I'll not have a daughter of mine running off behind my back and behaving like some common whore!" He stood over her, his great fists clenched, his face contorted with uncontrolled rage. "And I promise you one thing, girl—I'll see to it your mother pays for her part in this little escapade. I'll not have my wife and daughter disgrace me in the eyes of this community."

Jette only half heard the words, but his meaning penetrated her dizziness and confusion. Dimly she was aware of the door slamming and the metallic click of a key in the lock. Slowly she pulled herself up onto the bed and stretched herself across the quilted coverlet, gathering the pillow to bury her sobs in its softness. She could hear her father's boots pounding down the stairs. Outside her room Pecky and Buff returned to keep vigil and scratch disconsolately at the door. Having once given way to weeping, Jette found it impossible to stop.

It was almost noon when Jette awakened. She felt exhausted and dull as she rose from the bed and looked at herself in the mirror over the washstand. Her eyes were reddened, the lids puffy and pink. She fingered a discolored swelling on her left cheek. Taking a small linen handtowel from the rack, she dipped it in the water pitcher and held the cool compress to her face.

At the sound of footsteps on the stairs she ran to the

locked door. "Mother? Is that you?" she called, her hope for release rising.

The steps advanced along the second-floor veranda and toward the short hallway. As she listened, Jette realized the tread was much too heavy for Verdie's. Whoever it was, stopped outside the window of her room—the window which took its light and air from the veranda. The girl pulled back the curtain and peered out.

"What are you doing?" she cried out in alarm.

"Doing what I'm told, Miss Jette. Just doing what I'm told." Asa Beemer closed the outside shutters of the window, took several three-inch nails from his pocket and began to drive them into the wood, effectively sealing off the window. In between blows of the hammer he laughed, "I don't like this any more'n you do, but you know old Elias, once his mind's made up."

After the job was done, he leaned against the shutters and said quietly, "Now if you get too lonesome in there all by yourself. . ." He dropped his voice to a whisper. "Elias gave me the key to the door. You just say the word, and I'll come right in and see that you don't stay lonesome." He waited for her reply and getting none, he continued, "Elias, he won't mind . . . maybe tonight . . . ."

"Never! Not tonight . . . not ever!" She pounded with her fists at the shutters, her protest rising to a shriek, "I'd die first!" Beemer's soft laughter outside the darkened window brought her to tears.

"That'd be a terrible waste, Miss Jette," Beemer said as he turned to leave. "I'll come up this evening and see if you're still of the same mind. Who knows, maybe by then you might like to spend the night in my room." He tapped on the shutters with his knuckles and started down the veranda.

Daylight was now cut out by the closed shutters,

leaving the room in darkness. In complete despair, Jette crouched by the window as soon as Beemer left. The lower pane, closed early in the morning against the heat of most days, had been left open this morning in her haste to get away. She could feel the hot air rushing through the louvers, and from the front patio of the garden below she could hear men's voices. She strained to catch the sound. Carefully she pried at the louvers, expecting them to be nailed shut also, but was surprised to find them still movable.

Asa Beemer had neglected part of his chore.

Through the lower slits she could look down into the flagstone patio where Elias and Asa were standing. Asa still held the hammer. Beside him stood Elias, his shock of gray hair and heavy, powerful build contrasting Beemer's dark leanness. Their laughter was loud in the quiet noontime. Elias gestured toward the upstairs bedroom. Jette held her breath for fear he would notice the opened louvers. He did not. Instead, he reached into the breast pocket of his leather vest and offered Beemer a cigar. Striking a match on the seam of his rough trousers, Beemer held the light for Elias, then touched it to his own cigar. Pungent smoke wafted upward. Although Jette could hear their ridiculing laughter and smell their cigars, she could not be sure what they were saying. Just enough breeze disturbed the live oak leaves to drown out their words, but she could guess at their conversation.

"I will *not* marry him. I will not!" she whispered aloud. Rage grew within her as she watched her father clap the younger man on the shoulder and then shake hands with Beemer as they parted, Beemer heading for the cattle barn and Elias back toward the house. Beemer's swagger infuriated the girl. Its implication was obvious.

Somewhere downstairs a door slammed. A woman's

voice, shrill with fear, rose in a wail, then dropped to a moan as something thumped solidly against a wall. Jette wanted to scream out—but to whom? Who was there in the house—or on the entire ranch—to rescue them from Elias' cruelty? For several minutes the voices continued, punctuated by the sounds of blows.

Jette threw herself on the bed and held her hands over her ears, overwhelmed by the utter helplessness of her situation.

Was there never to be an escape?

Chapter 2

The train from San Francisco, a few minutes ahead of schedule, rumbled to a stop at San Genaro Station. Elias Allenby stood back from the railbed only far enough for safety. No other passengers were boarding, none disembarking, but there was a great commotion at the end of the loading platform. A consignment of tackle blocks, sulky plows, grub hoes, and manure forks for Joe's Hardware and Ranch Supply were being off-loaded and shunted into the storeroom at the far end of the building. Lanterns shed yellow pools of light in the immediate work area, and lamplight shone from a few of the scattered houses west of the rail yards, but a moonless dark engulfed the sparsely inhabited east side of town. To the north on Hurley Road, Harriet Selby's establishment blazed with a brilliant glow from the lower floor while a tinny roller piano hammered out mechanical, jazzy rag. Upstairs, the windows remained discreetly draped and curtained.

Elias, impatient to board and complete the first leg of his journey, paced alongside the passenger car. If he were not headed for Iowa, a night at Harriet's would be an allowable diversion. She ran an honest enough game—faro, stud, fan-tan—and her girls were reasonably clean. But the magnificent Aberdeen Angus bull up for auction in Osceola took precedence over Harriet's pleasures.

"You understand, Benito, the ladies are not to have any of the buggies or wagons?" Elias Allenby asked.

"Oh, yes, sir. And we are not to saddle horses for them." The slight Mexican handed the last piece of luggage to the porter and turned back to his employer. "I understand perfectly." His naturally grave demeanor obscured the fact that he had no desire to smile. He removed his floppy straw hat and said, "Goodbye, Mr. Allenby." He then glanced at the younger man waiting in the vestibule of the railway coach and added, "Mr. Beemer, have a good trip."

Beemer nodded and said, "Thanks, Benito. Keep a sharp eye on those new heifers in the east pasture, hear?" The ranch foreman, uncomfortable in a narrow-lapeled suit which he reserved for business and funerals, adjusted the angle of his new wide-brimmed hat and opened the door to the passenger compartment. "And tell the men to shoot those damned dogs from La Coruna if they start bothering again. If the sheriff doesn't like it, tell him to see me when I get back."

"Yes, sir, I'll do that," Benito agreed.

Elias hesitated before boarding the train. He was reluctant to leave his wife and daughter alone on the ranch, not so much because of any danger to them—there had been neither Indian nor Mexican troubles for two decades—but because both Verdie and Jette were becoming openly defiant of his authority. Their growing independence disturbed him, especially when threatened—or actual—physical reprisal no longer controlled them.

"Neither one of 'em, Benito," Elias admonished the old man.

"Yes?" Benito called back, wondering what Allenby meant.

"Neither of 'em is to leave the ranch. You see to it," Elias commanded, then swung himself up the metal steps.

"Yes, sir, I'll do that," Benito Galvan repeated as he stepped back from the train and held his hand up in farewell. The engine thundered to life and roared steam into the crisp night air. "Don't worry about the ranch, sir. Have a good trip," he shouted as the train began moving from the station.

Elias' tall, heavy figure disappeared into the car, followed by Asa Beemer, who held the door open for the rancher to enter. A red lantern at the far end of the train ceased its waving gyrations and the sliding door to the station warehouse shut, its noise silent within the noise of the rolling train.

Until the red lights of the last car disappeared behind the live oaks south of the sleeping town, the elderly man stood by the rails, watching. He must return to the ranch and tell Mrs. Allenby what her husband had decreed. Shaking his dark head, he climbed into the surrey and gently urged the magnificent sorrels into a slow trot.

* * * *

"Mrs. Allenby, please don't ask me to do it," the elderly servant curled the straw hat brim in his gnarled hands. "Mr. Allenby was very positive. It would mean my job—and my wife's too—if I went against his orders." There was pain in his deep-set eyes, pain both for himself and for the wife of his employer. Lines from private sorrow which creased his thin face deepened with sympathy for the woman.

"All right, Benito. I won't press the matter. I can't have you or your family suffer for our sake." Verdie Allenby touched the old man's arm. "I understand how it is. It isn't your fault. Thank you anyway. I know you'd help us if you could." She turned from the door and walked slowly into the front parlor.

Early morning sunlight brightened the silvery tops of the eucalyptus hedge which bordered the road. Splashes of cool light spilled into the patio just beyond the front windows. Heat was already building up outside, but the adobe house retained the chill of night. Verdie stood by the window which looked into the dusty patio. In an iris bed which lined the flagstones, purple finches and white-crowned sparrows darted about like nervous, feathered mice. She pulled back the lace curtains and watched the birds, her face registering no emotion.

"They're so free. . .they can fly away. . .no one can stop them if they want to go. . ." The woman's voice was flat, as unexpressive as her wan, immobile face.

Jette came to stand by her mother and watched the fluttering, chattering flock. For a long moment they observed the busy searching and scratching amidst the debris. The girl sighed and turned from the window.

"I'm not flying away, Mother. I merely want to be around other people, to hear other talk and laughter. I want something—anything—to get me out of here for a while every day. And a chance to be with people my own age, too."

"I know, dear. I meant that the birds. . ." Verdie stopped and looked confused, as if uncertain as to what she had meant. Blankness became bewilderment.

"I know what you mean," Jette hastened to say before her mother became more uneasy. To change the trend of Verdie's tangled thoughts she asked, "Will Benito have the buggy ready for me by eight-thirty? I want to be in town by half-past-nine or so." She stopped as she saw the look on her mother's face. "Mother, what's wrong?" she asked.

"Benito can't hitch up the buggy for you, Jette."

"Then one of the other men . . ." the girl said, then stopped in mid-sentence as she saw Verdie shaking her head. "Why not?"

"Your father left orders with Benito that we're not to have the buggies or the horses—not until he gets back. None of the men is supposed to help us . . . we're prisoners . . ." Verdie wrung her hands and began pacing the length of the parlor.

"Then I'll have to walk," Jette said quietly. She could quite easily harness the horses herself, but knew only too well the viciousness of her father's retribution when crossed. She would not risk causing trouble for any of the hands.

It was well past ten o'clock when Jette paused in front of the angled display windows of Raizes Department Store on McKinley Street. She glanced into the wide glass to inspect her reflection. A small teal blue grosgrain hat brought out the rich auburn of her hair; a deep brown daytime suit with ruffled lace jabot and snug bolero emphasized her slim, high-bosomed figure. Since she was in town strictly on business, she carried no parasol, only a neat handbag of tapestry cloth in shades of teal and maroon. The hems of her skirt and petticoats were dusty from the long walk into town, as were her kidskin boots, but it could not be helped. With one final surreptitious look at her image in the window she opened the door and went in, head high, chin tilted to convey confidence she did not feel.

"Where is Mr. Raizes' office, please?" Jette asked of the lanky young clerk who appeared from behind the men's shirt counter.

"I'll be happy to show you, Miss Allenby," he replied and smiled. "Right this way, please." He sidled in front of her and took the lead to the rear of the store and up a short flight of steps. Glass-enclosed offices lined one side of a narrow balcony where the proprietor might survey the main floor without rising from his desk. Several men bookkeepers, bent over accounts in the office adjacent to the owner's, looked up as the clerk conducted Jette to the door. He knocked sharply, waited briefly for a loud, "Come!" which was shouted over noise of typewriters and hand-cranked adding machines.

"Ah, good morning, Miss Allenby." David Raizes rose from his wide roll-top oak desk and pulled back a chair for the girl, then dismissed the young clerk with a nod. "Won't you please sit down?" Raizes waited for her to be seated before he resumed his place behind the cluttered desk. "How may I be of service to you?" he asked.

"I want a job," Jette said with a directness that the man found amusing.

"What? In my store?" He chuckled at the idea.

"Yes, I want a job." She looked across the room at the stenographers and bookkeepers who in turn were staring at her. Elias Allenby's beautiful daughter was known by sight to almost everyone in San Genaro, and the fact that she would come to David Raizes for a job was worthy of attention. Jette smiled back at them and turned to their employer. "I'm willing to learn anything at all. I could clerk—sell ladies' clothing, children's things. Or perhaps I could do office work," she continued.

"I believe you're in earnest, Miss Allenby." Raizes leaned forward on his desk, hands clasped, eyes twinkling with his unvoiced laughter. He could not picture wealthy Elias Allenby's sole heir selling underwear and corsets or sitting at a typewriter from 7:30 in the morning until 6:00 at night.

"I am very much in earnest," Jette assured him.

"But why? Why should you want to take a job, my dear? Surely it isn't for necessity." The merchant shifted in his chair and shuffled a few papers which lay on the desk top. His aristocratic face betrayed his discomfort.

"Perhaps it isn't necessity as you mean it, Mr. Raizes, but it *is* a necessity for me." She longed to explain to him her desperate need, but only continued, "I'm willing to undergo an apprenticeship period, working and learning until I can prove myself capable."

"You put me in an embarrassing position, I'm afraid," Raizes said. "I might put you on—purely temporary, of course—to replace one of our young ladies who must take a leave of absence to attend to family matters."

"Then why should you be embarrassed? I ask no special consideration."

"Miss Allenby, unless I knew your father completely approved of the arrangement—approved, and was in no way opposed—I couldn't possibly promise you a position with us." The man adjusted his pince-nez spectacles on the thin bridge of his nose and peered at the girl. "Tell me the truth, please. Does he approve?"

"I haven't asked him. I don't see how it matters one way or the other whether or not he approves." Jette was close to anger not because she was being refused, but because even in this mild attempt to gain a measure of freedom for herself, her father stood in her way. The frustrating unfairness of the situation incensed her.

"My dear Miss Allenby. . ." The man gestured with his delicate hands to illustrate his helplessness. "Your father is a . . . a . . ." He found it necessary to choose

23

his words carefully. " . . . a very influential man. A very positive one. He is powerful in this valley and I must endeavor to keep on good terms with all our businessmen, ranchers and townspeople alike, for my own trade to prosper. You will forgive me if I speak frankly?" He waited for her assent.

"Of course. I'd appreciate your being honest with me," she replied with a touch of rancor.

"Should I do something—anything—to displease your father, take some action which would bring down criticism upon my establishment, I should endanger the livelihood of not only myself, but of every one of my employees." There was no longer any hint of humor in the man's expression. Across the room the machines had become unnaturally quiet as their operators found reasons to postpone their tasks to listen. Jette became aware of their near-hostile glances as they heard Raizes' explanation. It was obvious to them that Jette Allenby had no need of a position, but would, indeed, take away the livelihood of one who really did need it. Just a lark, they would later tell their friends as they recounted her visit.

"And if you hired me, gave me a job—any job—it would hurt your business?" Jette asked in surprise.

"I'm afraid it could. Yes, it more than likely would," he agreed. "Now if your father wholeheartedly approved . . ." He did not finish. Jette rose from her chair, her face flushed with disappointment and anger.

"I see! Since I'm Elias Allenby's daughter, I'm not to be given a chance to prove myself," Jette said quietly. She turned to leave the office. "Yes, I see very clearly how it is."

"That is not quite what I mean," Raizes protested.

"But that is how I must take it. I'm sure my interpretation is close to your intent." The girl reached for the door knob. "I don't wish to cause you any trouble.

Thank you for your time.''

Four hours later as she walked along Union Avenue toward the Central Ranchers and Shippers Bank, Jette mentally cataloged the results of her efforts. Five interviews—five refusals. Even Abe Marley at the county courthouse had refused to add her name to his list of applicants for county positions.

"Now, Miss Allenby, first thing you know, you'll be married and busy raising a family. All that good training the county would give you would just go to waste," Marley had said as he rolled a thick green Cuban cigar between his long fingers, held it to his nose and sniffed. "Your father would never in this world hold for you becoming an ordinary working girl. You know that, don't you?" He refrained from lighting up while she remained in the office, but he was not impatient for her to go. Marley had dealt with female job applicants before and found it congenial enough. The trouble this time was that it was not a militant suffragette or overeducated schoolteacher with ambition, but old Elias Allenby's daughter. Trouble came too easily in San Genaro County without courting it. He would be charming, polite, and gentle, but he would send Jette Allenby home.

"It seems everyone has far greater consideration for my father than for me," Jette said hotly. "Are my wishes of no consequence?" Then more calmly she asked, "What if I agree to stay a certain length of time on whatever job is given me? I may sign an affidavit to that effect, may I not?"

"Child, you could sign it, but most likely it wouldn't mean a thing. You're a mighty pretty girl and some man's gonna . . ."

"In other words, my guarantee is suspect—and I'm not to be given a chance." She was now hurt and furious. If Abe Marley would not, or could not, help her, to whom could she turn?

Marley's shrewd eyes caught the slight trembling of her chin as she strove to master her disappointment. He rose from his chair behind the desk. "Believe me, I'm sorry this is the way it has to be. You must try to understand my position." He sat on the edge of the desk and crossed his arms as he looked down at her. "To put it bluntly, your father is a difficult man at best, and I can't afford to get on the wrong side of him. As chairman of the Board of Supervisors I need his support on some measures the county is proposing."

"But what has that to do with me?" Jette asked.

"I know Elias well enough to realize he'd take it as a very personal affront if I went behind his back to give you a job." The politician paused in his explanation long enough to grip the girl's shoulder and say, "If you can get him to agree to your working for me, you bring him around and we'll work something out between us. Is that fair enough?" There was always an outside chance the old man would come around; it would be wise to have a point of obligation between them, and Marley had to admit it would be pleasant to have the lovely Jette nearby. "Well, what do you think? Is that fair?" he asked.

"I don't term it fair, but I do see what you mean, Mr. Marley," she answered. "You've been very kind to see me, at least you told me the truth. For that I'm grateful." Jette arranged her skirts preparatory to leaving and noticed her dusty boots once more. Her long walk to town, her canvassing the larger business establishments and offices, had all been in vain. "Thank you for talking with me," she said as she rose to go.

"A privilege, I assure you, Miss Allenby," the man smiled and ushered her out the door into a polished marble hallway. He waited until she was far down the

26

staircase before he struck a match to his cigar.

Jette retraced her steps to the corner of Grant Street and Union Avenue where the Central Bank dominated the district. It was almost three o'clock, nearly closing time, but if she hurried she might be able to see Ainsworth Millege before returning home. She was too tired and disheartened to bother looking at her reflection in Raizes Department Store windows as she passed by.

The afternoon had grown progressively hotter, with a dry desert wind whipping down from mountains east of the valley. Dust swirled along the narrow sidewalks and wide streets. She regretted not bringing her parasol, for the sun would still be blazing during her long walk home. The bank's cool interior was welcome relief as she entered and headed for the president's office.

Jette paused uncertainly before the low oak rail which enclosed a small, open waiting room occupied by a low settee, a pair of grotesquely-upholstered leather chairs and sand-filled urn from which protruded the day's collection of cigarette and cigar butts.

"Did you want to see Mr. Millege?" asked the chief teller as he stuck his head around the pillared and grilled counter which abutted the banker's private office. "He has someone with him right now."

"Yes, I would like to speak with him, please," Jette replied and turned to one of the bulky chairs as the teller pressed an electric buzzer to let Millege know he had a vistor.

The door to the office burst open suddenly, barely missing the girl. A young man stepped from the office just as she pivoted to avoid the door. For a brief moment Jette stood looking up at him, annoyed at his clumsiness—until she saw the crutches from which he swung his weight. She stared, not from rudeness, but from surprise. His tall, muscular frame and wide, lean

27

face seemed incongruous with infirmity.

"I'm so sorry," she stammered, flushed with embarrassment.

"You needn't be. It's my fault entirely. I beg your pardon . . . I always seem to forget there may be someone on the other side of a door," he laughed. His smile pulled at his wide jaws and square chin, lifting his full lips unevenly in an expression of both amusement and pleasure. He shifted his weight and sidestepped out of the entry.

Ainsworth Millege joined them from inside his office. Holding the door open with one hand, he extended the other to the girl. "Such a pleasure to see you, Miss Allenby." The banker glanced at the young man and continued, "Have you met our new doctor? He's taking over Doctor Hill's practice."

"No, I haven't," she answered. She did not wait for Millege to introduce them properly—did not even see the banker's welcoming hand. She offered her own hand instead to the stranger and said, "I'm Jette Allenby."

"Hello, Jette Allenby." The young doctor leaned heavily on one crutch and took her hand, his deep blue eyes memorizing the oval of her face, her dark eyes with their message of trouble. "Miles Hunter," he stated his name without relinquishing her hand. "I'm delighted to meet you." Afternoon sunlight, sifting through slatted blinds at the west windows, ignited gold and copper in her halo of auburn hair.

Millege allowed them only what he considered a proper time before he interrupted their meeting. "Don't hesitate to call on me any time, Doctor," the banker said, dismissing the young man diplomatically before he turned to Jette and asked, "And now, my dear, may I flatter myself that this is a social call—or is it to be business?" Millege had to wait for a reply.

"Good day, Miss Allenby. I hope to see you again soon," Miles Hunter said as he pushed the low, swinging oak gate back and headed for the main entrance.

"Goodbye, Doctor Hunter," Jette said, and found herself smiling for the first time that day. She looked after him as he maneuvered through the wide double door and out into the street. Ainsworth Millege cleared his throat and pushed the door to his office back with just enough force to make it bump against the door stop. Jette looked around, the smile fading as she recalled her mission to the banker.

"Please come in," Millege invited as he closed the door behind them. He pulled up a plush-cushioned chair and placed it close by him. "Do sit down," he urged.

"Won't it be hard for him?" Jette asked.

"Hard? I'm afraid I don't understand." Millege was puzzled.

"For Doctor Hunter to take over Hill's practice," Jette explained. "How can he manage to get around? I mean, just getting in and out of a buggy would be so difficult." She felt color rush into her face as she asked about the man.

"I would imagine it would prove most awkward," Millege agreed. He had not missed the sudden blush and realized its meaning. "Fine chap, that Hunter." He looked closely at Jette and saw that it pleased her to hear him praised. "Hurt in a railway accident back in Ohio, but it didn't stop him from finishing his internship and starting his practice. Good stuff," he said.

"But will he be that way always?" Jette asked.

"The experts he's consulted say yes; he says no. I'd place my bet on him." Millege smiled at the girl. "He felt the climate out here in California would be better for him and made arrangements to buy out Doctor Hill. Simple as that." He knew that was what the girl wanted

29

to learn. "Now then, young lady, would you like a cup of tea?"

"Oh, no, Mr. Millege, I'm afraid I've come purely on business," Jette said as she seated herself and straightened her skirt beneath her. "I've been trying to find myself a job today." She seemed to expect Millege to fathom her meaning from her statement.

"Did you indeed?" The banker suppressed amusement at the idea. "And did you succeed?" he asked as he resumed his place behind the elaborate mahogany desk.

"No," Jette replied quickly. "I've been given the same advice by everyone I talked with today." Anger snapped in her expressive black eyes.

"And what would that advice be?" he asked.

"To go home and get married!" Her fury was obvious. "I even went to the courthouse to see Abe Marley."

"You'd take a position with the county?" the banker asked with surprise.

"Mr. Millege, I'll take any job short of Hurley Road," she said defiantly. Even the mere pronunciation of the notorious street's name raised Millege's eyebrows.

"But you were turned down?" he asked to cover his embarrassment.

"By everyone, yes," she answered.

"Are you qualified in any line of work? Aside from managing a household, which I'm sure you could do admirably." There was affectionate condescension in his question.

"No, I suppose not, but I'm willing to learn and nobody will even consider me," Jette replied. "Mr. Marley would only go so far as to say if Father gave permission for me to work, a place might be found for me with the county."

"That sounds reasonable to me," Millege defended the politician's suggestion. The banker, too, knew Elias Allenby.

"Well, it doesn't sound reasonable to me!" Jette countered, her chin close to trembling once more. "It's humiliating. Why on earth should I be required to have his leave?"

"Didn't they explain their reasons?" Millege queried, but he could imagine what they might have told her.

"Yes, they did," the girl said. "They feel Father would be against it and they don't want to do anything that would anger him. But it isn't fair! I have a right to a life of my own choosing, haven't I?"

It was a moment before the banker could phrase his answer properly. "I'm certain your father has your own good in mind. Perhaps he feels you're not accustomed to the life of a working girl . . . he wouldn't want to see you disadvantaged. And, of course, your father has mentioned several times to me that you're to be married soon to Asa Beemer . . ."

Jette jumped to her feet, her fists clenched in fury. "Never!" she almost shouted. "Never. How dare he tell you such a thing?" She gripped the back of the chair. "Oh, don't you see? That's why I must have a job—to get away from both of them." She turned to the elderly banker, her beautiful face pale with rage. "I despise Asa Beemer! I want my *own* life, not one arranged by Father. I will *not* be parceled off like a piece of property." Despite her defiance, the tears she had fought off all afternoon now welled in her dark eyes.

"Now, now," the man put his arms about her and eased her back into her chair. "I'm sure your father only wants what's best for you. Asa Beemer's a dependable, hard-working man." He did not need to add that Elias Allenby would never tolerate a ranch foreman who did not measure up to his qualifications.

"You said this was to be a business call," he reminded the girl. He was uneasy with her outburst. "What was it you wanted to see me about?" The banker was eager to lead the conversation onto safer ground.

"According to Grandmother's will, I'm not to inherit until I'm twenty-five." Jette dabbed at her eyes with a lace-edged handkerchief. "And I know there's nothing you can do to alter that . . ." She paused, as if hopeful he would contradict her.

"No, under specific terms of her will you can't touch any part of the estate until you reach the age of twenty-five or are married, whichever comes first. And it's most unlikely any of the terms would be set aside by the court," Millege stated.

"But isn't there something? Mother says she's sure there's a clause which stipulates that you have discretionary powers in handling the estate until that time, and that under certain circumstances I may be able to withdraw funds if it's for my betterment or for an extreme emergency." She leaned forward, tense in her eagerness, and asked, "Isn't that so?"

"Yes, there is that stipulation." Millege met her intense eyes, suddenly understanding their meaning. He grew alarmed. He swiveled his chair a bit to the left, just enough to avoid facing her directly, then asked, "You have in mind using discretionary funds?"

"I want to go to San Francisco and enroll at Ladies' Commercial College. They have a dormitory for students right on campus. I could live there. It would be perfectly respectable. And it wouldn't take too much money. The principal wouldn't have to be touched, and only part of the interest would be needed." Her enthusiasm was apparent.

Ainsworth Millege remained silent for an awkward minute, causing the girl to ask with concern, "It would be proper use for the discretionary funds, wouldn't it?

And it would be for my own betterment.''

"Miss Allenby, if your mother were strong I'd prefer to talk with her about this matter,'' the banker began. "But I know she's not been well—your father mentioned her illness to me—so I must speak to you instead. After all, it's to be your estate in a few years and you may as well begin learning about it now.''

He settled back, one arm resting on the desk, the other doubled over his wide front. Something was bothering him. His fingers drummed on the desk top as he looked across at Jette. "It would be impossible for me to obtain funds for you at this time unless you went to Judge Killigrew.''

"But I thought you had the authority . . .''

"Up to a point, I do,'' he affirmed.

Jette's apprehension grew as she watched the elderly banker's face which now no longer held a smile, but furrows of consternation. "I understand your father is away on a buying trip to Iowa, that is, he and Asa Beemer . . .''

"Yes, to look at some breeding stock. A prize bull was up for sale and Father wanted to make a bid on it.'' Jette's frankness in speaking of herd building was disconcerting to the old-fashioned Millege, who was accustomed to discussing such matters with women in much more evasive terms. "But what has that to do with it?''

"A short time ago Elias applied to the court for use of a considerable amount of funds from your trust,'' he said. "He'd come to me first, but I couldn't grant the money under the circumstances, and certainly not the large amount he wanted. I had to refer him to Judge Killigrew.'' Ordinarily a fluent man, Millege found it difficult to put the situation into words the girl would clearly understand.

"But I knew nothing of that! Why should he do such

33

a thing?" She sat back in her chair, a soft smile suddenly brightening her face. "He must have found out I wanted to go to Ladies' Commercial. He was going to let me go after all!" She seemed elated.

Ainsworth Millege squirmed uncomfortably. The girl did not comprehend. "That may be, Miss Allenby, and for your sake I hope it is. But the funds he withdrew were far greater than needed for that purpose." His fingers again drummed at the desk top. "Your father stated need for the money in somewhat other terms. Judge Killigrew granted his petition on the basis that the . . . the . . . animal . . . was necessary to establish a herd for you and Asa, and was to stand at service, with the fees going to Elias himself. Seems he's been dickering to buy the La Coruna Ranch next to yours and has most of his own money pledged in the transaction. He intends for you and Asa to live at La Coruna."

It pained the old man to watch the girl's facial expression change. Jette remained silent as the import of his disclosure dawned on her. Not only was she not to have a job or go to San Francisco, but was to be given away to Asa Beemer—along with her inheritance—as a pawn in Elias' schemes. Even in Jette's rights to her grandmother's estate she was to have no say over how it was to be spent, or by whom. It would be useless to protest to Judge Killigrew, since he usually found it prudent to acquiesce in favor of Elias Allenby. Indeed, as many defeated litigants could testify, Killigrew found it expedient to bend—even to strain—the law if necessary to render decisions favorable to the powerful rancher.

"I can see that this is all news to you," Millege continued. "But I'm sure I'm not betraying a confidence by telling you of your father's plans." He rolled his chair a bit closer to the girl and placed one hand on hers. "He had good legal ground for obtaining funds from the trust, but you should have been consulted. If not for legal reasons, at least for common courtesy. Miss Allenby, I must tell you very frankly, I did not approve of such action. And now, knowing how you feel, I'm only sorry I didn't protest the allocation." He patted her arm, his stubby fingers enfolding her slim hands. He was as angry now at his own ineffectualness as he was at the time of Elias' request. "Will you take advice from an old friend?"

"Advice? How can advice possibly help me now? Don't you see what Father intends?" Jette was plunged once more into despair. "I'm not to have any rights at all—no choice, no say, not even in things that most directly concern me. Several weeks ago I tried to go to San Francisco. Father stopped me." She saw by the banker's expression that he had heard of the affair.

"Yes, I'm aware he prevented your going," he said.

"Mr. Millege, you've known our family since before I was born; you must know what Father is really like. He demands his way in everything, no matter how trivial. He can't stand opposition. Did you know he punished me for trying to get away? He locked me in my room for a week. And did you know he beat my mother senseless for helping me?" It was a rhetorical question; the banker made no reply, but waited for her to continue. "Mother used to be a lovely woman. Lots of people have told me so. You know what's become of her. Father not only took all the spirit out of her, but he assumed complete control of her money and used it to suit only himself."

"He's used it well, though," Millege interrupted. "Even you must admit he's certainly managed her estate efficiently."

"But what good has it done Mother? He's a violent man, and cruel. He's almost succeeded in destroying Mother. Now he wants to do the same thing to me. And there's no one to stop him. You couldn't . . ." Jette spoke with a rising inflection that signaled increasing anger. "What advice can you give me—when Father can always rely on people like Judge Killigrew to get what he wants?"

"You and your mother ought to see an attorney," Millege said quietly. "Perhaps someone from Los Angeles." His implication was clear: A San Genaro attorney would be intimidated by both Elias Allenby and Judge Killigrew.

"And with what could we pay a lawyer?" She spread her hands in a gesture of futility. "You know better than anyone else that neither Mother nor I are allowed to handle our own money."

Jette was aware that she spoke the truth, and so was Ainsworth Millege. For a moment they sat in silence, the man wondering what he could say or do that would, without jeopardizing his position as Allenby's banker and business associate, offer the girl and her mother remedy. He could prudently go only so far.

"I'm sure your father would do nothing to endanger your welfare," he said. "He is, perhaps, high-handed in his methods, but you must admit the La Coruna ranch and a fine herd of blooded Angus is a pretty solid base for establishing your economic security." He tried to sound logical and hoped to persuade Jette of its reasonableness. "You may wish to take steps to safeguard your trust from any further allocations of funds to Elias, but if it is truly for your own future good . . ." He stopped as he realized he was trying to convince himself also.

"And is forcing me to marry a man I detest a solid base for my happiness?" she countered with an intensity that surprised Millege.

"That's a matter between you and your father, but the trust is something else," he said.

36

"If I marry Asa Beemer, do you think for one minute I'll be allowed control of my own money? Father is determined to increase his holdings along the east slope of the valley. He can't manage that unless he has my money to work with, too. Don't you see what he intends?"

Millege hesitated before answering, his stubby fingers pulling nervously at his close-trimmed beard as he considered his reply. "I believe I do, Miss Allenby, but it will be up to you to take proper action." He worried that he might have been too outspoken already and would have an unpleasant confrontation with Elias should he learn of Jette's visit to him.

To broach the subject of her inquiry, she asked, "You say there are no funds, no accrued interest, in the trust at present? Why is that?"

"The interest was depleted by the grant to your father. Judge Killigrew directed disbursal of the accrued interest to date plus a stipulated amount from principal."

"Then I could have no funds from the trust right now? Not until the principal accrues interest again? Short of an extreme emergency, that is?"

"That is correct," he replied.

"I see," Jette said. She gathered her skirt and petticoats and rose to leave. Millege rushed to open the door. "It seems I'm to be defeated by Father at every turn. That's been made quite apparent to me today." She stood for a moment by the door, then turned and looked squarely at the banker as she added, "But one thing I can promise you, Mr. Millege, he won't win forever. When he least expects it, just when he is most confident, he'll fail. He'll meet up with somebody just as ruthless—just as determined—as he is. And he'll lose."

Chapter 3

San Genaro Road still simmered in the late afternoon sun. To the north at a distance of several miles from town lay the Allenby ranch house, but from where Jette walked along the side of the road, it might as well have been in the next county. An arid wind still rustled down from the hills, carrying into the valley floor scorching heat and the scent of greasewood and dry sage.

Jette's delicate kidskin boots were little protection from the rough roadbed. Heat from the gravel penetrated the thin soles and made walking painful. As soon as she was well beyond the last straggling adobes at the edge of town she removed her tight bolero jacket and carried it over one arm. If no cooler, she at least could feel less constricted.

Where Calle Aluin intersected the highway a barbed wire fence on the west side of the road marked the southern boundary of Allenby Ranch. To the east lay the Baldwin ranch, but westward, extending across the valley and well into the coastal mountains, lay the western section of Elias' realm. At regular intervals were square signs affixed to the fence posts which gave notice that the property was posted and that trespassers would be prosecuted. As often as Jette Allenby had seen the signs, she had never thought much about them nor had she inspected them.

"No Trespassers!" the neatly lettered signs warned. Now as she looked, she saw them as an extension of Elias' power, another way of asserting his domination and ownership.

Jette crossed a shallow ditch which separated road from field, seized one of the white cardboard signs and tore it from the fence post. The air was ripe with the pungent smell of manure and hummed with enormous blue-green flies drawn by the fresh cattle droppings. She walked slowly along the fence row, tearing off the notices one by one and tossing them into the dry weeds.

"You think old Allenby would appreciate your doing that?" A man's voice startled her. She had been too absorbed in her occupation to hear the approach behind her of a phaeton and matched team of bays. The carriage pulled up beside her, the perfectly paired animals slowing to a walk as the driver reined them quickly. "Not that I'd mind in the least—a pretty girl like you could tear down my signs all she liked—but old Allenby might not take it too kindly."

Jette looked up at the man who laughed as he urged the horses nearer the west side of the road. His face was handsome, with finely drawn features and a pale blond moustache which rather than hiding his thin-lipped mouth, called attention to its perfect symmetry. "May I give you a ride?" he asked and tipped his narrow-brimmed fedora.

Although she continued to walk homeward, Jette returned his broad smile. "Are you sure I won't take you out of your way?" she asked as the man halted the horses and stepped out of the buggy to hand her up into the seat.

"I assure you, wherever you wish to go will not be out of my way." His eyes were a strange pale blue, with a fringe of dark, long lashes more appropriate for a girl than a man, but there was nothing effeminate in either his tanned face or his broad-shouldered body. Jette had not supposed him so large until seated beside him, nor had she thought him at first glance to be as old as he must be. Clearly he was not a local resident, for his clothing was of a cut fastidiously Eastern, his accent the clipped precision of New England.

"I'm Nate Trasker, and I'm very delighted to meet you, Miss . . ." he began and waited for her to finish his sentence.

"Allenby," Jette said and offered her hand. "Jette Allenby."

"Did I commit an unforgiveable gaffe?" Trasker held her hand in his and pulled it to his lips in graceful gallantry. "I should have known who you were."

"How is that?" she asked.

"I was told only this afternoon that the most beautiful woman in San Genaro County was Elias Allenby's daughter." He studied her face boldly, his pale eyes narrowing slightly as he smiled.

"Are you telling me that I was the subject of your conversation? How did that happen?" Jette settled into the seat, surprised at how weary she was.

"I probably should say it was some more romantic situation, but I'd be lying." He flipped the reins and the bays speeded their pace. "I stopped by the courthouse to see Abe Marley. When I said I was going to see Elias Allenby—on business—he mentioned that I'd just missed meeting his very lovely daughter." His smile revealed shallow depressions in the tanned cheeks, the strongly masculine equivalent to dimples. The effect was charming, but added little warmth to his expression.

"You're very flattering, Mr. Trasker," Jette said. She could not hide the blush which told him she was pleased.

"Not at all!" He continued to stare at her. "Marley spoke only the truth."

Jette looked away from the pale blue eyes in confusion. "You say you are seeing my father on business?" She wanted to turn the conversation to something more commonplace.

"Yes, I am. I plan to call on him as soon as possible."

"May I ask what about?" Jette could only wonder what Trasker and her father might have in common, or what business they might have to discuss.

"I represent Farrier Regional Development Corporation of Chicago. We're interested in funding and establishing various enterprises in the West as outlets for manufacturers and suppliers in the East. We feel that the growth potential, especially here in California, is unlimited. We intend to become an integral part of that expansion," he explained. There was no hint of condescension in his answer. On the contrary, he seemed happy to tell her of his mission.

"But of what possible interest would Father be to your firm?" Jette asked. "Or maybe I should put it another way—why should he be interested in your company? He's in the cattle business."

"Your father is an influential man, Miss Allenby. We feel it would be mutually profitable if we could reach an agreement in a few matters," the man replied. "Until I speak with him personally, you understand, I'm not at liberty to discuss any of the details."

"You anticipated my questions."

"Please forgive me. I meant no offense," he apologized.

"Then I shall take none. I was just curious." Jette looked away, up to the low, rolling hills beyond the fenceline. "Father would only tell me to mind my own affairs and stay out of his."

"I could never say such a thing to you," Trasker said and followed her glance to where a slow moving cloud of dust marked the progress of part of Elias' prize herd as it eased down the slope toward the watering pond. Jette turned to see the set hardness of his mouth. Undoubtedly he had learned a great deal more about her father from Abe Marley than the fact that he was influential.

"Father's in Iowa now," Jette said.

"So I was told. Something about a . . . a . . . herd sire up for auction, wasn't it?" Trasker phrased the question delicately.

"If you mean a breeding bull, yes," Jette put it plainly. " 'Herd sire' is a bit ridiculous, don't you think? This is, after all, cattle country—Father raises cattle—and I'm not one of those hypocritical women who are offended by honest terms." The defiance in her dark eyes was hard to miss. "Father went to Iowa to make an offer on a new breed bull."

"I beg your pardon, Miss Allenby," Nate Trasker said and chuckled. "I commend you for your forthrightness." He bowed toward her with mock dignity, bringing his face close to hers.

For that moment their eyes met. For that moment Jette forgot the dusty heat of the road and the rough jostle of the buggy; she became lost in the depths of the man's pale eyes. The warmth of his nearness, the faint smell of scented lotion that lingered about him as he bent close, the resonant gentleness of his voice, lent an irresistible fascination. Even as he bent nearer she closed her eyes and raised her face to his, receiving the kiss from his lips as though it were due regard being collected.

"You are so beautiful," he whispered. "You've every right to denounce me to your father. But it's all your fault, you know. No woman has the right to look as you do right now." He touched her face with his gloved hand and leaned down to kiss her again.

Even the slight caress inflamed her very being, stirred within her a new and strange passion she had never before felt. She hardly recognized the graveled drive that led up to the rambling Allenby adobe. She was lifted from the carriage and escorted to the door of the house in a delightfully confused dream.

* * * *

Verdie Allenby placed her daughter's clothing in an ornately carved walnut armoire and handed the dusty kidskin boots to Elvira. "I hear what you're saying, child, but you aren't telling me anything," the woman said.

"I've told you all I know, Mother," Jette protested. "I've only just met the man. How could I know more?" She loosened her masses of auburn hair, tossed the tortoise-shell pins onto the dresser top.

"He's so good looking!" Elvira could not bear to leave before she had heard all Jette had to say. She stood by the open door with Jette's boots in her hand. "Is he married?" she asked.

"I don't know," Jette replied and realized she really did not know. Only now did it occur to her that it was the one thing she most wanted to find out about Nate Trasker. She turned to her mother and repeated, "I don't know!"

"Well, no harm done. Not as long as your father wasn't here." Verdie had not missed the excited, breathless state, the animation in her daughter's face as Trasker bade her goodbye in the patio. Nor had she interfered. It was quite enough that she could see through the lace curtain at the patio window. But as she watched the tall blond stranger clasp Jette's hand in farewell she was seized with foreboding.

"And he'll come back to see your father soon?" Elvira asked, unable to conceal her curiosity.

"Yes . . ." Jette hesitated and dashed to the window. "I thought I heard . . ." She bent down and leaned out in order to see more clearly.

"What is it?" Verdie asked. "Perhaps Mr. Trasker's coming back already . . ." A look of apprehension flickered across her face.

"It looks like Father and Asa," Jette said.

"It can't be." Verdie drew back the curtain and peered past Jette's shoulder. "Oh dear Lord! It is! But they weren't supposed to be back until next week." She wrung her hands as she watched the hired carriage approach along the main road and enter the long drive.

"Hurry, Elvira. Get two of the men to see to their luggage. And run tell Socorro we'll have dinner early," Jette ordered the young Mexican girl. "Never mind my boots right now. Run along." As the girl dashed the length of the second floor veranda and down the steps, Jette grabbed a fresh white lawn guimpe and canvas-cloth jumper. Quickly she put them on, buttoning the jumper as she pushed Verdie before her and helped her down the stairs. "Remember, Mother, you knew nothing of my trip to town today."

"But I did, Jette. You told me all about it," Verdie reminded the girl.

"Yes, Mother, but you mustn't let Father know." Jette caught her mother's arm and pulled her to look directly at her. Childlike bewilderment met her eyes; a dark blankness had replaced the alert, inquisitive expression of only moments before. "Oh, Mother! Don't you understand? You mustn't let yourself take any of the blame for my actions. Promise me you'll tell Father you knew nothing of it."

Verdie stood at the bottom of the steps, her eyebrows drawn together, distress and confusion obvious in every gesture. Her hands went to her face, as if in covering her eyes she could escape the reality of Elias' return. Jette pulled at her mother's hands and at the same time guided her into the back parlor.

"You've got to promise me, Mother," she demanded. "Because I'll deny you knew anything." She shook Verdie gently and kissed her anguished face. "Please promise me."

"Yes . . . yes . . . I promise," the woman vowed as Jette eased her down onto a leather upholstered sofa. She lay back and closed her eyes against the waning light from the window. "I promise . . . I promise . . ." she repeated. Jette pulled a crocheted afghan about her mother's thin shoulders and sat beside her.

"There now, that's bettter. You just rest a while and I'll take care of Father. I'll call you before dinner. You'll be fine," Jette said.

More and more Verdie retreated to the darkness of the back parlor or the sewing room upstairs, the two rooms in the house where Elias was least likely to intrude. Slowly the anxious frown disappeared from her face as Jette stroked the graying hair and kissed her pale cheek.

At the front of the house the carriage crunched to a halt. From the kitchen rose the excited voice of Socorro as Elvira explained the family's requirements and warned that Elias Allenby had returned. Emerging from the shade of the patio the spaniel and mongrel barked protests against the incursion of strange horses and livery. They dodged Elias' boots and pawed at Asa Beemer as he descended from the buggy, both animals wriggling and yelping to welcome the foreman.

"Hello, old timers," Beemer said and affectionately cuffed the excited dogs. "Kept a good eye on the place while we were gone, did you?"

"Jette, call those damned dogs or I swear by God I'll shoot 'em both!" Elias' threat was the only greeting he bestowed upon the girl as she hurried down the steps toward the men. "Asa, pay the driver and come see me as soon as you're settled. I want the payroll squared away tonight. No sense waiting till morning. I'll not have the men asking for their pay." The old man ignored his daughter as he crossed the veranda and entered the house.

"Yes, sir. I'll check with Benito and bring you the pay sheets right away." Asa Beemer swung the luggage from the back of the conveyance, handed the driver several coins, flipped another and caught it in his palm before handing it to the man. "Many thanks, Howard," he said as the driver set the last suitcase on the steps.

"Thank you, Mr. Beemer," the man replied as he inspected the coin in his hand. "Yes, sir, thank you!" He was still grinning broadly as he coaxed the horses about the U-shaped turnaround and back along the main drive.

"Well, Miss Jette, I guess we surprised you coming back this soon." Beemer did not expect the girl to be overjoyed at their return, but he had hoped she would at least speak to him with less invective than customary.

"It might have helped if you'd telegraphed to let us know," Jette said. "I'd have seen your room was aired out. I'm sure it's stifling up there." She could not bring herself to look directly at the man. Instead she picked up one of the suitcases and headed for the front door.

"Oh no, Miss Jette. Don't you carry that. I'll send a couple of the boys over to take them upstairs." He took the heavy satchel from her. For an instant his hand closed over hers, but Jette withdrew her hand as if she found his touch repugnant. "I'm sorry we didn't send word ahead, but Elias felt we didn't need to."

"Yes, he would feel that way," Jette said with sarcasm. "Don't bother to send for the men—Elvira's gone to get them. I asked Socorro to fix dinner early. Will six-thirty be all right?" She turned abruptly from him as she became aware of his bold staring at the tight bodice of her jumper.

"That's fine. We'd both appreciate that. We had lunch in Los Angeles between trains, but nothing since." He stood aside and pushed open the front door which Elias had left ajar.

"Did Father buy his bull?" Jette asked.

"He did," Beemer replied. "Didn't get it at any bargain price, but he bought himself one fine animal."

"With my money!" Jette laughed, but without humor. She turned to Beemer and confronted him. "You knew that, didn't you? That it was my money he used?"

The door to Elias' office to the right of the front entry was standing open. For a moment the foreman did not answer. "Yes, I knew," he replied quietly. "But you won't have any cause to regret it, I promise you." He hoped Elias would not overhear and interrupt their conversation.

"How can you possibly promise me such a thing?" Jette demanded, the acid in her tone revealing all too well her contempt. "My own father robs me, cheats me—to add to his own estate! And I'm sure he had your approval." She started toward the dining room to see Socorro about dinner preparations, but Asa Beemer barred her way. "Why should I even bother to listen to your promises?" she asked.

"You're not being exactly fair to Elias, Miss Jette." He toyed with a wisp of hair that curled from her temple, but she darted away from him, her face white with anger. "What he's building up—land, herds, riparian rights, shipping yards—that's all yours in good time. You shouldn't hold it against him for looking out for your best interests, too." He followed her to the corner of the dining room and effectively blocked her way to the kitchen, one hand on her waist, his fingers feeling the soft swelling of her buttocks beneath the canvascloth skirt.

"Let me go, Asa. I have things to attend to," Jette snapped as she struck at his arm.

"And so have I, but what I have to say is important." He attempted to pull her to him.

47

"Important to whom? Certainly not to me!" She twisted from his grasp. "I'm sure Father's coached you on what to say. I can well imagine some of the promises he's made to you—all without so much as consulting me or asking my leave!" The girl's animosity was obvious; her eyes blazed with fury. "You say it's my future welfare he's thinking of? Rubbish! If it were, how could he possibly promise you that I'd marry you? I'm sure the prospect of falling heir to Elias' estate—albeit through a wife who would thoroughly detest you—might tempt any saddle tramp . . ."

"Enough, girl!" Elias' voice roared from the office across the front parlor. His bulk filled the doorway as he stood listening. With quick strides he crossed the wide room. Above his close-trimmed beard his face was red with rage; veins in his temples throbbed visibly.

Beemer stepped between father and daughter, caught ⸱ᵗ Elias' arm and turned him half around, facing away from Jette. "It's all right, Elias. I've got me a hide tougher than an old road-runner. Nothing she says can hurt me." Beemer's laugh was too loud even in the large room. "Women are funny sometimes, but just let 'em get the steam out now and again."

"I'll not have her . . ." Elias began.

"It's all right, Elias!" Beemer glanced uneasily at Jette who stood by the dining room door, her head cocked to one side, her chin tilted defiantly. It was plain to Beemer the quarrel could get out of hand if continued. Adroitly, so off-handed that the old man did not notice his deliberateness, the foreman maneuvered Elias back to the office. "Give me a few minutes to see Benito and we'll get to work on the payroll right away."

Beemer's ability to handle Elias only served to infuriate Jette all the more. There had been no words of greeting, no inquiry or concern about how Verdie might be. Straight to business, as usual with Elias. Jette

48

acknowledged she was partly to blame, but she was determined in her opposition to her father's will. Even to protect her mother she could not, *would* not marry Asa Beemer. There had to be another way.

"Which men do you want to go to the siding tomorrow? Think we ought to walk Old Max, or give him a ride in the wagon?" Beemer asked Elias as they disappeared into the ranch office. Despite the warmth of the late afternoon, Beemer closed the door behind them. Payrolls and the arrival of the Angus bull took precedence over all else.

Jette opened the dining room windows and looped the lace curtains back to let the breeze freshen the air inside. The huge adobe remained cool, especially on the first floor, but the interior retained the smell of all ancient buildings, the residual of decades of cooking, smoking fireplaces, and mildew that crept up from the foundation during the rainy season. She breathed in the hot, dry air as she waited to quiet her pounding pulse and calm her angry thoughts before speaking with the elderly cook about dinner. It was difficult enough for the help to satisfy Elias without an additional burden of hasty or thoughtless words from his family.

Beyond the windows the first-floor veranda extended to a dusty, hard-packed adobe service yard which in turn gave way to a fenced pasture enclosing the main cattle barn. A bit to the right was a sparse grove of live oaks which sheltered and hid from sight the stables and horse pasture. Halfway between the stables and the house a narrow, rutted lane branched off the driveway and led to the small shacks and cottages of the ranch employees. At the head of the lane a large, whitewashed, two-story building, the ranch store, dominated the tiny village as if to remind the inhabitants of Elias' omnipotence. No sign was painted on its wooden siding; there was no need for one. All the employees knew the building well, but if they were expected to buy from the ranch store, they at least obtained their needs at a fair price. Nor were they forced to plead for their wages. To his hands, Elias Allenby was fair and prompt. In such ways he bound their dependence and their loyalty.

Even Jette was forced to admit that her father, a hard and exacting employer, was far better than most in San Genaro Valley. And Asa Beemer had proven honest and trustworthy—to her father. She would go no farther, however, in praising either man.

From the window she saw Asa's familiar slouch as he crossed the lane toward the store. He had not bothered to change from his traveling suit, but had turned to ranch business immediately. Benito Galvan would have the men's work records ready as usual for Asa. As Jette watched Beemer's easy, self-assured gait she was again filled with resentment and despair. What other promises had Elias made to Beemer that made him so sure of his position in Elias' empire?

So the bull was coming next day. Jette was anxious to see the investment her money had purchased. It would be useless to ask Elias if she might go to the siding in the east pasture to watch the beast off-loaded from his rail car. She clenched her fists as she realized she must turn to Asa Beemer if she wished to witness the bull's arrival.

At the head of the lane Benito Galvan met Asa in front of the store. The elderly Mexican, whose courtly manners belonged to a gentler, more gracious age, respectfully removed his hat as he spoke with the foreman.

"Don't be so nice to him, Benito!" Jette murmured under her breath as she watched. She abruptly turned away from the window as if to thrust Beemer from her mind.

The girl touched her fingers to her lips, trying to recall

Nate Trasker's kisses, glad that he had missed meeting Elias. That meant he must return, and if he returned . . . She tried to imagine him near her again, bending to kiss her, to hold her softly in his arms.

"Miss Jette, Socorro wants to know if she should make apple cobbler for dessert." Elvira interrupted her daydreaming.

"Yes, we can have that with the rest of the ice cream, if it's still hard." Jette reluctantly put her mind to the practical matter of dinner.

"It will be, Socorro had me pack more ice and salt around it right after lunch," the young girl said.

"Good. That's one less problem, isn't it?" Jette said as she started for the kitchen.

"Yes, Miss Jette." Elvira stopped in the doorway. "Did you tell your father about . . ." She did not finish the question.

"No, I didn't," Jette said quickly. "I'll just let Nate Trasker come as a surprise. Who knows, maybe he won't come back at all." But even as she said the words, Jette knew in her heart that Trasker would return, if not to see Elias, then to see her. She was counting on it. And she was sure he would prove a surprise not only to Elias, but to Asa Beemer.

Chapter 4

"See to the payroll as soon as you finish with the lumber," Elias Allenby ordered his foreman. They sat in the cluttered office, their shirt sleeves rolled up, legs sprawled across woolen Navajo rugs on the floor. It was the one room in the adobe in which they could relax with no interference from any women of the household. The ranch office was neither entered nor cleaned by any of the females. Only occasionally did old Benito tidy up after the occupants. Dust accumulated unhindered on window sills and furniture. Elias poured another shot of rye whiskey and offered the bottle to Asa Beemer, who shook his head and rose to leave. "Tell Benito we'll get right to building first thing tomorrow morning," Elias continued. "Put his best men on it, but I want that pen up by tomorrow night, hear?"

"I don't think we can get it finished that soon. It'll take a good part of the day just to dig post holes and set the uprights. That adobe's as hard as concrete." Asa Beemer remained standing in the hall doorway. Already by mid-afternoon the east side of the ranch house was warm. Overhang of the veranda cut out direct sunlight, but a slight wind whipped end-of-April heat through every aperture in the building. Beemer wiped his face with a blue bandana handkerchief which he stuffed back into his hip pocket. "No use hurrying up the job and having Old Max bust out."

"All right, Asa. You know best about that. Just see to it." Elias tilted back in the desk chair and turned to the younger man. "I aim to run those advertisements in the papers all next month and I want that pen available from the first day."

"No problem there, Elias. It'll be ready." Asa started to leave by the hall door. "You want Benito to take the ladies to town this evening?" he asked.

"For that musical at the high school?" There was contempt in his question. He downed the rye at one swallow and set the glass atop the desk.

"Yes, sir," Asa replied. "Mrs. Allenby mentioned they'd like to go." Beemer did not need to add that Verdie preferred to ask him rather than her husband, since she knew in advance it would only serve to annoy Elias.

"Sure, let 'em go. Only you're to drive 'em in." Elias smiled. He knew Asa understood very well. "And on no account is Jette to have the team, understand?"

"Yes, sir," Asa grinned.

"Unless you already had too much traveling . . ." Elias chuckled.

"No, sir. That'd be a real privilege, taking the ladies to town." Beemer nodded his thanks and turned once more to go. "By the way, Elias, you've got to tell the women over by the store to keep their kids clear of that bull. They're cutting across the horse pasture, sneaking up to the barn to get a look at him. That animal's edgy enough after being cooped up in that cattle car without those kids worrying him. No telling what he'd take a notion to do if they started teasing him."

"That's your responsibility," Elias told him bluntly. "You tell 'em."

"I've done that, but by tomorrow those kids will just take it as a dare. You know how they are—all spit and spunk." Asa Beemer was genuinely worried. "Short of me taking a stick to 'em, they're not going to stay away from the barn."

"You think it's that serious, eh?" Elias asked.

"I do, yes, sir. What I say, the men will do and they'll see to their own womenfolks, but their kids are something else again."

"So you want me to handle the payroll and pass the word myself?" Elias asked. "That it?"

"Be a good idea if you did, Elias. Coming from you, they'll bust their kids' butts if they put a leg over that fence. I'm not going to have time to keep an eye on 'em and I sure as hell don't want anybody hurt."

"Christ! He's that mean, is he?" Elias seemed

reluctant to ask the question, but if Asa Beemer wanted him to speak to the women himself—a duty Asa would never under ordinary circumstances ask Allenby to assume—the Angus must indeed pose a serious danger.

"He'll settle down in a few days. Won't ever be a quiet little pussy cat, but that's not exactly what you bought him for, is it?" Asa smiled at his own joke.

"No, and I'm not holding up on those advertisements." Elias pulled down a green fabric blind to diminish the glare from the open window. Much as he disliked to interfere with the authority of his own foreman in relationship to the employees, he saw the wisdom of Asa's suggestion. The Iowa bull was a costly adjunct to ranch operations, and as such, deserved its owner's personal attention. Elias rose from his swivel chair, took his broad-brimmed felt hat from the top of the heavy safe in the corner and preceded Asa into the hall and out onto the wide veranda. "I'll see Benito right now. Is he at the barn or the store?"

"Up at the barn measuring off the post-holes," Asa replied. "You expecting somebody?" He shaded his eyes against the sun and looked down the long driveway. "Buggy just turned in from the road."

"Now who the hell?" Elias strode across the small patch of grass west of the pathway and waited beneath the live oak shade as a yellow-wheeled phaeton and glossy bays approached. From the service yard behind the house rushed the dogs, both barking furiously, the long-legged mongrel sprinting far ahead of the fat spaniel. Asa whistled them back to stand beside him as the buggy drew up.

From the corner of his eye Asa was aware of movement in the bedroom window at the end of the second floor veranda; within seconds Jette hurried along the hall and down the staircase. One quick glance at the young woman's face told him she was acquainted with the caller. Beemer advanced to the buggy and took the reins, holding the horses as the tall, blond man alighted. The dogs growled and bared their teeth as the man stepped forward.

"Pecky! Buff!" Asa snapped his fingers and the dogs retreated behind him, still protesting and sniffing the stranger's scent.

"Much obliged," the man said as he looked from one to the other, his restrained smile including both. "Mr. Allenby, my name's Trasker. . .Nate Trasker." At the county courthouse Abe Marley had suggested Trasker use a very direct approach and be certain to mention the profit angle immediately. Trasker ignored the scrutiny to which he was being subjected and continued quickly, "I'd like a few minutes of your time, sir. I think you might find it interesting—and possibly profitable."

Elias Allenby, not a man to give his hand in easy agreement, was not averse to the custom of shaking hands with a stranger who offered profitable conversation. He was surprised at the firm grip of the gloved hand extended to him. "Glad to know you, Trasker. This is my foreman, Asa Beemer."

"Mr. Beemer, happy to know you." Trasker made it a point to shake Asa's hand also.

Asa nodded and said, "Trasker you said your name was?"

"That's right." The stranger joined Elias in the shade.

"You the one's been trying to buy up the Baldwin place?" Asa queried.

"Yes, I am. I suppose that's no surprise, since you're neighbors," Trasker said as Asa led the horses nearer the side door and looped the reins to one of the hitching posts.

"Just because we're neighbors doesn't mean there's much communication between us. You get any farther with Lavinia Baldwin than the rest of us?" Elias asked, his cold blue eyes appraising the man's reaction to the question. If Trasker were after the Baldwin ranch, then he must have heard that Allenby also wanted the property.

"I'm afraid not," Trasker laughed. "Mrs. Baldwin is a difficult woman to do business with."

A hint of smile played about Elias' face at the man's candid admission. "I've got a good deal to do, Trasker, but if you'll come inside I can give you a few minutes." He turned and led the way to the side entrance. "Asa, I'll take care of that matter directly. Tell Benito I'll see him right away."

"Yes, sir," Beemer said, then added, "Good to meet you, Trasker." As he circled the house and cut through the service yard toward the barn, he glimpsed Jette through the parlor window. So that was the reason she had been wearing a new pink georgette blouse since mid-morning. She had been expecting the man to come.

Elias led Trasker down the side hall and into a large parlor at the center of the house. Originally it had been the old adobe's only room, but with additional generations of owners it had accumulated smaller rooms on either side, then a second floor complete with veranda on three sides. The massive walls, a yard thick, contained recessed windows which gave light and ventilation, while access to the upstairs bedrooms was afforded by an out-of-doors staircase sheltered by the porch overhang. The parlor, much too large to be intimate or cozy, had been made comfortable and pleasant in a plain, unadorned fashion. Upholstered chairs and sofas were placed in several groupings. Dark mahogany tables, gracefully free of the usual contorted Victorian tooling, displayed ferns and aspidistra and palms in brilliant, glazed pots. Two enormous mirrored wardrobes flanked the wide double front door and served the downstairs area as closets. Opposite the door was an oversized rock fireplace which was faced with rose-colored marble. Surmounting the mantel was a collection of rifles and shotguns, all carefully blued and oiled, completely at odds with the gentle quality of the rest of the room.

Trasker's eyes took in the furnishings and firearms at a quick glance. Elias' wealth was not displayed in his home, but in the other ranch buildings and the vast, seminal herds that spread from the coastal mountains to the foothills of the San Lucas range.

"Whiskey, Trasker?" Elias asked as they entered. He led the way and waved his guest to the long sofa placed before the fireplace. "Have a seat and we'll hear what you've got to say." The rancher turned from the liquor cabinet and added, "I've got brandy and port, too, if that's your pleasure." Elias gauged men by the choice of pleasures—food, drink, women. Therein were revealed to him both the strength and weaknesses of the individual. He was not disappointed when the stranger replied, "Whiskey's fine, thank you."

Instead of seating himself, Nate Trasker wandered about the room. "You've some fine old paintings here. Family heirlooms?" he asked. He leaned closer to inspect a delicate landscape mounted in a gold-leafed baroque frame. It was one of a pair which hung on either side of the door to the dining room. But it was not the pictures which held his attention.

Jette Allenby, auburn hair piled high atop her head, her skin pale against the pink blouse, dark eyes dancing, stood just inside the door. Her smile was unashamedly joyous as she stared back at him. He winked broadly, but quickly turned back to Elias, as if to allow Jette to either enter the parlor or take her exit, as she chose. He was aware from Abe Marley and others in San Genaro that Jette and her father were constantly at odds, and that an aroused Elias Allenby was not a man with whom one would wish to deal.

"Those pictures?" Elias asked as he took a glass from the tall cabinet near the fireplace and poured a shot for Trasker.

"Yes, sir. They look very old—very valuable," Trasker said.

"Come from my wife's family. Inherited them from some aunt back in Virginia. Can't say that I give a damn about such things, but they mean a lot to her so I let her keep 'em and hang 'em up where it suits her." Elias handed him the shot glass and waited for Trasker to be seated before pulling up one of the large chairs to face him. "Now . . . what's on your mind?"

"Mr. Allenby, as you already know, I made an offer to Lavinia Baldwin to buy her property. She refused, of course. I've also looked into the Rancho Mariano holdings in view of purchasing their western section, but with their lease agreements already existing, I felt it wasn't to my best interest and dropped the idea. I intend to settle here in San Genaro Valley and want to invest in farm or ranch lands. I can better represent my firm if I live here and have first-hand knowledge and experience with the territory. Abe Marley at the courthouse went over the maps with me, pointing out the various holdings in this end of the valley. He suggested I see you." Trasker tipped his glass slightly to salute his host, drank half the whiskey and waited to see if his words would elicit any response. Elias merely gestured for him to continue.

"Marely said you were going in for herd building—rather than the usual raising and fattening for slaughter—and that you intend to have the finest Aberdeen Angus sire west of the Rockies. That being the case, I thought you'd be interested in my offer." Nate Trasker had thrown out the bait. Now he waited to see if it would be taken. The silent pause was awkward as both men endeavored to read the other's expression, but in that, Elias was the more shrewd. He said nothing.

Trasker finished the whiskey and set the glass on a small marble-topped table beside the sofa. "Since your operation would entail less open range and more closed pasture, eventually you'll want to divest yourself of the northeastern section of your place," Trasker continued. "Shipping yards, siding, holding pens, feed storage facilities, plus this house and the buildings here—which represent the greatest share of your capital investment in the ranch—occupy a strip along Las Lomas Road which I propose you retain. This would assure you permanent access to rail transport and make any extensive moves unnecessary."

Elias sat looking at his caller as if he were waiting for him to complete the punch line of a bawdy joke. Only the faintest hint of amusement crept into his browned, leathery face. The eyes, so eloquent in command and anger, betrayed nothing of his reaction. Abe Marley had several times alluded to Elias Allenby's poker playing abilities; Trasker could well believe it as he observed the elderly man across from him. It was impossible to fathom the effect Trasker's offer had made on the rancher.

"That all?" Elias was abrupt, but not curt. He was willing to listen to more.

"In essence, yes." Trasker had no intention of elaborating or revealing more of his proposal until Elias had time to mull it over. Trasker knew the old man would not discuss it with anyone until he was sure in his own mind as to what he would do.

"You haven't talked money yet," Elias said and leaned back into the depths of the comfortable chair. "Seems that ought to come up front in the kind of proposition you're making."

"Later . . ." Trasker gestured with his hands and bowed his head slightly to signify he was ended. "When you've thought about it, we can resume our discussion." He rose to leave. "I'm staying at the Swift Hotel in San Genaro when you wish to send word to me."

Trasker's audacious approach and judicious leave-taking, which Elias recognized as being a more delicate behavior than he himself would follow in similar circumstances, amused the old man. He rose to accompany his visitor to the door. "While you're here—and since you've a mind to buy the place—why don't you stay, take a look around with me and have dinner with us tonight? I've got a little something up at the barn I'd like to show you."

"That's very kind of you, I'm sure, but . . ." From the dining room came the sound of windows being slid open. Jette was making her presence known. He waited, then agreed, "Yes, I'd like that very much, Allenby. That way perhaps I'll be better prepared for our next business conversation."

"Fine," Elias said and clapped a huge hand on the younger man's shoulder. "I've a few things to attend to. You may as well keep me company. Glad to have you." As they headed for the door he continued, "I'd like to hear about this firm you work for, too. You can tell me just how they fit into San Genaro Valley."

At that moment Jette entered the parlor and only for a moment hesitated. She did not wait for Elias to make introductions. "Mr. Trasker, how nice to see you again," she said and extended her hand to him. She was beautiful in pink blouse and maroon skirt.

Elias, caught off guard by both her sudden appearance and her greeting of the stranger, could only say, "This is my daughter, Jette."

"Yes, we met briefly yesterday," Trasker said as he

took her hand in his. "How are you, Miss Allenby?"

"Very well, thank you," she answered, her dark eyes meeting his over their handclasp. "Did I overhear you say you'd stay to dinner? We'd be delighted to have you. We seldom have guests." She shot a significant look at her father.

"If it wouldn't be too much of an imposition. . ." Trasker began.

"Not at all, I assure you," Jette smiled. "I'll tell Socorro." Her look returned to Elias as she added, "Mother isn't well—she's resting upstairs. I'll run and tell her we have a visitor. Excuse me, please." Her reprimand of Elias did not pass unnoticed by Trasker, who bowed courteously as she returned to the dining room and kitchen.

"I believe you had something you wanted to show me at the barn, sir," Trasker reminded his host. "I'm anxious to see what it is—you sounded a bit mysterious, and mysteries intrigue me."

If Nate Trasker entertained any doubt as to the severity of Elias Allenby's rule over his personal empire, it was removed after he had witnessed issuance of the ranch payroll. Although the system, typically Yankee and an innovation for the Hispanic West, seemed merely another routine task it yet smacked of an ancient feudalism. Elias, was, in reality, stern lord and dispenser of provender. Each man's account was posted on ledger sheets, his purchases at the ranch store debited to his credit for a full month's work; the remainder was paid in cash. Any question of accounts was settled by Benito Galvan's intercession. The process was swift, with no time wasted in discussion, but today Elias demanded—and got—the presence of the men's wives.

"So your fancy bull is that 'little something' you were going to show me, eh?" Trasker said as they walked up the dusty pathway which led to the cattle barn. The

Mexican woman had stared at Elias, intimidation making their expressive brown faces rigid with fear. "Is he really that dangerous?"

"Right now he certainly is. And I don't want him aggravated by those damned kids," Elias replied as he opened the heavy gate which gave access to the barn and pasture. The gate swung easily on inset metal rods, its fastening a sliding wooden tongue which fitted into a two-foot-long receptacle recessed into the upright posts at one side. The bar could be operated from either side, making it a simple matter to secure the gate. A chock dropped into place behind the tongue making it fast—and animal proof. Even the most inquisitive and ingenious would find it impossible to open such an arrangement.

For Elias there was no simple pieces of wire looped over a gate post for such closures; it was almost a fetish with the rancher. He caught Trasker eyeing the device and said, "I saw this type lock used by the Mexicans in Sonora and Arizona. Spanish, originally." He demonstrated the soundness of the device by hammering at it and rattling it in its grooves. "Used it around goats . . . you know how they can open damned near anything. Well, I guarantee not even a smart old billy could work this open."

"I've never seen a gate closing like it. But then, I've never seem much of the West." Trasker followed Allenby up the path toward the barn. Beyond the immediate lot which surrounded the extensive structure was another pasture, filled now with sleek black heifers. Trasker had learned of the Allenby herd through Marley and others in town. Seeing for himself the perfection of the animals bore out their information.

Late afternoon sunshine filtered through eucalyptus trees which edged the fence west of the barn. The wind remained hot and dry, sending dust and straw skittering along the hard adobe ground. Far to the east spread the Allenby holdings, beyond the gold-rimmed foothills. High above and to the north were a number of vultures wheeling in graceful arabesques, their circles tightening slowly as they descended. For a moment Elias watched, a look of satisfaction growing on his sunburned face.

"Asa, looks like you took care of those dogs from over at La Coruna," Elias said as his foreman emerged from the shadow of the barn.

"Yes, sir. Got five of 'em. That gets rid of the whole pack as far as I know. Boys didn't see any more of 'em and they rode all the way to the fence." Beemer carried a brass-jointed carpenter's rule which he was folding up.

"Find any more calves down?" Elias asked.

"Not this time. Guess we got that problem licked," Asa said and stuffed the rule into his trouser pocket.

"You mean you've had trouble with dogs?" Trasker asked incredulously.

"Running in packs—gone feral," Elias replied.

"Couple of 'em looked to me they were part coyote," Asa said.

"I warned Ed and Lodd Putnam," Elias explained. "They've been letting those damned dogs run loose the past three . . . four . . . years now. Killed some sheep over at the Larsons'. Ed and Lodd are just too old to run that place anymore. Sure as hell can't let the hired help run it." He shot a quick look at Asa and laughed, "Even with a good man like Asa here, I wouldn't give him his head and let him run things to suit himself."

Asa laughed easily with Elias. He understood and was comfortable with the remark. "They should've sold out when you made that last offer," Asa said.

"Should have—but didn't." Elias turned to Trasker. "Made a good offer; cash, no terms. Now it's going to cost them in court. Those dogs cost me three fine purebred calves."

Elias opened the sliding door on the south side of the barn and motioned for Trasker to enter before him. Low sounds of feeding cattle and a soft twittering of swallows broke the twilight silence of the interior. Nate Trasker, in his patent-calf bluchers stepped carefully as they headed for the far end, but it was unnecessary—the floor was immaculate, with stalls and aisles forked and swept as clean as a dairy barn.

Slowly the magnificent bull turned a massive head to watch them, his huge brown eyes in no way conveying hint of his present instability. The creature was blocky and square, its black hide glossy and smooth over solid bones and firm, hard muscles. Power and potency was evident in every line.

"A little something!" Trasker chuckled as he looked at the beast. "He is that, all right!" He moved nearer to the stall. Instantly the bull lunged toward him, smashing into the wooden rails with such violence the man retreated in sudden alarm.

"Easy big boy . . . easy . . ." Asa crooned and stood near the side of the stall. "Easy now . . . calm down, big fella . . ." he repeated softly. Then turning to the men he said, "Best we just leave him alone. He'll settle down, but it'll take a while. I don't want him busting out and getting hurt. He's got wind of those heifers, too, and that's not helping matters." Beemer checked the door to the stall, made sure it was fast, and led the way out of the barn. Behind them they could hear restive sounds of the huge animal and the response of cattle in nearby stalls.

"That's the largest bull I've ever seen," Trasker said as they retraced their steps toward the house. "Papers a yard long on him, no doubt?"

"Maximilian of Dundee . . . over a ton of him . . . best of breed. Gold medals and cash awards in a dozen shows. Got a reputation for the best calves—no dwarfism—passes on all the quality of the line.'' Elias was proud of his acquisition. "Yes, sir, I intend to have me the finest herd in the West.''

"From the looks of it, I'd say you've succeeded already," Trasker ventured. The lots surrounding them, and the range lands both east and north were dotted with the low slung, dark animals. It was impossible to calculate their numbers or worth, and he had learned long ago never to ask how many head of stock a man owns—at least not of the man himself. "Why'd you pick Aberdeens?''

"That's where the cattle business is heading. No more stringy range runners. Only thing that's good about the longhorn is its resistance to the fever. And of course its ability to feed off scrub land and survive. Blooded cattle, with more meat per dollar invested in feed and care—that's where the profits will be. Between the railroads and the government, the best land is tied up now and anybody wanting range lands has to pay their price.''

"And these animals solve the problem of extensive range," Trasker said. "Yes, I see what you mean. Of course there remains the cost of grain for finishing.''

"And we've got grain adapted to our needs," Elias replied. "Couldn't grow wheat here in the early days, but we've got high-yielding crops now for dry farming and irrigation. I figure the markets will be San Francisco and Los Angeles. Bound to grow. Man's a fool not to see that and put himself in at the ground floor.''

Trasker looked at the man closely. He was no fool. Of that much he was certain. "You've established yourself on the ground floor, as you put it, from the looks of all this.'' Trasker waved his hand toward the barn and holding lots.

"I saw the big die-ups in Texas and Wyoming in the

seventies and eighties," Elias went on. "And I was dragged into the range wars when the settlers began homesteading on the government lands. Made up my mind then that things would be different for me. I came here to San Genaro Valley and began building a business—as I wanted it, not subject to the whims of nature and vagaries of demand." The rancher opened the gate, allowing Trasker to pass into the rutted lane which led back to the house, then closed and relocked the closure. Asa Beemer had followed at a respectful distance, listening to the conversation, but not interposing his own.

Ahead of them they could see lamplight from the windows of the house. Some of the Mexican children were playing a noisy game beneath the oaks along the drive, but at Elias' approach they fell silent and watched from cover, their solemn eyes following the men as they disappeared into the brightly lighted parlor. Elias and Asa did not miss the children's behavior.

"You're not going to have trouble with those kids up at the barn anymore, Asa," Allenby said. He was pleased with the effect of his warning to the women.

"No, sir. Looks like what you told 'em did the trick." Beemer was relieved, because either damaged bull or injured child could mean trouble in their closely knit community.

"Jette!" Elias roared as he let the screen-door slam behind him. To Trasker he said, "I'll have Jette show you to a guest room upstairs. You'll want to wash up before dinner." It was a nicety he offered guests, but one which he did not observe himself.

"Very kind of you," Trasker said. Although he wondered why the daughter of the household should be called upon to serve in the capacity of one of the maids, he was pleased to see Jette alone once again.

From the kitchen came the rapid Spanish of Socorro

and Elvira and the clatter of utensils. Obviously the evening was to be an occasion. Jette, drying her hands on her apron, came to the door of the parlor, her smile brightening as she saw Trasker.

"Well, what do you think of Father's new pet?" she asked, pointedly ignoring Asa Beemer.

"A magnificent creature," he answered. "But pet—never! There is nothing in this world that could get me into the same stall with that animal." He shook his head emphatically.

"Show Mr. Trasker upstairs," Elias ordered his daughter. To Nate Trasker he said, "Soon as you're ready, come down and join Asa and me in the office. We'll have a drink and talk some more about your proposition." It was said banteringly, but a hardness about his face betrayed the fact that Elias was interested—and annoyed.

"Thank you, sir. I'd enjoy that," Trasker replied and followed Jette to the rear door of the parlor. Beemer opened the screen-door and stood aside, but Jette gathered her skirts tightly about her as she brushed past, giving him neither look nor thanks.

The outside staircase rose a few steps on the east side to a square landing, angled right and up to the second story. Two halls joined to form a 'T,' the foot of which opened to the right of the top landing. Down this passage were the doors to two bedrooms: the first, a guest room: the second, Asa Beemer's. Just beyond the landing and opening onto the veranda was another door, also to a guest room. Into this Jette led Nate Trasker, prudently leaving the door ajar as they entered.

"I'm sure you'll find everything you need, Mr. Trasker," Jette said as she busied herself refolding a linen hand towel which was draped over a rod above the metal washstand. "There's warm water in the washstand pitcher, and ice water in the water bottle."

Trasker smiled a slow smile and caught her about the waist. "I'm glad to have you alone for a few minutes. I don't want to waste them." He pulled her close and looked down into her dark eyes.

"You mustn't! Father's office is directly below this room!" Jette protested, but did not pull away from his embrace. She studied his face, handsome with its short-cropped blond hair, the wide, high forehead and close-set, thin ears. "No, no, you mustn't . . ."

"But I must," he said and kissed her, pressing her to him, holding her until he could feel the quick quivering response of her body to his. At the sound of footsteps on the stairs she sprang from him and out onto the veranda. Trasker made an exaggerated bow and grinned at her confusion.

Asa Beemer nodded to them and continued down the hall to his own room, but left the door open as he did so. Jette and Trasker listened as Beemer moved about, the sound of his heavy, oak-leather boots reassuring them he was not in a position to spy on them. Trasker took her in his arms again, his mouth hard on hers. Jette backed away, until the railing of the veranda halted her. His smile beneath his clipped blond moustache was more whimsical than passionate. When she fled, her heels drumming loudly down the broad wooden steps, he shook his head in amusement, and silently laughed.

* * * *

"When I was very young my parents took me to Chicago. It wasn't the city it is now, though. A good deal of lake commerce, and so many trains. I understand it's grown huge, almost like New York City." Verdie, pleased to have a guest at their dinner table, attempted to lead their conversation from talk of cattle, land, and politics. Jette had arranged her

68

mother's drab brown hair, helped her into a becoming lavender silk gown, and insisted she wear her amethyst necklace and earrings. Elias noticed, but said nothing; Asa Beemer, taking his lead from his employer, refrained from comment also. Nate Trasker, however, proved the gallant, and Verdie Allenby's vague mind focused intelligently during dinner.

"Chicago will be the hub of the world one of these days. The railroads are seeing to that. And automobiles . . . you should see the streets on Sunday afternoon." Trasker held his cup for Verdie to refill from the ornate silver pot. Elvira deftly cleared the table and brought Elias a cut-glass decanter and delicate, stemmed glasses from the sideboard. "Yes," Trasker continued, "I'm sure it's changed a great deal since you last saw it. You and Mr. Allenby owe it to yourselves to make a visit there and see how it's grown."

"Will that be all, Mrs. Allenby?" Elvira asked, her eyes surreptitiously studying the blond stranger.

"Yes, dear. That's fine," Verdie said. She was pleased the meal had gone well, not because it mattered to Elias, but for Jette's sake. While Elias might choose to dine in clothing still smelling of horse sweat and manure, Verdie and Jette attempted to maintain at least a veneer of refinement on the ranch. Silver, porcelain, crystal—inherited from Verdie's family—and fresh flowers from the carefully tended beds, represented their revolt against Elias' crude ways. By candlelight the adobe room could be any place where civilized people dined.

With no ceremony Elias poured brandy from the decanter, and for no more reason than that it was convenient, had Asa pass the first glass to Verdie. It was not courtesy, but a way to get it done. Thoughout dinner no word passed directly between husband and wife. It was as though a truce had been declared and was

69

being meticulously observed. There was no rudeness; neither was there politeness. Elias looked with disdain at the exquisite glass in his rough hand, raised it to his lips and drank the mellow brandy at a swallow.

"What's a proper stud fee for Old Max?" Elias asked abruptly. Verdie looked at him in dismay, but he only continued, "They've been getting two-hundred—two-fifty if he has to travel."

"Perhaps we should wait to discuss that after we leave the ladies," Trasker suggested just as bluntly. There was no open hint of anger, only a narrowing of his eyes and a straighter line to his lips.

"Hell, man, if they don't like the talk around my dinner table, they're free to go elsewhere!" Elias laughed, but the wine and brandy had ignited his temper.

To avoid unpleasantness Jette interrupted, "Mr. Trasker, what prompted you to try to buy the Baldwin property?" She knew Elias could not help but rise to the challenge; he wanted the Baldwin ranch, too, and if Trasker was his competitor Elias could not resist sounding him out. "From the little I've heard, mostly from Father, it isn't worth much as ranch land and even less for crops. Something about the wells, isn't it, Father?"

"That's right. Can't depend on the wells. Dry up every summer and water's got to be hauled by wagon. Land needs irrigation to get any real use of it. That's why old Seferino Aguilar gave up on it and sold it to Hiram Baldwin in the first place." Elias leaned heavily on both his arms at the table, his shrewd pale eyes intent upon Trasker.

"You planning to go to dry farming?" Asa asked. "That hasn't been practical for a good many years around here. Rains became too irregular ten, fifteen, years ago." Beemer was as curious about Trasker's

70

choice of the Baldwin place as was Elias.

"Perhaps at first," Trasker answered. "But with the phenomenal growth of Los Angeles, I feel truck gardening and citrus orchards will become extremely profitable in a short time. As you said earlier, Allenby, the old-fashioned cattle business is dead." Trasker sipped the brandy and enjoyed its bouquet as he warmed the glass in the palm of his hand. "The Baldwin place is close to San Genaro for workers—close to the railroad for shipping. Not inconsiderable advantages in the overall picture. With the addition of irrigation, that property would prove a valuable investment." Trasker's answer was candid and logical. He merely quoted Elias' own reasons for seeking to purchase Lavinia Baldwin's land—the exact reasons which Abe Marley had surmised and passed on to him. Trasker was gratified to see the old man nodding agreement.

"She's sure as hell not encouraging offers," Asa said. "How'd you hear about it?"

"Abe Marley told me about this young widow who had a ranch on her hands—didn't know what to do with it—and thought I might be able to pick it up at a good price." Trasker smiled ruefully. "It seems she's set on keeping her property, and didn't thank me for my trouble."

"You can just bet she's got something in mind if she's not selling to either of us," Elias said and poured himself another brandy, downing it as before.

"You'd think she'd want to get rid of that place," Jette said. "All alone like that, and right after her husband died. It might be some different if she were used to such a solitary life, but she's a city woman."

Asa Beemer's sudden laughter was infectious. All three men looked at one another as if debating silently among them as to what reply should be made. "Miss Jette," Asa finally said, "I've got a hunch Lavinia

71

Baldwin hasn't been left alone one solitary day in her life—at least not since she quit being a little girl!"

"Aren't you being a bit cruel?" Jette flared.

"Daughter, you've got a lot to learn about your own sex and one whole hell of a lot to learn about Lavinia Baldwin!" Elias laughed until his face grew reddened. "Don't waste your sympathy on that woman."

"But she was only married for six months. Then to have her husband die so suddenly . . ." Jette attempted to defend the woman.

"Damned thoughtful of old Hiram Baldwin to die off so quick. Saved Lavinia from wasting a lot of time in bed with him." Elias was beginning to show the effects of his drinking. His speech was not slurred, only a trifle louder. "Took an old fool like Hiram to think he could take care of a woman like her."

Verdie, accustomed to her husband's unpolished ways, was humiliated at his outburst in front of their guest. Her eyes clouded, her mouth worked to find something proper to say. Helplessly she looked at Jette for rescue.

"Shall we go into the parlor, Mr. Trasker?" Jette asked, and cast her father a withering look.

"Yes, of course, if you like," Trasker replied and pushed back in his chair, rose from the table and assisted Verdie. Jette hastened to rise before Asa Beemer could offer her his help.

" . . . and mind what I say, Trasker," Elias persisted, "that woman knew what she was doing. Coroner couldn't find anything to prove murder, but that's what it was all the same. Who the hell's the coroner anyhow? Just a damned mortician who couldn't rustle up enough buryings to make a living until Abe Marley gave him the job." Elias sloshed brandy into his water goblet, tilted it in a toast at eye level, saying, "Here's to old Hiram, who should have known better!"

Verdie and Jette preceded Nate Trasker and Asa Beemer into the parlor, but their ignoring Elias' tirade availed them nothing. He carried his goblet with him and stood before them, daring all four to try to stop him from finishing. "I knew Hiram from our days in Wyoming Territory. He wasn't a good man, not like you'd mean," he said and looked scathingly at Verdie. "But he never was a womanizer—never. That Lavinia, she set after him, and in five days she'd caught him. He couldn't wait to get her into bed at home . . . he took her right there at the hotel. Everybody in town knows about it." It was almost as if he were lecturing them. "Knew her five days before he married her. Five days, for God's sakes!"

Suddenly a man's shout rang through the evening quiet. No words could be distinguished; it had come from near the fence at the rear of the service yard. Pecky and Buff began wildly barking and dashed toward the fence. At the sound of running and more shouts in excited Spanish, Elias thrust his glass at Verdie and flung open the door to the rear patio.

"The bull, Mr. Allenby. The bull, he's loose!" Benito Galvan yelled as soon as he saw Elias' figure outlined in the doorway against the yellow lamplight. "He broke out of the stall!" The elderly Mexican was breathless as he ran to the house.

"Asa!" Elias grabbed Galvan's lantern and joined the men as they led the way up to the barn. The dogs rushed past them and into the pasture as soon as the gate was opened. From the number of hands already at the barn it was evident someone had raised the alarm in the workmen's village before informing the rancher and foreman. "If those kids . . ." Elias began.

"No, sir, it wasn't them," Benito said as they ran. "He just broke down the door to the stall—right off its hinges." Lanterns bobbed crazily in the pasture ahead.

From the horse barn emerged two vaqueros, hastily mounted, their lassos already whistling as they cut circles in the night air. A low roaring bellow issued from the dark as the huge animal, cornered by men and horses, defended its freedom.

Jette watched from the flagstone patio behind the house. Trasker came to stand behind her, his hands clasping her waist.

"Aren't you going to help?" Jette asked.

"No, I am not. I know absolutely nothing about blooded bulls, and that creature's far too dangerous for an amateur to try to corral." He gently pulled her to him and kissed the side of her cheek, his breath warm in her ear. "Besides, I want to be here with you. I rather doubt your father would approve of my doing this . . ." He turned her about and found her lips with his, his hands holding her body close.

"Oh, Nate, Nate . . ." Jette yielded to his embrace, her arms encircling him as she laid her head against his shoulder. "He wouldn't approve . . ." She clung to him, her body trembling with the sudden fires his nearness aroused.

"Is there someone else?" he asked. "Is that why he wouldn't approve?"

"No . . . yes . . ." she stammered.

"Which is it, darling?" His breath stirred a wisp of auburn hair which curled from her temple.

She raised her arms about his neck and replied, "Father's promised me to Asa." There was a note of desperation in her voice.

"And is that what you want?" His fingers touched her breast, softly, gently, in a caress she had never before known. "Tell me, Jette, is Asa what you want?"

Unheard were the shouts and yells of the men in the pasture, the defiant roars of the bull; in the dark seclusion of the patio Jette could only hear the beating of her own heart. Unseen were the wild gyrations of the lanterns; she was aware only of Trasker's face dimly seen in the darkness, his strong arms around her, his mouth on hers, his hands arousing in her a violent physical longing.

"No," she whispered. "No, Asa is not what I want."

Chapter 5

Verdie walked around her daughter and inspected the new linen suit and silk waist. The crisp ivory skirt and short, fitted jacket were edged with wide bands of black and white checked grosgrain, the same trim that embellished a straw boater which perched atop Jette's upswept masses of auburn hair.

"Is it all right? Does the hem hang evenly all around?" Jette asked as she twirled rapidly and craned her neck to see the back of the skirt. "It just has to be perfect." Her black eyes danced with excitement and anticipation.

"It's fine, dear. Now stand still so I can tuck the waist in properly. You've got it all bunched up in the middle." Verdie patiently evened out the pale yellow silk blouse and straightened the narrow waistband. "There . . . you're all ready," she said, wistfully envious of her daughter's prospective outing.

May Day had dawned clear and a trifle cooler, with a slight breeze from the west which died down shortly after sunrise. The San Genaro High School Marching Band and troops of gaily costumed Grammer School children would have a day perfect for their annual celebration. Local merchants donated prizes for participants; fraternal organizations provided materials and manpower for the noontime pageant and Maypole dance held on the county courthouse lawn. The natural exuberance of spring and pent-up enthusiasm—an enthusiasm spurred by the nearness of summer vacation—each year made the event a colorful, if slightly juvenile, festival.

"I'm glad you're going with the Larson girls," Verdie said as they walked along the veranda to the stairs. "That looks much more proper than attending alone with a man." She had worried that Jette would be asked to the festival by Nate Trasker. Not that it would prove scandalous for the girl to be alone with a man whom she scarcely knew, but that Elias would be angry.

"Lucy didn't mention in her note who all is going—just that they made up a small party. Now you won't forget, will you, that I'm to stay over for supper with them?" Jette knew her mother would fret about her when she did not return in the evening. "And remind Socorro not to set a place for me. Will you remember that?" She held Verdie's thin arm and steadied her as they descended the outdoor staircase. "Will you remember?" she repeated.

"Yes, I'll tell her right away," Verdie answered. "But I wish the girls wouldn't insist on coming up to the house. You could meet them at the road. Your father's apt to see them and make a scene." Her brow wrinkled in consternation as she imagined the probable diatribe. "I don't want him to embarrass you in front of your little friends."

"Mother, they aren't little anymore. They're the same age as I," she reminded Verdie. "And they would be more angered than embarrassed—just as I should be. After the way Father's carried on his feud with their father they wouldn't be surprised by anything he might say or do." Jette had to admit to herself that she had misgivings about Elias encountering the Larson girls on his own property, especially after his last court battle which had cost him the friendship of other ranchers in the valley.

Verdie glanced uneasily toward the ranch store and barn as they entered the parlor through the east door. Immediately after breakfast Elias had gone with Benito to check supplies and issue purchase orders for the store; then he intended to oversee the construction of the bull pen adjacent to the cattle barn. He had merely ridiculed Jette for her job hunting efforts—since they availed her nothing—but should he discover with whom she was going to the May Day Fete, Verdie shuddered.

"Just because Father hates Jacob Larson gives him no right to interfere in my friendship with Margaret and Lucy. Their quarrel has nothing to do with us," Jette said as she held the door open for her mother.

"That may be true, Jette, but you know how he is." Verdie paused in the middle of the parlor and looked into the dining room. There was something she must tell Socorro. From the graveled drive came the sound of the Larson's buckboard-surrey and high-stepping chestnuts. Buff and Pecky abandoned their watch at the kitchen door and scurried to meet the callers with a series of frantic yelps.

Verdie rushed to the front door which gave onto the curved drive before the house. "They're here, Jette," she called to the girl and flung open one side of the wide double door.

The large surrey, decorated with rainbow-colored bunting and rosettes of white crepe paper, approached the house with a jangle of polished brass harness bells and laughter of the group of young people crowded onto the shallow seats. Lucy Larson smiled and waved to Verdie as the woman stood timidly in the doorway.

"Jette will be right here," Verdie said, only vaguely wondering where Jette had gone when they came down-

77

stairs.

"Mother, I told Socorro I won't be here for dinner," Jette said as she came running from the kitchen. She knew her mother could not remember to tell the elderly cook. "Bye bye," she whispered and kissed Verdie's cheek before she ran down the steps to the waiting carriage.

"Have a good time, dear," Verdie called as one of the young men helped Jette into the surrey. Instantly the beribboned whip cracked and the team pranced about the arc of driveway and back into the lane toward the road.

Lucy Larson bent across the back of her seat and grasped Jette's hands. "You made it! We were afraid you wouldn't. Jette, I want you to meet Henry Stebbins. Henry, this is Jette Allenby." The young man sitting beside Lucy turned about and smiled, first at Lucy, then at Jette. It was clear why he was sitting beside the younger Larson girl, for his glance crept away from Lucy's face as if he were loathe to look at anyone else even if that person were as strikingly beautiful as Jette Allenby.

"Hello, Henry. I've heard a lot about you from Lucy. I'm so glad to meet you at last." Jette offered her hand to him.

"Miss Allenby . . ."

"Please call me Jette. All my friends do," she said.

"Then Jette, I'm happy you could come with us. And I'm just awfully glad to meet you." He looked shyly at Lucy whose face flushed pink beneath her flower-decked blue hat. "Lucy and I want you to be among the first to know . . ."

"We're going to be married!" Lucy burst out and giggled. "We just decided on the way over from the house now."

"Oh, that's wonderful news!" Jette leaned forward

over the seat and hugged Lucy. "Congratulations, both of you."

"Before we forget our manners completely . . . what with all this commotion . . ." Margaret Larson, a larger, more robust version of Lucy, interrupted, "Jette, I don't believe you've met Doctor Hunter."

Jette turned to the back seat in surprise. So hurriedly had she climbed into the surrey, and so anxious to get away from the house, she had not taken notice of everyone in the group. Had his head been turned away from her as she got into the surrey? She could not remember, but now as their eyes met she wondered how she could possibly have failed to recognize his presence immediately.

"We met briefly a few weeks ago," Jette said. "How are you, Doctor Hunter?" She averted her eyes from his crutches, but her concern showed in her face. She really cared about how he was.

"Much better; improving steadily, thank you." He had caught her meaning by the subtle inflection she gave the words. Sincerity was in her intense black eyes. "I'm happy to see you again." He took her hand in his, the warmth and gentleness of his grasp communicating far more than he intended. Hunter laughed and hastened to explain, "You might say I quite literally ran into Miss Allenby at the bank. That's really what happened. I'm not a thing of grace and beauty with these . . ." He tapped the crutches propped beside him in the wagonbed.

As they all joined him in his easy laughter Margaret looked puzzled, aware that there was something portentous in their meeting. Except for Lucy and Henry, the young people were not paired off. Margaret Larson, although pretty in a plump, pink-cheeked way, was pale competition for Jette's vibrant beauty, and the mannish, severely tailored ecru suit she wore did nothing to enhance her unruly brown hair and hazel eyes. A pang of jealousy made her suddenly regret Jette's presence, since she had pictured Doctor Hunter leaning on her arm, looking at her as he now did at Jette.

As the right wheels of the surrey bumped into a hidden rut and jostled the passengers, Margaret exaggerated her bouncing and nudged Hunter with her hips, then settled closer to him. "Henry, you're a wretched driver," she chided her sister's beau. "I'm sorry, Miles," she apologized to Hunter as she peered coquettishly from beneath the brim of her tan straw boater. Her efforts to gain his attention were in vain, however, for he sat gazing at the russet-haired beauty in the forward seat.

Hunter's broad shoulders occupied a great deal of the narrow space, while the young man on the other side of Margaret was quite content to crowd close to her and feel her thighs alongside his own. Margaret was delighted with the seating she had arranged, but grew resentful as she followed Hunter's glance toward Jette. Although scarcely believing the gossip the Allenby servants had whispered about a stranger paying court to Jette, Margaret was comforted to know that the couple had been spied on the upstairs veranda together. Kissing and hugging right out in the open—or at least so it was said. If that were so, Jette could hardly be interested in the young doctor. Margaret relaxed back into the seat, somewhat reassured at the thought.

She moved her leg, ostensibly to brace herself against the swaying as the team swung them into the main road and headed south. Hunter shifted slightly to reposition his body. At least he had feeling in his legs. Margaret smiled to herself at the revelation.

"Jette, what's this we've been hearing about some man from back east visiting at your place?" Margaret eyed Hunter as she asked the question. "From all we hear, he must be quite dashing. Is he here on business?" She was annoyed as the merest shadow of a frown passed over Doctor Hunter's face. "Who is he?" she demanded.

"Trasker—Nate Trasker," Jette replied. She had not missed the sharpness that whetted an edge on Margaret's voice. "He has business with Father. Seems he wants to buy property and settle here in San Genaro Valley."

"Is he married?" Lucy asked.

"Now why on earth would you want to know that?" Henry gathered Lucy to him with one arm and held the reins with one hand as he kissed her flushed face. "You're already spoken for—remember?"

"Do be careful, you two! People will see you." Margaret scolded from the back of the surrey, but she tittered behind her gloved hand and smiled into Hunter's amused eyes.

"Tell us all about him, Jette," Lucy begged. She had, of course, also heard the gossip and was as curious as her sister, but for vastly different reasons. "Is he a drummer?"

"Oh, no, nothing like that. He's connected with a development company in Chicago," Jette replied. "I'm afraid I don't understand what it is they do. For that matter, he hasn't really said much about it to me."

"Ah ha! Just what has he been talking to you about?" Margaret asked. She did not dare ask Jette what the man's intentions were, but she was determined to learn.

"It's Father he talks to," Jette answered. "And Asa Beemer. He tried to buy Lavinia Baldwin's place, but didn't have any more luck with her than Father did."

"Say, speaking of the devil, if you ladies will pardon the expression . . ." Henry Stebbins, since his hands

81

were full of Lucy Larson and reins, nodded with his head toward the junction of Las Lomas Road where a buggy was approaching the highway. "Isn't that Mrs. Baldwin?" They all turned to look as the fancy phaeton and beautifully matched bays entered the roadway.

Clad in tight black silk with clusters of black-beaded flowers and soutache braid, Lavinia Baldwin was a study in contrasts. Beneath an enormous black maline and ostrich feather hat her face was white, her lips bright crimson. Amassed about her head was a wealth of straw-blond hair, caught into a fantastic coiffure of poufs and swirls which were held in place with hairpins demurely ornamented with polished black onyx cabochons. She was small, but buxom, her breasts lifted and waist modishly cinched by corset and laces. The black of her costume proclaimed her to be in mourning, but everything else about the woman was a paean of voluptuousness.

"Should we speak to her?" Lucy asked her sister.

"Certainly not!" Margaret hissed. They watched in silence as the carriage continued toward town ahead of them. "Can you imagine? Her husband's only just been buried, and she's out sporting with another man!"

Miles Hunter ignored the girls' remarks as he saw the sudden pain in Jette Allenby's face. There was no mistaking either the passenger or the driver; obviously Jette had recognized the man.

"Who's that she's with?" Lucy asked. "I've never seen him before."

For a moment Jette did not reply. Then she said. "That's the man we've been talking about—Nate Trasker."

* * * *

"Surely your father isn't as formidable as that,"

Miles Hunter said as he handed Jette into the buggy, a feat made more awkward by his crutches. "An innocent day spent with friends—he couldn't object to that."

"Oh he couldn't, could he?" Margaret Larson's voice had become more shrill throughout the evening as she had observed Hunter's attentions to Jette. She strolled from the front porch steps into the yard where several buggies awaited departing guests. "I'm afraid Mr. Allenby has an abiding grudge against a good many of us here in San Genaro Valley. You'd be well warned not to get on the bad side of him, Miles."

"Jette's had simply a miserable time of it—what with her mother and all." Lucy caught herself and said quickly, "She's not well, you know. Poor Jette's had to be doctor and nurse—and run the house, too."

Henry Stebbins held the horses, then stood aside as Doctor Hunter wrestled himself into the Concord buggy beside Jette. Henry made no attempt to assist Hunter, rightly sensing that the young doctor preferred to manage by himself. "All set?" he asked.

"All set, thank you," Hunter replied as he took the reins. "Good night, ladies."

"Bye, Jette," Lucy called from the porch.

"Margaret, Lucy, thank you for having me with you today. It's been one of the happiest days of my life. It's meant a great deal to me—more than you can possibly know. Thank you." Hunter was surprised at the intensity of Jette's farewell. He could only wonder why such a lovely girl should have experienced so few outings and parties. He clucked the horses down the drive and for the time it took them to reach the road neither Jette nor he uttered a word.

The night had remained balmy, although a slight breeze from the south heralded a change in weather. Overhead the midnight sky already was starting to cloud over and lightning flickered in the distance. The buggy's acetylene lamps made splotches of light on either side of the horses enough for the creatures to see the road and maintain a decent trot.

"Why do you put up with it?" Hunter suddenly asked.

"I'm not sure I know what you mean," Jette said.

"Come now, you're not a Lucy or a Margaret. You needn't play games with me." He was quite serious.

"I'm not sure if that's flattering to any of us," she laughed.

"They're very nice girls, both of them. I'm sure you don't misunderstand my meaning."

"No, I don't really. I know what you mean." Jette sighed and looked at Hunter. "And you're nothing like Henry or Martin or . . ."

"Or?" he interrupted her.

"Or any other man I've known," she said.

"Have you known so many men then?" he asked.

"No," she admitted slowly. "No, I've had little chance to become acquainted with very many people, men or women."

"It must be a lonely life for a girl like you."

"Sometimes . . . yes, it is," she replied.

"Then why?" He did not apologize for his curiosity, but insisted upon an answer. "Why do you remain in your father's house?"

"Mostly for Mother's sake," Jette said. "I don't mean that to sound heroic. It's nothing of the sort really—it's just that I'm all she has. I don't know what would become of her. I tried several times to go away; she insisted I must for my own sake, but Father has always managed to force me to return. I'm afraid for her safety if I left."

"But that's not all?" Hunter sensed there was yet another reason.

"Money," she answered with open candor. "Does that shock you?"

"Do you think it should?" he parried.

"It sounds a bit too honest put so bluntly. When I say it out loud I remind myself of a lot of women—and men, too—whom I soundly criticize for putting money first." She laughed again. "I guess I'm not so much different after all."

"Money's very important. There are a lot of profligate souls who don't appreciate it."

"In my case it's important for many reasons." Jette turned to face Hunter. "My grandmother established a trust fund for me, but until I either marry or reach the age of twenty-five I have no control of it." She added with unaccustomed intensity, "I want control!"

Hunter looked at her. "You're terribly unhappy. I'm sorry. We shouldn't even be talking of such matters." He reached across and took her hand in his. "I've no right to comment, much less pry. Perhaps it's because I've become sensitive to others' pain."

"That's a fine quality in a man—sensitivity," she said quietly. Even in the dim light she could see the lines that his own pain had cut into his face and the gentleness it had left in his deep blue eyes. "You're not ashamed of it, are you?"

"Certainly not. This world has enough suffering and cruelty. Maybe if everyone became a bit more conscious of it around them we could eventually have less." In her face he saw his own pain reflected. "Can't you leave your mother? Are you afraid for her physically? Is that it?"

"Yes," she said. Then suddenly she wrenched her hand from his grasp and leaned away from him. "It's hideous. Hideous!"

"Have you no relatives? Can't you arrange for your mother to go to them?" Hunter was startled by her reaction.

"No immediate family—only distant cousins in Virginia. And Mother is in no condition to go anywhere. Father would never let her go anyhow. It's hopeless!" She looked away to the south where lights shone, sprinkled across the lower valley. Far beyond was the city of Los Angeles. "Do you know any lawyers in Los Angeles?" she asked.

"No. I'm really not acquainted in California at all." He made no attempt to take her hand again. "Do you think that's what you need?"

"I was advised . . ." She hesitated before repeating the banker's name. "I was advised by Mr. Millege at the bank that we might be able to get some of the stipulations set aside, or at least prevent depletion of the trust until I can legally claim it."

"If that's what's holding you here against your will, I'd have to agree with him. Would that enable you to take your mother away? To provide for her elsewhere?"

"Yes, if there's any money left by that time." She removed her hat and placed it on the floor by her feet. "But Father would stop us. He'd find some way."

"Tell me about your mother. Doctor Hill hasn't seen her in a long time, but he did mention her to me. How is she?"

"She's not crazy," Jette said quickly. "No matter what anyone says—she's not really crazy."

"From what little I know of her, I must agree." Hunter's reply encouraged Jette to continue.

"I'm sure you've already heard about Father. And it's all probably true." She laughed bitterly. "I'm learning things about him constantly. He's dominated Mother completely. Right from the start he hasn't allowed her to have an opinion of her own any more than he's allowed her the use of her own money. Her dowry went to him—he saw to that. And he's beaten and threatened her until she's so cowed and confused . . ." Jette shook her head. "I think she mentally blocks things out so she can't be hurt any more."

86

"But physically she's well?" he asked.

"Remarkably so, considering her age," Jette replied.

"Have you considered petitioning the court for a restraining order against your father?" Hunter's suggestion was reasonable.

"You're new here. You aren't aware yet of how things work in San Genaro County."

"I don't understand," he said.

"Judge Killigrew's the court and law in this county—and he and Father are close. He'd never issue such an order against my father. Besides," Jette paused and looked squarely at Hunter as she went on, "If we were to do such a thing we'd never live to see the benefit from it."

"Aren't you exaggerating, Jette?" Hunter asked. "Surely he's not as violent as that."

"Miles, Miles, is your Ohio so far from our West? Don't you know—haven't you ever heard about what goes on out here?"

"But that was long ago, Jette. Decades! This is 1901, not frontier days," he said gently. "Men don't sport side arms and settle disputes by calling each other out."

"Husbands still beat wives—fathers still batter children. Murder is still committed and goes undiscovered and unpunished. Once a man like my father is accustomed to such behavior, will a mere piece of paper issued by a court stop him?" The enormity of her despair suddenly overwhelmed her and she buried her face in her hands.

"Darling . . ." Hunter took her in his arms, his lips pressed her forehead, her eyes, her mouth. "I don't want you to be unhappy—not ever." She clung to him and laid her head against his shoulder, finding comfort in the strength of his arms, the gentleness of his hands. They rode in silence, the horses steadfastly trotting between the two bobbing pools of light.

"I'm so glad you asked to see me home," Jette

87

whispered as they neared the Allenby ranch drive. "Margaret didn't take much to the idea, but I'm glad you did. She's quite jealous, you know."

"Margaret has no claim on me, Jette," Hunter said. "No one has, except you." He hugged her to him and bent to kiss her upturned face, his hands exploring the softness of her breasts.

"Let me out at the drive," she said as they drew even with the eucalyptus hedge that lined the road west of the ranch house. "I'll walk the rest of the way."

"You'll do nothing of the kind."

"But Father may be . . ."

"What? Waiting up for you? Fine!" Hunter reined the horses to a walk and turned into the driveway. From the road no lights were visible, but as they approached the adobe a glimmer shone through the shrubs and trees from the front parlor. "I'd like to meet him. When I ask him for your hand I'd rather it not be as a total stranger."

Jette drew away from him abruptly.

"Does that surprise you?" he asked. "For people who love one another it's still the custom, isn't it? Even here in your West?" He laughed, but ceased when he saw her face.

"Do you love me, Miles?" she asked. "Do you?"

"Darling, of course I do," he replied. "From the first time I saw you at the bank . . . with the sunlight blazing in your hair and your face so sad and beautiful." He kissed her tenderly. "Being with you today was an answer to my prayers. I want you, Jette. I want to marry you."

"But he'll never agree." Her glance fell on the crutches at his side.

"Because of these?" Miles kicked impatiently at the crutches which were propped against the seat. "They're not a permanent part of me."

"Oh, Miles, no! I didn't mean that at all," she protested and cradled her head in the hollow of his neck. "I'm promised already to Asa Beemer!"

Hunter stiffened and looked down at her. Dogs in the workmen's village yapped alarm at the strange carriage and horses; the only other sounds were the plodding of the horses and crunch of wheels in gravel as they pulled into the arc of drive before the house.

"I see," he said and turned his face away.

"No, you don't see at all!" Jette retorted. "Father promised me to him. I had no say in it—nobody asked me. I loathe the man." She threw herself into his arms and coaxed his lips down to meet hers.

"Do you love me?" he asked.

"How can I answer you?" She touched his face with her fingertips, tracing the lines about his mouth. "If I knew, I'd tell you." As he started to say something she placed her fingers on his lips. "Shhhh . . . please, just listen . . ." She waited until he nodded assent. "I'm fond of you—that much I know. And I care a great deal about what happens to you. I like being with you. But I also care too much about you to say I love you, let you belive it, and maybe it wouldn't be true."

He said nothing and reined the horses to a stop before the shallow steps leading to the house. "Please don't be angry with me for being honest with you, Miles," she pleaded.

"Darling, I could never be angry with you. Perhaps I'm disappointed—even a bit hurt—but angry, no." He wound the leather reins about the whipstock and reached for his crutches.

"No, Miles," Jette said. "Please don't get out. I can see myself in all right." She placed her hand on his arm to halt him. "Everyone's in bed and it would only disturb them. Mother's left a lamp downstairs for me. I'll be all right."

He turned to take her in his arms and pulled her close, his fingers tangled in her auburn hair as she brought her face to his. For long moments he held her, feeling the vibrancy of her young body against his. "Good night, Jette," he whispered. "Shall I see you again?"

"Oh, yes, soon . . . please," she replied, breaking from his embrace to take her hat and descend from the buggy. She turned from the second step and said softly, "Good night, Miles," before she fled into the house.

Jette fitted the brass key into the lock and entered the parlor. A white-globed kerosene lamp glowed from the center-table at one side of the door. Only as she picked up the lamp and relocked the door did she realize Pecky and Buff were silent. She smiled to herself. Verdie had undoubtedly shut the two dogs up in the wash house behind the kitchen. No watch dogs guarding Elias' domain? How furious he would be if he knew.

Through the day she had crowded all thought of Nate Trasker from her consciousness. In the company of the Larson girls and Miles Hunter she could almost forget the sight of Trasker and the newly widowed Lavinia Baldwin as they bent, tete-a-tete, over luncheon on the grass at Lagunita Park. Now as she stood alone in the silent parlor she remembered his laughter and gallantry as he had amused Verdie at dinner a few nights ago. She remembered, too, the feel of his hands upon her body, the strong fingers that communicated an ardent desire as they embraced in the secrecy of the dark patio.

Unconsciously she touched her fingertips to her lips, recalling the hard, sweet possessiveness of his kisses. Surely by now Lavinia Baldwin must also have felt the warmth of his attention—if he was charming, he was also generous with his affections.

What did I expect from him? Jette asked herself. Lavinia Baldwin's property certainly constituted a surer attraction than Jette's naive, virginal infatuation. *Why should he be in love with me?* Still, as she thought of Trasker, she felt a desolation that was akin to physical pain.

And Miles Hunter—what of him? Jette refused to compare the two men who had so suddenly thrust themselves into her life. They were as disparate as earth and air. Resolutely she forced herself to cease thinking of Trasker.

Opening the rear parlor door which gave access to the patio, she placed the lamp on the flagstone step and relocked the door, then, holding her hat and skirts with one hand, lamp in the other, started up the outside staircase. From the back parlor she heard the wall clock strike one.

As she reached the top of the stairs she halted and listened. Somewhere the floor had creaked. She waited, straining to hear. Carefully she turned down the wick and blew out the flame. Darkness was almost total beneath the roof overhang. Had Elias known of her dereliction—that she had spent the day with Jacob Larson's family—he would have confronted her immediately upon her return. With the dogs in the wash house, a prowler could easily gain access to the upper veranda. Plentiful as his enemies were, it would not be unreasonable to discover one skulking about, taking advantage of the dogs' absence. Cautiously she advanced to the door of the guest room and waited again, scarcely daring to breathe.

As her eyes became adjusted to the dark she could make out familiar shapes of wicker chairs and table at the corner of the veranda. Dogs in the workmen's quarters had ceased their alarm, and from the interior of a viburnum bush off the patio a tree frog resumed its rhythmical trilling. The sound for which she listened did not recur.

It's just the old floors settling, she told herself. Feeling foolish for her fright, she gathered her skirts once more and tiptoed past her parents' bedroom where a loud snoring assured her that Elias slept soundly.

Using the same brass key as for the downstairs doors, Jette entered her own bedroom, located the small marble-topped table to the right of the door where she deposited the lamp. She groped for the door, found the lock with her fingers and inserted the key preparatory to securing it for the night. Despite the veranda window being open, the room remained stuffy. She found her way to the window and eased the lower pane all the way up. For a moment she stood in the slight draft the opening made, then turned and propped the door open for more air.

At the edge of her consciousness fear once more began to grow, as if the creaking of the old timber flooring had been a warning. She returned to stand at the open window, half expecting substance to materialize from the dark. Wearily she sighed and yawned, then tiptoed to the tall walnut armoire in the corner of the room and threw open its paneled doors.

Rather than relight the extinguished lamp or light a candle, she began undressing in the dark, removed the grosgrain-trimmed suit and yellow blouse, and placed them on hangers in the wardrobe. Shutting the armoire doors made a loud double click as the latches caught, but there was little chance that any noise from her room would disturb Elias across the hallway. She unlaced and removed her light corset and black hose and draped the ruffled petticoats over a chair before feeling her way to the chest of drawers for a fresh nightdress.

With a quick gasp of fright she stopped. Out of the blackness in the far corner the floor creaked as from a stealthy tread. Within the shadows she sensed movement although nothing was visible. She clutched the gown before her, a pitifully inadequate defense against the unseen menace.

"Who's there?" she whispered, too frightened to raise her voice. A vague form separated from the corner and slowly crossed the room. Suddenly the door swung shut, its key twisted in the lock with metallic finality.

"Who's there?" Jette demanded, her terror mounting. She darted for the door, tried the knob, fumbled for the key. There was none.

A rough hand closed over hers in a vise-like grip. Another hand stifled the scream in her mouth as she was thrown onto the bed. Pinioned beneath the weight of her assailant, she thrashed wildly with her free hand, pushing at the face that bent over her. The instant her other hand was released she felt a vicious groping at her breasts. Hard fingers tore away her thin chemise and grasped at the tender softness. She writhed in revulsion as strong legs impinged upon hers, forcing them apart.

Jette pummeled the man's head, her fingers raking the mouth that sought her breast. As she weakened she felt a hand go to her naked groin. Summoning a last desperate burst of strength she wrenched sideways and bit at the hand covering her mouth.

A smothered growl of anger and pain issued from the man's throat as she rolled free of him and fell to the floor. Unable to scream and call for aid, Jette uttered only a low, choked cry. She struggled to reach the open window, but the man threw himself upon her. She twisted from him, and from the washstand seized the heavy water pitcher. Sensing danger, he ducked to his right, taking the blow upon his left shoulder and back. Water exploded across the room as he staggered.

"You bitch!" he hissed and stumbled erect. "You murderous little bitch!" He grabbed at the table to steady himself as he reeled toward her.

In her rage and humiliation she could make no sound. At her feet lay the nightdress. Shuddering uncontrollably, she could neither retrieve the garment nor continue the struggle. She slumped against the wall by the window, dim light outlining the smooth curve of her hips and thighs. The man stood before her, so close she could smell the whiskey and feel his panting breath on her flushed skin. In that instant she recognized him.

"I could kill you for that!" he said in a hoarse whisper. Jette waited silently for the inescapable, but refused to cringe. He lurched toward her, took her in his arms, pressed her naked body to him, his mouth covering hers in a kiss, violent and hard. At her total lack of response, neither yielding nor opposing, he released her with a snort of disgust. She turned her head from him and wiped the back of her hand across her mouth.

"Not good enough for you, am I?" Asa Beemer snarled. "Maybe if I got me a couple of sticks and went around on gimpy legs . . . maybe you'd like that better?"

"Nothing you could ever do would make me stop despising you!" Jette spat out at him. Frantically she tried to think of anything within reach which might serve as a weapon. Without it, there was no use in further resistance. Asa was not only strong and could prevent her escaping through the window, but he had the key to the door.

"You think I'm gonna leave without getting what I came for?" He stood threateningly close, between her and the open window, as if anticipating her thoughts.

Jette sidled toward the window, but he moved slightly, effectively blocking her way. "Get out!" she commanded. She felt his hands touch her hips and slide upward, exploring roughly as they made their way to her hard-nippled breasts. His breath, sour with liquor, was coming shallow and fast. Slowly she inched away, edging toward a small desk in the corner, leaning her body into his embrace, teasing him to follow.

With one swift move she broke from him, grabbed a

letter opener which lay on the desk, and stabbed wildly. A sudden gasp told her the blade had found its mark. She retreated to the foot of the bed as Asa clutched at his arm and backed away from her.

"You she-devil!" He felt a warm smear where the paper knife had penetrated. "You'd kill me, wouldn't you?"

"Yes!" She held the knife ready to strike again. "But I'll let Father have that pleasure."

Asa laughed quietly as he placed his blue bandana handkerchief up his sleeve to staunch the wound.

"You won't laugh after I tell Father you tried to rape me!" She was furious that he would dare to ridicule her, but as the insinuating laughter continued, realization of its meaning slowly dawned on her. "My dear God . . . it can't be . . ." she whispered. "Father wouldn't . . . he couldn't . . ."

"No?" he taunted. "Well, you just go on thinking that way if it's any comfort to you. But it isn't so, girlie, and you might as well know it right now." He waited a moment before he continued, "That fancy doctor of yours hasn't got a chance—not with Elias, anyhow." Asa could hear the catch of her breath. "It's me—or nobody!"

"Get out!" she almost shouted. In a daze she realized that he unlocked the door and closed it behind him, leaving her sobbing alone in the dark. She turned the key and tested the door, half expecting Asa to return, then lowered the window pane, setting the locking peg to leave an eight-inch opening at the bottom. There was no use in calling her parents; her mother could do nothing. And her father . . . .

Jette threw herself across the bed and gave way to her anguish. As the raking sobs subsided she became aware of her nakedness. A chill wind had sprung up, moving the lace panels at the window and making goose-flesh of her skin. Too exhausted to move, she pulled the quilted coverlet about her and lay awake, awaiting the storm. Thunder rumbled over the mountains and within minutes rolling clouds obscured stars and distant hills, leaving the valley enveloped in total darkness. The room momentarily brightened with sporadic bursts of lightning, only to be engulfed in shadows even more intense.

She had preserved her virginity. But for how long? She was pledged to Asa Beemer. What he considered his—by right of Elias' promise—he intended to take, and obviously with Elias' blessing. She shuddered as she remembered the feel of his lean, hard body in its rough clothing as he struggled with her. She pressed her fingers against the bruises his heavy turquoise and silver belt buckle had made on her rib cage and belly.

Elias had turned Asa loose upon her just as he would turn his prize Angus bull into the heifer lot.

"He will not!" Jette sobbed aloud. "He will not breed me like some animal!" Doubling her fists, she struck with all her remaining strength at the quilt, the pillows, the mattress, in a frenzy of anger and humiliation. Sweat poured from her body. As she collapsed in sheer fatigue, she found herself unable to weep or even move.

Asa was right about Elias never accepting Doctor Hunter. To hope for such a thing would be not only useless, but foolish. And she had already been too foolish about Nate Trasker. Their secret, stolen kisses had meant nothing more to him than flirtatious amusement. She had taken him too seriously, ignoring the possibility of a rival for his love. It was a logical, practical move on Trasker's part—his attentions to Lavinia Baldwin. He had failed in his attempts to purchase her property. How better to obtain it than by marrying the owner?

Jette tried to put from her mind the memory of
Trasker's mouth on hers, his gentle caresses, so
different from Asa's brutal assault, and the scent of
bergamot toilet lotion, soft leather, and expensive
tobacco that lingered about him.

She buried her head beneath the pillow, but could
neither stop her turbulent thoughts nor block out the
sound of the storm. She lay listening as the violence
came nearer. Fierce squalls blasted against the old
adobe, pried at the tiled roof. Lightning exploded the
night with dazzling brilliance followed by resonant
thunder which shook even the thick mud walls.

Suddenly it seemed to the girl that her own life was as
besieged by uncontrollable forces as was the old adobe
by the wild, unseasonable spring storm. Her young
world of eager hopes was being overpowered by
malignant darkness.

"As some dark world from upper air
'Were Stooping over this . . ."

Jette recalled the poet's vision of an impending
storm. As some dark world. . . .

Chapter 6

"Miss Jette, why don't you let the men do that? Benito
can tell them how to do it." Elvira wrinkled her nose at
the pungent smell of liquid manure in the stained
wooden barrel. Flies edged the damp rim where the flat
oak top was askew. "You don't have to get all dirty like
that—just look at the back of your skirt," she scolded.

Jette straightened up and pulled the back of her dress
up to inspect the damage. "It's percale. It'll wash out."
She fluffed the wet hem and brushed mud from the

cambric hem lining.

"Why don't I go get Benito?" the small Mexican girl insisted. "I'll go over to the barn . . ."

"No, no," Jette protested. "This is one chore I want to do myself."

"But the men get paid for doing things like that," Elvira said as she stepped over a pile of debris in the pathway.

"This much I can do for Mother." Jette fished in her deep apron pocket for the pruning scissors and snipped off five perfect blooms and several buds. Making a compact bouquet, she inhaled the fragrance, as much reminiscent of delicate spices and fresh cut apples as of roses. Petals of clear deep yellow blushed rose at their crisp, ruffled edges, almost appeared luminescent against their black-green leaves. "Put these on her luncheon tray."

Elvira took the flowers gingerly to avoid the thorns. Her brown face grew sad as she looked at the roses. "These are the ones from her home, aren't they?" she asked.

"Yes, from Virginia." Jette replied.

"Do they have many flowers there?"

"Oh yes, whole gardens full of them. And blooming trees and shrubs . . . things that we can't grow here." Jette hacked at the hard adobe soil with the hoe.

"It must be a beautiful place." Elvira looked at the roses in her hand. "She misses it so much."

"Yes, she does." Jette hammered at the soil, managing to break up only a few unyielding clods.

"Please let me get one of the men to at least help you, Miss Jette," Elvira pleaded.

"If you can find Benito—without having to run out to the pasture—you could tell him to have one of the men take the barrel back to the garden shed for me." Jette would give the girl the satisfaction of doing that much to aid her this morning.

Elvira nodded. "He's down at the store. I saw him from the kitchen a while ago. I'll go tell him right away." She hesitated, her face straining into a scowl before she continued, "Socorro wants to know about lunch. Will you eat downstairs? Mrs. Allenby's lying down upstairs and says she isn't eating." Her dark face mirrored the fright and upset of the morning's quarrel between Elias and Jette. She jumped the shallow ditch beside the path and made her way through the beds of purple alyssum and white petunias.

"I shouldn't wonder she's not eating," Jette said. "It's my fault I guess. Is Father coming back for dinner at noon?"

"No, he says he'll want supper early. He had Socorro put up bread and bacon and pie for him and Mr. Beemer. They went out to the east pasture right after . . . after . . ." The girl faltered as she attempted to put the morning's events into proper English.

"Then tell Socorro to fix a light lunch and put it on trays for Mother and me. We'll eat on the veranda upstairs. Some cheese, a few slices of the roast from last night, horseradish sauce, green salad with vinaigrette. Is there some cake left over from last night?"

"Yes. Would you like a raspberry sauce for it?"

"That sounds good. Mother's fond of it."

"And bread or biscuits?"

"Plain buttered bread will do." Jette wiped her forehead with her voluminous blue cotton duck apron. "I'll try to get Mother to eat something."

"Shall I put the roses in the little crystal bowl?" Elvira asked.

"You're sweet to remember," Jette smiled. "Yes, that's her favorite. That's very thoughtful of you," she agreed. "Ring the dinner bell for me when you're ready."

"Yes, Miss Jette." The little maid turned to go, stopped, and retraced her steps. "I'm sorry about this

99

morning. I just want you to know it wasn't me or Socorro . . . or Benito, either, I'm sure. We didn't say one word to Mr. Allenby." She twisted the rose stems in her fingers and looked down at the hard-packed adobe pathway. "We don't know how he found out about yesterday. But it wasn't any of us . . ."

"I know, Elvira. Don't worry about it. It wouldn't matter if you had anyway," Jette said. "He'd have found out one way or the other. There aren't any secrets from him around here. But I do appreciate your not saying anything." Jette was aware the household servants were placed in an untenable position in the Allenby family, partly from her own rebellious behavior and her stubborn defiance of Elias. "It was probably Asa Beemer again. He seems to know everything that goes on."

"But how could he?" Elvira asked.

"I don't know, but he must have seen me come home with Miles Hunter and told Father. That would be just like him," Jette said bitterly. "There's no use in speculating at this point. It's done and over." Even though she knew in her heart it was not over, she felt she must allay the girl's fears.

"Yes, Miss Jette." The girl started back toward the house. "I'll tell Socorro about lunch. We'll ring the bell when it's ready." She lifted her bright blue skirts and hopped over the shallow irrigation ditch and hastened back to the shade of live oaks nearer the house.

The air was perfectly still—not a leaf of oak or eucalyptus or pepper tree moved. Distant mountains wavered blue and purple in the late morning heat as Jette returned to her garden chores. To finish raking up the debris meant working in the hot sun, but a sunburn made little difference now. How she might look no longer mattered. Elias was influential enough to do just as he threatened—to ruin Doctor Hunter and see him driven out of San Genaro. Perhaps it was just as well this way.

Did she love Miles Hunter? Through a restless night she had debated the question with herself. She was certain he loved her. But did she love him? Since she must put Nate Trasker from her mind, did Miles Hunter only represent a convenient way out from under Elias' domination?

Miles was kind and gentle, his kisses warm and tender, but he did not ignite the furious spark of passion in her body as did the merest touch of Nate Trasker.

Whetting the edges of the arrowhead hoe on a bastard file she thought of the differences in the two men. Just thinking of Nate Trasker disturbed her. She cut viciously into the hard soil with the hoe, working near the base of the roses. It was not a necessary task. Benito would see that the job was done regularly as with all usual maintenance and gardening around the ranch. Hacking at the resistant adobe took her mind from her jumbled thoughts and gave satisfaction as it broke and crumbled with her onslaught.

The rain had dampened only the surface of the soil, and already foliage and mulch were drying in the heat. Mugginess, the sort that shortens tempers and wilts starched collars, hung in the air. Deliberately she would not allow herself to think of Asa. Would an arrowhead hoe kill a man? She slashed at the sprouts of dock and mustard that clung to the edges of the watering basin beneath the bushes. Would it kill Asa? No, she would not let herself remember!

Jette carried a pitcherful of the reeking liquid manure from the barrel and poured it in the basin beneath the rose, then raked compost back over the basin. She tapped back into place a sliver of white wood upon which was written the rose variety: Mlle. Claudine Perreau. Gracing each side of the driveway where it

101

joined the road, the flowers represented the gentility and graciousness Elias had forced Verdie to abandon when he chose to marry her. Jette had learned to prune and care for the bushes, to coax the delicate buds into bloom for her mother—it was the one task on the ranch which she reserved for herself.

Jette hung the tin pitcher on a metal hook affixed to the barrel, replaced the heavy oak lid and trundled the garden cart out of the flower bed and back into the drive. Later in the day Benito would have one of the men wheel it back of the adobe wash house near the kitchen garden and put it in the shed.

"Pecky . . . Buff . . ." Jette shouted as the two dogs raced past her down the drive and onto the highway, their frantic barking announcing the approach of a buggy. She whistled to them, but they only turned to look at her and continued their dash down the road. "Pecky, get back here!"

From the road came the sound of wheels in coarse gravel and the nervous whinney of a horse as the dogs persisted in their alarm. Jette propped the hoe and rake on the garden cart and ran to the road.

There was no mistaking the man driving the new phaeton. The fair hair, the fastidious Eastern cut of his clothes, the soft yellow chamois driving gloves . . . her breath caught in her throat as she realized who it was. She ran a few steps as the buggy neared, then abruptly stopped, her hands going to her flushed face, as if she were totally undecided whether to remain or flee. With a pang of humiliation she smelled the pungent fertilizer on her hands and remembered the sorry state of her apron and skirts. She looked down at the rough boots she reserved for her gardening, tears welling suddenly in her eyes.

"Jette! Don't go. Wait, Jette!" Nate Trasker whipped the little bays to a faster trot. The dogs ran beside the buggy, the fat spaniel ceasing its noise in order to better keep pace with the horses. Jette hurried down the driveway toward the house, her dirty skirt flapping about her ankles. The buggy turned into the drive and suddenly she was in his arms, his mouth on hers, all else forgotten but the joy she found in his nearness.

"Darling, darling . . ." He held her to him as the dogs yelped about their feet. He pushed back the errant auburn curl that insisted on straggling across her forehead. "Why did you try to run away from me?"

"Can't you imagine why?" Jette allowed him to hold her, but stiffened as she recalled yesterday. "I didn't know if you'd want me to welcome you . . . like this." She looked up into his pale eyes as if in them she might find an answer.

"If I'd want you to welcome me?" He pushed back from her to stare into her face. "Jette, what do you mean? What's happened?"

"Yesterday is what happened," she said, making an effort to not reveal the despair she had felt. "Yesterday . . ."

"What about yesterday?" Trasker took her elbow and walked her a few steps to the side of the buggy. "You're angry with me—I want to know why."

"I spent the day with the Larson girls," she began. "We went to the May Day celebration in town . . . and picnicked at Lagunita Park . . ." She hung her head, but he placed his hand beneath her chin and forced her to look at him. "Oh, Nate . . ."

"Darling . . ." He laughed and hugged her to him, rocking her in his arms. "Is it Lavinia Baldwin? Is that what's upset you?"

Jette could only nod her head and cling to him, her arms about his waist.

"Oh, you sweet, silly, foolish child." He indicated he wanted her to get into the buggy but she shook her head

103

stubbornly. "I'll drive you back to the house," he insisted. At his action Pecky and Buff edged nearer, the huge mongrel lowering his head and growling deep in his throat as he eyed Trasker. "Can't you tell your dogs I'm a friend?" he laughed, but looked warily at the animals as they circled him.

"Pecky! Buff! Behave yourselves!" The dogs stepped back, glanced at her face for reassurance that all was well, then slunk around the buggy and sniffed inquisitively at the mares. "They're usually very friendly," she said. "I don't know why they're acting this way."

"Perhaps they sense you don't consider me a friend anymore." He made her look at him. "Could that be it?"

"Please, Nate . . ." She wanted to leave, to turn her back on him and walk away, but found she could not go. She wanted to tell him of her heartache at the sight of him and the widowed Lavinia Baldwin at Lagunita. She wanted to tell him of Asa's attack, but there was no way to begin.

"Lavinia Baldwin . . . Mrs. Baldwin . . ." he started to say.

"You don't need to explain to me," Jette interrupted.

"But I want to, sweetheart," he said as he placed one hand on her arm. There was no use in her trying to leave. Just the touch of his gloved hand inflamed her very soul; the scent of bergamot on his skin as he bent to kiss her made her forget everything but him. "Mrs. Baldwin hinted she might be willing to consider my offer for her property. *Might be*," he emphasized. "By my going to see her, being kind to her, showing her the little courtesies she's been accustomed to in the past—just being pleasant company—I may be able to persuade her to sell after all. It is strictly business, Jette."

"Business?" Jette sounded hopeful, eager to believe him.

"Just business," Trasker replied. "I drove her to town yesterday and took her to the parade. We had a box luncheon at the park and tea late in the afternoon at the hotel. All very proper. She is a widow, you know. The people around here haven't been kind to her. You heard Asa Beemer and your own father when they spoke of her."

"Yes, I remember. It was cruel of them," she agreed.

"She enjoyed her outing yesterday, and for a few hours seemed quite happy again. Considering all that's happened to her since coming to San Genaro, I'd say she had a bit of fun coming. Wouldn't you say so?"

Jette looked a trifle chagrined and nodded assent.

"It was no assignation, believe me," Trasker said. He pulled her to him and whispered in her ear, "It would have been entirely different had she been you—I'd have scandalized the town."

His breath on her neck and his strong fingers in the small of her back aroused a desire that was strange and exciting. "I want to believe you, Nate, only . . ."

"Only?"

"Oh, I don't know what to believe anymore."

"Then believe in me," Trasker pleaded. "Look, darling, I have plans—I want the Baldwin ranch. I want it for us. Do you understand? I want it for us. We can build on to the house and remodel the interior, put in water, and when they get the new electric plant operating we can run electricity out there. I want the Baldwin property for you and me."

"Oh, Nate, do you mean that?" Joy lighted Jette's sunburned face as she flung her arms about the man and pressed her head to his shoulder. "Do you really mean that?"

"Indeed I do mean it. And if Mrs. Baldwin won't sell,

it will be another place—La Coruna perhaps."

"But Father . . ." Her face clouded as she thought of Elias.

"Your father has nothing to do with it, Jette. I know what you're going to say, and no doubt you're right. He wouldn't approve, but there isn't one thing he can do about it. I love you, Jette, and I intend to marry you." As if to amend his declaration he added, "That is, if you'll have me."

"Yes, darling!" Jette sighed and yielded to his embrace.

"Does that make you happy?"

"Of course it does. I'd been so . . . so . . ."

"Hurt?"

"Yes, I guess that was it."

"I want to make it my life's business to see that you're never hurt again." He looked down at her and chuckled. "Did you think that one day you'd accept a man's proposal of marriage with a smudge on your face, a sunburned nose, and straw in your hair?" He picked the stalk from her hair and held it for her to see. She remembered her dirty hands and hid them behind her.

"I've been working in the flowers," she explained. "I'm sure I look a sight." She rubbed the back of her hand across her face, smearing the smudge even further. "I'd pictured myself in my most elegant gown, with moonlight, in a garden perhaps . . . but never like this." She wiped her face with her apron. "There, is that better?"

"You could never look anything but beautiful." He lifted her into the buggy, then drove to the house, leaving the horses tied in the shade beneath the oaks. Pecky and Buff accompanied them to the corner of the adobe with a series of yelps, then flopped in a cool spot under the veranda, their tongues lolling from their exertion. Pecky eyed the man with suspicion, but ceased his growling at a pat from Jette.

"I'll change my boots and take you up to see Mother. We're having lunch on trays upstairs. Will you join us?" Jette led Trasker to the rear patio where she removed her work boots and slipped her feet into ones of tan kidskin.

"I'd like that very much, if it wouldn't be an imposition." He sat beside her on the long bench. "And I don't want to cause trouble between you and your father."

"He's with Asa for the day. Culling the herd in the north pasture, Benito said." She fastened the first three buttons of the tan boots and took off her apron. "They won't be back for lunch."

"Then I'd be delighted to stay," Trasker said. "I'll let you break the news to him or come to see him myself, whichever you think best."

"I'll tell Mother and ask her what she thinks about it." In her haste and excitement Jette was too happy to give it much thought. They could decide what to do later. "I'll run upstairs and tell her you're here." Before he could rise she dashed away and up the stairs.

Nate Trasker strolled to the edge of the patio, his hands in his trouser pockets as he wandered past the adobe wash house. He gazed beyond the eucalyptus hedge toward the cattle barn and the low hills dotted with Aberdeen-Angus, his thin lips parting slightly in a slow smile.

* * * *

Elvira handed the tack hammer to Jette. "Benito says he has some brass tacks that are just a little bit longer if we need them. He has all sorts of iron nails, though."

"The iron ones rust and make stains on the fabric,"

107

Jette said. "We'll have to make these do." She held two tacks between her teeth and tapped a third into place on the curtain stretcher, then repeated the repairs on the opposite side. "That should do it."

"I'll go help Socorro take down the rest of the panels if you don't need me here," Elvira said.

"Yes, run along. I don't want her climbing on any chairs." Jette straightened up and shielded her eyes from the mid-afternoon sun. "The way the wind's coming up I think we can get them all finished today if we hurry."

"I'll be right back." The young girl's brilliant blue skirts billowed in the breeze as she ran up the staircase to the second floor. Spring housecleaning was well under way despite Jette's dereliction the day before.

The sun dropped below the coastal mountains to the west, summoning blue-purple shadows that brought relief from the spring heat as the horizon still glowed rose-gold. Down in the workmen's village eucalyptus wood smoke lifted only a few yards from the chimneys before it was dissipated by the brisk wind from the ocean. Benito Galvan shuttered the ranch store, locked the front door, and trudged up to the main house to deposit the key in Elias' office safe.

"Good evening, Miss Jette," the old man said and doffed his wide straw hat. "Will you want anything before I go home?"

"No, thank you, Benito." Jette removed the last lace panel from the stretchers and folded it loosely before laying it lengthwise on the long wooden bench in the patio. "We're all finished. Elvira and I can put the stretchers away."

"It would be my pleasure," he said. "I'll put the key in the office and be right back."

"All right, if you will, please." Jette could see the lines of weariness in his dark face, but knew it was a matter of pride with him that he could still be of service at the main house.

"Yes, Miss Jette." He bowed slightly, turned and made his way to the south side of the house.

Elvira came from the back parlor, a curtain rod in her hand. "Is this the last one?" she asked.

"Yes, all done. Did you have enough old newspapers to finish cleaning the windows?" Jette lifted the lace curtain from the bench and handed it to the girl.

"There was plenty. Socorro had some in the kitchen, too. We did them all except the wash house." She was in no hurry to hang the last panel, and stood watching a pair of mourning doves that flew down from the oaks and teetered on the rim of the pump trough that was now brimful of water. Finches performed on the flagstones. "Are you going to tell Mr. Allenby?" she asked.

"You mean that I'm going to marry Nate Trasker?"

"You know what I mean!" Elvira laughed. "He won't like it, will he?"

"I'm afraid he won't, but it doesn't make any difference whether he does or doesn't." There was a new note in her defiance—a quiet determination rather than the usual challenging scorn. She looked up at the sky to watch swallows circling against the darkening blue. An unaccustomed sense of happiness overflowed in a laugh and pirouette, as she extended her arms in a childish imitation of the birds.

"I'll be free . . . free!" Jette twirled about, her skirts and petticoats whirling about her ankles. "I'll marry Nate Trasker and be free!" She caught Elvira and they clung to one another, laughing uncontrollably. "Come on," she said as they stopped. "We'd better finish this before Father gets back."

Elvira picked up the lace curtain from the bench where she had abandoned it. "Let's see how you look as a bride," she giggled. "Here, let me put this over your head." She arranged the panel in much the same fashion as she had seen at San Genaro Church in town when her cousin had married. She stood back to admire the effect. "Oh, Miss Jette, you'll make such a beautiful bride."

"Elvira!" Both girls started with surprise as Elias' voice cut through the twilight. "You've got better things to do than play silly games out here." He lumbered toward them, his leather vest in his hand, his shirt stained with perspiration and dust. "Get into the kitchen and see if Socorro needs any help."

"Yes, Mr. Allenby." The Mexican girl cast a look of apprehension at the rancher, then hurried across the patio and into the kitchen. There was no point in telling Elias that she was supposed to finish hanging the freshly laundered curtains.

"You needn't frighten the poor girl, Father." Jette resented his authoritarian commands.

"She's no business wasting time with you. You'd do well to remember that." He snatched the lace panel from her head and held it out to her. "Go hang this where it belongs."

For a moment Jette refused to take the curtain. Now, she realized, was not the time to tell him that they had not been just playing a silly game. When the time was right, she would inform him of her decision to marry Nate Trasker. She took the curtain, picked up the enameled rod and without a word retreated to the rear parlor.

* * * *

Dinner that night and breakfast the next morning were silent exercises in restraint. Verdie looked anxiously from Jette to Elias, her consternation misinterpreted as confusion by her husband. After Asa's behavior and the violent scene it had provoked, Elias had felt it prudent for Asa to ride in to town for the evening rather than tangle with Jette in the confines of the dining room. Elvira Mireles served the meals with more than customary deference to Elias, her dark eyes wide as they met Jette's from behind his back during breakfast.

"I'll have my coffee in the sitting room, Elvira," Verdie said after waiting for Elias to be served his steak and eggs. "I must write a few letters this morning.

"Yes, Mrs. Allenby. I'll take it in right away," the girl replied as Verdie rose from the table.

"If you'll excuse me?" the woman asked her husband. She could not bear to look directly at him. At his grunt of assent she carried her cup and saucer to the door which led to the parlor.

Elvira looked at the woman's plate and saw the food untouched. "I'll bring you some toast and marmalade. Maybe you'd like that better?"

Verdie's glance wandered to Elias, who frowned at her over his cup as he finished his coffee. "Take it in for her, Elvira, and you stay to see that she eats it." He turned to his wife and went on, "Do you hear that, woman? I expect you to eat something."

"Yes, Elias. I shall." Fear flickered a moment in her eyes, but she mustered a smile. "Now if you'll excuse me, I'll see to my letters." She paused in the middle of the parlor as if not sure where she was going. Elvira saw the look of bewilderment and took her by the elbow.

"I'll go with you to see if you have everything you need in there," Elvira said and looked back at Elias, but he was busy helping himself to a second piece of dried-peach pie. She gently guided the woman into the sitting room and seated her by the west window, placing paper and pen on the small desk to help Verdie remember

111

what she was there to do.

When they were gone Elias turned to Jette. "I aim to have Asa take his meals with the family. That's been the way since he came with me, and it's going to remain that way." He forked a mouthful of pie, washed it down with coffee which he poured from an ornate silver pot. "What a man does when he's roaring drunk isn't to be held against him when he's sober. At least not by me." His brows drew down over his narrowed eyes, giving him the look of a grizzled bird of prey. He waited for Jette to reply. "He's apologized—to both of us. That ought to be enough for a man to do."

Jette pushed her chair back and began stacking the dishes, a chore she usually allowed Elvira to do, but which now gave her a reason to leave the table and cut short her father's speech. "Whatever I might say has already crossed your mind, Father. If I had been successful, I'd have killed him." Her voice remained calm, cool, even detached, as if she were considering a point of debate. "If I were given the chance again, I'd do a better job of it, believe me."

"I'm sure you'd do just that, girl. There's just enough hell in you that you'd do it. And I'm just as sure you'd hang for it." He tilted his chair back against the window sill and held his cup in both hands as he watched the girl. "Even if he'd took you, there'd be no harm done." His laugh implied he had discussed the episode with Asa. "He's going to marry you—make it right."

Jette looked down at the plates and sauce dishes on the tray as she gathered the breakfast service. It was a moment before she could trust herself to reply.

"Never, Father," she told him. "Never!"

* * * *

112

"Your father said he and Asa would be in for dinner at noon. He wants to write out some more advertisements for the Los Angeles and Santa Barbara papers." Verdie could not say out loud that it was the bull he would be advertising, announcing it was up for service and listing the stud fees. "Promise me you'll not cause any trouble, Jette," she pleaded.

"Only for your sake, Mother, I'll try." Jette held the sealing wax over the small candle on the desk, daubed a drop onto the envelope and handed it to her mother to impress with her seal. "I don't know how I can possibly face Asa and be civil to him. Father expects too much of me!"

"You intend to tell him about your plans soon?"

"When everything is all arranged . . . the license, a place to live. . . ."

"Are you sure it's the right thing to do, child?" Verdie's face mirrored her agitation. "Is he really the right man for you?"

Jette toyed with the sealing wax over the candle, turning the scarlet stick about in her fingers. "I'm not sure I can put into words how I feel about Nate, but I know I love him, Mother. I know when he touches me . . ." How could she tell her mother?

"You want to . . . to . . . lie with him?"

"Yes, Mother. I want to have him make love to me, to make me into a woman—his woman. I want to be with him every minute, to feel him close to me. When he walks away from me I feel such an ache in my body I want to run after him, tag at his heels like a puppy." Her face, still ruddy from the slight sunburn, glowed with her youthful rapture. "Oh, Mother, I love him so very much."

Verdie rose and parted the curtain at the window to see the garden outside with its iris and roses—red California roses, not the soft hued Perreaus. She put her arms about her daughter's shoulders, hugging her gently. "I know, dear," she said. "I know how it is."

"Do you, Mother?" Jette could not picture her mother ever having loved Elias as she now loved Nate Trasker.

"Once, long ago . . . It was like that with me, too. When I first saw Elias standing in the doorway of the grand ballroom . . . nobody else was there even though the cotillion was in progress and the floor was so crowded one could hardly move about, much less dance. He was so tall and handsome, so tanned and strong. Nothing like the boys I'd known all my life. His beard was short and close trimmed, so different from all the dandies that came to call. I was only twenty—younger than you are now. He was a grown man. Middle-aged, some said, but to me he was all a young girl could want . . . all she might dream a man should be . . ."

Verdie was carried away by her reminiscences. As she turned to Jette again she looked amazed to find herself not in the old Virginia mansion, but in the sparsely furnished sitting room of the adobe. Her hands flew to her face, covering her eyes, blotting reality from her sight.

"What happened to change it all?" Jette guided her mother back into the settee, placed a cushion behind her back and folded her shawl about the thin shoulders. "Tell me what happened."

"We were married . . ." Verdie could not pull her thoughts together as she mulled it over. "Yes . . . that's it . . . we were married." She closed her eyes and let her head fall back onto the settee's rose damask. "Oh, Jette, don't do something you'll regret later."

"No, Mother, I won't." Jette held her mother's cold hands for a few minutes as the woman drifted off into sleep. She was filled with compassion as she looked at

Verdie, seeing in her the lovely southern girl who withered into forgetfulness in Elias' violent and uncivilized West.

It wasn't just the West, Jette knew. It was mostly Elias. Something had occurred to wreck her mother's sanity and happiness, but each time Jette questioned her about it, Verdie eluded the answer by retreating into an unfeeling world of numbness and void. It was useless to pursue the matter further. If she was to find the truth, it would not be through her mother.

"Is she all right?" Elvira had tiptoed into the room.

"Yes. She's just resting." Jette collected the addressed envelopes from the desk and handed them to the girl. "Will you see that Benito takes these by the post office when he goes in to town? Father said he was sending him in with the advertisements, so he may as well take mother's letters, too." She was glad it was Benito to whom she could entrust the mailing, and not Asa Beemer.

"I'll take them right over. He should be leaving in a few minutes. I saw Severo bring the buckboard to the store a while ago." She looked around the door into the front parlor to make certain no one was near enough to overhear. "Benito said he'll take your note to Mr. Trasker himself, first thing when he gets to town. I told him you wanted him to wait for an answer. He says there'll be plenty of time since Asa isn't going in with him."

"That's thoughtful of him." Jette brightened at the possibility of hearing from Trasker again. "Tell him I'll appreciate that."

"I will. And Miss Jette . . ." the girl began. She tapped the envelopes on the palm of her hand and half turned to leave the sitting room, but seemed to have a question she was reluctant to ask.

"I know what you're going to ask, Elvira," Jette

115

said. "But, no, I don't know when I'll get around to telling Father about Nate."

"Wouldn't it be better if Mr. Trasker told him?"

"I don't know. Perhaps it would." Jette opened the door to the north patio, propped it wide with a weighted procelain cat and draped back the window curtains allowing the warm noontime air to circulate in the cool adobe room. Where flies had begun to cluster on the outside of the screendoor, she set them into buzzing flight by thumping the screen with her fingernails. She silently wished the problems with which she was beset would be as easily dispersed. She turned to Elvira and said, "No matter how it's done, there'll be trouble." Both girls knew it was only too true.

It was past mid-afternoon when Benito Galvan returned from San Genaro. Jette was arranging a large bouquet of white and yellow gladiolas on the center table of the parlor when she heard the sound of the buckboard coming down the drive. Quickly she dried her hands on her apron and dashed out the front door and down the shallow steps of the entry. She ran to the driveway before Benito pulled the big bays to a halt outside the ranch office.

"Did he . . ." She did not have to finish the question. Her dark eyes danced with anticipation as Benito reached into his shirt and handed her a small envelope with her name written boldly across it.

"He did." Benito laughed at her eagerness. He glanced somewhat apprehensively at the office window with its drawn blind, but Jette shook her head and took the letter from him.

"Father and Asa are still out in the east pasture," she reassured the old man. "Oh, thank you, Benito!"

"My pleasure," he smiled, watching her tear open the envelope. He stepped from the buckboard, tied the horse, and lifted several small boxes from the wagon and placed them in the shade. "Mr. Raizes sends his best regards to you and your mother. He says to tell you they have in a new shipment of summer cottons." He set aside a paper bag containing lengths of ribbon, soutache trim, buttons, and thread. "That's for Mrs. Allenby," he explained, but Jette did not hear him. She was absorbed in Nate Trasker's note.

"Thank you, Benito," she said without the slightest idea of what he had been saying. She was merely grateful for his help.

"You mean he's coming here—this afternoon?" Verdie asked in surprise when Jette read her Trasker's note. "He intends to speak with Elias about you?" She looked alarmed and sat down quickly on the chaise, her hands working nervously in her lap. The prospect of an encounter between Trasker and Elias frightened her, for better than Jette she realized the two men were dangerously similar.

"Yes, Mother. And it's probably the best way." Jette looked at her mother, studied her worried expression and fathomed its meaning. "But remember, Mother, not one word about Benito carrying notes between us. Not one word to Father, hear?"

"But he'll wonder how we knew he was coming . . ."

"Let him wonder."

"I don't want to lie to Elias." Verdie knew from experience when he demanded the truth he could extract it.

"Just tell him you don't know. Tell him to ask me."

"But you'll tell him it's none of his business . . ." Fear crept into Verdie's eyes.

"Yes, I shall tell him exactly that," Jette said quietly. "Promise me you won't say anything about Benito."

"All right, dear, but please don't bait your father. Especially not now." Verdie agreed readily enough, but her fingers continued to move in agitation.

"I'm going to go talk to Socorro and see what we can arrange for supper. I want it to be special." Jette handed her mother the new McClure's Magazine that had fallen to the floor. "Here you are—I'll let you finish your story."

Verdie took the magazine and thumbed through the pages, her brows pulled together as she tried to recall what she had been reading when Jette burst into the back parlor with news of Nate Trasker's visit. Jette patted her mother's shoulder and smiled. She would let Verdie find her place in the magazine by herself rather than remind her that she had turned down the page to mark it.

Shadows began lengthening and the afternoon breeze from the ocean rustled down from the western hills carrying with it the smell of mesquite and sage. Jette and Elvira had laid the table with their finest Dresden, linen, and silver, and in the center placed a graceful cut-glass epergne cascading with white philadelphus and pink roses.

In the kitchen Socorro's shrill voice rose in command as she began preparing a joint of beef, browned potatoes, broccoli and asparagus with hollandaise. From the garden Elvira picked lettuce, washed it under the pump and picked it over before putting it to chill in the pantry refrigerator. It was to be an occasion, with even the household servants caught up in the excitement.

Jette poured hot water into the wash basin in her room and drew the drapes across the open window. She unwrapped a cake of violet-scented soap and opened the walnut armoire, inspecting her garments to see which would be the most appropriate. Finally she chose the deep-teal skirt and pink silk georgette blouse. On the Allenby ranch she had little need of a dinner gown, although Verdie retained the gracious custom for Sundays, holidays, and guests. Rummaging through a small ebony and mother-of-pearl casket she found her crystal necklace and earrings. She held the long strand of beds up to the georgette, studied the effect, and, satisfied, placed them on the dresser.

As she bathed she became aware of a strangely new sensuality—a not unpleasant consciousness of feeling—the cool, smooth soap on her naked body, the violet scent, the roughness of the coarse linen washcloth as she ran it over her breasts, across her thighs and the soft, secret place between her legs. Bathing, touching her own body, had never before evoked such sensations, but now the ordinarily prosaic act was coupled with thoughts of Nate Trasker, thoughts that aroused a desire in her that she found impossible to ignore.

All was premature twilight inside her room, a twilight partaking of the crimson color of the drapes. The lowering sun struggled through the fabric, casting a subdued ruddy glow over her body. It was not female vanity that caused her to tilt the mirror and gaze at her own image. Was this how she would appear to Nate—to her husband? Would he see her with eyes that thought her beautiful, or with eyes that examined for every flaw, every imperfection? Men said she was beautiful, but they had never seen her naked. Even Asa Beemer had not seen her so. Would she still be as beautiful to Nate?

Taking the rough towel she rubbed herself dry, deliberately trying to hurt herself to blot out the doubts that bedeviled her. Quickly she hooked and laced the light corselet, pulled up the black silk hose and fastened them to the elastic straps. She would hurry and think no more about it. Even as she hurried, however, she found herself wondering if Lavinia Baldwin looked the same . . . and did Lavinia feel the same when she thought of Nate Trasker?

Jette removed the tortoise-shell pins from her hair and combed it forward, letting it fall over her face. As she brushed it back over her hand it fell into wide auburn waves which she coaxed into a full, soft halo about her head, then twisted the ends into a high chignon, and secured it with a pair of garnet and pearl Spanish combs.

The tall clock in the front parlor chimed six-forty-five as Jette made one last check on the dining room. Socorro was humming in the kitchen—a mournful dirge of unrequited love and pining which she accompanied by the clatter of sauce pans and much shaking of the stove grate. Through the dining room window Jette could see Severo Mireles cranking the handle of the ice cream freezer out on the rear patio. All was well with the meal preparations.

"Do I look all right, dear?" Verdie stood before her daughter and slowly turned about for her inspection. "I wore my amethysts. I remember you wanted me to wear them when Mr. Trasker was here before." She was pitifully eager for Jette's approval as she smoothed the tight bodice of the ivory silk gown. "Perhaps you might need to comb my hair a bit, just to tidy up the back?"

Jette sleeked the few stray hairs back into her mother's upswept arrangement and tucked them in. "You look lovely, Mother. Elvira did a nice job of pressing the flounces." Verdie smiled, her faded hazel eyes alive with expectation. In her hand she carried a painted ivory and lavender silk fan which she fluttered in nervous bursts.

"Shall I select the wine for dinner?" Verdie, although long in the West, still referred to the evening meal as dinner regardless of its being the main meal of the day or simply a light repast. "One of the nice burgundys, don't you think?"

"I'll leave that to you. There are several bottles in the cooler. Do you want to decant them or do you want Elvira to help you?" Jette wanted no wine stains to ruin

120

her mother's careful toilette and preferred that Elvira do the chore. "Perhaps since you have on your gown . . ."

"Yes, you're right," Verdie agreed. "I'll have her do it."

They had not heard Elias enter the parlor from his office. He stood watching them before he walked across the room to the liquor cabinet.

"Elias! I didn't know you'd come in." Verdie was frightened and almost dropped her fan. With an effort she composed herself and said, "We're having a guest for dinner, Elias. You might want to freshen up before dinner. I laid out a change of clothes for you upstairs. I'll come up and help you with your tie when you're ready." She reached into the cabinet, found a glass and handed it to him as he poured from the rye decanter.

"Company coming?" he grunted. "Who?" He downed the rye and poured another shot. He smelled of horse sweat and his face was grimy with dust. "Why the hell would I want to change clothes for a guest who's eating free at my own table?" He was already truculent and would probably soon be drunk since he was taking his rye neat and on an empty stomach. Verdie looked anxiously at Jette before replying.

"Mr. Trasker is coming," she said. "I should think you'd want to meet him looking your best." She closed the cabinet with the rye on the inside shelf, but Elias reopened the door and took the decanter over to the sofa and sat down.

"If I feel like it, I will." He sprawled, glass in hand, the rigors of a day in the saddle pulling fatigue lines into his leathery face.

"Humor Mother this once, will you?" Jette came to stand in front of the fireplace to face him. "It's not much to ask and it would mean a lot to her."

"To her—or you?" He was comfortable on the sofa

and tired, his temper ragged from the rye. He had no intention of acquiescing to their suggestion unless it suited him.

"Mother cares what impression you make on people. It matters to her." She turned from him, knowing if she did not leave they would be at each other's throats once more. "It doesn't matter to me one way or the other." She purposely did not sweep from the room and slam the door—that was sure to ire Elias. Instead she calmly went through the sitting room and out into the north patio where the dogs joined her as she wandered through the lemon trees and into the apricot orchard. She did not want to goad her father into a fury before Nate came. It was pointless, would do no good, and quite possibly could do much harm. She would have to suffer Asa's presence at the table—there was nothing she could do about that. Soon, she mused, she would never have to see his face or hear his voice again. And should she ever reveal to Nate that Asa had attempted to rape her . . . what would he do? What would he do to Elias, should he learn her own father had condoned and pardoned such an act?

A jackrabbit exploded from the brush at the side of the fence and ran a zig-zag course through the apricot trees, Pecky and Buff yelping and losing the chase as the creature squirmed under the wire fence and loped across the field. It was Jette's favorite time of day, when daylight mellows to gold and rose, intensifying the blues and greens of pasture and hills. The air was sweet and beginning to grow cool. She would walk off her anger and disgust and return in humor good enough to see her through the evening, perhaps good enough to allow her to enjoy it.

Nate said that they would live nearby—at La Coruna or the Baldwin place—near enough that she could look in on Verdie to see that she was all right and was being cared for properly. There was to be escape after all, and without having to abandon her mother.

She whistled for the dogs, who came obediently and ambled beside her as she headed back to the house. "See, old fellows, how things can work out if we just wait?" She rubbed Buff's tawny ears and scratched Pecky's chin. "I'll miss you two," she said. "But I promise to come see you every chance I get."

The mongrel pricked up his ears and cocked his head as if to listen, his gaze intent upon the north side of the house.

"You hear another jackrabbit?" she laughed.

The dog growled, lowered its blocky head and broke from her, running toward the patio off the sitting room. The spaniel whined and followed, taking the path that led directly to the house. Jette listened, trying to catch the sound that triggered them on their mad dash. Above the whisper of the lemon leaves and remote cattle sounds came an indefinable note of terror.

Lifting her skirts above her knees she ran blindly toward the sound, hoping it was not what she thought. She stumbled, falling against the low-pruned lemon tree, tearing the silk of her blouse, the thorns on the branches drawing blood as they scratched her shoulder.

"Oh dear God, don't let it be!" she prayed as she ran.

The dogs were worrying at something in the deep shadow of the patio, their gutteral snarls confirming what she most feared. Suddenly the spaniel yelped, a shriek of pain and fury as Elias' boot slammed in to the dog's flanks. The huge mongrel tore frantically at the man's sleeve and arm, but Elias flung the animal from him. He seized Verdie, shaking her until the woman could no longer shout for help or scream in terror.

"Let her go!" Jette screamed. "Stop it!" She flew at Elias, her fists pummeling his broad back, but he only turned and with one push thrust her from him. Off balance, she fell to the flagstones and shouted, "Benito! Severo! Help!" She staggered erect and screamed, "Please . . . someone help us!"

"Lie to me, will you? I'll teach you both this time!" He struck Verdie with one hand, his great, hard body behind the blow. She fell to the stone pavement and lay still. Jette seized a rock from the edging of the flower bed and lunged at Elias, striking at his head as he bent over Verdie. Caught off guard, the man lurched toward his daughter, blood trickling down his forehead from the wound she had inflicted. Both dogs returned to their attack, the mongrel leaping at him, tearing at his inert arm. For a moment he looked stunned, his eyes unfocused, as he leaned against the wall.

"Murderer! Killer! That's all you know, isn't it?" Jette hurled the words at him, the rock still in her hand. She circled him, warily waiting for a chance to strike should he move again toward her mother. "I wish I were a man and I'd kill you with my own hands!"

Unseen, the Mexican workers came from the rear of the adobe, but such was their fear of a drunken Elias Allenby that they waited, trying to determine the safest course to take. Any precipitate move on their part, they knew, might endanger the women even further.

Slowly Elias shook his head as if to clear his senses, one huge hand clinging to the window sill, the other fending off the dog. Jette moved between him and her mother as he took a step forward.

"Don't touch her!" Jette shouted. "Get away from her!" She saw the men at the corner of the veranda and called to them, "Severo, Benito, take Mother into the parlor. Put her on the sofa and put the big lamp on the table beside her. Elvira . . ." Jette was not certain in the half-light that it was the girl, but continued when the little maid sidled nearer, "Elvira, run over to the village and get one of the men to ride into town for Doctor Hunter and the sheriff." Her voice was cold and commanding, no longer sibilant with fear. The shock of drawing first blood had fled, leaving grim confidence. "Quickly, Elvira!"

The young Mexican girl picked up her skirts and ran to the cluster of cottages down the lane, raising the alarm as she sped to obey Jette. Her brother and old Benito, keeping their eyes on Elias, moved toward Verdie while Jette stood sentry, rock in hand, facing her father. With one quick catlike lunge, Elias grabbed her and sent the two men sprawling before they could rescue Verdie.

"You'd bring the sheriff down on me, girl?" His huge hand hit her face, snapping her head as if she were a rag doll. She lashed at him with her free hand, her fingernails gouging into his face and neck. "So you'd kill me, would you?" He struck at her again. She managed to slip from his grasp, but fell over Verdie's unconscious form.

"Yes! Yes! I'd kill you!" Jette shouted and tried to get up as Elias moved toward her.

"I'll drop you where you stand, Allenby!" The phaeton had come down the driveway, but no one had heeded its sound. Elias took two strides toward the women. "You're a dead man, Allenby." Nate Trasker stepped before the rancher, but had no gun in sight as Elias had expected. The rancher slowly shifted his weight and drew in his elbows as if preparing to strike Trasker.

"Allenby, one move and I'll split your skull," Trasker said quietly. The menace in his voice halted the man. Trasker carried his walking stick, slapping its lead-filled silver head in the palm of his hand. He was as tall as Elias, his shoulders as broad, but his lighter build made him no less a match for the older man. He did not settle heel to the ground, but balanced lightly on the balls of his feet, a suggestion of his intent to spring upon Elias in the slight forward bend of his body and thrust

125

of his head.

"Jette, are you all right?" Trasker asked, moving deftly between father and daughter.

"Yes, Nate . . . I think so," she replied as she bent over Verdie. "It's Mother who's hurt."

"You . . ." Trasker said and motioned to Severo and Benito, "Get the ladies into the house." They lifted Verdie, and Socorro took Jette by the waist and helped her in the sitting room door. From the lane to the south a horse and rider sped down the drive and out onto the highway, heading south to San Genaro.

"I don't know what the hell's going on here, Allenby, but there's not going to be a repeat of it. Not now . . . not ever!" Trasker continued to tap the weighted head in his hand, the gesture emphasizing to Elias that what he had said was a command, not a suggestion or request. It was impossible to distinguish between Elias' and the mongrel's growls as the man grabbed the dog and hurled it at Trasker. Trasker dodged, and although the dog scrambled to its feet it was too stunned to resume the attack. Elias wiped the blood from his face with the back of his hand and edged toward Trasker. Even in the poor light Trasker could see by the man's expression that he was completely out of control, his face convulsed by pure savagery. He wasted no more words on Elias but clutched the stick tighter and maneuvered to have the advantage when he swung.

"Elias!" Asa Beemer's voice cut through the twilight as he ran around the back of the house from the cattle barn. "Elias!"

"Stay out of this, Asa!" the old man yelled and lunged at Trasker. The cane flashed in a vicious slice as he sprang at Trasker. The blow caught Elias just below the ear, the aim deflected by only inches. He crumpled to the ground at their feet.

Asa was out of breath from his sprint from the cattle

barn. He turned Elias over and inspected the wound on his head and the already reddening welt on his neck. "What the hell's going on here?" Asa managed to ask between gasps for breath.

"I'm afraid I can't help you there, but from the looks of it, he was well on his way to killing Jette and Mrs. Allenby." Trasker stood over them, his stick still in his hand, ready to use on either man if necessary.

"God! Why didn't somebody send for me?" Asa asked.

"I'd guess it happened too quickly." Trasker stepped back far enough to allow Asa to roll Elias face up and straighten his legs out on the stone floor of the patio. "I'd heard of his violent temper, but hadn't been led to expect anything like this." His contempt was obvious. Asa stood up, still breathing heavily. "Does he act like this often?" Trasker asked him. "And if so, why hasn't something been done about it?"

"No, he doesn't do this often," Asa shot back. He eyed the man suspiciously, but held his tongue. "Did he hurt either of them?"

"It would seem so. They took Mrs. Allenby inside. She was unconscious." Trasker watched Asa closely. The ranch manager's loyalty was to Elias, but he was genuinely upset that the women had been injured. "They've sent a man for the doctor . . . and the sheriff." There was utter scorn in his voice.

Asa turned to Trasker. "Who the hell sent for the sheriff?"

"Jette." He waited for any comment. Asa said nothing. "I think she was justified from what I witnessed. The man is dangerous." He walked over and stood looking down at Elias.

"Only when he's drunk."

"And he's drunk often?"

"Lately—yes." Asa was honest in the admission.

"Then it's a case for the sheriff." Trasker opened the

door to the sitting room. "If you'll excuse me, I'll attend the ladies."

"Sure. I'll see to Elias." Asa motioned to several of the men standing nearby. "Here, help me get him into the office." He took Elias by his shoulders. "Take his feet . . . there . . . yes, that's right." They lifted the man, waited for one of the children who had gathered timidly on the veranda to open the door to the sitting room, then carried him through the house and into the office.

Nate Trasker held the lamp close to the sofa. "How is she?" he asked.

"I don't know." Jette caressed her mother's face and pushed back from her forehead the once carefully arranged graying hair. Livid red marks attested the breadth of Elias' hand and fingers as they had struck Verdie. "She's hardly breathing." She turned to Nate, her eyes cold with hatred as she asked, "Where's Father?"

"In his office. Asa and the men took him in there." At the question in her look he said, "Don't worry about him, darling. He's in no condition to start anything now."

"You . . . you . . ." Jette could not bring herself to ask what had happened.

"I clipped him a good one when he came at me. I warned him." Nate stepped aside as Socorro brought a tin basin full of cold water from the kitchen. She handed Jette a folded linen napkin snatched from the dining room table and hovered close to the girl. Jette dipped the cloth in water and dabbed at Verdie's pallid face.

"Can you find the smelling salts Mother keeps in the back parlor?" Jette asked the woman. "I think they're on the top shelf inside the cabinet by the window." Without a word the elderly cook hurried to find the ammonia.

128

Asa Beemer came from the office, his heavy oak-soled boots loud on the polished floor. "How is she?" he asked as Jette looked up at him, her face set with shock and anger. She refused to answer and turned away lest she make matters worse by raging at him.

"We don't know," Trasker answered him. "Frail little woman like that, he could have killed her." He glanced at the open office door. "Can you handle him when he comes to? I'll not have him start any more trouble, drunk or sober." His tone implied that he would not stop with only a blow from his loaded cane should Elias resort to violence again.

"I can handle him." Asa sounded surly at the other man's intrusion into what he considered his own area of interests. "What started it?" he asked.

"You mean what started it *this* time?" Jette retorted sarcastically. "He'd just come in and began with two shots of whiskey. Isn't that all he ever needs?"

"Must've been something more than that. Elias holds his whiskey . . ." Asa ventured to wonder aloud.

"It might be something more than that, but it's family business, none of yours." She would not look at him. Her hand shook as she wrung the cloth out and placed it on her mother's forehead. Asa's face darkened with anger, his brows drawing together as he glanced from the girl to Trasker. Her new silk georgette blouse, Verdie's amethysts, the elaborately set dinner table, flowers in the parlor—they were enough for him to make some shrewd guesses. He glared at Trasker, but said nothing before he retreated to the office. Socorro returned with the smelling salts and handed them to Jette.

"Thank you," Jette said and uncorked the small flat bottle, sniffed to test its potency, then held it beneath Verdie's nose, wafting it back and forth so it would not be too strong. "Mother . . ." There was a faint flutter of Verdie's eyelids and her lips parted as if to form

129

words. "Mother . . ." Jette said to Trasker, "I think you can put the lamp on the table now. We can't do anything more until Miles . . . Doctor Hunter . . . gets here." Trasker did not miss the familiarity and glanced at her curiously.

"When she's conscious, give her a brandy," he said as he placed the lamp where it would not glare into the woman's face. "I recall she mentioned she didn't like hard liquor, but it'll do her good. Strengthens the heart."

"I'll get it," Socorro said and went to the cabinet by the fireplace, bringing back a small crystal glass with the potent brandy. Fear lingered in the woman's black eyes. She constantly watched the door to the office. "I'll put it here, Miss Jette. Let me take care of your arm and shoulder," she pleaded. "I have iodine and cotton in the pantry."

"No, Socorro, not yet. But thank you—I'll be all right." She saw the pain in the woman's face and surmised she thought it Elias' handiwork. "I fell against one of the lemon trees," she added. "It's really nothing but scratches." She tried to smile. The Galvans had known enough trouble in their lifetimes without sharing Allenby problems. "You run along and see to the dinner. Just put things back for the time being."

The old woman nodded, her eyes filled with pity as she looked at Verdie before fleeing back to her kitchen. Elvira, still mirroring her fear, opened the door to the rear patio and waited before venturing into the parlor.

Jette looked up and called, "It's all right now. Come in." The girl stood ill at ease, seemingly prepared for immediate flight. "Elvira, do you remember that folding cot upstairs?"

"The one in the storage room off the sewing room?"

"That's the one. Do you think you can get one of the men to help you get it out and put it in my room?"

"Yes, Miss Jette. Severo's just outside. He didn't

want to come in . . ." She looked back at the patio where her brother's face could be seen peering through the screen door.

"Make the cot up for me, will you? Take a pillow and some blankets from one of the guest rooms. That'll be easier than getting them out of the storage chests and having to air them first." She tried to think of what else she might need. "And bring in the little table from the sewing room. Put it at the head of the cot. Move the furniture around any way you have to."

"Yes, Miss Jette." The girl was eager to leave.

"And find a clean nightshift for Mother . . . and her robe and slippers." Elvira and Severo ran up the staircase and soon could be heard moving things about in the upstairs storage room. "I'll not have Mother stay one more night with him," Jette said to Trasker.

"Have you thought out what you're going to say to the sheriff?" Trasker pulled a chair closer and sat beside the two women. "He'll want you to file a formal complaint. It's going to be nasty, Jette."

"I don't care. I hope he rots in jail." She was beginning to tremble. "He's always been so concerned about his reputation in the community—I'll see that he gets the one he deserves!"

"No . . ." Verdie raised her head and looked in horror at her daughter. "No! You can't do that to him!" She pushed the smelling salts away. Too weak to rise, she fell back into the cushions. "You mustn't . . ."

"Mother, please . . ."

"No, Jette! I won't let you do such a thing." Verdie groped for Jette's hand and clung to it as if it were her only reality. Her eyes refused to focus and she turned her head to look away. "You mustn't do such a thing. I couldn't bear it." Her voice was scarcely more than a whimper.

"But the sheriff . . ." Trasker began.

"Send him away!" Verdie was desperate in her opposition.

"No, Mother. I won't. I can't." She took the glass of brandy Trasker handed her and held it to her mother's lips. "Sip some of this . . . there, that's right . . . just a bit more . . ."

"Is Elias all right?" Verdie whispered. "He ain't . . ."

"I wouldn't know. And I'm sure I don't care one way or the other." Jette was surprised at how callous she sounded—even more, that what she said was quite true.

"Where is he?"

"In the office. Asa's with him," Trasker said, then added, "He won't abuse you any more, Mrs. Allenby. I'll see to that."

"But you don't understand," she protested.

"Mother, this is the last time . . ." Jette was almost angry with her mother. She could see no reason why she or her mother should worry about Elias.

"Do you care to tell me what happened, Mrs. Allenby?" Nate Trasker could well imagine what had triggered Elias' wild behavior, but wished to know with certainty.

Verdie looked fearfully at Jette as if she expected another outburst if she revealed what had occurred. "It's all right, Mother," Jette reassured her. "Please tell us . . ."

"He suspected about you and Mr. Trasker." Verdie's knuckles were white as she held her daughter's hand. "He asked me directly, and I told him he should ask you, that it wasn't up to me to speak to him about it when you had specifically asked me not to."

"He struck you and made you tell him anyhow?" Trasker waited for her to reply, but she only nodded her head, tears welling unchecked as she touched her bruised face. Trasker got up from his chair and began pacing. Several times he moved toward the office door which Asa had shut, then seemed to reconsider and sat down once more.

"Mother, I'm so sorry." Jette buried her head on Verdie's shoulder, wanting to weep, but too angry to find relief in doing so. "I didn't want you to be hurt."

"It's all right, dear," the woman said and enfolded Jette in her thin arms. "My poor little girl, my poor little baby," she crooned. "Promise me you'll send the sheriff away. Don't hurt Elias any more, please, for my sake if not for his. You don't understand . . ."

Verdie's arms slackened their hold, falling limp. Her head fell back into the cushion, her eyelids closing and reopening as if she were making an effort to remain conscious.

"Mother?" Jette cried out. Nate Trasker pulled her away and knelt beside the sofa, putting his head on Verdie's chest, his ear to her heart.

"Give me the smelling salts!" He held the bottle under her nose, but there was no response. He looked at Jette. "That doctor had better get here soon," he said.

Chapter 7

La Coruna Ranch spread east to the San Lucas Mountains, its boundary lines still in doubt since the title's description—in flowery antique Spanish—established those lines by referring to "an oak with three trunks" and "a split rock with an indentation like the Blessed Cross." Such transient and fanciful markers had, indeed, on some ranchos and haciendas caused bloodshed when the land was partitioned or willed to succeeding generations of beneficiaries. La Coruna had been part of an immense grant that had been parceled off to satisfy debts and obtain cash for improvements. Its fields now lay fallow, its grazing lands barren and baking in the California sun.

Lodd and Ed Putnam sat beneath the shade of the old three-trunked oak in their piano-box buggy. Behind them in the hauling space was a collection of small trunks and on the seat was a large leather satchel. The men, balding and white-whiskered, gazed back toward the ranch house, their expressions mingled with sadness and relief. The afternoon was still, with only the sound of an occasional ambitious bee to disturb the quiet.

Ed Putnam wiped his bald head and neck with a soiled handkerchief and loosened his shirt by pulling an extra six inches of it out of his trousers. The ride to town, their last ride away from the ranch, would be hot and uncomfortable. "What time you got, Lodd?" he asked.

"Near one o'clock, I make it." He took out a fat gold-cased railroad watch, flipped open the cover and grunted. "Yep, five to one."

"Ought to be here by now, I'd say."

"One o'clock is one o'clock. No need to be impatient now. Don't have to wait for 'em, if you don't want to." Lodd bit off a piece of plug, chewed it, spat, and pushed it to one side of his cheek. "Rather go on?"

"Nope. Might as well wait and wish 'em luck."

"Think they're gonna need luck?" Lodd laughed and jabbed his brother's ribs.

Ed laughed, too, but replied, "They're gonna need plenty, never you mind. Elias ain't gonna take too kindly to Trasker buying La Coruna right out from under him. Not even if it's for his own daughter. No, sir, he ain't apt to take it kindly at all."

"We give him the chance, fair and square," Lodd reminded him.

"Yeah, but that was twenty years ago," Ed chuckled. The joke, it seemed, was on Elias Allenby.

"I ain't sorry to be leaving, to tell the truth, Ed."

Lodd Putnam leaned back, crossed his long legs and rested his left arm on the back of the seat. He turned to look at the rambling house and the outbuildings on the gentle slope beyond. "Now we got money, I'm gonna be content to loaf, believe me."

"Like hell you will!" Ed laughed again. "We got a sight of work to do on that house in town."

"Maybe we'll just hire it done, now we got money." Lodd, the older of the brothers, was still lean and wiry at seventy-three. "You hear a buggy?"

Ed raised his head and listened, cupping a gnarled hand to his one good ear. "Think you're right." He looked across at his brother, eyeing him closely. "You sure you ain't sorry we sold?"

"Course I ain't, you damned old fool," Lodd grumbled, but he looked away from the house and barns. "We're too old to stay on out here much longer. And no telling what Elias might be up to one of these days." He spat a thin stream into the dust of the rutted road. "Might us wind up like them poor wild dogs."

Ed nodded. The thought had often crossed his mind. They had known Elias Allenby in Wyoming Territory and had heard of his reputation in Texas.

"You think Jake Larson had the story straight?"

"About Elias almost killing his wife?"

"Yeah. Don't seem natural, a man beating his women folk like that." Lodd shook his head as he pondered the gossip.

"He never quibbled who he took on, but he wasn't no coward. Not that I ever heard anyhow. And beating women is the act of a coward as I see it." Ed batted at gnats that floated in the still air beneath the tree. "If what Jake and Anna said about the girl marrying that drummer from Chicago is right, that must have been what set him off."

"He ain't no drummer," Lodd contradicted his brother.

"Well now, sir, you don't know that, do you?"

"Sure I do. Jake Larson said he's representing some big development company out here. They got a mind to do some trading and building here in San Genaro Valley." He shifted in the seat and tossed the satchel behind them, fastening it by a loop of twine to the rest of the baggage. "Them Larson girls must've had something mixed up, though. They've been telling around that Jette and that new doc in town was pretty thick."

"Neither of them girls h.has got the ense to come in out of the wet, Lodd. I doubt they got their own names right half the time." Ed Putnam had little use for flighty women, as he termed them. "Now that Allenby girl, there's a different matter."

"How you figure she's different? You don't know her."

"Don't have to. Not personal. What folks say about anybody ought to be listened to. If it's just plain gossip, forget it. That don't mean much. But if it's like what's said about Jette Allenby, it means something and you ought to pay attention." Ed shook out his handkerchief and spread it over the leather dashboard to dry. "I told you before, I heard Ainsworth Millege at the bank tell Abe Marley she's got a better head for business than most of the men he knows. Smart and independent."

"You was eavesdropping, Ed." There was little disapproval in Lodd's comment. Information garnered, no matter how, was at least interesting.

"I never said I wasn't," Ed said with some irritation. "There was something about Elias wanting her to marry that hired man of his, too."

"Well, pretty girl like that, she's bound to have more'n one fella hanging on the gate." Lodd spat into the dust beside the wheel. "Funny thing about that girl . . ."

"How's that?" Ed fished in his vest pocket and

found a small fat panatela, bit the end off it and rolled it in his fingers, listening for the dryness.

"Must take after her mother's side of the family, with that dark red hair of hers. Regular spitfire, from what I hear."

"Now, Lodd. I know what you're thinking, but Verdie Allenby ain't that kind. Never was—you should know that better'n anybody else. As to her being peppery, she could come by that righteously enough!"

"Amen to that, brother." They both laughed until the buggy shook. "Say, who's Elias gonna sue now?"

"Being a son-in-law don't exempt nobody—not with Elias."

As a shiny, yellow-wheeled phaeton turned from the highway and into the lane both men jumped out of their buggy and waited by the tree, their stained, wide-brimmed plains hats in their hands.

"Afternoon, folks," Lodd called as the buggy neared. His face broke into a wide smile that multiplied the wrinkles in its tanned surface.

"Mr. Putnam, how are you?" Nate Trasker pulled the mares to a halt and extended his hand first to Lodd, then to Ed. It was a matter of seniority, and although one could not distinguish the elder by appearance, one might presume Lodd was the older since he seemed to handle the business and have the final say. "How are you, Ed?" He turned to Jette and said, "Darling, you know Ed and Lodd Putnam? Gentlemen, Miss Allenby."

"I've seen them in town—and in court, of course, but I've never actually met them," Jette replied. "I'm so glad to meet you both at last."

"Honored to meet you, ma'am." Lodd held his hat to his chest and gave a short, old-fashioned bow.

"Real pleasure, Miss Allenby." Ed grinned broadly, showing the gaps in his back teeth. "Sure want to congratulate you two and wish you all the luck in the

137

world.''

"Thank you, Mr. Putnam. That's very kind of you," Jette said.

"I have all the luck I need right here," Nate said and put his arm about her waist. "But thank you, gentlemen." Beneath his narrow-brimmed city hat, Trasker's eyes squinted against the sun. "I hope you'll drive out and visit us now and then. We plan a housewarming party and you're most welcome."

The two old bachelors looked embarrassed, Ed looking to Lodd for an answer to the invitation. "We'd be mighty pleased to attend, Miss Allenby," he addressed his reply to the girl. "But since Elias and us . . .''

"He won't be there," she interrupted him. "All our friends will, however." The implication was not subtle. She did not consider Elias, her father, to be a friend.

"Then we'd be pleasured to come," Lodd said. "That'd be right nice." The brothers beamed their agreement.

"Good," Nate said and extended his hand to both men again, as if impatient to be on his way. "I'll stop by your place in town and let you know when it will be."

Jette leaned across and spoke quietly. "Please don't be strangers in our home, either of you. My mother will be very happy to see you after all these years."

"Verdie . . . Mrs. Allenby . . . will be at the party?" Lodd asked.

"If she's well enough by then."

Both men were silent for a moment, again looking at one another. Finally Lodd said, "I'd appreciate it greatly if you'd give her our best regards. Tell her I . . . we . . . hope she'll be real fine right soon." Even at seventy-three he was still a fine looking man, erect, handsome, and proud.

"I shall, Mr. Putnam," Jette said. "Thank you."

"Gentlemen, if you'll excuse us, we'll get on down to

the house. Jette's anxious to see it and begin planning where to put things." Trasker nodded and clucked the horse to a fast walk. Jette waved to them and settled into the seat close to Nate's side.

"That must have been some feud your father had going with them," Nate said.

"Oh, it was so silly. So ridiculous," Jette exploded. "Something to do with riparian rights . . . which they won. And then about questionable boundary lines. As if a few yards one way or the other makes any difference when there are thousands of acres involved."

"It's according to where the extra yards are . . . and whose water's threatened," Nate said.

"You may be right, but all the same, Father could have settled the thing out of court." Jette was annoyed that Nate did not consider Elias' contests trivial. "Right now he has a suit pending about some calves that were killed by wild dogs he says came from La Coruna."

"He has a point at law there, Jette. If the Putnams allowed those dogs to roam at will and made no effort to stop their depredations . . ."

"Well, it's past bothering about now. Asa saw to that."

"But, darling, you simply can't have the feral dogs pulling down livestock. They run like wolves, but with none of the natural restraint of the true wild animal."

"I'm not expert in animal behavior, but I can't see much difference between the way they act and the way a lot of people behave."

"You mean your father?" He glanced at her face and saw the rigid set of her features.

"Yes, I mean Father!" She twisted her parasol handle in her fingers, twirling the ruffled shade as if in protest against such things. "All my life I've heard about how he settled his disputes. Long after the law said no one was supposed to wear side arms, he kept right on. Only when the sheriff told him he'd put him in jail did he

139

quit."

"I've heard about a few episodes in Wyoming and the Dakotas. He was a good man with a gun, I guess."

"A good man with a gun—but not a good man, Nate," she replied. "Violence . . . it's in his blood. It seems to be all he knows."

Nate Trasker did not wish to continue the discussion lest it usher forth a quarrel, a quarrel he was unwilling to take sides on at present. It had been enough for him that he had balked Elias and announced that he intended to marry Jette. Given time, Elias might be reconciled to the inevitable, but he wanted no further antagonism between them which might make their relationship even more difficult. He hurried the mares along the narrow lane to where it dipped into a shallow stream bed then veered slightly north toward the old ranch house.

"Ah, there it is, sweetheart—our home!" He pointed with the whip to the one-story adobe that sprawled beneath a cluster of ancient live oaks.

Jette tilted her parasol to shade her eyes, her face mirroring her excitement as they pulled into the rustic yard. The squat structure was constructed in a U-shape, its wings centered about a tiled patio. A well, off to one side, still displayed yellow and cobalt Mallorca tiles, imported to Alta California by Spanish ships in exchange for cattle hides. The Putnam brothers had sensibly converted the well from its more charming—but totally undependable—early form to an efficient American pump which required no priming. A wooden trough channeled waste water into a patch of yellow and russet wallflowers beside the well, and a brilliant vermillion rambling rose, carefully tended and pruned to shape, arched above the front door. The wide courtyard was swept clear of debris, its hard-packed adobe soil barren of fallen oak leaves or burr clover.

Doors and window frames sported a fresh coat of

carmine paint, while the house itself reflected the glaring sunlight from stark, white-washed walls. Shutters once strong enough to withstand Indian attack, now hung on rusted hinges. Long since rotted to pith by a searing sun and arid winds, the shutters served only as an ornament now, their carmine coat already curling back in spots to reveal the Putnams' choice of colors over the past decades. Blue jays shrieked in testy argument as the buggy drew up into the patio, and a tiny blue lizard scuttled into a shadowed crevice under the foundation.

A slight, middle-aged man and plump Mexican woman approached from around one wing of the house. The woman timidly fingered her long apron as she watched the arrival of the new owner. The man took his wife's hand and led her to the buggy as Nate halted the mares at the far end of the courtyard.

"Good to see you again, Mr. Trasker. We been expecting you," the man said as he took the reins and tied the horses to the hitching rail.

"I've brought someone to meet you and your wife," Trasker said as he stepped from the buggy and handed Jette down. "Darling, this is Mr. and Mrs. Scott."

"Just Seth, ma'am," the man explained. "And this here's Tecla." His inelegant introduction was nevertheless warm and hospitable. The woman smiled and curtsied, her eyes modestly averted.

"Welcome to La Coruna," Tecla said. "Welcome, and may you find only happiness here."

* * * *

Jette poured another cup of green China tea and nibbled at a sweet cinnamon and pecan biscuit. She could not completely hide her disappointment. The adobe ranch house, although immaculately clean and comfortable in a primitive way, had none of the

141

amenities she had for in her first home.

"Well, sweetheart, what do you think of the place?" Nate was obviously pleased with his purchase. "You haven't seen the outbuildings yet, but what do you think of the house itself?"

"With proper paint and fresh wallpaper, it will be lovely." She would not dampen his enthuisasm by telling him exactly how she felt. It would be their home and she would dedicate herself to making it perfect, no matter what obstacles she encountered. "We can use the furniture that's here for the time being. Perhaps the little spare room next to the first bedroom could be made into a bath."

"Anything you say." Nate buttered a slice of bread, placed a slab of cold roast beef on it and bit into it hungrily. "The Scotts seem to be very pleasant people. I'm glad they're staying on."

"You say she's the daughter of the original owner?"

"Oh no—the great-granddaughter of the original owner," he corrected her.

"It goes back that far?" Jette was surprised.

"It's been in the Calderon family since the early eighteen-hundreds." Nate finished the salad of fresh greens and pickled beets.

"What happened to the rest of the relatives?"

"When the old man, Matias Calderon, had to sell to Lodd and Ed most of them drifted off to other ranches, taking what work they could find. One of the sons became manager for a meat packing outfit down in Los Angeles." He helped himself to a wedge of lemon pie, tasted it and said, "You should really try some of this. Tecla is a marvelous cook."

"I'm much too full already," Jette laughed.

"You do like Seth and Tecla, don't you? I mean, I don't want to turn them out, but if you'd rather hire someone else . . ."

"Oh, no, Nate! I'm glad they want to stay on with us.

I know how hard it is to find good help. Father's taught me one thing: cherish a good worker as you would a friend."

"You admit then that he does have some good points?" He held his cup to indicate he wanted more tea.

"I've never denied that fact. Yes, I'd admit it." She poured, filling the cup. "But please, don't let's talk about Father." She looked about the room, envisioning what changes she might want to make. The china service, stored in an ugly oak cabinet, was like the old adobe, sturdy and utilitarian. The tea pot was of brown stoneware and did not match the plain white dishes, but it held the heat well and contained plenty of tea. Luncheon had been laid as a surprise for them, its simple provender a welcome from the Putnams and the Scotts.

Nate reached across the starched cotton tablecloth and took Jette's hand. "Whatever isn't just right, I want to make it over just to suit you." He had watched closely as she inspected the house and grounds, and had noticed her disappointment. "If you'd rather, we can have it fixed up before we move in." He knew the place fell short of her expectations with its low ceilings and small, deep-set windows.

"No," she protested quickly. "I don't want to put off the wedding just for a little paint and wallpaper. It will be fine just as it is. We can do our remodeling gradually, a bit at a time." She looked into his face and found in it a smiliar eagerness. "I'm so happy, Nate."

"All right, darling, whatever you wish." He glanced about the sparsely furnished dining room, noting its dark, varnished wainscoating and gray painted pine flooring. "This isn't the most cheerful place to eat I've ever been in, but that red toile paper on the walls and a decent lamp over the table . . ."

"I think perhaps it's wiser to live here a while—then

decide what needs to be done. One afternoon isn't enough to tell us what we want." Already in her mind she was redoing the entire adobe, but was sensible enough to be reasonable. "When will the Scotts be back from town?"

"Oh, probably by sundown. Certainly not much later," Nate replied. He laughed at her look of consternation. "If you're worried about your reputation, we can run into town right now." He tilted her chin with one finger, forcing her to look at him. "You can be a respectable old married woman by nightfall."

Jette laughed with him, her eyes dancing as she considered the dare. She rose from the table, taking her cup and saucer with her as she went to the uncurtained window. Suddenly Nate took the dishes from her hand, replaced them on the table, and drew her close.

"What do you say?" he breathed in her ear as he bent to kiss her. "Shall we drive in right now? Abe Marley can fix us up . . . witnesses . . . Judge Killigrew . . ." Jette found herself responding, yielding.

"Nate . . . no . . ." she protested as he unbuttoned her pale green silk blouse and loosened it from her skirt, his fingers caressing and stimulating her young body, coaxing her to desire. "We mustn't . . ."

He did not answer, but lifted her in his arms and carried her into the parlor. All the rooms of the old house opened, Mexican style, onto the courtyard, with the broad veranda serving as communicating hallway. He opened the front door with one hand, thrust it wide and proceeded to the first door to the left—the main bedroom, and closed the door behind them with his foot.

"Don't say no, Jette. Not now," he begged as he lowered her onto the elaborately carved mahogany bed.

"But the Scotts . . ." she began.

". . . won't be back until sundown." His mouth

144

covered hers, his kiss hard and searching as he untied the blue ribbon that bound her camisole beneath her arms. "I want you, Jette." Her arms encircled his neck, pulling him closer as she writhed in arousal. She closed her eyes and denied all sensation save the touch of his hands on her body, the feel of his lips as they explored her neck, her shoulders, the firm softness of her young breasts.

She broke from him and rose from the bed, turning from him as she stepped out of her white linen skirt and petticoats, draped them on the back of a chair. Slowly, deliberately, she loosened the lace-covered corselet, then returned to him. No word was needed. He unfastened her hose and unhooked the garment, took it from her as she moved into his embrace.

* * * *

The marble and ormolu piano-clock on the shelf above the corner fireplace struck four. Surprised, Nate Trasker rolled over and glanced at the clock. Four. It would still be a while before the Scotts returned from town with the toile wallpaper and unbleached muslin for window curtains. Jette was determined that the renovation project would begin next day.

He sat on the edge of the bed for a moment. It was cool inside the thick-walled adobe, and only the erratic twitter of finches and swallows broke the utter silence of the place. He pulled on his silk underwear and trousers as he stood looking down at the sleeping girl. Her perfect body with its delicate lavender shadows, her heavy auburn hair spread across the pillow . . . she was all any man could wish. Even as she lay for the first time with a man she had exhibited a wild, natural excitement—an inborn sensuality that promised to make the physical aspect of their marriage pleasurable.

"What time is it?" Jette asked sleepily.

145

"Just past four."

She yawned and stretched out her arms to him. "Kiss me, Nate," she demanded. "Kiss me as if there would never be another time like this."

"Sweetheart—don't say such a thing. We have all our years before us."

"But this time will never come again," she said. "Not for me . . ."

"You're so beautiful lying there," he said as he sat down beside her and took her in his arms. "The first time I saw you I told you that you had no right to look so beautiful." He pushed back the errant curl that fell across her forehead. "You're all I've ever wanted in life . . . more than I ever dared dream of . . ." Her lovely nakedness aroused him once again. "You wicked little Lorelei!" He broke from her and laughed. "We'd better make ourselves presentable and I'll take you home." He backed from the bed and finished dressing quickly. She watched him, her eyes growing solemn.

"I love you, Nate," she breathed softly.

"And I love you, darling." He accumulated her discarded garments and placed them on the bed. "But if you don't want to be hopelessly compromised, you'd better get dressed. I'm not at all sure the Scotts would approve . . ." He gestured toward her and the rumpled bedclothes.

"All right." Jette slid from the bed. "I'll hurry."

Trasker kissed her and left abruptly. She could hear his boots on the terra-cotta tiles of the veranda as he wandered back to the parlor. She looked at herself in the mirror when she had completed her toilette. She had recombed her hair and pinned her manila straw and maline hat back atop her loosely massed topknot. She had bathed herself, using the water from the pitcher on the wash stand. It did not matter if the Scotts discovered the towels and wash cloth had been used, or the linens on the bed. She was to be her own woman now, and

146

would answer to no one but Nate. *Her own woman*, she thought and smiled.

Was it possible that no one could tell she was now a woman? Could there be no outward sign? She spread her hands across her abdomen, a thrill coursing through her, causing her to shiver in remembered ecstasy. Nate had so gently, sweetly guided her from girlhood into womanhood, giving her a joy she had only dreamed of before. Again she inspected her image in the mirror. Was there a special gleam in her eyes? Perhaps a different smile on her lips? She shrugged as she saw nothing unusual to indicate her new status, but her heart sang a passionate new song and beat to a new and exciting rhythm.

"Jette?" Trasker tapped at the carmine door. "Ready?"

"Yes, come in." She looked about the room, saw it was all in order. He opened the door and held it wide for her.

"Do we lock up?" she asked as they walked across the courtyard to the waiting mares and buggy.

"No one ever has out here," he replied.

"Never?" She was amazed that it would be so. Elias had locks and keys for everything on the ranch. "It seems peculiar that they would leave the place open all the time."

"Lodd says they never have since they took over La Coruna. And the Calderons before them didn't either. Old Matias Calderon took pride in the fact that his home was always open to travelers and visitors." He handed Jette up into the buggy. "Besides, if someone wanted to rob the place, they'd manage to get around any locks in the way." He backed the carriage until he could negotiate a turn, then climbed into the seat beside her.

As they drew away from the courtyard, Jette looked back at the house. In the distance where her father's property adjoined the southern boundary of La Coruna, she could discern the shifting black forms of Aberdeen Angus as the dominant cow led her herd to their watering pond. Farther east and south a series of wire fences cut across rolling slopes, separating the various herds. Almost due south she could see white tops of the lofty silos near Elias' cattle barn.

Slightly higher than the Allenby ranch, La Coruna had the advantage of looking down on San Genaro Valley. It was a peaceful—if not too profitable—stretch of land.

"It's lovely out here," Jette sighed. "I can see why Father wanted La Coruna so badly. It would make a nice addition to his own property."

"And it has water he wants, too," Nate reminded her.

"But not enough to rely on year 'round," she said.

"I understand the Putnams gave up dry farming when the rains went bad—they should have tried irrigation." Trasker tightened the reins just enough to turn the bays into the highway. "I suppose they were too old to make such a big change."

"But if the water can't be relied on, what will we . . ."

He looked strangely at her, a hint of annoyance in his expression. "Darling, you're not to concern yourself about such matters. That will be my job . . . mine alone."

Jette did not miss the suddenly narrowed eyes and the taut set of his lips beneath the trim blond moustache. She had observed her own father react the same way. Trasker, sensing he had offended her, took her hand in his and pulled it to his lips.

"You're to be my wife. I'll not have your pretty little head worried over running the ranch," he chided. "Seth Scott comes highly recommended as an experienced, knowledgeable manager. Been on La

Coruna since before the Putnams and knows everthing there is to know about the place. You and Tecla can run the house and whatever else you'd like to keep you busy and happy. Just let Seth and me run the ranch." He looked at her. "All right?"

"All right, Nate," Jette answered. "Just please don't expect me not to take any interest in the ranch." She was as much hurt as angry. It was one thing for her Father to issue orders and dictate to her. It was quite another thing for her future husband to do so. "All of La Coruna will be our home—not just the house and its grounds. What touches you—whether in running the ranch or in your business—will also touch me. If I'm to be your wife . . ."

"If?" He turned to her in alarm, saw her smoldering resentment and drew her to him. "Of course you're going to be my wife! And of course you'll be involved in everything." He kissed her cheek and held her close. "I just don't want you to ever have to worry about anything again. I want you to let me take care of you. Understand?"

Looking into his smiling face, she laughed and thrust aside any lingering doubt. "That's sweet of you. Forgive me. But you must promise me you'll let me share in everything, let me help in any way I can."

He bent to kiss the tip of her nose. "Request granted." As their phaeton topped a slight rise in the road they could see a buggy heading toward them. "Anyone you know?" he asked, glad for the interruption.

"I don't recognize the horse or the carriage, but that's Margaret Larson I think. Can't tell who else it is." Jette watched the approaching vehicle. "Yes, that's her tan boater and suit. Oh . . ." She stopped abruptly.

"Would you rather not meet them?" he asked as he saw her anguished face. "We can turn into this road here. Where does it go?"

149

"That's Alisos Road . . . part of our ranch. It leads over to a few cottages in that grove of alders about half a mile west." She was tempted to tell him to turn. "No, don't turn off. I want you to meet her."

"But what's wrong?"

"Margaret's been gossiping . . ."

"Then by all means, I must meet her." Trasker smiled and urged the mares to one side of the road as the heavy black Concord buggy drew near.

"Jette!" Margaret Larson called out. "I told Miles I thought that was you." She snuggled closer to Doctor Hunter, linking her arm in his, her face unnaturally pink with sudden pleasure that neither of the men could fathom. Hunter doffed his hat and reined his blazed black and chestnut geldings to a halt beside them. Something was missing. Jette looked for his crutches. Propped against the dashboard was a brass-ferruled cane.

For a brief moment her eyes met Miles'. He smiled, acknowledged the introduction to Trasker, congratulated him, wished them luck, but always his eyes were on Jette. *Could he see? Could he sense what had happened in the bedroom at La Coruna?* The joy she had felt as she lay with Nate was now nothing compared to the wretchedness in her heart as she looked at Miles.

Hunter and Margaret continued north toward the Larson ranch. An afternoon off from his work, he had said. Margaret was elated, inordinately pleased. Jette dared not look back at them as they drove on. If Nate Trasker had noticed anything during the encounter, he wisely refrained from saying so.

"Seems a nice girl," he finally said to break the silence.

"Margaret? Yes, she's very nice."

"Are they engaged?"

"I don't know . . . I don't think so." The thought was painful.

"Hunter didn't seem too thrilled with her attentions, did he?"

"I'm afraid I didn't notice." It was the truth. She had not noticed Margaret's clutching at Hunter or her awkwardly coquettish conversation. "Engaged?" she asked aloud, but had no answer. Why should she feel hurt? She had chosen Nate Trasker over Miles. She could not expect him to remain a celibate just because he'd said he loved her and she had taken someone else.

A sudden desolation overcame her. She longed to run back to Miles and kiss away the pain from his eyes. He had loved her and wanted to marry her. But now she was to marry Nate Trasker . . . Nate Trasker, the man beside her, the man with whom she had committed unforgiveable sin. Could Miles forgive her?

* * * *

"Nate, won't you come in and have tea with Mother and me? That would please her so much. She has so few visitors." Jette held her skirts and allowed Trasker to lift her from the buggy and deposit her on the front steps. "Please stay."

"All right, darling. Just long enough for tea, though. I've got to see Abe Marley this evening in town." He took her elbow and escorted her into the house. As they entered, the door to the office opened. Asa Beemer took a step into the parlor and stopped. He was dressed in rough canvas trousers stained with horse sweat and high-heeled stoga boots chafed from stirrup wear. Jette could not help comparing the men by their attire and giving the advantage to the nattily dressed Trasker.

"Afternoon, Miss Jette . . . Trasker." Asa seemed to want to say something but hesitated, looking significantly at Trasker.

"Well, what is it?" Jette asked impatiently. When he remained silent she said, "You can say whatever you wish in front of Mr. Trasker. He'll be a member of the family soon." She could not stop herself from emphasizing the fact that she had triumphed in her determination not to marry Asa. "What is it?"

"Mrs. Allenby's acting real strange. I think it's time you took her down to Los Angeles to a new doctor. I read in the paper they have some sort of fancy doctor there—he's from Germany, I think it was. Don't know much about him, but he's supposed to be good at helping folks like her." He waited before going on, as if debating whether to continue.

"Well, do go on, Asa," Jette prompted him irritably.

"It isn't just that beating she took, Miss Jette. It's worse." He took a deep breath and expelled it before answering her unvoiced question. "Benito caught her wandering around out at the big barn, trying to get into that stall where we keep Old Max."

"What in the world would she want to do that for?" Jette was horrified.

"He couldn't make any sense out of her. Seems she told him she was testing the will of the Lord." He shuffled his feet as if reluctant to finish. "You'll have to keep somebody with her, right around the clock, or she'll have to be put in some hospital where they can look after her."

Trasker seated Jette before the fireplace and took a chair beside her. "I had no idea she was that far gone," he said. "Is she a danger to others?" He did not try to disguise the cold objectivity in his inquiry.

"No! How could you even think such a thing?" Jette asked.

"No, sir, Trasker, that woman couldn't hurt a fly. Matter of fact," Asa said and chuckled, "She gets upset when Elvira and Socorro go around swatting bugs inside

152

the house. And we don't even tell her when we have to kill off gophers and squinnies. She's no harm—except to herself."

"I'll have to have Elvira . . ." Jette began.

"She's got as much as she can handle right now. Look . . . this ranch is no place for her to be after you're gone. And I can't look after her, that's for sure." It was a plea for Verdie that Jette could not ignore. "If she gets into that pen with Old Max, I can't be responsible for what might happen. He's settled down some, but he's over a ton of meanness when he's riled up and I'll tell you right out—he's nearsighted like most blooded bulls are and anything flapping, he'll go for it, head down and pawing for China."

"You mean women's skirts?" Nate Trasker guessed the problem.

"Yes, sir," Asa nodded. "Don't get the idea Old Max would do it for plain cussedness. He's no killer by nature. I don't aim to have anyone get hurt by him. And I don't want Old Max hurt either. He's got a right to serve his purpose and not be pestered and spooked."

"You make yourself very clear." Jette sounded sarcastic.

"Mrs. Allenby just doesn't belong out here." He met her eyes straight on. "And I don't want to see her get any worse."

"You seem fond of her, Beemer." Trasker was intrigued by the man's solicitude. "That's very commendable."

"I am fond of her, yes, sir. She's a fine lady." He turned to go back to the office. "And I'm fond of Elias, too. He has his ways. You have to take him as he is. He's fair to me, and that's a lot more than some I worked for in my time." He nodded and said as he left, "Trasker, good to see you again."

It was past six-thirty when Nate Trasker left the Allenby ranch. Although Socorro Galvan had hurriedly prepared a light tea of bread and jam and fresh strawberries with thick cream, the event had been disastrous, both for Verdie and her daughter. He had been polite and attentive, but shrugged with exasperation as Verdie could not follow the conversation and instead drifted off into her own world of silence.

For the time it took the buggy to cover the distance to the main road, Jette stood at the sitting room window, watching until Nate was out of sight. Their tea service remained on the center table, bread beginning to curl at the edges as it dried, tea cold in the silver pot. She and Nate had walked to the front door where she bade him goodbye beyond Verdie's hearing. He had agreed with Asa Beemer—Jette must see someone about her mother. In Nate's attitude she detected something that bothered her, not something said outright, but an indefinable irritation, possibly even resentment. She turned now from the window and faced her mother.

"Why don't you like him, Mother?" she demanded. Verdie looked up in surprise as Jette sat beside her. "I can tell—there are subtle signs—and I know you so well." The girl poured cold tea into a cup and sipped it as she settled back into the rose damask settee. She was suddenly very weary. "Please, Mother." She tried to keep her own irritation from her voice.

"What shall I tell you, dear?" Verdie reached for the tiny silver bell to summon Elvira, but Jette took it gently from her hand and replaced it on the tea tray.

"Not yet . . . I want to talk to you first." She was determined to find out why Verdie had become cool to Trasker. It had been subtle, as she said, but apparent. "You don't like Nate, do you?"

"No!" Jette was startled by her mother's abrupt reply. "He is totally charming. His manners are above reproach. And he is certainly one of the handsomest men I've ever seen. But, no, I don't like him." Verdie rose and went to the north door, the one leading to the patio, opened it and called softly, "Pecky . . . Buff . . . you can come in now." The dogs scampered into the sitting room and waited expectantly as Verdie broke the buttered bread into bits and fed it to them from her fingers. "I'm not saying a dog's instinct should be the criterion upon which we should base our human relationships, but don't you think it strange—the way Pecky and Buff behave around Mr. Trasker?"

"Embarrassing, to say the least," Jette agreed. "But hardly strange. Some people seem to put animals off."

"But Pecky and Buff love everybody."

"Except Father."

"Yes, except your father." She sighed as if it pained her to admit such a thing. "They are good watch dogs, but if it came down to attacking someone, even in defending us . . . Well, I'm not sure we could count on them. And yet, I have the feeling they might set on Mr. Trasker if he gave them the opportunity."

"That's hardly a reason to dislike him, Mother. You're keeping something back. What is it?" Jette pleaded. "He's the man I'm going to marry. I want you to love him, too."

It was a moment before Verdie answered. She allowed the black and white spaniel to crawl up onto the settee and cuddle in her lap. "Are you certain you want to hear what I may have to say?"

"Yes, I do. We mustn't have any secrets between us."

Verdie waited, watching her daughter's face, as if undecided whether or not to reply. Finally she said, "He is an imposter." For once her own face contained none of the vagueness that so frequently betrayed her wandering state of mind. Her hazel eyes were bright and sharp, her words precise as she continued, "Don't ask me to explain, for I can't. I only say he is not what he seems. He is not what he wants you to think he is,

Jette."

"How can you say . . ."

"He's studied manners and speech, child, but he's playing a role, acting a part. Can't you see it?"

"No, I cannot!" Jette flared impatiently. "He's been a perfect gentleman. He is a perfect gentleman!"

Verdie stared at her daughter, her expression part sad, part reproving. She shook her head slowly and glanced away. "You've never lied to me before, please don't begin now." She rolled the spaniel's ears and scratched his black pate.

"I don't know what you mean." Jette was clearly annoyed.

"Of course you do, Jette." Verdie turned to the girl and sighed. "But then, no one could talk to me when I was your age either. No one could convince me that I knew nothing of men. I don't want to see you repeat my mistakes!"

"Marrying Nate is not a mistake!"

"Think, think, child! He hardly knew you before he announced he was going to marry you. Asa says he was telling it all over San Genaro only a few days after he met you on the road. Why?"

"Mother, young people do fall in love. It happens. And they do marry because they are in love." Jette was exasperated.

"I'm not so old yet that I can't remember how it was when I was in love and full of hopes and dreams." Verdie turned away and for a moment Jette feared she would retreat into silence once again.

"I'm sorry, Mother. I didn't mean it that way." She had never really quarreled with her mother and was reluctant to do so now.

"I know."

"I don't want us to quarrel, especially about Nate."

"Jette, you know absolutely nothing about him. Does he speak the truth? I doubt it, and yet I must admit I have no reason not to believe in either him or in what he says.'' She smiled and patted her daughter's hand. ''He has not been a perfect gentleman, now has he?''

Jette looked at her mother before replying. It was not possible that she could know about what had happened this afternoon. And yet she did know. Jette refused to lie about it. ''I'm going to marry him, Mother.''

''Then at least wait until you know him better. Wait until you can know for certain that he is an honorable man—someone you can trust as well as love.''

Jette sipped the cold tea, her eyes closing as she recalled Nate's love making. ''I know him very well right now,'' she said.

''Yes, I know.'' Verdie nodded her head. Jette looked away as she realized her mother had guessed at what went on in the bedroom at La Coruna. ''You love him that much then?''

''Oh, yes, I do, Mother. I want to be with him always. He makes me feel as I've never felt before—alive and free. I want to be his wife.''

''And what about Doctor Hunter?''

''I don't love him. It's as simple as that.''

''Ah . . . and you do love Mr. Trasker.''

''Yes!'' Jette was angry that her mother could doubt it.

''Are you sure you don't see marrying Nate Trasker as the means to get away from your father? Remember, while it may not be common knowledge that you'll come into your grandmother's trust when you marry, there are enough people around San Genaro who know about it and that it could be a factor in his courting you, wanting you to marry him.''

Verdie had struck a nerve. Her daughter stood up, placed her cup on the tea tray and rang the silver bell to call Elvira from the kitchen. Verdie pressed the advantage and continued, ''When you marry you'll be well off financially. And one day, when your father and

157

I are gone, you'll be wealthy. I'd ask myself if these were Mr. Trasker's considerations. You are a lovely young woman, dear, but make certain first . . ."

"Mother, I think I should tell you the trust fund was looted by Father in order for him to buy Old Max. I didn't want to tell you and get you upset, but when I saw Mr. Millege at the bank and tried to get enough for tuition I couldn't get a penny. Millege says Father had Judge Killigrew arrange it. Since he'd tied his own money up in his property offers, he took mine." At her mother's look of indignation, she added, "Oh, it was all very legal, all properly done—and signed by the judge."

Verdie grew white, her lips compressed into a tight line. "How could he?" she asked.

"Very easily, as a matter of fact," Jette laughed. "So you see, if Nate is seeking a fortune he's going to have to wait for it."

Elvira Mireles hurried into the sitting room, a freshly starched and ironed white apron tied over her wide blue skirt. Without waiting to be told, she began collecting the tea dishes and tidying up the room. "Will there be anything else, Mrs. Allenby?" She dropped a crust of bread to the mastiff mongrel on the floor by Verdie's feet.

"No, dear. Just take the tea tray." Verdie seemed relieved to have her thoughts on something else for the moment. "And please tell Socorro we'll have dinner a bit later tonight. Mr. Allenby won't be back until after seven."

"Yes, ma'am. I'll tell her." The girl stepped around the huge dog and returned to the back of the house. She did not remind her mistress that she had already instructed Socorro about this evening's meal. She wondered if Mrs. Allenby could even remember being out by the bull pen earlier in the day.

Jette purposely avoided mention of the incident. She did not wish to agitate her mother. First she would

158

speak with Benito, try to find out what exactly had happened, and much as she hated doing so, would talk with Asa once more. Elias would never learn of his wife's foolish attempt to enter the Angus' stall. She could at least rely on Asa to see that the story was kept from him. For that, Jette was grateful.

After taking her mother upstairs to rest until dinner, Jette sought out Benito. He was still working in the ranch store, directing two boys in rearranging shelves of tinned foods, sacks of fine-ground *masa harina*, pails of lard, barrels of beans and rice. He wiped his hands on his canvascloth apron and came out to stand on the porch. He could not, however, add substantially to Asa's report of what had occurred at the barn.

"What reason did Mother give for being out there?"

"Please, you'd better ask Mr. Beemer." Benito's old face evidenced the pain he felt for his employer's wife.

"I'd rather you tell me, Benito."

"Mr. Allenby won't find out?"

"No," Jette was quick to say. "I promise you he won't know anything about it."

"She was talking wild. It can't mean much, not the way she was. She was crying . . ." He waited, not wanting to tell the rest. "She said she was a sinner in the sight of God and had to know if He had forgiven her." The old man was puzzled. "I suppose she had in mind the story of Daniel and the lions in the Bible."

Jette leaned against the porch railing, sick at heart. "Thank you for rescuing her and getting her back to the house without Father finding out." She touched his wrinkled hand and turned to leave. He nodded, understanding her heartache. "Thank you for telling me about it."

Asa Beemer was coming from the office as she returned to the main house along the graveled drive. He slouched against a pillar on the veranda and waited for her. "Seen Benito?" he asked.

"Yes," she replied with a weariness strange to her. Pecky and Buff ran from around the patio and pranced about them, licking at Asa's hands as he gently cuffed their ears. Buff nuzzled the girl's skirts and promptly sat down on her feet, content to be as close as possible. "It's just as you say, insane."

"Now just a minute there! I never said anything of the kind!" His thin mouth pulled back to show large, even teeth as he set his jaw in anger. "That's a cruel thing to say and it isn't like you to say it."

"It was an insane thing to do." She refused to look at him and grew red with anger of her own.

"Whatever's wrong with her, it comes and goes. She has good times, when she's just fine. That's not what I'd call insanity. If you go around taling like that, there's no telling what harm it could do her." He blocked her way in the side door, one arm across the entrance. "You of all people, shouldn't even think such a thing, let alone say it out loud. If it's Trasker got you to thinking that way, he ought to be shot."

Jette stood looking at the man. His brown eyes were almost hidden by his prairie squint as he stared down at her. He was a taller man than he appeared at first glance. Years in the saddle had given him a perpetual slouch, but he had the build of a lean, wild animal. He was not loud, as Elias was, but was quiet, saying little unless it was necessary and to the mark. Vaguely she felt a threat in his stance, and heard it in his voice.

"Mr. Trasker has nothing to do with it," she said.

"Then maybe you'll take her over to La Coruna to live with you. You discuss it yet with Trasker?"

She resented his familiarity. "No, I have not. If it gets to a point where it becomes necessary, I'm sure he'd be happy to do all he could."

"I don't believe that."

"I don't care what you believe." She attempted to get past him, but his arm barred the way. She turned to go by way of the rear patio. He caught her, his work-calloused hand tight about her wrist.

"Now you're gonna listen to me, whether you like it or not, by damn!" He spoke quietly, scarcely moving his thin lips.

Fear shot through her as she tried to escape his grip. In spite of her father's bullying violence, she did not fear him. Asa Beemer was another matter.

"Let me go, Asa!" She glanced at the dogs, but they merely watched, wagging their tails. "Let go of me!"

"Not till you hear me out." He pushed her to the wall, pressing her to the adobe with his hard body. "There, that's better," he grinned as she stopped struggling.

"Say what you've got to say and let me go," she spat.

"This Trasker you're so set on marrying, has he told you about him and the widow Baldwin?"

"Of course he has." She glared at him in defiance.

"Did he tell you about him staying all night with her over at her place? And about the times he runs down to Los Angeles and stays with her at the Imperial Hotel?" He could see he had piqued her interest. "Now if you already know all about it, and you want to go right ahead and marry him, that's your business, but I'd say you're a goddam fool."

"I don't believe you!" She kicked at his legs, but her long skirts prevented any effectiveness. Pecky barked and jumped out of the way as she wrestled with Asa. "You're a liar!" she cried.

"Listen, little lady, there's a whole hell of a lot you don't know about Trasker and you better find out before you go do something really insane like marrying him. He's Lavinia Baldwin's man. Do you understand me?"

He released her and she swung her hand at his face, slapping him hard enough to cause him to duck the second time. He sidled away, but added, "I had that coming. You have every right to take a gun and shoot me if it'd make you feel any better." He ducked as she lunged at him again. "God knows I'm sorry about what happened, but I probably would try it again." He laughed as Jette's hair, loosened by her efforts, fell in disarray about her shoulders. He stooped to pick up her hairpins that had fallen to the veranda floor. As he did so she aimed a kick at him, tripped on her skirt and fell. He caught her in his arms and held her, his face close to hers as he whispered, "You know damned well I love you, Jette. Maybe I'm no prize in your book, but I'm honest with you."

He almost threw her from him and turned from her, walking quickly down the path to the cattle barn. "I'm honest with you," he called back to her. "You remember that."

Chapter 8

"The Glorious Fourth—Celebrate in San Genaro—Freedom Parade—Noon" *"Fireworks at Lagunita Park—8:00 P.M."* Red-white-and-blue banners stretched the entire width of McKinley Street and San Genaro Road, proclaiming on all four sides of the square that the town was prepared to welcome the holiday in style.

Bunting in patriotic colors was bunched and draped to lamp posts and porch pillars, ruffled and frilled on balconies and railings. Raizes Department Store featured cotton nainsook in white, percale in guaranteed-wash-fast brilliant red, and Hamburg flouncing in cobalt blue. Across the street Murdock's Pharmacy filled its front windows with crayon and watercolor illustrations of patriotic motifs created by grammar school pupils of the town. Flags of every dimension flapped from poles or were strung in doorways, inconveniencing customers.

Spit-devils and sparklers had already burned the fingers of children too eager to wait until the Fourth to do their celebrating. For a week ahead of time the evenings were noisy with the bang and sizzle of firecrackers and snakes, and the air reeked of powder and scorched paper.

Middle-aged and elderly veterans of the War of Secession brushed their faded blue uniforms and aired the camphor and cedar resin from the fabric, then polished the buttons in anticipation of trooping behind the Masonic Lodge's brass band. Young men, fresh from Cuba and the Philippines, some on leave from active service, overburdened the cleaning establishments with their khakis and worried if they would have them back in time for the noontime festivities.

The ice-house added five additional men to its routes for a few days before the holiday. Wagon-loads of crushed and block ice trundled down every street, much to the delight of thirsty, thieving small boys. Watermelons, ripened in the hotter inland valleys and off-loaded from the train the night before, were cooling in ice-water in barrels, buckets, and troughs, and Fee's Dairy had a run on whole milk and thick Jersey cream as housewives traded recipes for ice-cream.

By eleven o'clock the streets along the parade route were lined with celebrants. Frantic last minute tootling of cornets and trombones, wetting and trimming of new reeds in clarinets, tentative thumps on drums, and an impatient turmoil all along Lopez Street presaged the start of the procession. Extending almost to the railroad tracks beyond Oneill Road were decorated buggies, wagons, and pony carts interspersed between the bands. A few automobiles, sporting crepe paper and bunting, carried dignitaries to lead the parade, and streetcleaners called to holiday duty were positioned along the route with manure shovels and brooms. All awaited the firing of the old cannon on the courthouse lawn to signal the start.

Jette Allenby, radiant in ashes-of-roses watered silk, tilted her parasol against the sun, grateful for the tiny spot of shade it created. The pedestal clock on the cement sidewalk in front of the bank showed one minute before noon. Everyone on the wooden grandstand waited in hushed expectancy as the hands of the clock marked another minute. Lucy Larson, in pale blue ruffles and ivory lace, giggled and swung her parasol to shade both Henry Stebbins and herself, forcing him to move closer.

Boom! The antique cannon blasted its blank charge and recoiled into silence until needed at election time next fall. A cheer rose from the spectators and countless small flags on blue dowel sticks fluttered in the stands and along San Genaro Road. From the area of Van Vliet's Feed and Grain Supply on Lopez Street the first oom-pah of tubas and clang of zealously slammed cymbals let the crowd downtown know the parade had begun.

"Comfortable, darling?" Nate Trasker adjusted the rented pillow behind Jette's back.

"I'm fine. Thank you for getting the pillows." She turned to Ziphia and Ainsworth Millege, who occupied the seats directly behind them. "As soon as they come in sight I promise I'll put down my parasol," she laughed.

"Quite all right, Jette." Ziphia Millege fanned herself with a colored cardboard and peel fan purchased from the Civic Beautification Club's fund raising booth on the corner. Resignedly, she sat in the hot sun before her husband's bank, strickly from a sense of duty rather than desire. "I'm sorry your mother didn't feel up to coming along today," she said to Jette. "We see so little of her these days. You must bring her to tea the first afternoon she's well enough.''

"That would be nice,'' Jette said. "I'll tell her you asked about her.'' She knew, of course, that Ziphia Millege would have heard about her mother's condition, although she tactfully refrained from mentioning it. Gossip in San Genaro, especially about the more prominent and affluent members of the community, spread quickly if not accurately.

"Have you two young things decided on a date yet?'' Ainsworth Millege asked Jette as he handed an iced lemonade to his perspiring wife. He flipped a nickel to the boy vending the drink from a portable stand. "Abe Marley tells me it won't be long now until you're Mrs. Trasker.''

Before Jette could reply Nate said, "We've selected a dozen dates, and each time Jette's changed her mind.'' He was dapper in white summer-weight linen trousers, navy blue yachting style blazer, and stiff-brimmed straw hat. His golden moustache was meticulously trimmed to a narrow inverted-V, its shine almost equal to the brass buttons on the coat. He took Jette's hand in his and asked the banker, "Can't you say something to persuade her to make it soon?''

"I've found it the better part of discretion to avoid any sort of coercion or influence when it comes to the ladies,'' Millege replied with a wink. "I must say, I am delighted she's made such a good choice.'' He looked significantly at Jette as he added, "But then, I never doubted she would.''

Millege nudged his wife as the lovers on the seats below them put their heads together in a quick kiss behind Jette's parasol. As outrageous as the display of affection was, since it was in public, the older couple found it touching. Ziphia smiled and sighed behind her fan.

Millege was uncomfortable on the hard boards of the

grandstand, and had decorum and civic responsibility not dictated his remaining to view the parade, he would have preferred to escape to the cool, copa de oro-covered porch of his home. He wiped his face with a rumpled handkerchief and stuffed it in his coat pocket before Ziphia could reprimand him. "You're a lucky man, Trasker," he said. "I'd wager there must be a dozen men in town who'd like to call you out for taking Miss Allenby out of circulation." His laugh was hearty in spite of his acute discomfort.

"Lucy and Henry have decided on the first Sunday in August," Margaret Larson volunteered. She sat next to Jette, with Miles Hunter to her right. Knowing she could not compare in her severe white dimity dress to the titian-haired Jette, she smoldered with resentment as all conversation seemed to be centered on her friend. Bereft of attention, she continued in a voice a bit too loud, "Father's inviting half the county and making such a fuss. I'm really a bit put out by Lucy stealing the march on me." Hunter refused to meet her adoring glance.

"Well now, congratulations, Stebbins." Millege reached down and shook the boy's hand and patted him on the back. "Seems like we're apt to have a rash of weddings this summer, doesn't it?" he beamed. "Glad to hear it. Good for the community."

Margaret looked sideways at Miles Hunter, disturbed to see him staring at Jette, a slight frown fleeting across his face. Rearranging her skirts and the pillow upon which she was seated, she moved closer to Hunter, linking her arm in his to distract his wandering attention. Flushed with pique, Margaret leaned forward and looked at Trasker saying, "We all thought for sure Jette would marry Asa Beemer. How ever did you manage to take her away from him?" The question was filled with acid. Lucy jabbed her sister, hoping to shush her, but Margaret went on, "From all I've heard about

166

Asa Beemer, he's nobody to fool around with. Father says he was involved in some shootings in Kansas or somewhere. Isn't that so, Jette?''

Lucy glared with disapproval at her older sister. "You just never know how to keep a hold on your tongue, do you?" she hissed under her breath. But Margaret, intent upon disillusioning Miles Hunter, made a face at Lucy. "Don't tell me you've never heard such tales, Jette," she said.

"I've heard all sorts of tales about all sorts of people, and prefer to ignore them. Just because they are told doesn't mean they're true." She turned to Millege and smiled, "Isn't that so? Just look at our local paper! It said today would be overcast and cloudy, and here it is—a beautiful day."

Lucy snickered and made a face back at her sister. In order to defuse the situation Jette continued, "Are we all going out to the picnic after the parade?" She had no intention of letting it become necessary for Nate to answer Margaret's remarks.

"Oh my, yes!" Mrs. Millege put in quickly. She had no way of knowing what had caused the barbed exchange, but could guess simply by the way Hunter gazed at Jette Allenby. "Everyone must help us eat all that potato salad I spent half the night fixing. I made bushels of it and four cakes. I was icing them at two this morning and don't intend to take a morsel of it back home. I'll be angry with you all if you don't help us." She laughed easily and with good natured generosity.

"It's settled," Millege said. "She's a tiger when anyone crosses her and I advise you all to come along quietly."

"Mrs. Howard, I suppose our little celebration can't compare to the ones you're used to back east." Henry Stebbins turned to the older woman seated beside the banker's wife. She was a tall, Junoesque woman of indeterminate age whose pure white, carefully arranged hair was totally at odds with her pink complexion and dark brows.

"Frankly, Mr. Stebbins, I attend such things as seldom as I must. I let Mr. Howard do the honors for both of us and plead a headache." Her laughter was solid, earthy, and in it one could discern a resemblance to Ziphia Millege, her cousin. "I must ask you all for a few new excuses that I may use when I return to Cincinnati."

At the name of the city Nate Trasker gave a perceptible start. Jette looked at him in surprise. "Pesky fly!" he muttered and waved his hand in front of his face.

"They get bad this time of year," she said. "Oh, look! here they come!" She collapsed her parasol and leaned it against the seat between Nate and herself.

Chugging into sight in the next block was the contingent of automobiles, their gears grinding as the slow speed kept them shifting to maintain proper spacing. Harvey Cutsworth, the mayor, waved to the crowds in grandiose style from the lead vehicle, his top hat and cutaway coat ludicrous in the noontime heat. Following his automobile was Abe Marley's, festooned with as much bunting and crepe paper as could reasonably be tied to it. Marley, as chairman of the Board of Supervisors, drew second position in the procession, but far more people recognized and cheered him than the mayor. Sure of perpetual reelection, he had no need of silk hat or cutaway coat. Nor did he need to wave. He knew the citizenry; they knew him. He smoked his long green Cuban cigar and with an occasional nod of his head recognized whom he would among the massed crowd.

In bare feet and overalls small boys ran alongside the noisy vehicles, the more audacious of the youngsters darting between slow moving machines, daring the attendant law officers to give chase. Now and then one held a lighted stick of punk to a firecracker and howled with glee as the ensuing bang drew shrieks from girls who pulled their skirts tight and screamed abuse at them.

As the rag-tag tail of the parade—consisting of every boy in town who had a pony to ride and those who wished they had—filed by the reviewing stands with all the solemnity of a small riot, the spectators began leaving and started their own trek toward the park. Soon only the sanitation workers and a few stray dogs patroled the deserted streets.

Ziphia and Ainsworth Millege skirted the business section and drove their phaeton down Campbell Avenue to Lagunita, thus avoiding the confusion of carriages and pedestrians which followed the parade route. In honor of her cousin, Mrs. Millege had invited a few dozen appropriate guests to participate with them in the communal picnic that took place between the parade and the endless soft-ball game. It was understood, of course, that all were welcome to remain the entire afternoon and evening, view the fireworks, and finish the refreshments.

A central bandstand erected in the center of the picnic area was the hub of the afternoon's entertainment, with the municipall brass band alternating with those of the lodges and local high school. Near enough to hear the concert, but far enough away that conversation was possible, the Milleges had arranged a group of tables and benches beneath the oaks. The small lake, fed by surrounding hills, shimmered in brilliant sunlight. Low during the summer, its ready margins were alive with the flash of red-winged blackbirds whose shrill notes could be heard above the shouts and laughter.

By late afternoon even the most exuberant picnickers were beginning to weary. By twilight a second round of sandwiches and ice-cream was accompanied by respectful attention to the silver cornet band hired for

169

the day from Los Angeles. No one went home, save those who had livestock to attend. Not until toddlers became obstreperous from lack of their customary afternoon naps were they put down on blankets in the grass. Too tired to resist, they slept soundly despite the band's most thunderous military marches. Eight o'clock would come, although it seemed to the children that darkness would never fall. Sparklers twinkled about the lake, and pin wheels tacked onto tree trunks whizzed around, showering golden and orange sparks in whirlagig circles.

The fire department deployed its several units about the park, leaving only one man to sound the alarm at the station should an emergency arise in town. Summer in San Genaro was dry, with only a stray spark needed to touch off the hills. Ranchers, fearful of such an event, had posted a perpetual reward of $10,000 for the conviction of anyone—adult or child—who was instrumental in starting such a fire. Parents, mindful of the vengeance possible, had put the fear of sudden death in their offspring lest one of them be responsible. In more than one home the admonitory name was Elias Allenby.

Scheduled for eight o'clock, the pyrotechnic display would take place near the water's edge, with aerial features over the lake. In case of wind, it would be cancelled completely. As the time drew near, however, not a leaf was astir.

Huddled in the dark on benches and sitting in the deep shadows on the grass, young couples made the most of the occasion. Lucy and Henry, mindful of her reputation, chose a spot near the Milleges, who were irreproachable chaperones. Miles Hunter and Margaret Larson played Parchesi and Flinch with various partners throughout the afternoon, with one interruption to watch a few innings of the soft-ball game. Jette and Nate Trasker excused themselves and walked toward the lake, arm in arm. Until they had turned the path and disappeared, Hunter watched them, a frown creasing his wide forehead. Margaret shuffled the cards and began to deal again, tears of anger and frustration welling as she surreptitiously observed him.

Nodding greetings to passing couples, Nate encircled Jette's slim waist with one arm as they made their way slowly around the water's edge. The evening air retained July heat, unrelieved by a breeze. Mosquitos sang about their ears, and in the lake carefully-nurtured bass leaped after low-hovering insects and fell back into the water with a loud slap. Beside the walkway frogs croaked until approaching footsteps stilled them, then resumed as they departed. Jette was content to enjoy the dusk, to be by Nate's side and feel his arm about her.

"What must I do to get you to set a date, darling?" he asked when they were out of earshot of the others.

"I have to know Mother will be all right, Nate. I can't leave her now." Jette was reluctant to go over it all again and risk spoiling what had been a perfect day.

"Are you taking her to see that new doctor in Los Angeles?"

"Yes, next week, if she's well enough. We're going down by train on Tuesday."

"Good. It's the right thing to do. Then perhaps we can see just where we are." He tightened his grip on her, bringing her closer. "I don't want us to wait any longer. I love you too much." He bent to kiss her and she turned to his embrace.

"Nor do I, but I have no choice," she said. "You do see that, don't you?" She studied his face, disappointed to see his frown.

"Frankly, no. You have a life of your own to lead. You can't continue to be responsible for your mother. I appreciate how you feel, but you must understand my position, too." He felt her body stiffen and he added quickly, "But I shall leave it up to you, Jette."

171

In silence they wandered at the water's edge until they reached the end of the pathway where an upthrust of granite blocked the way. From above them they could hear the voices of a few of the more adventurous young people who had clambered up the jumbled heap of boulders for a better view of the fireworks.

"Shall we join them up there?" he dared her.

"I'd love to, but I'm not dressed for it this time." She looked upward and smiled at the faces peering down at them. "Next time I shall come dressed for the climb."

He pulled her to him again, oblivious of the onlookers. "Darling, please be honest with me . . . will there be a next time?" His face was drawn and serious, unsmiling. "Is there to be a next time for us?"

"Nate . . . what do you mean?" She grew alarmed as she peered into his pale eyes and found there an emotion new in their relationship—anger.

"You've got to tell me, Jette. I must know where I stand. When we were over at La Coruna, I thought . . ." He hesitated and turned from her, unwilling for her to see his lingering resentment. "If you mean to marry me, then set a date. Don't go on torturing me like this."

"Torture?" She put her hand on his arm and coaxed him around, then pulled his face down to hers and kissed him. "Oh, my poor darling, how could I ever do such a thing to you?" She touched his sun-tanned face with her hands, fingering the lines that marked his frown. "I love you beyond anything else in this world. How could I ever hurt you?"

"Then you will set the date?"

"Yes, Nate. One way or another, after I take Mother to Los Angeles, I'll set a definite date."

"Regardless of what you may find out?"

"Regardless."

He hugged her to him, sweeping her off her feet and swinging her about, sending her rose skirt and petticoats flying. His straw hat flew off into the cattails, and from above them came hoots and whistles from their viewers. Before retrieving his hat he looked up and waved to the sight-seers on the rocks. Jette stooped and picked up the straw boater. Something inside the hat, on the silk band, caught her eye.

A silver hat-marker glistened in the waning light as she tilted the straw boater to decipher the engraved initials. As Trasker saw her reading the marker his frown returned and deepened. Jette extended the hat to him and he replaced it on his head at a jaunty angle.

"Thank you, my sweet," he said as he took her elbow and prepared to escort her back to the picnic grounds. She did not look directly at him, but watched him from the corner of her eye. It was apparent something had annoyed him, but he gave no outward indication.

"Someone's going to think you're a thief," she laughed.

He looked obliquely at her, his thin lips curved into a smile. A wariness, however, had crept into his eyes. "I'm afraid I don't follow you," he said. The pressure of his hand on her arm was enough to tell her she was right in assuming he was irritated.

"The initials inside your hat . . . on the little silver marker," she explained. "They say 'P.B.' "

His fingers flexed tighter, almost imperceptibly, and his eyes narrowed, the lower lids all but obscuring the cold blue iris. He halted, removed the hat and inspected the marker.

"Hmm. Well, I'm afraid a Mr. P.B. and I have crosed paths somewhere," he admitted with a show of chagrin. "Anyone you know?"

She tried to think of anyone with those initials whom she knew. "No, I don't think so."

"Must have been in the barber shop," Trasker speculated. "Or maybe in the hotel dining room."

He put it back on and cocked his head to one side for

her inspection. "But it fits pretty well, doesn't it?"

"Beautifully, darling. I think I'd keep it, if I were you," she told him. "There's no telling what shape yours will be in by now . . . or where it's been," she laughed. "I must remember this the next time I see a hat I like better than my own."

"You're incorrigible!" he chuckled as he guided her past flat-bottomed boats tethered by frayed ropes to a flimsy wooden dock.

Out on the lake rowers and passengers, dabbing citronella on their exposed skin or fanning briskly at swarms of mosquitos, circled the small lake, the splash of oars and paddles echoing across the still water. From the bandstand came the opening bars of *Flow Gently Sweet Afton*, followed by the words sung slightly retard by the crowd. Far to the west a dull mauve afterglow silhouetted blue coastal mountains while overhead a few early stars pricked the darkening sky with pinpoints of brilliance.

"They've started the community-sing already," Jette said. "Let's hurry." As they came to the Milleges' party Lucy beckoned them to sit beside her and Henry in the grass. Quilts had been spread to shield the ladies' dresses from dew. More from their desire to obey Ziphia Millege's suggestion that they serve as chaperones than from an actual wish to spend the evening on the damp ground courting sore joints, a few of the older women joined the young couples on the lawn. Propriety must be maintained.

Henry Stebbins' high tenor rose above the voices, carrying treble harmony, while Ainsworth Millege tried bass with wavering success. Jette and Lucy, an octave apart, took the melody. For an hour, old, well-loved selections rang through the park as the celebrants waited for eight o'clock. It was a quiet hour after the activity of the long afternoon and evening, with only an occasional fingercracker or one-incher touched off.

174

"Five to eight," Millege announced as he opened his gold key-winder. The municipal brass band went into its final number, a rousing rendition of *Patriots' Promise*.

"Let's go down by the water to watch the fountains," Henry suggested. "They're first on the show. Then we can come back up here and see the rest." For a few minutes he wanted Lucy alone, away from the sharp eyes of their chaperones. All day their decorum had been proper to a stifling degree. Now he wanted to take a few of the liberties to which he was entitled as an officially engaged man. "Come on," he coaxed until most of the group had joined them.

Eugenia, daphne, pyracantha, oleander—placed according to light requirements of each plant—created an uneven hedge behind rows of green slatted benches near the shore. Accompanying the younger people, Ziphia Millege and Daisy Howard accepted a seat when occupants of a bench moved to make room for them. Within seconds an aerial bomb burst aloft, spattering rainbow-hued comets overhead. A cheer rose from the viewers. At last the show commenced.

Nate Trasker led Jette to an advantageous spot where the fireworks fountains could be better seen. He felt the grass with one hand and said, "Let me go back up and get one of the quilts. It's damp down here. You'll ruin your dress."

"Thank you, Nate." She stopped and watched the first fountain ignite, its fiery shower rising and falling, changing from gold to pink to green. As Nate returned up to the picnic tables for the quilt she wandered closer to the shoreline. In front of her, their wide, high-crowned hats rendering them anonymous, sat five women on one of the benches. Jette moved to go, but halted as she heard a name spoken.

"Trasker . . . Trasker . . ." She could tell it was Daisy Howard speaking. "No, Ziphie, that wasn't his name. I'm sure of it. But Trasker's close."

175

Jette wanted to go, but something rooted her to the spot as the woman continued, "I'm just as certain of it as that I'm sitting here. I have a good memory for faces and I know I've run into him somewhere before."

"But Daisy, you couldn't possibly. He just got in town a short time back." Mrs. Millege was as positive as her cousin.

"You say he's from Chicago?"

"That's right. He's with a firm called Farrier Development Company in Chicago." Ziphia Millege sounded a bit exasperated. "He's established quite a line of credit at the bank, so he's no fly-by-night. I think you must be wrong."

"No, I'm not! It's his eyes, and those dimples of his." She laughed girlishly. "You have to admit he's a fine looking boy."

"Hardly a boy, Daisy. He must be thirty-four or five."

"At my age, anyone under forty is a 'boy' or a 'girl.' " Then she said in defense of her opinion, "He's striking enough in appearance, heaven knows. Anybody would remember him."

"Yes, but that doesn't mean anything, Daisy!" Ziphia insisted. "What makes you remember him so clearly? Or whoever you think he is?"

"Now I'm not betraying any confidences—it was all published in the Cincinnati Globe when it happened so it's public knowledge. There was this widow—old enough to know better—who had valuable riverfront property there in Cincinnati and she took up with some fellow much younger than herself . . ."

"You don't have to tell me that. She got flim-flammed by some good looking young fair-haired chap with dimples and a yellow moustache." Mrs. Millege was amused at the familiar story.

"Yes, I do mean to tell you that!" Daisy retorted. "He promised to marry her—at her age, mind you—and said he needed money for some scheme he was promoting. Supposed to be a sure thing."

"So she sold some of her property to help him?" Mrs. Millege guessed the ending of the tale. "And then he disappeared like smoke on a windy day. Am I right?"

"You are so right. Police looked into it, of course, but what could they do? A foolish older woman head over heels in love with a younger man. I suppose they hear of such things all the time." Mrs. Howard sighed audibly. "I must admit he's enough to make any woman lose her head."

"If it's the same man, you mean."

"Well, yes, if it's the same man."

"But didn't you say the other man had a moustache and beard? Nate Trasker doesn't, in case you hadn't noticed. Just a thin little moustache. Besides, the beard would have hidden dimples."

"Oh, for goodness sakes, Ziphie! Haven't you heard of razors? He had it trimmed just enough to show his dimples—and it was very attractive, believe me. And remember, a man can alter a moustache or beard—or eliminate them completely—in far less time than it takes us to change the color of our hair."

Both women laughed, their heads close together under bulky, flower-bedecked hats. "Besides, I met him one time at this woman's home," Daisy went on. "He was all sweet smiles and soft words, very stylish and attentive." She stopped and thought a moment. "No, Ziphie, I'm sure it's the same man. A little older, more suntanned, and minus the beard and southern drawl he had then, but it's the same man. I could swear it."

"If you are right—and mind I only say 'if'—he must be a changed man because he's marrying that pretty Allenby girl. You know, the one in the ashes-of-roses silk dress and with all that dark red hair."

"I know the girl you mean. She's lovely and seems to

be a fine young lady." Daisy turned and asked in a confidential tone, "Now she's the one whose father is the holy terror? And her poor mother's a bit addled?"

"Yes. Isn't that a pity?" Mrs. Millege clucked her tongue in sympathy. "Verdie Allenby was the prettiest little thing, so gay and happy. They came here about the same time we did. Came from a fine old Virginia family. Of course, they'd lost a good deal during the War of Secession, but they still had their home and its furnishings, which was a lot more than most of the rebels had by the time it was over."

Ziphia Millege bent closer to her cousin as she noticed the other women on the bench eavesdropping. "Jette Allenby's a real catch, believe me, what with the ranch and all that fancy blooded cattle. Elias Allenby never let any young fellows come courting her though. Kept her practically under latch and key. Ainsworth was upset a while back that she was going to make a bad marriage—I asked him what he knew about it, but he refused to say, so I guess it had something to do with bank business. We're just happy to see her get away from Elias at last."

"But what if this Nate Trasker . . ."

"Oh, Daisy. That child's all spunk and vinegar, as Ainsworth says. Do you think Trasker could fool her?" Even as she said it, Ziphia Mellege realized it was ridiculous. If he had deluded a worldy-wise older woman, could he not do the same with Jette, who had had no experience at all? "But I'm sure you're wrong."

"All the same, I'd like to know the truth about that man."

"I tell you what, Daisy: when you get back home, you send me a clipping of that newspaper article you mentioned. And didn't you say there was a picture of the two of them taken at a lawn party or something?" Mrs. Millege threw down her challenge.

"Yes, there was. You can't tell much what he looked

like, but it's a good picture of her. When the police asked the photographer if he had any more of the man, he said he was lucky to get one at all. Seems the man didn't want his picture taken. After the story came out it was apparent why he didn't want any photographs made of him."

"Will you send it?"

Daisy Howard nodded agreement. "I'll go see Palma Owens the minute I get home. I'm sure she'll give me a copy of the picture when I tell her what I want it for. Then I'll go right down to the Globe and see if someone there can resurrect a copy of the paper with the story for me. Then you'll see I'm right."

Jette could not utter a sound. What she had heard was not intended for her ears. Perhaps it served her right, she thought. She should not have listened. She looked back up the hill and saw that Nate was coming with the quilt. Silently she moved away, walking up to meet him and away from the gossiping women.

"Trasker? No, that's not the name, I'm sure." The words echoed again and again. The description fit him perfectly. and there was the silver hat-marker with the initials "P.B."

Daisy Howard was wrong. She had to be!

Chapter 9

Asa Beemer shifted the lock pin into place on the heavy wagon and rechecked the harness on the dappled Percherons before climbing up on the seat beside Severo Mireles. Maximilian of Dundee stomped the wagonbed and lowed his discontent at being transported to La Coruna Ranch. High sides, reinforced against Old

179

Max's displeasure, surrounded the bull and shut from view the awed youngsters who gathered along the driveway to catch a glimpse of him.

"Why didn't Mr. Allenby let us walk Max over to La Coruna?" Severo relinquished the reins to Asa and turned around to peer through a crack in the siding at the huge animal.

"He all right back there?" Asa asked.

"He's fine," Severo replied and settled back for the ride over to Trasker's place. "Wouldn't walking him over be a lot easier?"

"Elias figures this would be better for Old Max. Those short legs of his don't make it easy for him to walk too far. He's no range-runner like longhorns."

"Yeah, he's a gentleman cow!" Severo laughed at the idea. "He gets treated better than most people. You know that, Asa?"

"Reckon you're right." Asa nodded agreement. He knew the youth referred to Verdie Allenby.

As the wagon turned into the highway the bull slid on the strawed flooring and snorted, rattling his wide nose ring on the boards behind the two men.

"It's all right, old fella. Just you settle down and we'll let you out in a little while," Asa called over his shoulder. He took two thin black Mexican cigars from his vest pocket, handed one to Severo and opened a small, closed tin container of matches. "You're gonna have the best damned time of your life with all those ladies, Max," he comforted the animal. Old Max's breathing was loud in their ears as Asa calmed him. Severo leaned across the seat and accepted a light from the match Asa struck, sucking pungent smoke in great mouthfuls.

"Thanks, Asa." The cigar was strong, but Severo was too proud to admit he did not care for it, and too polite to refuse. Rather, he assumed a pose of dignity and adjusted his manner of smoking by observing Asa

180

Beemer. "Benito says that man, Trasker, just has a bunch of scrub cows and heifers. Bought 'em over at the auction at El Puente. Is that right?"

"Haven't seen 'em yet, but from what I hear they don't amount to much. Reds and crossbreeds mostly." He clamped the cigar between his teeth and employed both hands in slowing the four horses as a motorcar came from behind and chugged on, raising clouds of dust in its passage. He scowled at the noisy machine and allowed the dust to settle before continuing.

"If he's got scrubs, how come he wants Old Max?" Severo persisted with his question. "Any old bull—maybe Jake Larson's—would do for a herd like that. How come Trasker don't get a cheaper one?"

"You're asking the wrong customer," Beemer replied. "He could buy a bull for what he's paying Elias. He's bound to get a crop of calves, but if they'll be good stock—considering the cows he's got—well, that's another matter." He flipped the reins and let the horses know it was all right to resume their stately plodding. "Crossbreeding's fine—if you have good cows to start with. That's what they're going to have to do down in Texas if they want to stay on in the cattle business."

"They still got a quarantine on stock from Texas?"

"Damned right they do," Asa said. "Splenic fever's a real killer. Don't want it spreading west if they can help it."

"Benito says now that Jake Larson won't be selling horses to the British for replacement mounts he's got to go back to raising cattle. Says he'll maybe go into dairying." Holding the cigar down to the wagonbed he tapped off the ash and squashed it to nothingness with the sole of his boot. Grass, gone brown in the rainless season, was too dry to risk a spark. "I heard Nate Trasker fought in Africa. Did you know that?"

"I'd heard it in town. Some say he was with the

181

British, some say the Boers. Either he's telling two stories or they aren't listening right." Beemer's face set, the muscles working in his lean jaws as he thought of Trasker. He stuck the cigar in his mouth and squinted as the smoke blew back into his eyes. "After seeing him handle Elias, I can believe he was a soldier. Never batted an eye."

"You think he'd have killed Mr. Allenby?" Severo looked worried as he considered his position on the ranch should such a thing have happened. "Would he really have done it?"

Beemer's laugh was closer to a snarl and contained no humor. "You're just damned right he would, boy. I saw the look on his face." Asa shifted the cigar to the other side of his mouth and spoke between his teeth. "Didn't have any feeling in it. Now a man gets in a fight, he usually shows something. Not Trasker, No, sir. I'd just about bet he was one of those they call commandos and guerillas. That'd most likely be his style."

They rode on in silence. Each pondered the possibility of another confrontation between the two men. It mattered little that Elias' and Trasker's differences were smoothed over—in the interest of a mutually beneficial business relationship, if for no other reason. Both Severo and Asa knew it was inevitable that the two men would again clash.

* * * *

Seth Scott swung the pen gate shut and tested the lock. It was a duplicate of the fancy Spanish gate latches that Nate Trasker had first seen on the Allenby ranch. Sent over by the new owner of La Coruna to study the mechanism, Scott made a few sketches of it and obeyed Trasker's orders to manufacture and install them around La Coruna. Since even the doors of the ranch house had never been locked from the days of the

Calderons until the present, Scott could see little reason for such precautions, but carried out Trasker's wishes.

"Maximilian of Dundee," Scott said the name with respect. "That's some fancy name."

"That's some fancy bull, Seth!" Asa watched Old Max wander about the strange pen. One foot up on a low rail, Asa put his arm through the fence, a fistful of sugar cubes on his extended palm. "Come on, old fella. Here's your treat for being a good boy. And just you look at all the nice heifers over there in that pasture." Asa laughed quietly as the animal took the sugar, its raspy tongue slobbering over Asa's hand. "Atta boy, Max. Good boy."

"I never seen a critter that big, I tell you." Seth Scott was properly awed. He dropped his voice lower as he added, "Them heifers and cows is going to go plum wild when he gets around to 'em." He chuckled and slapped Severo Mireles on the shoulder. "Your Aunt Tecla's wanting to see you, son. If it's all right with your boss here, why don't you run along and say hello to her. She's out back of the house, scrubbing clothes."

Severo looked to Asa, who nodded assent and said, "Better go see her for a minute before Elias and Trasker get here." When the boy was gone Beemer asked Scott, "You and Trasker getting on all right?"

"Yes, real fine, praise be." Seth accepted a cigar from Beemer and struck a match on the gate post, lighted the cigar and ground the match beneath his boot. "Many thanks, Asa," he said. After a few drags he sighed, "My wife don't hold with smoking, but it sure is good to have one now and again."

"Place looks pretty much the same since he moved in. Not making many changes, is he?" Beemer had visited the Putnams with Elias and saw at a glance that only the carmine paint was new since he'd last been there. Curtains hung at windows that had been bare when Lodd and Ed Putnam lived in the house, but otherwise all remained unchanged.

"Few things . . . mostly inside the house," Seth replied. "His lady friend's got some things she wants done, of course, but seems she'd rather live here a while before they do any real work on the place. She's sensible, that Allenby girl."

Beemer walked over to the wagon and rubbed the foreheads of the lead Percherons. He would not speak of Jette with anyone. The wedding was within a few days and if he were a reasonable man he would admit defeat. But in respect to Jette Allenby, he could not be reasonable. When it actually took place, he would have to accept her loss. Until then, he still considered Jette to be his.

"Aren't these Percherons real prize-takers?" He dug into his hip pocket and extracted more sugar cubes, held them under the dappled horses' muzzles on the flat of his palms. He wiped his hands on his trousers and grinned. "Elias says these four eat more than they're worth, but he's not getting rid of 'em." The near horse nickered and butted Asa's shoulder. "No more sugar, boys. All gone . . ."

"Sets a store by good stock, don't he?" Seth's expert hands ran over the horses. "Mighty fine animals. Must of cost Allenby a mint of money. Where'd he get 'em?"

"Come by train from Los Angeles," Asa said. "I told him he'd do better to get himself one of those new tractors. You know—the ones you can use for stump pulling and threshing . . ."

"Use 'em for most anything you set your mind to, I guess," Scott interrupted. "I seen posters in town telling about 'em." He shook his head and said, "I'd take these here Percherons to any stink-belching machine. Like as not it'd set a fire first time out."

"You could be right, Seth," Asa had to admit. "Where can I put the wagon? I'd like to get the team out of the sun." He pointed to a shady spot under the oaks near the stone-walled granary. "All right if I pull 'em over there?"

"Sure. Trasker likes to put his team over there, but he ain't using 'em today." Scott slouched against the sturdy fence, thumbs in his wide black leather belt, one boot heel hooked on the lowest rail. The valley simmered, the horizon dancing in heat waves. Everything that could escape the heat had already sought shade. Horses clustered beneath oaks accepted the company of several gray mules as they stood nose to rump, tails switching at flies. Scott waited as Beemer drove the team and wagon into the deep shade.

"How come Elias has got to oversee this business?" Scott asked as Asa returned. "He ain't exactly the kind likely to get no kick out of watching a bull set onto a bunch of heifers."

"Guess he wants to see Trasker's set-up for himself," Asa replied. "I already told him about those scrubs, but he says if any man pays for Old Max, he gets him, so I know it isn't that he wants to see the stock." The two men strolled to the barn. "No, I suppose he wants to look the place over, maybe see what he missed out on."

"You mean Lodd and Ed not selling to him?"

"He wanted La Coruna mighty bad. Pure cussedness, those three old men." He could not resist smiling, even at the expense of his employer. "Could have been good for all of them, if they'd not been so damned pig-headed all these years."

"Well, Lodd and Ed was good to work for," Scott said in defense of the Putnam brothers. "Never made much off the ranch, though."

"Way I hear it, they didn't exactly need to."

"No, I suppose you put it that way, they didn't." Scott gazed from the cool interior of the barn and scanned the tawny gold hills that sloped up to the San Lucas Mountains. "Pity they didn't do more with the ranch. Hurt Tecla to see it get so run down . . . no

185

cattle anymore, no big parties, no weddings . . . things like that.''

"Real pity was that the Mexicans never learned the cattle business. Hell, they couldn't run forever on just selling hides." Asa sat on a bale of hay placed near the door in lieu of a bench. "Elias says if they'd let the Indians have the meat, they'd have been able to settle all the way up to Oregon."

"The Calderons said it was more the fault of them Spanish ships and no free trade." He laughed and pulled up a wooden keg to sit near Beemer. "Matias Calderon used to tell about them Yankee schooners putting in over at San Gallan, and the soldiers doing most of the trading, instead of tending their job and putting everybody in jail." He pointed toward the house with his cigar. "Most everything they had in the house come around the Horn on a Yankee ship. Dishes . . . furniture . . . lamps . . .''

"Things will be different around here from now on," Asa ventured. "Can't see why Trasker paid for an Angus bull for those scrubs of his. Jake Larson's bull, you know the one I mean . . .''

"Big Hereford?"

"Yeah, that's the one . . . he'd be good enough for Trasker."

"Trasker ain't no cattle man. Won't listen much to me, neither, not when it comes to that. Running the ranch, feed, things like that, but not the breeding." Seth Scott pulled a cheap nickel-cased watch from his waist pocket. "Don't know what's keeping Trasker." Reluctant to start back to the house in the broiling sun, he wiped sweat from his hat band and off his face and neck. "Maybe I'd best go find him," he said, but remained seated on the keg.

From the lane leading to the road came the sound of a solitary horse approaching the ranch at a fair gait "That's Elias now," Beemer said. Both men rose and went to the door to watch the rider. There was no mistaking either horse or rider. Elias sat erect and loose in the high-cantled working saddle, his wide-brimmed hat pulled low over his eyes against the glare. He was at ease on the black stallion, as only a man accustomed to many hours a day spent in riding could be. He moved in rhythm with the horse, their bodies seeming to be in close communication.

Elias did not pause as he came into the ranch house yard, but guided the stallion to the barn at the rear. Seth Scott seized the face straps and held the horse as Elias swung from the saddle.

"Allenby, good to see you, sir," Scott said, then took the reins and looped them about a rail on the shady side of the barn. Allenby extended his hand in greeting, a smile broadening across his face.

"Scott, it's been a time," Elias said.

"Yes, sir, it has at that." Seth Scott did not remind Allenby of their last encounter at the courthouse when—for once—Elias had lost his case against the Putnams.

"Where's Trasker?" Elias asked as he looked around the barn yard.

"He'll be along any time now," Seth replied. He turned and started for the house. "I'll tell him you're here."

"Stay where you are, Scott. He heard me ride in," Elias said. "We don't need him anyhow." His animosity was apparent as he scowled toward the ranch house. He spied the heifers and cows in the lots and walked toward them. "You were right, Asa. This stock isn't worth a good damn. What the hell does Trasker expect out of such a bunch of culls? These aren't any better than the culls we cut out of the north pasture." He spat into the dust at his feet.

"Maybe he plans to fatten steers for the Los Angeles market," Asa suggested.

"Scott, what's Trasker doing here?" Elias roared. "These scrubs aren't fit for the slaughter-house."

"I told you, Elias," Beemer reminded the rancher. "He's paying for Max, so let it be at that."

Elias regarded Seth Scott with evident suspicion and planted his feet wide, arms folded as he demanded an answer. "What's Trasker up to, Scott? This doesn't look like herd building to me. Most likely damn foolishness from the look of it."

"Like I told Asa here, he ain't no cattle man. Don't know one thing about stock." Scott was uncomfortable as he tried to form a coherent reply. Allenby had always respected Seth Scott even though he worked for the Putnams, but Scott's respect for Elias was tempered with a certain amount of fear. "I reckon he just bought what he could afford over to the auction barn and plans to do the best he can with what he's got."

". . . and he intends to bring the quality up when he has enough money to buy blooded cows—after he sells off the first crop." Nate Trasker came from around the barn, his impeccable Eastern tailoring at odds with the rough gear of the three cattlemen. His blond hair and moustache shone like burnished bronze as he stood bare-headed in the sunlight. "Good morning, Allenby . . . Beemer." He included the two men in his greeting as though they were indistinguishable and inseparable. "I may be new at your business, Allenby, but at least give me credit for using the best sire available for my first efforts."

Trasker approached slowly, watching his step in the yard. "I have neither your money nor your credit with which to buy my cows, but I do have enough to meet the stud fees for Old Max."

Seth Scott eyed both men anxiously for signs of their repeated antagonism. "We figure to put him to them cows first off," Seth said to break the building tension. "Old Max will sure enough know what to do." His

188

laugh was a womanish titter.

"Hold him in the stall inside until you're ready," Trasker ordered his manager.

Severo Mireles came running from back of the house, his wide hat in his hand. Timidly, not sure she should join them, Tecla followed for a hundred yards, then seeing Elias, she retreated again to her laundry. Something in the very appearance of the tall, heavy rancher intimidated the woman. She pumped fresh water into the wooden tub and began to rinse the bed sheets and table cloths.

Tecla could not help wondering what Elias Allenby would do should he learn of the soiled sheets she had found in the main bedroom after his daughter had made her first visit to the ranch. Seth had cautioned her to say nothing, but the warning was unnecessary. She dared not reveal their secret, not only from fear of Elias and Trasker, but from pity for the girl.

* * * *

"That should hold Maximilian until we're ready for him." Trasker fastened the stall latch. "You see, Allenby, I've learned something from you already—I had Seth copy your animal-proof Spanish locks." He slapped his hand on the gate lock to demonstrate how well the improvisation worked. "If the most successful rancher in the valley stands by them, I thought I could do no less." His face broke into a disarming smile, showing the shallow dimples in his tanned cheeks. Even Elias Allenby had to admit Trasker could be most ingratiating.

"Very flatttering, but it'll take a hell of a lot more than fancy locks to build you a good herd." Elias ran a finger around the neck of his shirt. His cotton flannel shirt under the leather vest was wet with sweat. His only concession to the changing seasons was to shift from heavy woolen shirt to heavy cotton, the vest relinquished only as one would wear out and be replaced by another of exact duplication. His temper increased with the heat. "Damned foolishness, putting Max to those scrubs."

Trasker pointed through the barn door to the far side of the pen. "I adapted that lock out there myself, from the drawings Seth made. It's quite an improvement over yours."

Elias raised his eyebrows in surprise. "An improvement, you say?" He passed the stall where Old Max had been confined preparatory to transferring him to the larger lot beyond the barn. "I'll be with you in a minute, Asa," he said as Beemer and Scott left for the lots accompanied by young Mireles.

"Perhaps you'd like to take a look at that one," Trasker said. Aware of Elias' passion for keeping everything under lock and key, he was certain he could pique the rancher's curiosity by challenging the original design. He joined Elias in the pen, walking with him to the far side where the new latch had been installed on the gate. "It's a simple adaptation. but most efficient." He turned his head quickly as if listening. "You'll have to excuse me, Allenby. I heard Seth calling me." He hurried back to the barn, passing through the open door by Maximilian's stall.

Absorbed in the gate latch, Elias paid no attention to Trasker's leaving. He worked the latch, inspecting the positioning of the bar, intrigued with the change.

A bellow of rage rumbled from the barn and Elias looked up just as the bull burst through the stall door and into the pen. The huge animal dashed a few yards closer, but now stood, waiting . . . watching. Behind the bull the barn door slammed shut as if caught by a sudden gust of wind.

The bull sidled across the dirt, keeping close to the high fence. Elias moved carefully toward the door

190

which was a safer exit than the huge reinforced gate which would have to be swung wide. There was a chance that the bull would escape that way. Elias must get to the door. Slowly, so as not to excite the animal, he eased to the door, keeping his eyes on the beast. He reached blindly for the door, found the latch and triggered the release. Nothing happened. He tried once more, but the door refused to open.

His back to the rails of the enclosure, Elias made his way back to the gate. Certainly it would be safer to open the gate and chance the bull getting loose than trying to scramble up over the high fence. The bull could be on him before he got halfway up.

Elias groped for the wooden tongue that locked the massive gate. His fingers seized the bar. It would not move. He repositioned himself, reached through the fence, hammered with the heel of his hand. It was useless. The bar refused now to budge.

Cautiously, always keeping his eyes on the animal, Elias side-stepped a few yards to the left of the gate where a heavy upright post made a shallow angle in the fence. Each movement provoked a responding motion in the enormous beast. Sweat erupted from every pore of the man's body. It trickled down his face, drenched the grizzled beard. Despite the heat of the morning Elias Allenby shivered.

"Trasker!" he called out in anger. The bull flattened its nostrils, snorted its fury as it studied Elias with malignant gaze. "Trasker! God damn you, Trasker!" the man yelled in rage.

As the animal pawed at the dirt, throwing dust on its shoulders and lowering its massive head, Elias looked wildly about him. None of the newly-hired hands was anywhere in sight. Trasker had sent them out early in the morning to mend fences and check for signs of wild dogs or coyotes. Not even Tecla would hear him, much less respond to his cries for help.

Carefully, inching his way, Elias felt for the lower rail of the fence with his foot. Placing the heel of his boot against the rail, he pivoted slightly. With one furious roar the bull lowered its head and charged, crushing the man to the rails. Elias slumped against the fence, a great wave of pain obliterating all but the will to remain upright and face the beast.

As the bull drew back, preparing to renew the attack, Elias flung himself up the fence. Desperately scrambling for foothold, he turned his back to the bull. Instantly he realized his mistake. Grabbing for the top rail he raised himself about a yard and a half above the ground, the pointed toes of his boots finding the rails only by luck.

The bull slammed upward at him, twisting and lunging at his legs. Elias groaned, fighting to keep back the blackness that edged in around his pain. From the corner of his eye he was conscious of Tecla running and screaming, her apron and skirts flying as she came from the house. He pulled himself up to the top rail just as the animal crashed into the fence, its one-ton weight of fury-driven force cracking the poles and crossbars. Elias wondered why he could not use his left leg, why it was not obeying his will. He looked startled as through the mist he saw blood just above the boot.

Heaving himself over, he clung for a moment, then dropped to the ground, unable to get his feet under him. Again and again Maximilian plunged at the fallen man, bloodying his own head as he spent his rage on the rails that separated them.

"Bring a wide board from the side of the shed over there," Asa yelled to Severo. "Seth, is there a good riding horse here?"

"None special, but Mr. Trasker's mares is saddle broke. They'd be faster than the others." Seth Scott knelt beside Allenby, straightening out his uninjured leg before Asa helped turn him over. "His other leg's broke, Asa. Broke real bad, too."

192

"Seth, you'd better saddle up one of the mares." Beemer ignored Trasker, who came running from the direction of the east lot. Severo grabbed a long, one-by-fourteen board from a pile of lumber stacked against the tool shed, and laid it beside the prostrate man. "Severo, you ride as fast as you can to town. Send Doc Hunter out here. You high tail it right back here and don't say anything about Elias—not even to Mrs. Allenby or Jette. No use getting them upset until we know how he stands. Is that understood?"

The youth paled as he looked at Elias' leg and turned away quickly. "Yes, sir, I understand," he said. He raced after Seth, who had headed for the stables. Tecla, her face mirroring the agony of the old man, stood aside as Asa bent over Elias.

"Trasker, you have whiskey up at the house?" Beemer asked.

"My God, what's happened?" Trasker was breathless from his running. "Whiskey? Yes . . . I'll go get it." He continued on toward the house. The answer to his question could come later.

"Elias . . ." Beemer waited until he saw the man's eyes open slightly. "We're going to take you back to the house. Trasker's bring some whiskey and you'll have to take a lot of it before we can move you." He took the man's rough hand in his own. "You'll be just fine, Elias. Just fine." He looked up at Tecla Scott and asked, "Is there a room we can put him in?"

"I think maybe we should put him in Mr. Trasker's room. It's bigger and the light's better." She knelt beside Elias and wiped his face with her apron. "He's so cold. . . ."

"Likely he's in shock," Asa said. "Have any hot water at the house?"

"The wash water out in the yard. I'm boiling clothes . . . the water's clean . . ."

"That'll do fine. Now, Mrs. Scott, I want you to put

on every pan you have in the place and get the water boiling and keep it that way. Soon as Hunter gets out here, we're going to need it. First off, though, better put some papers out on the bed. You have any papers?''

"Yes, Mr. Trasker brings them from town.''

"Well, you put them on the bed and put a couple of sheets over 'em. All right?'' He watched her face as realization of what might happen dawned on Tecla. She covered her face with her hands and sobbed quietly.

"Yes, yes . . .'' she nodded. "I'll do it.''

"Before you do that, bring me something to tie his leg with and tie him onto the board. Hurry . . .'' He wanted no hysterics before they got Elias back to the house.

"I'll bring you a sheet and the clothesline.''

"That'll be just fine. Run along now . . . hurry,'' he urged the woman. She ran to the rear of the house where the laundry was stretched across lines between the adobe and the poultry house. She seized a sheet, untied one of the lines and hurried back to the bull pen as Trasker brought the whiskey.

Asa cradled Elias' head in his arms, elevating it so the man could drink. "You think you can manage, Elias?'' He waited for the man to nod his head, then put the bottle to his lips and tipped it up, letting it spill into Elias' mouth. The whiskey trickled down the grizzled beard and onto the flannel shirt. For a moment Tecla watched, then raced back to the house to prepare the room.

After the liquor had dulled Elias' eyes even further, Asa pased his hand in front of the man's face. Seeing no response as he moved his fingers close to Elias' eyes, he said to Trasker, "We can move him now.''

Asa took his shoulders while Trasker shifted Elias' good leg and hips onto the board. Asa moved the injured leg, watching for any sign of pain in Elias' face, and seeing none, moved it onto the board. Carefully, gently, Beemer passed the clothesline beneath the board as Trasker raised it, and within minutes had secured the heavy body. The torn sheeting grew red and dark drops sank into the dust.

In the bull pen Maximilian of Dundee stood in the center of the enclosure, pawing and chuffing deep in his throat, never once taking his eyes from the men outside the fence. Trasker glanced at the beast and spied the damaged rails.

"Was Allenby caught in the pen? How the hell did Old Max get out here?" Trasker grunted with exertion as he hoisted his end of the board.

"Afraid I can't answer that. Looks like the bull took out after him and he legged it over the fence. He didn't get that leg smashed up like that falling over the fence, though. Guess we'll have to wait to hear it from him as to what exactly happened."

"I've seen legs mangled like that by shot," Trasker said. "He'll be damned lucky if it can be saved." They rounded the corner of the courtyard, passed the well, and crossed to the bedroom. Tecla Scott threw open the carmine door as she heard their footsteps on the terra cotta tiles of the veranda. She had drawn back the drapes and muslin curtains, admitting as much light as possible from the two windows. Quilt and coverlet were tossed in a heap in the corner of the room; a small center table had been cleared, covered with a clean towel and placed near the head of the bed.

"Easy now . . . easy . . . there, yes, that's right . . ." Beemer and Trasker placed Elias on the bed, released him from the flat board and slid the ropes from under him.

"Tecla!" Asa snapped as the woman teetered uncertainly near the window. They would need all of the help she could give them and Asa wanted no fainting women on their hands. She steadied herself and swallowed hard a few times before trusting herself.

"I'm all right," she assured them and busied herself unbuttoning Elias' shirt, loosening his belt and trousers. "I put the scissors and some knives to boil."

"Good girl." Asa took his pocket knife, opened out the thin, razor-sharp blade and began cutting away the trouser leg. "Tecla, do you have a box or something we can use to put this in?" He hoped to get her out of the room while he inspected the wound.

"We have some cardboard boxes in the poultry house. The hens like to nest in them," the woman said. "Will that do?"

"That would do just fine," Asa replied and waited for her to leave before he removed the cloth and exposed the torn leg. He shook his head as he looked at the damage.

"One good thing—there isn't much bleeding. That would be just one more problem," Trasker observed. "You notice how gray his face is?" His attitude was one of dispassionate objectivity.

"I have a hunch it's more than just shock." Asa held Elias' hand and examined the fingernails. "Hands are getting blue. See the fingernails . . ." He put his ear to Elias' chest, catching the sound of an erratic heartbeat. He straightened up and looked at Trasker, his eyes grave with concern.

"Heart?" Trasker asked.

"Might be. Doesn't sound regular."

"Heart attack then?"

Asa nodded. "I'd guess that. I hope to God I'm wrong, but it isn't just shock." He stood up and leaned against the window, looked out at the rear yard where russet and black chickens were investigating Tecla's laundry which was spread on the ground where she dropped it. "I guess all we can do now is wait. Nothing more we can do. I wouldn't risk trying to set that leg. Not the way it is."

"I feel we should send for Jette and Mrs. Allenby."

196

Without turning around Asa shook his head. "Not yet. As soon as we know something for sure . . . You have a man you can send if we need to get them over here?"

"I can ring the bell and get the men back to the house. Seth says the sound carries out to the east pasture. They know to come when they hear it."

Beemer's body sagged as from exhaustion, lines deepening in his dark face. He took off his hat and wiped his forehead with his sleeve. "I'd sure as hell like to know what happened out there," he said.

* * * *

"It's as bad as that?" Nate Trasker shoved the cardboard box aside with his foot. Flies, lured by the scent of blood, hovered about the discarded trouser leg and strips of sheeting. Trasker glanced at the gray face on the pillow, then back at Doctor Hunter.

"It is." Miles Hunter rose from the bedside and faced the three men. "You'd better send for the women right away. He may have moments of lucidity, but it can't be long now. There's nothing to be done for him except to keep him as comfortable as possible. I've taken care of that for the moment and he'll drift in and out of consciousness."

"I'll send Severo," Asa said. "I'll see that your horse is brought back tomorrow, Trasker."

"Any time. As long as I have the bays I don't need the others." Then as if to explain, he added, "I'm not a riding man anymore. I had quite enough of that in Africa."

Seth Scott passed a hand over the stubble on his chin and shook his head. "I'm damned if I can figure it out."

"At this point it makes no difference, Seth." Trasker led them from the room and out onto the tiled veranda.

Gray and brown sparrows flitted in and out of the roof tiles, their activities sounding like mice overhead. "Saddle up one of the horses and tell Severo to hurry."

"I already got one ready to go. It's tied yonder," Scott said and motioned with his head to the side of the house. He beckoned to his nephew, who sat in the shade by the kitchen door. The youth came running, his eyes round with apprehension. "Ride over to the Allenby place and fetch the women folks, son." He placed an arm around the boy's shoulders. "Old Elias is in real bad shape, but you be careful how you tell the ladies, hear?"

"Yes," Severo said. "I understand." He waited for Asa to affirm the directions.

"Go see Benito first of all," Asa said. "Tell him to hitch up the Rockaway. And he's to drive, you come along with him. Tell Socorro and Elvira, but nobody else. Leave it to me to pass the word to the rest of the men. I don't want any panic. Nobody's going to lose his job. That's the way Elias would want it." Beemer looked back at the bedroom door, then walked with Severo to the waiting horse.

"Is he going to die, Asa?"

"He's real bad," the ranch foreman replied quietly.

"But is he going to die?"

Asa Beemer nodded his head and loosened the reins from the rail. "Looks like it," he said.

* * * *

For a long moment Verdie Allenby sat looking at her husband, her face immobile. Elias' eyes stared vacantly at a corner of the ceiling. Doctor Hunter reached across the bed, touched the eyelids, gently closing them, then drew the quilt up over the still face.

"I'm sorry, Mrs. Allenby . . . Jette," Hunter said and walked around the bed to the women's side. "I'll

198

take care of everything here if you'd like to go on home. There's nothing more you can do."

Verdie rocked to and fro, her arms tightly wrapped about herself as if in a agony of pain. She uttered not a word.

"Mother . . ." Jette began, but realized her mother wasn't hearing anything being said to her. To Miles Hunter she said, "We'd be very grateful if you'd see to . . . to . . . everything. I'll drive in to town as soon as I can and make funeral arrangements." Somehow she was surprised that she experienced no more emotion than the initial shock and horror of the accident. Something more should be felt at the death of one's father, but even the sight of Elias' huge inert form failed to do more than evoke pity.

"Mrs. Allenby, ma'am . . ." Asa Beemer spoke from across the room, reluctant to move closer to the women. "I'll take you home, ma'am. As the doctor says, there's nothing more to be done for Elias." When Verdie ignored him—indeed, did not hear him—he turned to the girl. "Miss Jette, can you get her to leave? Staying here won't do her any good. The carriage is just outside the door, if you can manage her."

"Yes, thank you, Asa," Jette replied. "You go on out. I'll bring her." Benito Galvan, hat in hand, waited outside the bedroom door, his face deeply etched with the sorrow that brought no tears to his old eyes.

"If you need me . . ." Asa began.

"No. We'll be fine," Jette insisted. Now was no proper time to argue with Asa, but neither was it a time to permit him to assume more authority. Beemer hesitated, glanced at Hunter and Trasker, and left the room.

"Perhaps you'd like me to make the funeral arrangements for you?" Nate Trasker asked. "It's the least I can do." He placed an arm about Jette's shoulders and drew her to him. Doctor Hunter turned abruptly from them and replaced the stethoscope in his bag, snapped shut the brass locks, and from the back of the chair took his coat.

"I know you mean to be helpful, but this is something I must do myself," Jette answered as she allowed Nate to kiss her.

"Of course, darling. Whatever you think best. But you know you can ask me to do anything—anything at all," Trasker whispered to her.

"I know, Nate." Jette suddenly felt awkward in his embrace, perhaps because of the circumstances, perhaps because of the presence of Miles Hunter. She edged from Trasker and turned to her mother.

"We must go home, Mother. There's no reason for us to stay here, nothing more we can do," Jette said. There was no response, only the rocking back and forth. Jette touched her mother's arm, and repeated, "Mother, we must go now."

The motion ceased. Verdie looked in surprise at Jette's hand, her anguished eyes traveling up the arm to her daughter's face. A confused expression crept over Verdie's own face. She squinted her eyes, her brows furrowing as if in puzzled thought. "Go home?" she muttered half aloud. "Home? To Virginia? To Collyer Meeting?"

"Oh, Mother!" Jette knelt by the woman, her hands enfolding Verdie's. She looked helplessly at Trasker. "What shall I do?" she asked.

Trasker's annoyance was obvious, but he only shrugged his shoulders and replied, "Your mother is not a well woman, Jette. Surely you realize that." Miles Hunter buttoned his coat and glanced at Trasker, then the women, as if he intended to interfere, but turned away when Jette rose to face Trasker.

"I know what you mean, Nate," Jette said so her mother could not overhear. "And you're wrong!" She turned her back on him and looked to Hunter.

"Come along, Mrs. Allenby." Miles Hunter took the woman by her thin shoulders and lifted her from the bed. He avoided looking at Trasker, but was aware of his scowl as he guided Verdie toward the door and signaled Jette to follow. "You've had a dreadful shock, but you'll be just fine." He spoke in low, reassuring tones as they crossed the veranda and headed for the black-enameled Rockaway.

"Miss Jette, may I see you for just a minute before you leave?" Asa Beemer waited by the carriage with Seth Scott and young Severo.

"Miles, will you stay with Mother? I won't be long," Jette said.

"Certainly." Hunter handed Verdie into the carriage and lowered the glass window all the way down to rid the interior of the intense heat which had built up in the sun. Jette joined the three men as Nate Trasker came from the bedroom onto the veranda, his eyes following Jette as she accompanied them to a spot of shade beneath one of the oaks.

"We been talking . . . the three of us . . ." Seth Scott began.

"We think you have a right to know a few things," Asa said. Both Seth and Severo nodded their heads, nervously glancing back at the house where Trasker stood watching. "I want you to act just like I was telling you the time of day . . . don't let on anything to Trasker. Understand?"

"No, I don't understand. And why should I act any way you tell me to?" Jette flared at Beemer, hatred plain in her black eyes as she turned away from him. Asa stepped nearer and took her wrist.

"This is one time you're listening to me, young lady." His strong fingers were like vises, his dark eyes narrowed to slits.

"Let go of me this instant," she exploded, but Asa only tightened his grip. She turned her head toward the house and started to call out to Trasker.

"No! Please listen to Asa," Seth Scott pleaded. He positioned himself so Nate Trasker could not see that Asa grasped the girl's wrist. "Please . . . you got to hear him out, ma'am!"

"For once don't give me any back talk—just listen and don't go yelling for Trasker. If he starts anything with me, he's the one'll be the loser. I'll guarantee that. It's one thing for him to take on a drunk old man, but it's something else if he goes for me. Are you understanding me, girl?" He jerked her arm and made her look directly at him.

"I am," she said, not trying to hide her contempt. "Get on with whatever it is you have to say and let me go." When Beemer felt her relax, he released her arm, took her by the elbow and led her down the lane toward the bull pen. "Seth here served as scout and tracker for the cavalry . . . now that won't mean much to you, but it ought to if you use your head for thinking instead of spouting off at me." He saw he had caught her interest as she glanced at Scott and back at the ranch manager. "Seth can read the ground as well as any redskin and what he saw out where Elias got mauled by Old Max says it wasn't any accident your father's lying stone dead on Nate Trasker's bed."

"I don't know what you're talking about!" Jette pulled away and took a step toward the house.

"You just shut your mouth and listen if you know what's good for you . . . and your mother." Asa confronted her, his back to the house where Trasker still stood in sullen silence. Jette was alarmed beyond her usual antipathy by Asa's vehemence. One look into his face made her chill with apprehension. "There, that's better," Beemer said and led her further down the path to the barnyard. He had to be certain Trasker could neither overhear them nor read the expressions on their faces.

"What are you trying to tell me?" she demanded.

"I don't know how he did it, but Nate Trasker got Elias into that pen and cut Old Max loose on him, deliberately."

"That's ridiculous. It was an accident."

"It was murder." Asa said it so quietly she had to look at him to make sure what he said. "I don't call that very damned ridiculous. I call it a hanging matter."

"You can't be serious," Jette almost laughed, her voice a bit too high and edgy. "Run tell that to the sheriff and you'll find yourself either behind bars or laughed out of town."

"Maybe we got nothing much to go on, nothing a jury could act on, but it's all there in the dust, telling the whole story. Only we don't know all it's saying." Seth Scott was as deadly earnest as Beemer, his face pulled into a worried frown under his battered hat. Jette halted in the shade and waited for the rest of their revelation.

"Trasker had Seth here make up some special gate latches—just like the ones Elias was partial to." Seth nodded confirmation of what Asa said. "Only Trasker worked out a couple of his own and put 'em on the barn door that led into the bull pen and on the gate to the pen from the barnyard. We put Old Max in the pen—didn't see any reason to put him in the barn—but Trasker insisted he wanted him in the stall. He was showing Elias those locks while the rest of us went out to the east lot."

"Ma'am, them locks worked just fine. I worked 'em myself," Seth interrupted. "There ain't a thing wrong with them locks!"

"What have the locks to do with it?" Jette might doubt Asa Beemer's accusation, but when Scott attested to the truth of his story, Jette was obliged to listen and pay heed. "How do the latches enter into what happened?"

"By the way Elias circled that pen, right next to the

rails, facing inward, going to the barn door, then back to the gate, and having to leg it up and over the fence—you have to take it the locks wouldn't work for him." Asa held out a tiny sliver of wood. "Seth and I took a look at those locks first chance we had after he read the tracks in the pen." He held the bit of wood for her to inspect. "We found this sticking in the one on the gate." That the sliver was significant became apparent when Asa wrapped it carefully in his handkerchief and replaced it in his vest pocket. Jette looked bewildered.

"And there's more . . . it looks like a wedge was dropped into the thing to keep it from opening," Severo spoke up for the first time. "You can see where it was by the marks it made."

"And you found the wedges, of course?"

"No, ma'am, we didn't. Ain't likely to, either, the way I look at it." Seth was reluctant to admit they had failed to discover conclusive proof.

"But you're trying to tell me Father was trapped in the pen?"

"Yes, ma'am," Seth said.

"Isn't it just possible Father didn't know how to work the locks? And being inside the pen, maybe he couldn't get it to work from inside?" Jette was anxious to find a logical explanation that obviated Asa's charges against Trasker.

"Hell, use your head, girl!" Beemer was furious with her. "He knew 'em backwards. Truth is, he couldn't get 'em open because Trasker didn't want him to. He'd put a piece of wood in to block the bar from moving. Wouldn't be hard to do if Elias wasn't paying too much attention to Trasker." Beemer paused and waited for her to think it over. "I call that murder."

"I don't believe it!" Jette was now furious. "Why would Nate want to do such a thing? He had no reason!" Her face flushed with anger. "Take that story to the sheriff and you'll be locked up for a lunatic." She turned to Scott and Severo and continued, "I don't know what Asa is up to with such a fabrication, but he seems to have convinced you both. He's a jealous, vicious man, capable of anything if it serves his purpose!"

"Please, Miss Allenby, he ain't making anything up," Seth pleaded. "I seen it all on the ground . . ."

"A few tracks in the dirt?" She was contemptuous. "That's hardly conclusive evidence."

"If a wedge was put in to keep the bar from moving, there ain't no way Elias could have opened them latches from inside the pen." Scott was desperate in his attempt to make her believe. "Way Old Max acts, I plumb think he was goaded into attacking. That ain't natural behavior. No sir!"

"Mr. Scott, I'm sure you're upset about what happened, but don't let Asa Beemer influence you in making false accusations against an innocent man." She turned to leave, but he caught at her sleeve.

"You ain't gonna tell Trasker, are you?" There was abject fear in Scott's face. "If you don't believe us, for God's sakes don't tell him. Ain't no telling what he'd do." His voice trailed off. "My wife and me, we been on La Coruna a long time and it ain't like we could go out and get new jobs at our age . . . 'specially if Trasker had it in for us."

"For your sakes I'll say nothing about it. It's too ridiculous. And you're right, I don't know what he might do if he learned of Asa accusing him of murder!" Her icy stare at Beemer caused him to shift uneasily and turn away. "Thank you for doing what you could for Father, Mr. Scott."

"What you aiming to do with Old Max?" Scott asked.

"His stud fee is paid, isn't it?" she countered.

"Yes, ma'am. Trasker paid it cash to Elias," Scott replied.

"Then use him." She took a few steps and returned to the men. "I'd advise you all to drop your accusation . . . say no more about it to anyone. I promise I shall forget it, but if you insist on carrying it further you'll have to answer to Mr. Trasker." She eyed Beemer and taunted him, "I rather think you'd want to avoid that, Asa."

She left the men and hurried back to the waiting carriage. There was so much to be done—and one of the first things must be to replace Asa Beemer as foreman. If he dared conspire against Nate Trasker in such a fashion, if he could convince a sensible man like Seth Scott that Elias had been lured to his death by Trasker, what else was he capable of doing?

And yet there was Daisy Howard's gossip about the man. She had been so certain he had another identity. And there was the silver hat marker with the initials P.B. So many questions, so many doubts.

Jette slowed as she neared the house, her mind in turmoil. It was not possible! She recalled his arms about her, his mouth on hers, the joy she felt the day she became his woman.

He was too gentle, too loving. No, it was not possible that Nate Trasker would do such a thing.

But Asa . . . Asa Beemer was capable of anything!

Chapter 10

Doctor Hunter closed the door behind himself and crossed the parlor to where Jette sat before the fireplace. A log fire warmed the east end of the parlor and cast a ruddy glow in the gloomy room. It had grown almost dark enough for lamps, but none had been lighted as yet. Pecky and Buff lay before the hearth, absorbing the heat, comfortably lazy, impervious to the trauma of the past few days. The spaniel looked up, yawned and wagged its tail as Hunter stooped to pet both animals.

"I've given your mother chloral hydrate," Hunter said to the girl. "That should see her through till morning." He pulled a low stool from beside the hearth and placed it by the sofa. "Do you feel you can handle her by yourself?" he asked as he sat down.

"I've taken care of her up to now," Jette said. "Nothing has changed in that respect." Weariness had tightened her beautiful face and even in the dim firelight Hunter discerned signs of exhaustion. She sat in the dusk, staring into the blazing logs as though finding solace in the dancing flames.

"I'm worried about you, Jette." He took her hand and felt its coldness. "You can't assume responsibility for everything all at once like this without wearing yourself down physically and emotionally."

"Have you any suggestions to remedy that?" She was not being sarcastic, but asking a valid question.

He shook his head. "No, since you're going to marry Nate Trasker I have no right to suggest what I should like. I'm sure you know what I'd say if circumstances were different." She did not pull her hand away and he did not relinquish it.

"Yes, Miles. Perhaps I do know." Her sigh was as much from weariness as sadness. "Poor Miles . . . you've been so kind. How can we ever thank you enough?"

"There's no need. I'm only glad I was able to help." He stood up as Elvira Mireles came into the parlor from the dining room.

"Shall I light the lamps now?" the girl asked Jette.

"Yes, please," Jette replied. She rose from the sofa and went to the door of the back parlor as Elvira began

207

a circuit of the ground floor, lighting the oil lamps one by one.

"Your mother's already asleep," Hunter said.

"I'll just go light a candle for her. I don't want her to waken and find it dark." She opened the door and tiptoed into the room. Verdie lay on the chaise before the window, her slight form covered with a light blue down quilt. Jettie listened to her deep, heavy breathing, then struck a match and touched it to a candle on the mantle over the small fireplace.

"You can't let your mother refuse to go upstairs forever, Jette," the doctor remonstrated. "She's got to face it sometime."

"For now, this is the way it must be," Jette said firmly. "When she's ready to go upstairs again, ready to go back into their bedroom, she can go. Until then, we'll take care of her down here."

"Jette, you won't be helping her if you do that." Hunter leaned on his cane as he stood by her side in the makeshift bedroom. "She must be made to face reality. The sooner she can do it, the sooner she'll get better, believe me."

"I'm sure you're right, Miles, but I simply won't force her. She's suffered enough. I'll not make it worse by insisting she do something she's not yet capable of doing." They left the room, leaving the door slighly ajar.

"Wouldn't it be better if you put her in a hospital for a short time? There are several fine ones where she'd be well cared for. The one in Santa Barbara is excellent." He followed Jette back to the parlor and into the dining room where a light supper was laid for them.

"I couldn't bear to send her away," Jette replied and sat down, at the same time indicating his place beside her at the end of the table. The place had been her father's, but she felt no qualms in seating the doctor there. She poured sauterne for them and tasted it before helping herself to the cold meats and cheeses. "I shall keep Mother with me," she said with finality.

"But you can't devote all your time to her, Jette," Hunter protested. "You have your own life to live." He hesitated before asking, "Are you going ahead with your wedding?"

Jette toyed with the thinly sliced roast beef and cheddar cheese on her plate. "No," she admitted. "Nate wanted to, but I thought it best we wait a decent interval—not because of tradition or how it would look to others, but because of Mother." She cut the meat and daubed on peach-and-raisin chutney. Hunter said nothing, waiting for her to continue. He had sensed something was troubling Jette and hoped she would confide in him. "Nate is angry about my putting him off after he'd gone ahead and planned everything for us. He wanted to move in and get settled at La Coruna right away."

"But he surely doesn't resent a postponement under the circumstances," Hunter said with surprise.

"He feels I'm just being arbitrary." Her hand shook as she lifted the crystal glass of wine to her lips.

"You are the last person I know who would be arbitrary. Surely he apprciates the fact that you aren't free right now."

"Free?" Jette considered the word and laughed. "My freedom seems gravely in doubt, doesn't it? No matter what I do, no matter what happens, freedom seems to always be just out of my reach." The candlelight's soft glow revealed her desperation. She shook her head as she passed Hunter a basket of warm cornbread muffins. "No, I'm certainly not free right now," she agreed.

Elvira entered the dining room and paused on her way to the kitchen to ask, "May I bring you anything, Miss Jette?"

"I think we have everything, thank you. You run along and help Socorro. I'll call if we need you."

"Yes, Miss Jette." The girl hurried back to the kitchen, shutting the door behind her. With visitors coming to express condolences and from curiosity, Elvira and Socorro were kept busy arranging and replenishing the buffet that all were invited to share. Abe Marley, the last caller for the day, had left just before sundown. Now in the kitchen the two women washed and rinsed dishes in wide pans atop the wood range. Tonight there was no chatter of rapid, lilting Spanish between them. Elias Allenby was dead—uncertainty over their continued employment in the household precluded merriment.

After Miles Hunter had departed, Jette wandered alone in the garden with only the dogs accompanying her as she strolled in the moonlight. She pulled her shawl about her shoulders against the slight wind that had sprung up. Overhead a pair of owls rustled in the tops of the eucalyptus, their soft hoots echoing hauntingly down the long driveway. She walked as far as the highway and stood in the middle of the road, feeling the clean, cool breeze on her face. To the south, scattered lights of San Genaro winked like flickering beacons in the dark. From the north came the remote rumble of the evening freight train as it crested La Cumbre Pass and dropped down into the valley.

She waited, listening, almost feeling the invisible pulsations of life surrounding but excluding her. Overcome with a sense of suffocating frustration, she ran in the direction of the lights, racing blindly, her eyes fixed on the glimmering pinpoints that represented life and freedom and fulfillment.

Gasping for breath she stopped, unaware of how far she had run, uncaring that her hair had come undone and had fallen in wild abandon about her shoulders. Tears that she had denied so long welled in her eyes and flowed down her cheeks, sobs previously unuttered found outlet that only the dogs would hear.

Sitting in the grass at the side of the road she gathered Pecky and Buff to her and buried her head against their warm, wriggling bodies. The mongrel licked at her face, the salt from her tears on his tongue, the spaniel whimpering in sympathy as it crawled into her lap. She shivered in the wind and realized she had lost her shawl in her maddened run. No matter—she could find it again.

The dogs stiffened in her arms, their heads turning to catch a sound only they could hear. Both animals looked south, down the road. If someone should find her alone on the road, in the dark of night with only the two dogs for company, her hair disheveled, boots and skirts covered with dust, it would soon be whispered in San Genaro that the Allenby ranch harbored two insane women.

She had come to the junction of Las Lomas Road. There was no chance of getting back to the house by the road before being overtaken. She rose up and listened. A team and buggy were coming from the direction of town, the sharp clop of trotting horses' hoofs carrying in the crisp night air. Quickly she made her way to a clump of pepper trees that shadowed the fence corner. Holding the dogs by their studded collars she prayed they would stay quiet as she crouched concealed behind the drooping, feathery branches. She held the dogs close, willing them to remain silent.

The buggy topped a shallow rise beyond the junction and continued toward her. In the moonlight she could make out the vehicle, a shiny phaeton pulled by a team of matched bays. Twin acetylene lamps bobbed circles of light on each side of the horses, but the night was bright enough to travel by moonlight alone.

Pecky growled, a low throbbing vibration deep in his throat. Jette gently shook the dog and shushed him. The spaniel was rigid, its teeth bared as it looked past the pepper tree into the roadway. With growing dread Jette saw the carriage begin to make a left turn. It would pass within a few feet of where she was hidden. She could hear the wheels leave the graveled highway and enter the rutted dirt of Las Lomas Road. She grasped the dogs' collars more tightly as the buggy came abreast of them.

The horses shied nervously and nickered, not as they would at another of their kind, but as they would when alarmed. The solitary driver flicked the reins and spoke reassuringly to the mares.

Instantly Jette recognized the voice. In a moment the phaeton had passed the pepper trees and continued east. Only one ranch could be reached in that direction of Las Lomas Road.

Jette waited, holding fast both dogs until she was certain the buggy was out of sight and hearing. Troubled and uncertain before, she was now sick at heart. She refused to believe anything Asa Beemer had said, but what was she to think now?

There was no mistaking who the lone driver was. The man was only a few feet from her, the moonlight clear and bright on his pale moustache. Nate Trasker was on his way to see Lavinia Baldwin.

* * * *

Judge Booth Killigrew unfolded the legal papers and spread them on the desk. A slight breeze riffled the new curtains at the windows and the air smelled of furniture polish. An unaccustomed woman's touch had come to the formerly males-only ranch office. A bouquet of white and yellow roses and cobalt-blue bachelor's buttons graced the table before the newly shined window. There remained none of the disorderly clutter of Elias' handling of business matters. A fresh coat of white-wash had been applied to the walls, and several small reproductions of Constable landscapes in narrow, gold-leafed frames echoed the fresh greens and ivory of

212

the draperies and upholstered divan and side chairs. The room was light and pleasant, a place where work could be done in comfort, with touches of beauty to relieve its plainness.

Jette turned the pages of the documents, reading the words one by one. Killigrew seated himself at one end of the divan, his fingers drumming on the doily-covered arm. He had been told by Abe Marley that the Allenby girl was no fool. Her questions so far had put him not only in an awkward position, but on the defensive. Although he did not relish dealing with Jette, it had become necessary when her mother was unable to carry on the ranch business. If she were like her father, he could very well have earned himself a dangerous antagonist. The adobe house was still cool, but he was sweating as he watched Jette peruse the dry legal phrases.

"Everything seems in order, Judge," she said at last. "It is exactly as I specified." She took a straight pen from the pewter and crystal desk set, dipped the nib in the inkwell and signed the papers.

"You understand as conservator of your mother's estate you will be able to handle only the funds . . ."

". . . from the ranch itself. Yes, I understand." She folded the documents and returned them to Killigrew, keeping her own copy to place in the safe. The man winced inwardly as she turned her black eyes on him, her expression one of utter contempt. "You and Father nicely arranged my own funds for me." She spoke with an edge to her words. "And you are partly responsible for his buying the animal that killed him."

"But how can you possibly . . ." he tried to protest.

"Because it's true." With no other trace of emotion but disdain she met his glance, daring him to deny it. He could do nothing but agree, and nodded his head.

"Yes, you're right, of course," he admitted. "But you must understand your father set a great store in that

213

. . . that . . ."

"Oh do say bull!" she prompted him. "Why must you men evade honest terms?" She was impatient with him. Everything about the man annoyed her, from his fastidious brocade vest to the jowls that overhung his high collar. "If you mean bull, say it."

"I beg your pardon, Miss Allenby," he apologized, his face growing red. "Your father set a great store in that bull. He assured me it was for you that he was acquiring it." Killigrew touched his heavy white moustache and removed his gold-rimmed pince-nez glasses, letting them dangle from their black ribbon. "It was all quite legal and above board."

She rose and went to the safe, placed the document in a compartment and slammed shut the steel door. She could not trust herself to answer him.

Killigrew had come to the Allenby ranch for the sole purpose of sizing up Elias' daughter. Had it not been for that, he would have sent the papers by his clerk. Now that he had met the girl he would never underestimate her. Abe Marley had been right—she was completely capable of running the ranch, either with or without the help of Asa Beemer or any other man. However, the question remained—how would her forthcoming marriage affect the arrangement? He could only wonder.

"My mother would be pleased if you'd stay for dinner," Jette said. She knew her irritation must be apparent to the man. Rudeness to visitors was an unforgivable social transgression, not only in her mother's more gracious Virginia, but in rural San Genaro County. "We have several other guests coming this evening. We'd be delighted to have you stay." For her mother's sake, and for diplomatic reasons, she would welcome the judge into their home.

"I'd planned to return home." He mustered the genial smile that had aided him in his rise from obscure

214

law clerk to gubernatorial candidate. "But how can I refuse an invitation from such a lovely young lady?" He bowed slightly from the waist.

"You'd be most welcome, Judge." She returned his smile. He was, after all, a friend of her family. "The Putnam brothers and Nate Trasker are coming. And Ainsworth Millege and his wife." At the banker's name Booth Killigrew brightened.

"I'd be most happy to join you," he beamed. "Most happy."

"May I offer you a drink?" Jette led the way from the office into the parlor where she said, "Please do sit down. Which do you prefer, bourbon, brandy, sherry?" She went to the liquor cabinet and opened the faceted-glass doors. "Or perhaps rye?" She was new at entertaining her father's friends.

"I'd like to say rye, but sherry will have to do," he replied. "Doctor Hunter has convinced me I must forego stronger stimulants at my age." He seated himself facing the fireplace, his bulk sagging into the down cushions. "Thank you, my dear," he said as he accepted the delicate, fluted sherry glass. He held it to his nose and sniffed the nutty bouquet, then said, "Now tell me about your mother. How is she taking your father's death?"

Jette selected the easy chair opposite the judge and sat down. She was not prepared to discuss her mother's condition, but knew it must be a matter of much speculation in town. If she told the judge she was certain it would be relayed with variations to the entire community. Almost any response was better than silence.

"Not too well, I'm afraid," she replied. "You can readily understand that it's been a terrible shock to her. Had Father died peacefully in his own bed it would have been another matter, but being attacked by Old Max . . ." She could let the judge image the impact of the occurrence on Verdie.

215

"Terrible thing. Just terrible," he commiserated, the folds of his face drawing into a deep frown. "What do you intend to do with the creature?" Both eyebrows went up to emphasize the question.

"The same as my father planned," she replied. "I can't blame the bull. Asa Beemer assures me that Old Max is not a killer. If he were, I wouldn't think of breeding him. Besides, had he proven to be unmanageable in the past, he would never have been allowed to breed." She gathered her skirts and crossed her legs as she relaxed into the chair. "No, I intend to breed him, just as Father would have."

"That makes sense," Killigrew agreed, but added, "It takes a lot of courage to pick up where your father left off. I can't envisage Elias planning for you to handle ranch business yourself . . ." He was instantly sorry he phrased it that way.

"I have no choice, have I?" Jette was surprised that his comment did not arouse resentment in her, but rather an appreciation that he was concerned with her attempts to carry on the business affairs of the Allenby ranch by herself. He probably was not the ogre her imagination and prejudice had conjured. "Father had advertisements in papers up and down the coast. I see no reason to alter his plans," she said.

Due in part to sincerity, part to the sherry's glow, Judge Killigrew said with admiration, "You're a remarkable young woman, Miss Allenby. Not many young ladies would be able to take over the way you have."

Jette glanced toward the door to the back parlor where Elvira was helping Verdie dress for the dinner party. "As I said before—I really have no choice, have I?"

*　*　*　*

Socorro Galvan dipped red currant sauce over the roast quail and arranged them on plates hot from the warmer over the range. Elvira ladled hollandaise over broccoli and tiny new carrots. Just before serving she decorated the plates with watercress and parsley, then wiped spills from the rims of the delicate Haviland china. Everything—for Jette's and Verdie's sake—must be perfect.

After sampling the bird Ziphia Millege proclaimed, "Marvelous!" She tasted the vegetables and sighed. "You're fortunate to have competent help, Mrs. Allenby. I've had a steady stream of girls, and I tell you quite frankly, it's a trial." She dabbed at her mouth with the embroidered white linen napkin. "We've had Irish girls from Boston and Swedish girls from Dakota. They're much more interested in finding a husband than learning how to be of service."

"Elvira's family and the Galvans have lived on this place all their lives," Verdie said. "I'm sure I don't know how we'd manage without them." She passed the silver-handled pickle dish to Mrs. Millege. "In the old days this was known as Rancho Felicciata—named after the youngest daughter of Lorenzo Moraga. He was given the ranch by the Spanish government when he retired from his military command at San Gabriel." She turned to Killigrew. "Surely you remember the family, Judge."

"Yes, indeed." Killigrew deftly separated breast meat from the bone and tasted a morsel. "Delicious. But then Socorro Galvan would know what to do with quail. Any game, for that matter. Her people lived by beef cattle, but they had a fine appreciation for what variety the land offered." He settled back into the uncomfortable straight-backed chair and glanced toward the door to the kitchen. He lowered his voice as he continued, "The Galvans were entitled to share in the property through

217

the female side of the Moraga family, but old Don Lorenzo didn't leave a will. Attorneys took sad advantage of both sides when it went to law." He wagged his head as if in sorrow for old misfortunes, but did not let it interfere with his enjoyment of the meal. He speared into the broccoli.

"I recall hearing about what happened when I first came to San Genaro," Ainsworth Millege said. "Something about one of the sons—Patricio, I think it was—mortgaging the place for cash to some Los Angeles lawyer."

Killigrew nodded. "That's right. Interest compounded weekly, and no real chance to repay the debt." He pulled his face into a look of stern disapproval. "Needed laws to prevent such practices. Abominable," he pronounced his judgment of the usury.

"But it made a lot of Americans rich." Nate Trasker had to smile at the judge's pompous righteousness. Everyone in the county was aware of Killigrew's profitable dabbling in distressed real estate. "Had Don Lorenzo paid more attention to his ranching and less to playing the grandee, perhaps the property would have remained in his family."

For a few moments there was silence in the dining room. Nate Trasker spoke the truth, not as an affront to the judge, but as unemotional observation of fact. Killigrew studied Trasker over the rim of his wine glass without betraying his irritation. Unwilling to either contest his statement or agree with it, Verdie glanced uneasily toward Jette at the end of the table.

"Wasn't one of the purposes of the census last year to compile data about land ownership?" Jette initiated a new subject not too far removed from the former, and one sure to garner comments from everyone present. The census had been hotly contested and debated from mining camps and back fences all the way to the halls of

Congress. Verdie smiled almost imperceptibly, relieved that Jette had maneuvered talk from parlous matters.

"I must say I rather resented being questioned—and by a man, at that," Ziphia Millege said. "I know the government must have cerain information, but it does remind one of the neighborhood snoop who delights in knowing every last bit of gossip."

"A frightfully expensive snoop, my dear," her husband countered. "Waste of the taxpayer's money, I say."

"When the poor census taker came to us—wasn't it in June, Mother?" Jette waited for Verdie's assent, then went on, "Father was pretty quick with the shotgun. If Mother and Asa hadn't stopped him, I swear Father would have shot the man."

"Don't swear, child." Verdie was quite serious, but she smiled at her daughter at the far end of the table. "Never swear unless you know certainly and of your own knowledge." To Verdie, Jette was still a young girl who needed occasional guidance.

"Yes, Mother. I'm sorry," Jette laughed. "But I'm certain they know what I mean." She was pleased with her mother's improvement and enjoyed humoring her. The way Lodd Putnam watched his hostess' face and relished each word she uttered, Jette felt his presence at the dinner was probably responsible for her mother's animation. She could only guess at their relationship years ago, but was sure that at one time they had been close.

"Just think of it—seventy million people and four million square miles to be canvassed!" Judge Killigrew was properly impressed with the dimensions of the undertaking, and proud he knew data to quote which he hoped would impress others. And it seemed a safe subject for discussion. "Monumental task, especially in view of the country's growth since the one in '80."

"Didn't Congress stipulate that the four principal

reports must be published by next July?" Ziphia asked.

"Don't rightly see how they can get it done by then, but of course they got the manpower and the money—right out of our pockets." Lodd Putnam had remained quiet in the company of the judge and the banker, but as the wine thawed his reserve he spoke up. "Might do to know who's gonna profit from the whole thing. You can bet somebody's gonna make money out of them reports, too."

"You say four reports—what are they?" Verdie asked. "I know population count is one purpose, the main one, but what else?" She poured more wine for Lodd and passed the glass back by way of Ziphia and Ed.

"Population, as you say," Nate Trasker replied. "Plus data on manufacturing, agriculture—and mortality." He paused, wondering if such a word would upset Verdie.

"Oh, yes, I'm certain our legislators are vitally interested in mortality." Verdie's hazel eyes twinkled. "They demonstrate by their actions that they have little concern for immortality."

Jette's infectious laughter brought a look of disapproval from her mother, but it was obvious she was pleased.

"I suppose the taxpayers got something for their money," Millege said. "It gave forty thousand men jobs, and at fifty to a hundred-fifty per man for two or three weeks' work, it was bound to be a stimulus for commerce." The banker thought in solid dollars and cents. He rearranged his napkin to cover his vest to the top button as he attacked the vegetables with their hollandaise.

"But after it's all finished, what do all these men do to continue feeding their families?" The thought distressed Jette.

Trasker in turn laughed, displaying the shallow

220

dimples that softened the expression of his handsome features. "The same men who recommended them for the census jobs will no doubt find something for them to put their hands on—or into—and see that they are paid from the public purse."

"Good heavens, is that how it was done?" Mrs. Millege asked.

"I'm sure the judge knows more about it than I do." Trasker almost seemed to be baiting the judge. "As I understand it, Congress asked prominent businessmen in each community to recommend someone for the position of census-taker. This was to create good will for the political machinery at all levels." He smiled disarmingly at Killigrew. "Gratitude spills over into even the most remote, unlikely places. I saw it at first hand in Chicago." Trasker drained his wine glass and handed it to Jette with a knowing grin. "You see, my pet, that is how great things are accomplished in our republic."

"So Father said many times." Jette refilled the delicate goblet and presented it to him. Between them she and her mother had poured several bottles of the cold sauterne, and the mood about the table was already mellow, so different from the times Elias had presided over a gathering. "Father said the fifteen million dollars it was supposed to cost would benefit only the politicians. A bit like legally buying votes."

Killigrew spluttered a denial, but Trasker beat him to the words. "Your father was absolutely right," Nate said. His smile was broad, but his cold blue eyes betrayed no humor. Killigrew thought better of contesting him.

"But isn't there a better way?" Jette asked.

"Darling, the prizes always go to the audacious and daring." Trasker toasted her with his glass and sipped the wine. "Only in fictional drivel are honest toilers awarded keys to the city and hand of maiden-fair." He spoke with derision, as if he added his own personal condemnation to those who played the game by the rules or heeded Holy Writ.

"I wonder, though, is the prize they get worth it?" Trasker was puzzled by Jette's seriousness as she asked the question. "Is the loss of a man's honesty and integrity worth material gain?"

"My poor innocent, how much you have to learn in this cruel world." Trasker reached across the table and clasped her fingers. "I intend to make it my life's work to keep you from having to lose your beautiful illusions."

"Here, here!" Ainsworth Millege raised his glass and seconded Trasker's speech. "A worthy dedication, Trasker," he said.

Ed Putnam, who had been absorbing the conversation, but concentrating on his meal, wiped his mouth and looked to Trasker. "I always figure first hand knowing's the best. Reckon you learned a plenty when you was in Africa." He flushed crimson, not so much from the wine, but from having all eyes suddenly focused on him. "How come you to get mixed up with them Matabeles and Dutchmen?"

Nate considered a moment before he replied. He pushed back slightly from the table, his head tilted to regard his audience. "When I was a boy I used to look at all those pink and green countries on maps in my geography books and wonder what they'd be like. There were pictures, too, of strange animals and date palms and dark-skinned people in burnooses. I decided I wanted to see a good deal of this world of ours while I was still young." He leaned back in his chair, intent upon his explanation. "I grew up seeing all about me old men who knew nothing beyond their own hog lots and wheat fields and the county seat. The light of adventure, if it had ever been kindled in them, had long since died out, smothered by responsibilities assumed too young.''

"So you went adventuring?'' Ed Putnam made it sound easy.

"I'd heard tales of Indian fighting—Apaches, Navajos, Ogallalas, Utes. Two of my uncles were in the cavalry in the Oklahoma Territory. I saw little difference between settling our American West and settling the veldt in Africa. The problems were the same.'' He chuckled as he added, "And the pay was good.''

"You fought them black folks, too?'' Lodd asked. Having done their share of fighting as young men on the plains and in the southwest desert, the Putnams liked to talk of the old days—the one exciting period of their lives. "Guess there ain't much difference between them Matabeles and the Indians when it comes to fighting 'em, is there?''

"I suppose not, but the Boers—the Dutch settlers—were something else,'' Trasker replied. "They were dangerous enemies.''

"I was under the impression that the British wouldn't accept foreign volunteers,'' Killigrew said without allowing Trasker to reply further to Lodd's query.

"Quite true,'' Trasker said. "Foreigners couldn't join the British regular army, but a number of us found a way around such nonsense. A good fighting man is worth his pay in any nation's army.''

"And you joined?'' Ziphia Millege asked.

"Rhodesia Light Horse, yes, ma'am,'' Trasker answered. "And we saw plenty of action against the Matabeles and the Indians when it comes to fighting in '96 and '97.''

"You killed them—like in a real war?'' Jette was horrified.

"Dear innocent girl,'' he said softly. "It was fully as much a war as the one that sent us to Cuba and the Philippines.'' He smiled at her naive reaction. "And it

223

was fought for the same reasons: land, privilege, power."

"That's very important to you, isn't it?" Jette said it with regret since it was apparently true.

"Of course it's important to me," Trasker replied. "To any man with red blood and a drop of ambition those are the most important things in life." He saw he had blundered as Jette turned away from him. He blamed his outspoken admission on the sauterne and tried to ameliorate the effect by adding, "Only one thing can be more important—finding and keeping the love of that one perfect woman." The ploy was calculated, but it worked for the moment. Jette looked at him and smiled.

"Here, here!" Millege agreed and raised his glass to his wife, who stared at him across the table in fond amusement.

"Well spoken, young man," Killigrew said, his expression lapsing close to sentimentality as he gazed at the two lovers.

But Jette did not want to look longer at Nate. His eyes held that cold, practical appraisal which was so much a part of him, a part that she found so difficult to accept. Matabeles, Boers, Navajos, Calderons and Moragas and Lavinia Baldwin—to him they were all the same, fit only for conquest and profit. As she listened to him she could only wonder if he placed her in the same category.

Jette had not seen Nate since the night she had hidden in the shelter of the pepper trees and watched him drive east on Las Lomas Road toward the Baldwin ranch. She refused to ask him about it. Her own admission would be more damaging to their relationship than any of his. While he might claim business reasons, what could she possibly claim?

She was glad when the last guest departed. Shortly after Nate's buggy pulled away from the front veranda she had heard Asa Beemer ride in from the main road and return to the house. Until he could be replaced, Asa was essential to the running of the ranch. He had warned her against Trasker and she had discounted it as jealous retaliation. His allegation that Nate was responsible for Elias' death she still classified as purest nonsense. And yet as Nate Trasker had related his experiences as a trooper in the Rhodesia Light Horse, Jette almost felt frightened by his totally dispassionate attitude. Men, she reasoned, talk of war and killing in the same way women speak of childbirth and baking bread. There lingered, however, so many unanswered questions. Should she allow her doubts to destroy their love?

When she bade Nate goodnight she felt a resurgence of the wild, singing desire his nearness evoked. His embrace and kisses made her wish she could abandon doubt and reason and all responsibilities and flee with him to her own share of happiness. In her heart she longed for things to be as they were that afternoon at La Coruna.

"Come sit with me a while," Verdie said and patted the down cushion of the sofa. "I think I'd like a little sherry, please." She sighed with newfound contentment. Her evening had gone well. The company was pleasant, and the simulating conversation steered away from contentiousness by Jette's adroit intervention. Jette poured from the cut-glass decanter and handed a glass to her mother.

"Thank you, dear," Verdie said. "Now sit beside me and we'll talk."

"All right, Mother, for a little while. I'm very tired."

"I shouldn't wonder." Verdie sipped the sherry and smiled, her eyes still aglow with pleasure. "You are a fine hostess, Jette." She said it with undisguised pride and admiration. "It will be all over San Genaro in a few days." For a moment she looked distressed, her old expression of confusion clouding her face. "Was I all right? Did I . . ."

Jette gently kissed her cheek and hugged her. "You were perfect, Mother. Absolutely perfect." She did not care if she spilled her mother's sherry or not. "You looked so beautiful and I was so proud of you." Impulsively she hugged her again. "It will be all over town that you're feeling much better, too."

Verdie knew exactly what she meant and tears came to her eyes as she took another swallow of the sherry. "Yes, I suppose it will get about." She looked at her daughter, a flicker of confusion returning. "I am better, don't you think?"

"Of course you are, Mother! And you're going to get well—completely well—soon now. You'll see."

"Oh, I hope you're right, dear." Verdie looked up as Elvira came into the room with a tray and collected the last remaining glasses and demi-tasse cups. "Run along to bed, child. You can finish tidying up in here tomorrow. You and Socorro did so well this evening that I want you both to have a day off. Next time Benito goes to town, perhaps you'd like to go in with him. Or you can have your brother drive you over to see your Aunt Tecla at La Coruna. Would you like that?"

"Yes, thank you, Mrs. Allenby," Elvira hastened to say. She was tired, but brightened at the prospect of a holiday. "I'd like to go see my aunt."

"Then it's settled. I'll speak to Asa about it." Verdie stifled a yawn.

"Do you want me to help you undress?" the girl asked.

"No, no, you run along. Jette can help me. And we'll turn out the lamps. Good night, Elvira." Verdie was pleased that she could make a decision on her own without having to consult Elias first.

"Good night," Elvira included them both, and sidled through the door with the tray and shut the kitchen door behind her. In a moment the back door closed, the latch rattled as Elvira tested it, and the screen door slammed.

In the front parlor the standing clock chimed the quarter hour—fifteen to twelve. All was quiet in the old adobe. Even the dogs of the workmen's village were silent. Jette rose and began a circuit of the parlor and sitting room, extinguishing the lamps, testing the doors and windows to make certain all were safely locked. She opened the door to the office, checked the door to the hall, then the hall door to the veranda. She had seen her father do the same thing for many years, but doing it now by herself she had begun to realize what was entailed in being responsible for their property.

"That does the ground floor," Jette said and resumed her seat beside Verdie. "Are you sure you don't want me to stay down here with you? I can have a cot . . ."

"No, I'm not afraid. I find it rather nice, really," Verdie said. "With the dogs on the floor beside me, I feel more secure than I would upstairs." She left unvoiced her dread of sleeping in the bed she had shared with Elias, a bed shared not with love, but from a sense of fear and obligation.

"All right, as long as you're comfortable." Jette stretched and yawned, and bent to unbutton her high patent-leather shoes and slip them off her feet. "Tell me, Mother—what was Lodd Putnam to you?" She curled up on the sofa, tucking her feet beneath her.

"He admired me—many years ago." The question was too abrupt for Verdie to parry. It was an honest answer she gave, but she appeared pained by her reply. "What on earth makes you ask?"

"I saw the way he looked at you all evening." She touched her mother's arm and asked, "Was he in love with you? Was that it?"

For a moment Jette thought her mother would not answer, but Verdie finally said, "Yes, he was." She glanced away as if viewing an episode long tucked away in memory and only now recalled. "But it wasn't

227

proper, you see. I was a young married woman and he was very much older than I. To me he was more like a father." She paused to give emphasis to the point. "At first he was just worried about me being alone on the ranch. Your father was gone a great deal of the time, making trips for one thing and another. Lodd told your father he didn't like him leaving me alone, and me so young and inexperienced. Things were peaceable in this part of the West, but he felt Elias should stay here and look after me." Verdie finished her sherry and handed the glass to Jette. "Pour me just a bit more, dear."

"Was that the beginning of their falling out?" Jette poured half an inch of sherry and gave it to Verdie. "Is that what started their feuding?"

"It didn't help, but it didn't start there. They knew your father before he ever came to California." She took the glass, sipped from it, trying to order her thoughts before continuing. "It was terribly lonely for me at first. Your father kept on most of the Mexican help who'd been with the Moraga family, but he demanded they speak English if they wanted to stay. He said they were Americans now and should speak the language of the nation. I know it was more for my benefit than his, since he spoke Spanish quite well. Over the years he let some of the hands go, but we kept most of them. They were good people—still are—and very kind to me, although I'm sure they must have resented both of us."

Jette settled back to listen. They had never spoken much about early days on the ranch, but somehow with Elias gone it seemed proper, even necessary, for Jette to learn what had occurred. Verdie toyed with her amethyst necklace, twisting it in her thin fingers as she debated how much she should reveal to her daughter. She smoothed the deep lace flounce which encircled her shoulders and rippled down the front of her dress.

"Maybe you're too tired . . ." Jette saw her mother's distress.

"No, dear, it isn't that," Verdie replied. "It's just that it was so long ago, before you came along." She shook her head as though she were determined to finish the story, regardless. "Your father was not an easy man to live with or to stay in love with. I'd loved him when he came to our home in Virginia and I vowed to marry him the minute we were introduced. He wasn't gallant and polished as most of the boys I knew, but he had a quiet strength, a bearing, that appealed to me. My own father was an ineffectual man, given to daydreaming and living in fantasies. I thought Elias—being the opposite of my father—was the answer to all my own daydreaming."

"I think I know what you're going to say, Mother."

"I'm sure you do, Jette." Verdie seemed agitated as she went on, "It's just that I seem to see the pattern being repeated. I want you to be careful whom you choose to marry. I don't want you to live the life I have. You mustn't make my mistakes."

"You don't want me to marry Nate?" Jette could not keep her irritation from her voice. They had discussed the matter so many times that it seemed useless to go over it again. "He was a perfect guest this evening. You enjoyed him."

"I admit he is charming. And, yes, he is pleasant to have as a guest." Verdie paced before the stone fireplace and glanced at the gun collection impaled above the mantle. "I can't help feeling as I do about him. When he spoke of the war . . ."

"Please, Mother," Jette begged. "We were talking about Lodd Putnam. Tell me what it was you started to say about him."

"Very well, dear." Verdie could see Jette's annoyance.

229

"You were saying Lodd wanted Father to look after you . . ."

"When we came west, I began to see a change in your father." Verdie stopped and appeared puzzled as she sat down again. "No, I'm wrong. It wasn't a change in him—it was just that I began to see him as he really was. I had imagined him as a hero, a gentle lover." She turned away from her daughter in embarrassment. "He was not a gentle lover," she said with vehemence. "Nor was he considerate where my needs or wants were concerned. I just seemed to be something he owned—and used."

"Mother, why did you stay with him?" Jette could feel the disillusionment and heartbreak her mother was trying to express. She took Verdie's hand in hers. "Why didn't you leave?"

"I wanted to leave," Verdie explained. "But there was no chance of it. He had control of all my money. My family could do nothing for me. And Elias wasn't the sort to let me go. No matter where I'd gone, he would have brought me back. My dowry had been settled on him, and in my innocence and ignorance I had no idea what that might eventually mean for me." She hoped Jette would see the parallel between her experience and the one into which she might be led by marrying Nate Trasker.

"You could have divorced him."

Verdie looked dismayed. "No proper lady ever resorts to divorce!" She was horrified that the subject had been mentioned. "I'd rather have died than gone through a divorce."

With an effort to refrain from saying how foolish Verdie's attitude seemed, Jette merely patted her mother's hand. "I see," she said. "And then Lodd Putnam came along and you fell in love with him?"

"Oh, no, dear!" Verdie drew back in shock. "Whatever he may have felt for me, I swear I didn't

230

return it! You must believe me, Jette, there was never anything improper in my friendship with Lodd Putnam." Verdie fidgeted with her sherry glass, consternation cutting deep lines in her face. When she looked up at Jette, Verdie had once again retreated into muddled confusion and bewilderment.

* * * *

Jette placed her mother's amethyst necklace and earrings in the office safe and locked the heavy door. The small lamp she carried cast a dull yellow glow as she made her way back through the front room. Buff, the huge mongrel, ambled from the back parlor, his tail moving slowly from side to side as he awaited her caresses. She patted his upturned head and scratched behind his drooping ears.

"Good night, old fellow," she whispered. Before going upstairs she stood at the rear parlor door and listened to Verdie's soft, regular breathing, then satisfied that she was settled for the night, opened the patio door. Buff returned to lie at the foot of the chaise, his black muzzle resting on his outstretched paws as he resumed his vigil.

Outside, the night was still warm. A sliver of waning moon hung low in the sky, dimming the stars about it and doing little to alleviate the darkness. A mockingbird trilled in the oak by the lane and was answered from the depths of the orchard north of the house. Crickets chirred shrilly in the grass and damp flower beds. As she made her way up the steps Jette broke off a snippet of sweet jessamine and held its yellow blossoms to her nose. Inside the back parlor the vine's fragrance pleased Verdie, reminding her of her girlhood home. For a long time Jette stood at the veranda railing and gazed out through the live oaks, across the rolling hills to where a few lights from San Genaro twinkled in the distance.

"How'd the dinner party go?"

Jette almost dropped the lamp from her hand at the sound of Asa Beemer's voice. He was sitting in the shadow of the overhang, but he rose and walked to her side.

"I'm not sure it's any of your concern," she said.

"Just asking to be polite," he replied. "I saw Abe Marley in town tonight. Said he was right sorry he couldn't come. Had a supervisors' meeting over at the courthouse." Beemer sat on the railing, one foot on the lower rail, the other stretched out, almost touching Jette's skirts. "Mrs. Allenby have a good time?"

"I know what you mean, Asa. There's no reason to be devious," Jette said. "Yes, she had a very good time." She held the lamp to illuminate the man's face. "Mother was perfectly lucid, made intelligent conversation, and even joked with everyone. She did very well."

"I'm glad to hear it. I never thought she wouldn't be just fine."

By the lamplight Jette studied his rugged face. Since there was no reason for him to narrow his eyes against a brilliant sun, she noticed for the first time how wide-set and large his dark eyes were. Wrinkles from too many days in heat and dust etched crevasses across the sharp planes of his forehead and jaws and about the wide mouth. She saw with surprise that he was clean shaven and smelled of castile soap and lavender hair tonic. "You really mean that, don't you?" she asked.

"I do." His laconic reply made her look even closer at him.

"Thank you for caring," Jette said, abandoning some of her hostility. "You've been a great help to us both since . . . since . . . ." She found it difficult to finish.

". . . Since Nate Trasker killed Elias." Jette was startled by the intensity of Asa's voice. It was just above

232

a growl. She wanted to contest him, but thought better of it and turned instead to leave. "It's true!" He moved to her side, started to touch her arm, but pulled back his hand. "God in heaven! You know it's true. You can't go marrying him!"

In that instant she made up her mind. "Oh, but I am, Asa." His stubborn indictment of Nate Trasker only reinforced her wavering determination. She took the lamp and hurried down the veranda to her own room. As she stood in the doorway she flung back at him, "I intend to marry him as soon as possible!"

Chapter 11

By eight in the morning Los Angeles was already hot and bustling, its streets a cacophony of electric streetcars, horse-drawn delivery wagons and carriages. A few automobiles dared to thread their way through the slower vehicles, horns honking impatient blasts at each delay. Verdie Allenby pulled back the curtain and stared out the third floor window at the early traffic.

"Such a commotion! I wonder if it's like this every day?" She raised the venetian blinds and leaned forward to watch as the streetcar's passengers trooped down the steps and hurried across the street, dodging buggies and cars. "I don't even remember Richmond being like this."

"It's a good thing we didn't want to sleep late this morning." Jette skewered a navy-blue, narrow-brimmed straw hat atop her auburn hair with a pearl hat pin. She inspected the angle in the full length mirror which occupied the corner of the hotel room. One silk-petaled daisy which was misaligned on the brim she bent to shape, then tucked the coarse white veil over her hair in back and secured it with another pearl pin. She had slept badly in the hot, stuffy room and yawned as she turned to check her completed toilette. "Are you all ready?" she asked.

"Yes, dear," Verdie replied, but did not move from the window. "It's all so exciting, I didn't want to miss a minute of it." She gasped as two produce wagons laden with oranges and lettuce almost collided in the intersection below. There seemed to be no organized flow of traffic, much less regulation, but the wagons and pedestrians missed each other and continued about their business. "I declare, I've never seen so much coming and going!" Her soft Virginia drawl—almost lost after so many years in the West—surfaced in her excitement. She stood in the full light of the window and turned slowly. For their trip to the city she wore an old, but exquisitely tailored, white linen suit with wide tan lapels and graduated width bands encircling her skirt. A cascade of lace-edged ruffles spilled to her waist from the shell-pink blouse, the fresh color reflecting a blush into her face.

"Look me over good, Jette," Verdie said. "I don't want to disgrace you." She was as fearful of her appearance as a girl.

"You couldn't possibly do that, Mother," Jette laughed. It was what her mother wanted to hear and she smiled with pride. "Here, just let me do this," Jette said as she straightened the seam of Verdie's skirt to fall exactly right. "Perfect," she pronounced her verdict. "Are you hungry?"

"Ravenous! Do you suppose the food's better here at the hotel or over there?" Verdie read the name emblazoned in fancy gold-leafed letters on the window across the street, "Hotchkiss Garden Restaurant." She turned to Jette and asked, "Shall we try the dining room downstairs or go over there?" Their excursion, although made for the practical reasons of consulting a doctor for Verdie and buying a trousseau for Jette's marriage, was nevertheless a joyous adventure for the older woman.

"I'll let you choose," Jette replied. She could not suppress a smile as she saw the elation on her mother's face. Few had been the decisions, even in trivial matters, that were permitted her by Elias. There was hesitation, but only for a moment.

"Then I say let's try the Hotchkiss," Verdie said. "I've heard so much about it, but your father would never bring me here." Her delicately pointed chin was thrust outward with a touch of the defiance so characteristic of her daughter. "The Hotchkiss," she announced, relishing the opportunity to decide something for herself fully as much as the idea of break-fasting in the famous restaurant. She picked up her small handbag from the foot of the bed.

Arm in arm, Jette and Verdie hurried to the iron-grilled elevator. Potted palms and wicker chairs lent the halls and lobby an air of tropical relaxation, the turkey-red Oriental rugs underfoot constrasting not unpleasantly with the light, carefree feeling of the rattan-and-peel furniture. While not the finest or most expensive hotel in Los Angeles, the Imperial was the busiest and most comfortable. Since it was convenient to both train station and commercial center of town, Verdie had suggested they stay there. They strolled to the corner, waited for a pause in traffic and crossed, hastening their pace as an elaborate carriage hurtled past.

The Hotchkiss was the epitome of elegance. Its immaculate linen, polished silver, and engraved glassware were the envy of eating establishments throughout the Golden State. Waiters imported from the British Isles attended each diner with meticulous attention, never obvious, but always at hand.

Coaxed into glorious bloom beneath skylights two-stories above were blue agathea, crimson, clove-scented carnations, and white alyssum with its sweet fragrance of honey. The sunken central display was surrounded by a yard-wide apron of blue and white Delft tiles, and interspersed among the tables were columns of white ceramic brick crowned with brilliant blue falls of lobelia. Two tiers of private dining rooms ranged opposite one another on a balcony above the main floor, their doors sliding, Japanese fashion, rather than swinging on hinges, allowing diners a colorful view downward or discreet seclusion. Small palms in heavy glazed stoneware of pale blue and white were strategically placed to break the open expanse and provide a tactful screen for those sitting at tables on the main floor. Electric fans, installed inconspicuously overhead, revolved slowly to provide cooling air movement and prevent the incursion of flies from the manure-fouled street outside.

"Good morning, ladies." The head waiter, clad in black-and-gray-striped trousers and white linen coat, sported a fresh scarlet carnation in his lapel. His impeccable English accent was as foreign to Spanish California as the tourists who abandoned their break-fasts by the windows to stare as the women entered. "If you will follow me, please." The waiter bowed stiffly and led them to a central table, next to the flower beds, but out of the patch of sunlight which crept across the main floor.

The beauty of the younger woman, the mature hand-someness of the older, drew the attention of waiters, bus boys, and diners alike. Verdie made no pretense of reading the menu, but chose instead to look about the restaurant, her eyes gay with fascination. At a nearby table a group of businessmen turned to observe the women, their glances lingering with admiration on both mother and daughter. Suddenly aware of their staring, Verdie pretended to give her attention to the bill of fare.

"Iced cantaloupe sounds delicious for a start, don't

236

you think?" Jette asked. "Creamed asparagus on toast and thinly sliced ham frizzled in butter . . . and coffee . . ." She looked up to find the men watching. "Mother, I do believe you are distracting some gentlemen from their breakfasts," she whispered across the table. Verdie smiled over the top of the menu and nodded, her face alive with unaccustomed animation. With a pang of sorrow for her mother, Jette realized she had never before seen her so happy. It was not that Verdie was the recipient of approval, but the fact that she seemed alive again, eager for encountering life once more. She could only wonder as she watched Verdie how many years it had been since she had known such pleasure.

"It's been a long time since you came to Los Angeles, hasn't it?" Jette asked. Verdie nodded over a mouthful of coffee and averted her eyes from the gaze of the men. "You are glad you came, aren't you, Mother?"

"Of course I'm happy I came!" Verdie said with almost childlike enthusiasm. "Now let me think . . . how long has it been?" She put a finger to her chin and tried to remember. "You were five years old. Yes, you'd just had your fifth birthday and your Aunt Florie had come to visit." Her face clouded and she turned her head toward the flower display so Jette could not see her face. For a moment she could say nothing more, but finally asked, "Do you remember that summer, dear?"

"Indeed I do!" Jette replied. "That was the time Father was so insulting to Aunt Florie that she turned right around and went back to Virginia." She was instantly sorry she had said it. To change the drift of their remembrances, she continued, "Have you decided what to have?"

Verdie took a deep breath, as if determined to recapture the exuberant feeling of minutes before, but her face betrayed her effort. *Why*, thought Jette, *must Father still destroy Mother's happiness?* Her mother looked up and signaled to the waiter, saying, "I think we're ready to order now."

Dining was a leisurely affair at the Hotchkiss, although Los Angeles businessmen tended to bolt their sausages and steaks and dash away despite the quiet calm of the restaurant. Courses were served, dishes removed, all with such graciousness that one was hardly aware of the service. After finishing coffee and paying the bill, Jette and Verdie wandered down Broadway to the Fuller Building.

"Alienist." Verdie said the word with curiosity and a touch of concern. "It sounds so formidable," she sighed. She tugged at her gloves and fingered her rolled-brim scarfed hat almost as though she expected to pass an inspection. "I'm sure he will be critical of my not wearing mourning. Any respectable widow should, you know."

"You're perfectly respectable, Mother," Jette said with exasperation. "Mourning is an antiquated custom that should have been abolished centuries ago. You did your best for Father while he was living. Wearing black would be depressing—and would do neither Father nor you any good." In a gentler tone she added, "You look lovely. You'll make a very good impression."

"I'm not sure I want to talk to a complete stranger about such intimate, personal things."

"You just talk over your problems with him. He'll help you solve them—or forget them." Jette felt it could not possibly be as simple as that, but it would serve as an explanation. She knew little more than her mother about the doctor. Their exchange of letters did little to enlighten them. Although it had been Asa Beemer who first suggested the doctor, Nate Trasker had agreed, insisting that Verdie must see him as soon as possible. Nate did not issue an ultimatum, but had been demanding enough to cause Jette to wonder at his reasons.

"You're sure you'll remember to meet me back at the hotel?" Verdie was anxious about their arrangements. She passed through the revolving glass door into the lobby of the Fuller Building. On the wall to the left was a listing of occupants, with letters spelling out names and suite numbers inserted into a slotted board. "You won't forget, will you?"

"No, Mother," Jette reassured her. "I'll do some shopping and go back to the hotel. If I'm not in the lobby, I'll be up in our room." They had already discussed it, had already decided where to meet. Jette knew her mother only wanted to hear it once more before going to the office upstairs. They stepped into the elevator and Jette said to the uniformed operator, "Fourth floor, please."

* * * *

Until noon Jette was free to shop for her trousseau. Her mother, while not approving her choice of Nate Trasker, made no further objections and had given Jette a generous allowance toward the purchase of clothing and accessories for wedding and honeymoon. The ceremony was to be private, with only a few friends in attendance. To Verdie it was most unseemly to have the wedding before a proper mourning period had elapsed. She did not, however, insist that Jette and Nate wait and observe the traditional custom which they considered hypocritical and obsolete. Jette would have her way.

"I'd like to have these fitted." Jette turned to view the dinner gown in the triple mirror of the ladies' department. "Would it be possible to have them ready by day after tomorrow?" The saleslady pinched the waist of the garment in back, showing her how it would look after being taken in several inches.

"We can certainly make it a point to get them done by then," the woman replied. "With this large an order—

239

and considering it's for a wedding, we'll put a 'rush' on it."

"That would be marvelous of you." Jette had to smile at her image in the mirrors. The vibrant electric blue of the glistening silk was a perfect foil for her burnished copper hair and warm ivory skin. A wide fold dropped from the shoulders to form a deep décolletage which was filled with organza a few shades lighter in color.

"You couldn't find a gown more perfect for you, Miss." The saleslady stood to one side and considered the effect. "You have an incredibly small waist. We'll have to take in the waist and let down the hem by two inches." She took out her sales book and asked, "Shall I write it up?"

"Oh, yes! I love it." Jette resisted the desire to pirouette in the dress and returned to the dressing room. She could hardly wait to wear the gown with the pale aquamarine and gold necklace and earrings bequeathed to her by her grandmother. She had never yet worn the jewelry, never had the occasion to do so. San Francisco —that was the right place. They would honeymoon in San Francisco and she would wear her silk gown and jewelry for Nate. Perhaps when they had been settled for a while at La Coruna they would have a dinner party where she might again wear the beautiful dress and gems.

Jette had not told Nate that she and Verdie were going to Los Angeles this week. Tentatively they had set next week as the earliest they could arrange for Verdie to see the doctor. No matter. He would be pleased.

"I shall pick everything up Wednesday," Jette said. "I can either pay you now for the entire bill . . ."

The saleswoman looked at the floor manager and said, "Just a deposit is enough, Miss. You can pay when you come for them. Unless you'd prefer we deliver them to your hotel."

240

"No, I'll come by for everything. I think I should try on the gown and suits." Jette handed the woman a twenty and waited for the receipt.

"Yes, Miss. That will be fine." The clerk scribbled a receipt and handed it to the girl. "Thank you."

Jette took a slip of paper from her handbag and read the list of items she had decided upon: a Japanese kimono instead of a cotton wrapper, flesh-tinted hosiery, satin petticoats in navy blue and white, one in silk with morning-glory shape reinforced with buckram about the hem and the seams with whalebone; lightly boned corselet; cambric cotton nightshifts . . . she checked each one off with a silver-cased fountain pen.

Jette entered the elevator as the doors opened. As it gave an initial lurch upward she started in surprise. Absorbed in her list of purchases, she had taken the first elevator that had opened its doors, unaware that it was going up, not down.

On the floor indicator panel beside the operator a buzz alerted him that he should stop at four-down. An instant later the fifth floor rang. The cage was open on three sides, the ornamental work enclosing the cages to allow a clear view of street level and of the central corridors of stories above. The department store occupied the first three floors, business and professional offices the next four, an apartment-hotel the remaining five.

The smartly uniformed operator rotated the lever of the circular floor-stop control, halting the cage at three where several women exited and asked for the housewares section. Again the cage slid upward, heading for five. Slowly they passed the fourth floor.

Waiting by the doors in the poorly illuminated corridor was a woman, her black French walking suit and diaphanous black veil conveying their message of recent bereavement. Beside the woman, his back to the cage, stood a tall man. In that instant Jette stifled an urge to cry out.

"Something the matter, Miss?" The elderly operator turned to her in alarm.

"No, no," Jette replied. She was glad they were alone on the elevator. Her gasp was awkward to explain. "I thought I saw someone I knew, but I'm sure I'm mistaken." It was sufficient excuse for her inadvertent surprise. The cage rose to the fifth floor and Jette got out, her face crimson. Suddenly she felt ridiculous. How could she become so upset at the mere glimpse of a woman she could not identify?

A short, bowler-hatted man stepped aside for her as Jette left the elevator. It still had to call at the sixth floor and again descend. She hurried to the end of the hall, found the stairs and ran down to the fourth floor, peered around the corner just as the cage began its downward trip carrying the passengers from sight. Quickly she ran back to the high window at the end of the corridor which overlooked the congested street. Breathlessly she waited. People fanned out from the main entrance of the building, some crossing the street, others making their way to the intersection. As she was about to give up she spied the couple as they emerged from beneath the canopy of a nearby restaurant and disappeared around the corner.

At such a distance it was impossible to determine who they were. But she must know. Surely the answer lay in one of the fourth floor offices.

Beginning with the side hallway, Jette made a circuit of the floor. Carr Medical and Surgical Supply —National Body Brace Company—Cranitonic Products —Douglas-Lacy and Company—Montague-Cameron Trust.

Perhaps she had been wrong. The light, after all, was not good and the figures had been momentarily silhouetted against the window at the far end of the hall. Under those conditions it was most unlikely she could identify anyone with certainty.

Names of the offices gave her no information. She retraced her steps to where she had seen the couple. The closest door was the Montague-Cameron Trust. On the frosted glass was stenciled in black block letters only the name of the firm. No officers were listed as on other doors, no hint as to the sort of business it represented.

On the street below, people scurried along the sidewalks and crowded the crossings. There had been a slight decrease of traffic by mid-morning, but the noise continued. She could see a panorama of the city where it stretched to the dusty hills in the north and to the high mountains in the east. Mount San Antonio towered majestically above the foothills and valleys, its bald summit glistening in the cloudless distance.

"Darling, I'm a businessman," Nate Trasker had tried to mollify her. "I have to meet with all sorts of people, male and female. If you can't trust me, there's something terribly wrong with our relationship." Held tightly in his arms, his lips on hers, she had believed him. "If you're going to listen to every bit of gossip you hear—or misinterpret everything I do, what chance have we? Isn't it enough that we love each other?" he had asked. And she chose to believe.

She had not dared tell him she had seen him driving to the Baldwin ranch at night. There simply was no way she could rationalize why she came to be hiding beside the road. Nor was there adequate explanation as to why she should listen to the maligning accusations of Asa Beemer. Perhaps she—instead of her mother—was going mad. Just as soon as she began to make sense of a situation, as soon as she believed happiness was within her grasp, something happened to cause her to doubt, to question everything and everyone. Young and inexperienced, she found herself beset with problems for which there seemed no resolutions.

"Beautiful view from up here, isn't it?"

Jette jumped as the man's voice interrupted her thoughts. He was perhaps fifty, his crisply tailored lightweight suit and spats proclaiming him to be no mere bookkeeper or clerk from one of the adjacent offices. Flat-brimmed straw hat in one hand, silver-banded thorn walking stick in the other, he joined her at the window.

"I'm sorry," he said. "I startled you, didn't I?" Without waiting for reply he went on, "I must remember not to startle lovely young ladies who are standing near an open fourth floor window." He watched her closely, his eyes inspecting her minutely, looking for an indication as to her intentions. His face was tanned and just beginning to betray an indulgence in dining well and often. The shrewdness of his appraisal was not completely hidden.

"You thought I was going to jump?" She laughed and covered her face with one hand in embarrassment as her blush could not be concealed.

"The thought crossed my mind," he admitted.

"How silly I must look!"

"On the contrary, you're a most delightful sight." He adroitly turned her away from the window without her even being aware of it. "Are you visiting Los Angeles?" he asked.

"Yes, with my mother," Jette replied. She was surprised that she should want to speak so eagerly with a total stranger. Her forthrightness was a trial to her mother, who felt a proper young woman should under no conditions strike up a conversation with an unknown man. "Do you live here?" she asked, a plan suddenly forming in her mind by which she might learn something of the woman in black.

"Yes, out in the Westlake Park district." He smiled a bit ruefully. "I've neglected my manners; please forgive me. I'm Russel Carr. My offices are at the end of the hall." He gestured to the far end of the corridor.

"The medical supply?" Jette was gratified to learn he belonged on the fourth floor. "Then you're the right person to ask . . ."

"My pleasure," he replied with a slight bow.

"I wanted to get in touch with an acquaintance of mine and I've forgotten the name of the company she works for. I thought it was the Montague-Cameron Trust, but I tried the door just now and found it's locked. There's no one to ask if it's the right place or not." She hoped she lied well.

"What sort of company is it she works for?" He fell right in with her query. "I'm familiar with most of the firms in this building. Perhaps I can help you."

"I'm really not sure. I think she said it was a . . . a . . ." Jette groped for a plausible business for a young woman to be in.

"Montague-Cameron is a land speculation firm," he interrupted. "I'm certain they have no young lady working for them. In fact, there's rarely anyone in the office. It seems to be just a place they have their mail directed. Now and then someone drops by. One of the men and his wife were by only this morning. I met them in the elevator as we all came upstairs."

Jette looked away from the man quickly. She was determined to either confirm or allay her suspicions. "Was that the woman in black I saw in the hall?" she asked. "And the tall blond man with the moustache?" She prayed he would contradict her.

"That sounds like them," he said. "Lovely woman. Hate to see a woman in mourning. Terrible thing. Right out of the Dark Ages. Don't believe in it myself." He saw the stricken expression on her face and hastened to say, "I do beg your pardon. Perhaps I've been too outspoken?"

Jette mustered a smile. "Not at all. I happen to agree completely." With Carr's confirmation of the couple's descripton, she was determined to find out all he might know about them. She clutched her handbag as if by gripping the silver chain handle until her fingers ached she might maintain her composure. "Just what sort of business is this Montague-Cameron Trust?" she asked.

"Land speculation. Development. All that sort of thing." He spoke with disapprobation. He shook his head and added, "Not the kind of enterprise a nice young lady would want to be part of." He turned to her and asked, "What's your friend's name? I might recognize it."

"Margaret Larson." Jette uttered the first name that occurred to her. Perspiration beaded her forehead, not so much from the heat as from the anguish she must hide. The man considered the name for a moment.

"No, I'm afraid I don't know her," he said. "Sorry."

"I suppose I must make it another time then," Jette said. She turned to leave. She was aware of his continued scrutiny and could not trust herself to meet his sharp eyes. "I don't follow you . . . about the business, I mean."

"Shady dealings," he said in a whisper and jerked his head toward the locked door. "Real estate combines will be the ruin of California if we don't put a stop to them. Eastern capital—that's the real problem." It was obviously a matter he not only felt strongly about, but about which he was well informed.

He began to walk beside her toward the elevator bank. She wondered if he was still suspicious that she might jump out a window and intended to accompany her to the ground floor to make certain she would do no such drastic thing. She attempted to erase his doubt.

"I know nothing at all about real estate. You'll have to forgive my ignorance," she said. "I don't understand what you mean. What exactly do they do?" She hoped to steer him back to the company and the people involved in it.

"It's quite simple, really." They reached the vestibule and he asked, "Which floor do you want? Ground level?" She nodded and he punched the proper button before continuing, "They solicit Eastern capital, bring it out here, and invest in land—mostly ranch land. They do a certain amount of developing, just enough to be able to ballyhoo it, then sell off parcels to innocent investors or farmers. Usually there isn't enough water to do anything with the land, or if there is water, the rates charged for irrigation are so exorbitant that only the water companies can make any money. And," he added significantly, "the developers obtain riparian and water rights by fair means or foul." He had warmed to the subject. "Mutual ownership—that's the answer. Drive out the speculators. Kick the crooked ones right back to Illinois!"

"Illinois?"

"From what I understand, most of the money's from Chicago. This particular trust is chartered here in California, but all the backing, all the promotion, is from the East."

Jette was relieved that the elevator arrived at that moment. Some of the pieces to her puzzle were beginning to fit together. The picture that was emerging not only made her sick at heart, but frightened. Dare she ask a direct question about the people?

"You say you saw one of the men and his wife this morning?" They stepped into the elevator. She allowed the fancy grill to close before she went on. "Do you know who they are? I've heard of a developer out in San Genaro. Perhaps it's the same one."

"Afraid I don't," he apologized. "This outfit is pretty secretive, it seems to me. The way it usually works is that a firm like this does the preliminary work, then a subsidiary with a completely different name and no traceable connection to the parent company does the selling. Very devious."

"I see. Yes, I can see how it might work." She turned to Carr and asked so the operator could not hear, "Is it a swindle? Is that what they do?" Her black eyes were intense, her face a shade paler, but in the dim light of the cage the man could not discern the change. "Are they . . . criminals?"

"Got to be careful, alleging that," he replied. "Might be actionable in court. No, I wouldn't say outright that it's criminal, although some of our men at Sacramento are of the opinion it is. Unscrupulous or unethical is probably closer to the mark." He smiled at her absorption in the matter. "But don't worry, I'm sure your Miss Larson isn't mixed up with them. I'd have noticed a pretty girl about the premises if they'd had one." They reached the ground floor lobby and the doors opened with a clatter.

"Thank you so much for trying to help me," Jette said.

"Not at all," Carr replied. He fished in his breast pocket and removed a small flat leather case, withdrew a card and presented it to Jette. "Most happy to be of service to you."

"Thank you, Mr. Carr." She read the card and smiled up at him. She realized she was barely being polite, much less cordial—certainly not what the man deserved for his courtesy and concern. She extended her hand and said, "My name is Allenby. Jette Allenby. I'm happy to have met you, Mr. Carr."

"Pleasure's mine, I assure you," he beamed. They had reached the door and he put on his immaculate straw hat before going out. "I hope you never have need of my line of products, but if you should need assistance again, don't hesitate to call on me."

"Thank you. I appreciate your offer." She wanted it to seem that she was leaving, but was reluctant to actually go from the building. Somehow she must be rid of the attentive Russel Carr. "Oh, I almost forgot! I

248

have some packages to collect. If you'll excuse me . . ." She turned to go back into the department store. He tipped his hat and smiled, then made his way to the sidewalk outside.

From the children's wear department she could see out a display window. Carr still stood on the sidewalk, his gaze still upon her. He was curious about her. She thought it odd that she did not mind his observing her, and indeed, felt a trifle more secure under his surveillance. As their eyes met once more she waved gaily and smiled through the glass. He again tipped his hat, grinned, then disappeared into the crowd. As soon as she could be certain he was gone she returned to the lobby and consulted the directory on the red-marble wall.

"Manager of the building, Room 203," she read in a whisper. "Two, please," she said to the elevator man, who gave her an inquisitive look and muttered, "Yes, ma'am," and deposited her on the second floor.

Room 203 was a suite of well-lighted offices opening off the main corridor. A waist-high oak railing separated a narrow waiting room from the main office beyond, where desks were aligned beneath electric globes suspended by single wires from the ceiling. Several telephones lent prestige to the desks of a few men whom Jette supposed to be supervisors of the younger men and women sitting at less advantageous positions about the vast room. A glass-enclosed office to the right appeared to be the one she might want.

"May I see the manager, please?" she asked of the man nearest the railing. "It will only take a moment and it's very important." She had already lied a few times and a few more could not blacken her soul much more. She summoned her most ingratiating smile and waited by the oak divider. In a moment the man returned and motioned her into the separate office.

"Mr. Sandberg can see you. Go right in," the man

said. The office staff turned to watch the beautiful red-headed girl as she was welcomed into the manager's office.

"I'd like to enquire about one of the firms in your building." She saw no point in wasting time. If it were suddenly asked, perhaps she might get a more candid answer. "Specifically, the Montague-Cameron Trust." She did not wait to be seated, but confronted the man as he stood behind his desk.

"What would you like to know?" She did not miss the quick set of his facial muscles and narrowing of his eyes behind his gold-rimmed spectacles. "I'll be happy to help you any way I can. Won't you sit down?"

"No, thank you. I don't want to take up any more of your time than necessary." She smiled at him, but something in his manner seemed defensive—evasive. She wondered why.

"What was it you wanted to know?" he asked again and came around his desk to be nearer. A fringe of sandy hair beginning to gray was cropped close to his scalp, giving his head the look of being totally bald. Behind glasses which pinched the narrow bridge of his long nose his blue eyes were small and cunning. She concluded it was best to continue in an abrupt vein with the man rather than resort to any craftiness.

"Who are they? What is their business? Do you know the officers of the company? Can you recommend them?" She had caught him off guard. He blinked with each question.

"May I ask what your interest in them is?" He smiled when he asked it, showing teeth mended generously with gold, but his eyes betrayed a sudden arousal of suspicion.

"My mother and I have been asked to invest in some ranch lands and the name of this company came up in the discussion. Before we do anything, I insist on learning something about the firm." She must not appear too ignorant, but must seem to need his advise. "I knew that you'd have access to certain information since they rent from you. You'd know who leased the offices . . . who pays the rent. You'd be in a much better position to advise us than those who've been so quick to tell us where to put our money." She had surmised he would be susceptible to the right sort of flattery.

"I'd be delighted to help you any way I can, but you must realize there are certain matters about which we must be discreet," he countered, but Jette could see he had taken the bait. "Please, do sit down." He gestured to the leather-cushioned chair which faced his desk. Jette smoothed her skirts and slid into the chair. "There, that's much better," he said as he seated himself.

"You see, everyone is so eager to tell us what to do, where to put our money, but how do we know that they're right?" Jette went right to the point. "We've heard some rather strong criticism of these land specula- tions . . ." He raised his eyebrows. Jette now knew he was privy to the same information as Russel Carr. "What would you say about them?" she asked.

"I'm no financial advisor," he began a bit pompously and leaned back in his swivel rocker. "But I can tell you that I have a great deal of my own money placed in their hands." He tried to say it with confidence and pride. A tilt of his chin and the assuming of a superior manner did not convince Jette of his sincerity. "I certainly wouldn't put my own savings with them if I in any way doubted their ability to handle it wisely."

"What firm did you invest in, if I may ask?"

"Montague-Cameron, the very one you're speaking about."

"That's encouraging. But who are they?" she persisted.

"Well, I know I won't be violating a confidence if I

251

tell you at least that much. The president is, of course, Montague. Horace Montague. First vice-president is Beresford Cameron." Sandberg rolled the names off as though he were personally—and closely—acquainted with the founders of the trust. "One of their representatives made all the arrangements, leased the offices a number of months ago—in March, to be exact."

"And who is he?" Jette tried to make the question sound inconsequential, but her heart beat faster as she awaited his reply.

"A Mr. Clarence Pomeroy. From Chicago." He allowed the exalted information to have its effect, and when she looked properly impressed he continued, "But he's rarely in Los Angeles, you understand. Busy man. One of their other men is in and out of Los Angeles and San Francisco. Takes care of all the business until the company makes its final move West." He endeavored to convey his feelings of confidence in the company, but nervous picking at his fingers as he rocked in his chair belied the statements. Jette knew he was trying to convince himself as well as her about the legitimacy of Montague-Cameron's operations.

"And who is this representative?" she asked.

"Never met him." The fact made Sandberg squirm in his chair. "Can't say that I've ever seen the man myself."

"But they do pay the lease regularly?"

"Oh my, yes! Right on the dot every month. A bank draft comes right on the tenth of the month."

"From Chicago?"

"No, from here locally. I suppose they must have an accountant who handles the trivial details for them."

"Would this Clarence Pomeroy be a tall blond man, with a moustache? Perhaps in his mid-thirties?" She dreaded his answer.

"No, that's not Pomeroy. He's quite short and

heavy-set. Light brown hair. Wore right handsome burnsides, too. I remember because I thought he must have grown them to make him look older . . . more dignified, you know." A shade of concern passed over Sandberg's florid face. "Do you think you know him?"

She shook her head. "No, I don't think so. Is Pomeroy the one with whom you invested?"

"As a matter of fact, it is." The building manager appeared apprehensive. He chose to obscure his worry with a show of joviality. "Why, do you know he assured me my money would quadruple within a year! Can't beat that these days. Money to be made in open land." It seemed to Jette he might be quoting verbatim the trust salesman's persuasive slogans.

"You've had an accounting from him recently?" She recalled her father's constant demands for facts and figures when it came to business. "Has it doubled yet?" She was abashed at her inquisitiveness and apologized, "I'm sorry, I have no right to ask such questions. It's just that you seem to know more about such things . . . and having first hand experience, I thought you would be the best to consult."

"Quite all right," he smiled and accepted the flattery. "As to your question—yes, I had a statement of account just last month. He says it's going right along on schedule." Sandberg's optimism was forced. Jette resolved not to pursue the inquiry further. She rose to leave. "These things you've heard about the company . . . what are they?" he asked quickly.

"I'm sure it's nothing important." She hoped to leave without answering him directly. "Thank you for your time, Mr. Sandberg. You've been very helpful." As she reached the door she turned and said, "Good luck on your investment."

Jette hurried from the manager's office. He was uneasy about the situation, and yet the company paid its rent on time. As for facts, she had few. Only of one thing could she be sure: Nate Trasker was not the man who had set up the offices for Montague-Cameron Trust. He might, however, be the local representative who seemed a trifle elusive for a substantial tenant. Even that knowledge failed to be of comfort.

She did not wait for the elevator but used the stairs which paralleled the shafts. She opened the case of the pendant watch that hung from a gold filagree bowknot on her lapel. Almost noon. Verdie would be terrified if she were not back at the hotel as planned. Jette threaded her way among the pedestrians on the wide cement sidewalk in front of the department store windows. The hotel was too close to bother hailing a cab for such a short distance.

Concentrating on the possibility of missing her mother, Jette did not see the man as he sidled from the entry to a jewelry shop and fell into step behind her, his straw hat at an assertive tilt, his thorn cane tucked under his arm.

* * * *

Although luncheon in the Hotel Imperial dining room was not an event, it was more than adequate. It could not compete on the same footing with the Hotchkiss Gardens across the street and did not attempt to do so. Instead, it specialized in plain American-style foods of generous portions, with the main dining room devoted to family-style service. Jette and Verdie Allenby were ushered to a secluded table in a quiet corner, away from the crowded and noisy center.

Jette did not waste time looking about, but perused the bill of fare, ordered quickly, and returned the menu to the waiter. She wished she could return home. Had it not been that Verdie would be utterly panicked by being left alone in the city, Jette would have taken the afternoon train back to San Genaro. During their leisurely meal Verdie prattled about her interview with the new doctor. She seemed unaware that her daughter's thoughts were elsewhere. Nor did the food capture Jette's attention. Finally realizing her distraction, Verdie put down her lemonade and studied the girl's tense face.

"What is it, dear?" Verdie asked. "Something's bothering you. You've been so preoccupied all through lunch I dare say you didn't hear a word I said." She was concerned, not petulant.

"I'm sorry, Mother." Jette dabbed at her lips with the napkin. The cold sliced breast of chicken and tomato aspic remained almost untouched on her plate.

"Is it the heat?"

"No." Jette looked away, avoiding her mother's questioning glance. She hoped she might evade telling Verdie what she had learned. Why she wanted to withhold the information puzzled her. It would bolster Verdie's opinion of Nate Trasker—that he was not quite what he seemed. "Would you like some strawberry shortcake for dessert? It looks delicious."

"No, nothing more for me—not if we're going to have dinner this evening." Verdie leaned across the table and inspected the uneaten food. "I won't insist you tell me what's wrong, but I hope you will. This is no time to begin keeping secrets from one another." Jette made no reply, but toyed with the salad, cutting the lettuce to shreds with her fork.

"Did you finish your shopping?" Verdie asked.

"Not all of it." A look of pain crossed Jette's face and her chin trembled as she turned her head away. "I'm not sure I intend to finish it."

"Jette, I've never demanded your confidences. I don't think a parent should do that. If there is something I should know, I can only trust that you'll tell me in your own time." When she saw her daughter could make no answer, she changed the subject. "It's terribly hot in here. Let's take the trolley out to Westlake Park. The girl who works for Doctor Norris says it's pretty out there—and lots cooler in the afternoon. We can be more comfortable there than here in town."

The bill paid, and after freshening up in their room, they walked over a few blocks to catch the streetcar which turned onto Wilshire Boulevard. The early afternoon sun blazed relentlessly, simmering the congested downtown section with no relief from a west wind off the sea. The south side of the trolley had green shades pulled down to the sill, but that only aggravated the problem by preventing air movement inside the car.

Wet with perspiration, the conductor called out, "Alvarado! Alvarado!" He turned to the women and said, "The next stop will be yours, ladies."

They waited until the car halted, then climbed down, grateful to see fresh green lawns, bright red and yellow cannas in huge circular beds, and palms that drooped crowns of dusty fronds almost to the ground. Cement and gravel paths wound through the park in graceful arabesques studded with dark green, slatted benches. Clustered in shade were knots of women in light summer cottons and preposterous hats garnished with stiff bows and fictitious flowers beneath which their heads sweltered. Toddlers, male and female alike, fretted in long dresses and white cotton stockings, while older brothers ventured ankle-deep at lake's edge to push toy boats adrift. An ornamental drinking fountain on a raised platform of brightly colored tiles was in constant use, the spills about its base collecting yellow jackets and pigeons.

Verdie and Jette, accustomed to searing temperatures of San Genaro Valley, still found the heat intolerable. There was something in the breathless constriction of heat within the city that seemed to increase its penetration. Beyond the boathouse on a shallow point of land that projected into the lake was a group of sycamore trees. Dapplied gray bark and broad leaves combined with white gravel raked into concentric swirls made a cool, greenish-shadowed retreat. The spot was shunned by barefoot children, nor could anyone sit on the sharp gravel, which left its use to those who preferred to use the benches. The two women headed for the place.

It was a pleasant, quiet oasis from which to view boats and canoes on the water and the activity on the opposite shore. For a nickel Verdie bought a paper fan printed with pink cherubs and red roses. When the small Mexican boy smiled a toothless grin and murmured, "Gracias, Senora," she tipped him a dime, widening the grin from ear to ear.

"It seems to be cooler over here," Verdie said. She waved the cherub fan rapidly before her moist face. "I think the humidity must be higher here in the city." She glanced at Jette for any sign that she wanted to talk. Seeing none, she found an empty bench, dusted the seat with her handkerchief and sat down. Normally neither moody nor sulky, Jette had said hardly a dozen words since lunch. Several times her mother noticed Jette drawing in her lower lip, biting it to hold back tears, but she refrained from pressing for an explanation.

"Now tell me what you bought, dear. I want to hear all about it." Verdie settled back into the bench, unbuttoned her suit jacket and resumed fanning. "Would you like to use this?" She offered the fan to Jette, hoping to break her silence.

"No, thank you," Jette replied. Once started, she continued, "Mother, you were right about Nate." Her chin trembled, but she refused to lose control.

"In what way?"

"I saw him today."

"Here? Here in Los Angeles?" Verdie had guessed as much.

"Yes." It was almost a whisper.

257

"And . . .?"

"And . . . he was with Lavinia Baldwin!"

"Ah," Verdie said and nodded. "So that's it."

"I don't understand!" Jette was close to anger, but there was a catch in her voice. "All those things Asa said about Nate . . . can they be true?"

"I'm sure I don't know, child. Asa has never been one to talk much about anybody, let alone lie. God knows he has his faults, but lying isn't one of them." Before she blundered and said the wrong thing Verdie wanted to know the rest. "Where did you see them?"

"The building the department store's in . . . I took the elevator up instead of down. When we went past the fourth floor I saw them—or at least I think it was them—standing in the vestibule, waiting for the elevator to go back down. It went on up to five and I got off. I didn't want to be on it when they got on."

"Staying on and confronting them would have been a much more sensible thing to do," Verdie said. "You could have demanded an explanation right on the spot. They couldn't have time to fabricate a story that way." After a moment she asked, "Are you sure it was Nate?"

"I'm not positive it was Nate. But it was Lavinia Baldwin. And from what I learned, I'm almost certain it was Nate." Jette took an embroidered handkerchief from her handbag and dabbed at her eyes.

"Did you see him clearly?"

"I ran back down from the fifth floor, just to make sure that's who it was, but the elevator came and they were on their way down by the time I got there." Jette unbuttoned her suit coat and removed it, placing it on the back of the bench.

"Nice young ladies don't remove their coats in public, Jette," Verdie remonstrated with her daughter.

"I'm too hot and too upset to care, Mother!"

Verdie ignored the breach of etiquette and asked, "How can you be certain it was they? I mean, you say

258

you didn't get a good glimpse . . ."

"If you put it that way, no, I didn't. The light wasn't very good. But the woman was all in black, in mourning, and her figure was . . . well, full. You know what I mean."

"Yes, I know Lavinia. She's very buxom," Verdie replied. "She has a fashionable shape, even without corsets, so I've heard. That Mrs. Frielly who sews for us did some sewing for Lavinia this spring. She told me about her." Verdie did not go further into details, feeling it was not quite respectable to discuss such things in public. "What you're saying is that you think it was Lavinia and Nate, but you can't be completely sure. Isn't that so?"

"Yes, I guess so," Jette admitted. "But there's more . . . .I know Nate's involved with a development company, but as you know, too, he's never told us exactly what he does. Whenever I've spoken to him about his work he just tells me I'm not to concern myself with it, that earning the living is his business and I'm not supposed to worry about it—neither the ranch nor the development company."

"That's not too surprising for a man like Nate. He wants to be responsible for his wife and home himself. Any upright young man would feel that way." Verdie found herself defending Nate Trasker for no other reason than to ease Jette's pain.

"It doesn't matter that I resent his attitude. I can cope with that, if that's the way he wants it to be." Jette turned to face her mother, her dark eyes anguished. "Just from curiosity I wanted to see what they could have been doing on that floor and looked at all the offices, up one hall and down the other. Nothing really sounded the sort Nate would be interested in, until I got to the one nearest the elevator—Montague-Cameron Trust. I met a man who has offices on the same floor and he said . . ."

"You didn't strike up a conversation with a strange man, did you?" Her mother was aghast. She stopped fanning, her face pulled into a deep frown.

"I did!" Jette replied with a touch of rebellion. "And he said the description of Nate and Lavinia Baldwin fitted one of Montague-Cameron's employees . . . and his wife."

"Oh, Jette." Verdie was disturbed by the revelation. "Does this man know for sure?" She could only repeat the question. "Does he know these people? Does he know they are man and wife?" It seemed she must play devil's advocate.

"No, he doesn't know them personally. He's only seen them as they come and go."

"Nate Trasker is with the Farrier Development . . ."

"They must be related in some way. This man says they are engaged in what he calls 'unethical' land dealings." Jette did not know whether her mother was up to hearing the entire story, but having gone this far felt she might as well continue. "I spoke to the building manager, too, and he says they've only been here since March. That's about the time Nate came to San Genaro, isn't it?"

Her mother nodded and waited for her to go on.

"The manager, a Mr. Sandberg, told me he has his own money invested with this trust company. He was enthusiastic about it on the surface, but I had the feeling he has misgivings. He doesn't know the people involved, either, or anything about them except that they pay the rent on time. And Mr. Carr . . ."

"Who is he?"

"The man from the fourth floor. He has Carr Medical and Surgical Supply," Jette explained. "He says these land development companies are just short of being criminal."

Verdie gasped, her fingers covering her mouth. "That can't be true!"

"That's not all, Mother." Jette felt she must tell all. "I saw Nate on Las Lomas Road, heading east, a few nights ago." She could not meet her mother's shocked stare. "I just couldn't stand it inside the house . . . so much trouble, everything coming all at once. I ran down the road, all the way to the junction. I ran until I was out of breath and had to stop. I heard a buggy coming and knew how peculiar it might look if somebody saw me—you know how everybody in San Genaro gossips—so I hid in that clump of pepper trees you wouldn't let Asa cut down last year."

"And it was Nate in the buggy? You saw him?"

"Yes, I saw him."

"There was no doubt about it? It definitely was Nate?"

"There was no doubt about it, Mother."

Verdie fanned with agitation, consternation plain on her small face. For a long time neither said a word. Echoing across the water came shouts of children and the occasional bark of dogs. Over on Wilshire a trolley clanged warning as an empty freight wagon lumbered across the rails.

Wheeling in tightening circles as they descended, a flight of pigeons alighted in grass at the water's edge where an elderly man in threadbare canvas coat and trousers fed moldy bread crumbs to mallards and fat white geese. A few gray and white gulls glided down, yellow feet first, to join the alfresco banquet.

Once again Jette had the feeling of life eddying about her, washing about her feet, yet not quite touching her. Overhead, leaves began to quiver with a first tentative whisper of breeze. The hot resinous sycamore smell blended with chocolate-scented oleander. All around her was the city, teeming, noisy, quarreling and loving, but somehow she remained isolated and alone.

"Oh, Mother, what am I to do?" She burst into tears, unashamed as three elderly women on the next bench

261

stared and began to murmur behind their fans. "I love him so much . . ." Verdie took her daughter in her arms, suffering the inquisitive loungers and strollers to peer and speculate. When the paroxysm passed, Verdie handed Jette a clean handkerchief from her handbag.

"If you still love Nate and want to marry him, you're going to have to comport yourself like a real woman. You can't find answers by snooping around office buildings, talking to property managers or men who may just have offices there. And your behavior the night you saw Nate on the road is certainly open to criticism to say the least." Her small features took on an unaccustomed sternness, her chin thrust forward defiantly as had her daughter's.

"Look at me, Jette," Verdie demanded. "No marriage can withstand suspicion and doubt. If you have suspicion and doubt now, it will only get worse. If Nate's innocent of any wrongdoing—and it's just possible he is, in spite of what you've seen and heard—you're doing him a terrible injustice. If he's deceiving you, if he's guilty, then you should know it. You're a woman now, no longer a child. If you loved him enough to give him the most precious thing a woman can give to a man, then you're obliged to be woman enough to confront him honestly. Anything less than that is cowardly and despicable. Go to him, tell him what you've learned. Ask him to explain it, one way or the other. You can acccept what he says or not.

"You know how I've felt about Nate." Verdie took a crystal cologne flacon from her bag, twisted off the cap and shook a few drops onto her handkerchief. "Here, touch this to your face, dear. It will make you feel better." Some of the pain in Jette's face was replaced by a slight smile. Verdie's reliance on a simple dab of cologne to help solve her problems was absurd, but the gesture was loving. She took the bit of lace and embroidery and held it to her temples.

"I've told you how I felt about him," Verdie resumed. "I'll not insist you marry him for propriety's sake. If you truly love him, want to be with him, you must find the truth for yourself, then decide whether you still want to marry him or not."

"But if Mr. Carr says they are man and wife . . ."

"You said he doesn't know for sure. He's never become acquainted with them so he's in no position to know. It's something he has surmised. That's much like gossip, you know."

The wisdom of her mother's words was comforting. There was no solution other than an honest confrontation. "Even feeling the way you do about Nate, you'd want me to marry him?"

Verdie was not sure her advice was sound. Her own mistakes had been monstrous and had led to nothing but unhappiness. It was a while before she replied, "If you love him, yes."

* * * *

Russel Carr was waiting in the lobby of the Imperial. He sat behind a pillar where he could see both the elevators and the main staircase. As he glanced at the clock over the door to the dining room he crushed his second cigar in the sand-filled urn beside his chair. Despite his lounging about the lobby for several hours in the heat, he still maintained his dapper appearance, his high Hanford collar unwilted, his blue and white striped silk bow tie immaculately knotted and tucked beneath his coat. The spats, a dandyish affectation in the California climate, remained spotless below the neatly-creased trousers.

The sun had dipped low enough to create shade on the west side of the street, although the approaching evening did little to reduce the temperature. A slight breeze that swept dirt down the sidewalks afforded little relief either. Most of the shops had already closed and the streets of downtown Los Angeles were emptying of traffic.

Verdie and Jette lingered along the way from the trolley-stop back to the Imperial Hotel. Jette had no appetite for further shopping. Collecting a trousseau would be folly until she could learn the truth about Nate Trasker and Lavinia. Mother and daughter, arm in arm, strolled slowly, window shopping, keeping to the shade as much as possible, saying little to one another. The joy of their morning had been shattered.

"Room 301, please." Jette waited for the key at the desk.

"Miss Allenby?" The clerk handed her the key and smiled as she acknowledged her name with a nod. "A gentleman has been waiting for you in the lobby." He glanced over his steel-rimmed spectacles and spied Carr. "He's over by the stairs." He added as if to explain why the hotel allowed men to loiter in the lobby, "He says you know him."

"Miss Allenby!" Russel Carr rushed to meet them, hat and stick in hand. "Hello, remember me?"

"Of course, Mr. Carr. Mother, this is Mr. Carr, the gentleman who helped me this morning. Mr. Carr, my mother." Astonished to see the man again, Jette was pleased as he took Verdie's hand. His hair lay in waves that looked as if all attempts to comb them straight had failed. Thick and almost white, his hair and neatly trimmed moustache provided startling contrast to his tanned face and wide-set eyes. There was a comfortable hint of thickening about the middle, although he retained the look and movement of an athletic, active man.

"I'm delighted to meet you, Mrs. Allenby." He did not relinquish Verdie's hand until she began to appear flustered. "I should have known when I met your daughter that her mother would be equally lovely."

"What a charming thing to say, Mr. Carr," Verdie said. "I must thank you for coming to her aid this morning."

"Most welcome," he replied, not taking his eyes from Verdie. Then as though remembering what had kept him waiting to see them so long, he said. "That's why I stopped by to see you this afternoon. Miss Allenby mentioned you were staying at the Imperial and I took the liberty of dropping by."

"You mean you've been waiting for us?" Verdie asked.

"I confess I have. You see, your daughter asked me about one of the companies in our building—the Montague-Cameron Trust—and I managed to find out something that might be of interest to her." He turned to Jette and said, "You'll forgive me, my dear, but I didn't quite believe you when you told me you wanted to see your friend, Margaret Larson. I felt you were really interested in the Trust. When I discovered you'd been to the building manager, asking some very probing and intelligent questions, I thought I might do well to make a few inquiries of my own. Shall we sit over here, ladies?"

Carr escorted them to a secluded corner furnished with writing desks and rattan chairs. Without waiting for them to reply, he continued, "I was afraid you might have been approached by someone to invest in the Trust, and Mr. Sandberg, the building manager, confirmed my belief. Please do forgive my intefering, ladies, but I couldn't rest easy if you were to lose money in one of these development schemes due to my remaining silent."

"But that wasn't . . ." Jette started to interrupt.

"It's perfectly all right, Miss Allenby. You needn't tell me one word. Just let me finish and I'll bid you good evening and know my conscience is clear."

"Very well, Mr. Carr," Verdie said. "Please go on."

Jette was amazed at the warmth of her mother's smile. The man was extraordinarily attractive, but he was, after all, a stranger and Verdie had only hours before scolded her for speaking to him.

"I checked about with some of the building personnel and the secretarial service on the sixth floor. They do a lot of work for the smaller offices in our building, especially the ones that have no secretarial staff of their own."

"And you found . . ." Jette prompted him.

"You'd asked about the couple you saw," he reminded her. "I found they're both connected with the Trust in some way. They come here to Los Angeles frequently, I'm told. As a matter of fact, they stay right here in the Imperial. Have you run into them yet?"

For a moment Jette could not answer. "No, we haven't seen them," she managed to reply in a nonchalant way. Impatient as she was to hear the rest of his revelation, she dreaded what he might say. "Just who are these people?" she asked.

"The woman is from San Genaro. You undoubtedly know who she is—Mrs. Hiram Baldwin. The man's name is Trasker . . . Nate Trasker. I understand he is from Chicago."

Chapter 12

Maximilian of Dundee lowered his massive black head into the grain trough and scooped up a mouthful with his raspy tongue. His jaws worked sideways as contented sounds rumbled from deep in his chest. Severo Mireles scratched the huge animal's pate and gave him an extra measure of grain.

"You're spoiling that beast rotten, Severo," Asa

266

Beemer said.

Severo's grin was wide in his dark face as the ranch foreman made his way down the barn to Old Max's stall. "He was a good boy today." The Mexican youth caressed the animal's thick neck.

Asa slumped against the white-washed board wall, his lean frame sagging from shoulders to oiled stoga boots. "You mean the agents from La Maravilla?"

"You make a deal with 'em?" Severo asked.

"They have to make the deal with Miss Jette. I don't have any say in that part of it."

"She's going to keep Old Max, then? She won't send him to the slaughterhouse?"

"Not likely! She's a sensible girl." Beemer reached across the partition and scratched the bull's silky ears. "Now there're a lot of women who'd panic and make pot roast out of him, but she isn't cruel and she isn't foolish." Asa pulled a tiny cloth bag from his hip pocket, extracted a thin sheet of paper from the packet on the back of the sack and rolled himself a cigarette, wetting the paper on his tongue and pinching the wrapper closed around the crumbly tobacco. "She'll keep Old Max. He's gonna die of old age, just having the time of his life." The men chuckled as the bull raised his head and lowed, his mouth drooling saliva.

"You need me any more, I'll be up to the house," Asa said. "I'm going over the records with Miss Jette, then I'll see Benito about orders for the store."

"Yes, sir." The young man forked sweet-smelling straw onto the floor of the stall. "Miss Jette going to buy that new windmill for the west pasture?"

"The steel tower one?"

"The one that tilts."

"Yeah, she ordered it. She's not afraid to spend money on improvements. She's just like Elias that way." Asa found a match in his shirt pocket, but waited until he was well away from the barn before lighting it with his thumbnail. He shielded the flame with his fist

267

and paused long enough to light the homemade smoke as he ambled back toward the adobe.

He had asked no questions last night when Jette and her mother returned early from Los Angeles. He did not wish to be reminded by Jette again that such things were no concern of his. Nor had he missed Nate Trasker's look of well controlled surprise yesterday afternoon when he had stopped by to see Jette and found she had gone to Los Angeles. It had seemed to Asa that Trasker had become uneasy when told of their trip. A tightening of the mouth, an exaggerated steadiness of Trasker's eyes, convinced Beemer that the information had caught him off guard.

Beemer had never resumed taking his meals in the dining room with the women after Elias' death. His tenure was subject for speculation at best and he did not want to jeopardize his position further by antagonizing Jette. That they needed him, he knew. The pay continued as before; his room was comfortable and kept spotlessly clean for him; the food was plentious and good—even though he ate alone in the kitchen. Socorro and Benito Galvan and little Elvira Mireles treated him with kindness and respect. He would not complain.

The door to the office was propped open so what little breeze there was could air the small room. Jette, in pale pink blouse, gray skirt and cerise cummerbund, sat at the desk, account books lying open before her. It pained Beemer to see blue circles beneath her eyes and the still puffy, reddened lids. During the night he had tiptoed to her bedroom door and stood listening as she wept. Furious at his inability to win the girl for himself, more furious that she would not heed his warnings about Trasker, he returned to his own room and emptied a quart of bourbon.

Sitting at Elias' heavy oak desk seemed to reduce Jette's size. Now as Asa looked at her, she seemed small and delicate, her deep-red hair tucked into an elongated

French twist, the ends pinned in a small tight roll across her head. Severe and businesslike, the coiffure enhanced the perfect oval of her face. She glanced up without smiling as Asa came down the hall and into the office.

"Sit down," she said as she picked up a pen. "I'm just writing a check for the new windmill." She signed her name and blotted the ink. "Before I mail this, are you sure it's the right one for the west pasture?"

"Water's there, all right, but it's down pretty deep. This one has steel bearings and a good tower. Jake Larson has one in his feed lot. Says it does a real good job and doesn't take much maintenance." He heaved himself into Elias' old leather chair.

"I looked over the advertisements and specifications when Mr. Van Vliet drove out the other day," Jette said. "I'm learning, but I don't know that much about it yet. I'm taking your word, Asa." It was a challenge, not of his honesty as so often before, but of his knowledge.

"Like I told you, it just has to do with the best type for the location. You have to consider the angle . . . the curvature . . . amount of sail surface." Asa would not talk down to the girl. Not only would she recognize and resent such condescension, it would alienate him even further. This he wanted to avoid. "Then there's resistance of air to rotation . . . shape of the vanes . . . things like that. Now if the water table was deeper, or apt to drop much, we'd do best to take another kind. I think this one's what we need." He tapped a finger on the invoice that lay on the corner of the desk.

"Fine. That's settled." Jette placed the check in an envelope and sealed the flap. "Will we need any of our own men on the job?"

"No, ma'am. Old Van Vliet has a good crew to do it all—digging and erection. We don't need to do any more than keep an eye on things while they do the work." Asa could not suppress the urge that lifted his wide mouth into a lop-sided grin. Jette glanced over at him, annoyed by the expression she surprised on his face.

"Maybe you'd better tell me what's so funny," she said.

"I'm not grinning because it's funny, Miss Jette," he drawled. "It's just that it's mighty pleasant dealing with a lady. I have to tell you right out, folks weren't too sure you could take hold. I told 'em you could—and would. I'm glad you're proving me right." His long muscular legs were spread wide, his elbows on his knees, hands clasped before him as he leaned forward in the chair. There was a band of lighter skin on his forehead where the hat he habitually wore prevented tanning. Unruly brown hair, too long to be considered neat or fashionable, was creased flat by the hatband. Asa Beemer was —even at a casual glance from a city dweller—a ranch man. He was not the sort of man who could be comfortable either making or enduring polite small talk in a damask-and-mahogany parlor. Right now he wanted to say something nice, but facing Jette Allenby's black, intense eyes, he found he could utter no banal compliments. "You're doing real fine," he finally said. "Old Elias would be proud of you."

She looked quickly away and her fingers clenched into white-knuckled fists in her lap. "I take that as a consummate compliment, Asa."

"That's how I meant it." Usually closed in a squint against the sun, his eyes now were wide as he looked at the girl. In her pink blouse, her hair pinned tight to the top of her head, he wanted her. He wanted her so badly he could almost feel the smoothness of her naked body against him, feel the softness of her thighs and breasts beneath his rough hands. Aware of his stare, she turned back to the account books, her face flushing crimson.

From the highway came the sound of horses and buggy. Brass harness bells jingled down the driveway as the dogs ran out to greet the arrival. Jette swiveled in the desk chair and pulled back the curtain at the west window. She did not recognize the glossy black piano-box buggy or the pair of bays. The wide, fluffy sea-green hat, however, was familiar.

"We'll have to go over the books later," she said and pushed back from the desk.

"Who's that coming?" Asa bent beside her to look out the window.

"Mrs. Millege, judging by the hat," Jette replied.

"Handles those bays right well, doesn't she?" He watched as the woman pulled up before the adobe. "Didn't know she'd be out driving alone." He said it with admiration. "I'll go see to the team."

"Yes, please do." Jette smoothed her hair and tucked in the back of the pink blouse where it had worked out of the cummerbund. "Elvira!" she called out to the kitchen where she could hear the girl talking with Socorro. "Elvira!" She ran to the dining room as the girl came from the kitchen.

"Ask Socorro to make tea for us. Mrs. Millege just drove up." Jette opened the china cupboard doors and took down the silver tea service and put it on the table.

"You want the Darjeeling tea or the China-green?"

"The Darjeeling . . . and sandwiches."

Elvira bobbed her head in reply and dashed back to the kitchen. Jette crossed the living room and entered the back parlor where her mother lay napping. She pulled back the drapes and raised the blinds. "Mother, we have a visitor."

Verdie started from the chaise in fright. "Who? Who is it?" she asked, a shadow of the old confusion crossing her face as she struggled to rouse from her nap.

"It's Mrs. Millege."

"Ziphia?" Verdie slipped into her high, cloth-topped shoes and rummaged in the top drawer of a small escritoire which she was using as a dressing table.

Finding the pearl-handled button hook, she asked, "What on earth must she want? Is Ainsworth with her?"

"No, she's alone."

"Driving alone? That's not like Ziphia." Verdie's face grew red from bending over as she fastened her shoes. "She'd never come uninvited unless it's important."

"Hurry and come out when you're ready. I'll go let her in," Jette said. "I'll tell her you were resting."

Verdie searched for a comb and began to tidy up her disarranged hair. "Have Socorro make something to serve."

"Yes, Mother." Jette did not linger long enough to explain that she had already ordered tea and sandwiches.

Ziphia Millege accepted Asa's hand as she clambered down from the buggy. Walking up the steps, she removed a long chiffon scarf with which she had secured the mountainous hat to her head. Her ample figure, cinched about the waist by whalebone and laces, was all but hidden by a white muslin dust coat which enveloped her champagne-colored pongee calling suit. That she had set about her trip hastily was evident in the dusting of face powder which had been left in rachel smudges on her round cheeks and forehead. Nor were her tan leather driving gloves chosen to match her attire, but had been seized and donned without thought.

"Hand me that envelope from the seat, Asa," Mrs. Millege said. She stuffed the white chiffon scarf into the pocket of the dust coat and retraced her steps back to the buggy.

"Yes, ma'am." Asa gave her the large envelope. "Mighty nice team. New, aren't they?" He stroked the rump of the fat bay gelding, whose great gluteal muscle shivered under his hand.

"My husband just bought them through Abe

Marley," she replied. "It's an extravagance, but since he swears they're as much for my benefit as his, how could I disapprove?" She was in a rush, but did not wish to seem rude to the ranch manager. "Are Jette and Mrs. Allenby at home?"

"Yes, ma'am. Miss Jette will be with you right away," Asa answered. "I'll just put the horses over there out of the sun." He tipped his hat and led the team to the dense shade around the bend of the drive. He looped the reins in the hitching post's iron ring, then headed toward the cattle barn, cutting across the orchard behind the house. He smiled to himself as he wondered about the postmark he had seen on the envelope—the envelope that seemed to have precipitated the urgent journey of the banker's wife.

Clutching the envelope in her hand, Ziphia Millege hurried up the steps to the front door. Before she could twist the brass key of the door bell to announce her arrival, Jette flung open the door in welcome.

"Mrs. Millege, what a pleasant surprise!" Jette ushered the woman into the parlor and helped her out of the dust coat which she placed in the armoire beside the door. "Wouldn't you like to take your hat off, too?" she asked.

"No, dear, if I took it off I'd never get it back on right. I came out of the house so fast I didn't take the time to pin my hair up and just plopped my hat on willy-nilly." She was breathless with excitement. "You'll have to forgive my coming like this, but as soon as the mail came, I dashed right out."

"There's nothing to forgive. You're always welcome any time," Jette said. "Mother will be with us in a minute. She's been resting." Jette could not miss the incongruous tan gloves and the haste of the woman's toilette. "Won't you sit down?"

"May we go into the sitting room? It's so cozy in there."

273

"Certainly." Jette led the way to the left and waited for the woman to enter the smaller room. Afternoon sunlight made dappled patterns on the patio outside, and bouquets of roses and jessamine perfumed the air. It was a perfect room for an intimate chat.

"Oh, I do so love this room," Mrs. Millege said. "It's just like your mother—delicate and a bit fragile. Not at all like the rest of the house. These old adobes always seem so overpowering with their thick walls and so much stone and tile."

"The only time is isn't pleasant is in the winter when it rains. The fireplace doesn't draw too well and it's hard to get it warm in here." Jette knew she must make conversation until the woman could decide to approach the reason for her sudden visit. She waited for Ziphia Millege to be seated on the damask settee, then took a chair opposite her. "Isn't that a new team you drove up in?" she asked.

"Yes, it is. Abe Marley knew of one for sale over in San Gallan and arranged for Ainsworth to buy it. Traded our other team to Elmer Fee. I didn't like the idea of good carriage horses going to a dairy, but Ainsworth says Elmer Fee babies his route horses like a tender, loving mother. I do hope he's right." She sighed and relaxed into the damask cushions. "But that's not what I came to talk about, Jette." She held the envelope for the girl to see. "This . . . this is what I drove out for."

"I don't understand."

"Of course you don't, dear." Ziphia Millege cast an apprehensive look toward the parlor. "Is your mother well enough to hear, shall we say, 'unpleasant' matters?"

"I think so," Jette said. She could not help frowning as she glanced at the envelope in the woman's hand. "Mother is really much better, you know."

"I'm glad to hear it. I'm not one to speak ill of the

dead, but I must say your father—in my opinion—was a lot to blame for her troubles. He shouldn't have kept her so isolated out here on the ranch. It's just not a natural life for a woman who's used to city living.'' She removed the elastic band that closed the envelope and took out the contents. "Perhaps before she joins us we should discuss these.''

"What are they?'' Jette was mystified as she saw what appeared to be a letter and some newspaper clippings.

"You remember my cousin, Daisy Howard, from Ohio? She was visiting us over the Fourth of July . . .'' She waited expectantly.

Jette nodded, saying, "Yes, I remember her very well.''

"Well, she was certain she'd seen someone out here somewhere else.'' Ziphia laughed at her own awkward explanation. "That doesn't make much sense, the way I say it, does it?'' Without waiting for Jette to agree, she went on, "Daisy promised to look into a matter for me when she got back to Cincinnati—more to prove herself right than to actually do me any good. She said she'd go to the newspaper office and let me know what she discovered.''

"And she did?'' Jette pointed to the clippings.

"Yes, she did.'' Ziphia Millege was almost apologetic and hesitated uncertainly. "I'm not at all sure I should be doing this, but I think it's too important to ignore.'' She betrayed her consternation by shaking her head, all but toppling the sea-green hat. "After all, you are going to marry the man, so you have a right to know . . .''

For a moment Jette sat stunned. She had known it was something critically imperative to bring the woman out as far as the ranch so unexpectedly. Ziphia Millege was not an irresponsible, flighty sort, not the type to take off in late afternoon and travel many miles just to make idle gossip. Jette could now guess the reason for her errand.

"Daisy said she'd seen Nate Trasker before," Ziphia continued. "She couldn't place where it was, but she recognized him from somewhere. These clippings are the story of how some man bilked a woman in Cincinnati of a lot of money and then disappeared. It seems this woman was under the impression the man was going to marry her and she loaned him the money for some scheme he was working on. Then he upped and disappeared—taking her money along with him. No explanation, no nothing." She held the newspaper columns out to the girl. "I think you should read these for yourself, Jette."

* * * *

"Harness the buggy for me, Benito," Jette said as soon as the elderly man entered the office from the hallway. "I'll drive myself," she answered his unspoken query. "Have it brought around to the front as soon as it's ready."

"But Miss Jette, it will be dark before you can return. Let me or Severo drive you in." He knew it was useless to suggest she have Asa Beemer take her to town. He placed the key to the store in its customary place in the safe.

"Thank you. You're very kind," she said and shook her head. "This is one time I must do things for myself." She had already changed into a mannish beige suit, white lawn guimpe, and flat straw boater with blue band and rosette. Although her preparations were hasty, she was careful to select her wardrobe with restraint. Remembering the elaborately soutached and beaded black costumes of Lavinia Baldwin, Jette deliberately picked her most severely tailored, least embellished outfit. She pulled the shades in the office and rolled the desk top down.

"To please an old man, let me drive you to town," Benito pleaded. "Your mother will worry—and so shall I."

"No, Benito." To soften her refusal she said, "I do wish you and Socorro would stay up at the house for a while. I have no idea how late I may be. Mrs. Millege said I might stay overnight with them if necessary. I've already asked Elvira to stay all night with Mother, just in case, but I'd feel much better knowing you and Socorro were close by."

"Yes, Miss Jette." He looked downcast, his thin face evincing concern. "Which buggy do you want? The trap might be easier to handle alone, or do you want the phaeton and the sorrels?"

"The trap will be fine. And give me Blue, she's not so apt to give me any trouble." She knew the blue roan mare was the most reliable harness horse in the stables.

"Yes, Miss Jette." The old man turned to go. "I'll bring it around right away." As he left he asked, "Did you decide about the offer on Old Max from La Maravilla?"

"No, not yet. I think they'll come up to our price if we let them wait. They want to crossbreed those Hereford heifers to a good blood-line. I can't see any reason to lower his fees. If we do it for La Maravilla, we'll have to do it for everybody. They'll come around."

He nodded and left. How like her father she was, he thought. Even without being schooled in ranch business by Elias, his daughter had made the same decision that he would have made. And how like Elias she was in her decision to drive alone into town to settle her personal matters.

Elvira had heard only part of the conversation in the sitting room when she had served tea. She had only been able to relay the fact that Nate Trasker seemed to be involved in some sort of fraudulent land transactions. Mrs. Allenby, the little maid whispered, had remained in the sitting room long after the banker's wife had left—still was there, staring blankly out the window toward the sunset.

Benito did not hurry to the stables. He had no desire to aid the girl in her headstrong rush into trouble.

* * * *

The small gray mare trotted steadily south along the highway, her dainty, freshly-shod hoofs crunching lightly in the pea gravel. To the west a flaming sunset fired the sparsely-clouded sky a brilliant orange that faded quickly to crimson, then lavender. Meadowlarks sang from the fence rows and swallows plunged in vertical sweeps to capture moths and gnats in the calm evening air. Heat absorbed by day now radiated from the roadbed and a cloud of dust trailed the light two-wheeled carriage as it headed for San Genaro.

Jette held the long, flexible whip in her right hand, the harness reins in her left. Grasping something in both hands kept her mind off the envelope on the seat beside her.

Ziphia Millege was sure Nate Trasker was in town. She had seen him only that very morning in front of Murdock's Drug Store. *Why had he not returned to see her*, Jette wondered. He had called to see her at the ranch at the same time she and Verdie were on the train coming home from Los Angeles. They had missed him by only a few hours. Had Nate returned to La Coruna, he surely would have sought to see her on his way back to town.

Over and over in her mind Jette considered the bits and pieces of information she had gathered. Daisy Howard could not be positive Nate was the same man suspected of absconding with funds entrusted to him in Cincinnati. Indeed, Daisy admitted she could not identify him with any certainty even when she had spoken with him several times during her visit to the Milleges. And yet when Jette had mentioned that Mrs. Howard was from Ohio, Nate's reaction had been strange.

Too many things fit together. And there was voluptuous Lavinia Baldwin, lonely, beautiful, with property Nate coveted. If Asa Beemer were right in his accusations, Nate wanted—and got—more from Lavinia than Hiram Baldwin's ranch.

"You can't live with uncertainty, Jette," her mother had said. "You owe Nate at least the courtesy of hearing what he may have to say. Men have been hanged on such evidence. Men have died because of rumors and gossip . . . innocent men . . ."

Verdie had blanched white and turned away from her daughter. She clasped her hands in her lap, her fingertips red with the pressure exerted as she endeavored to maintain control. "If you mean to dwell in peace and happiness, you've got to face things honestly. You say you love Nate Trasker—then go to him!"

Jette had left her mother in the sitting room. She had sensed there was something else Verdie wanted to tell her, but seemed unable to continue. Far too upset about her own immediate problem, Jette had not pressed the matter.

It had grown dark by the time Jette reached the outskirts of San Genaro. Calle Aluin marked the limit of the Allenby holdings on the west and the Baldwin ranch on the east. Cornelius Van Vliet's Feed and Grain Supply spread to the left, taking up the entire block to Lopez Street. To the right Elmer Fee's dairy occupied acreage all the way to Keogh Street. Even with no wind to carry the smell, the air was heavy with the odor of cattle droppings. A huge manure spreader was parked in a corner of the feedlot near the fence, ready for loading next morning. Truck gardeners from farms on Rancho

Mariano south of town made Fee enough profit on the manure to keep barns, sheds, fences, and house immaculately painted. The dairy buildings loomed ghostly white as Jette drove past.

Across the street she could see the outlines of Van Vliet's warehouses. Lamplight shone from the lower floor of the Dutchman's house which sat apart from the storage facilities, but not so far removed that he could not keep an eye on his business from his dining room table.

Gas street lamps cast a weak yellow glow at the intersections beginning with Station Street. Soon electric lights would replace gas, and would be strung to the city limits. Abe Marley had been instrumental in getting the city to agree to contract for the electricity. It did not matter that he was a County man. That he was a major shareholder in the power plant did matter. San Genaro could soon boast of its municipal lighting system, and the newly expanded power plant of its increased dividends. Until then, however, the gas lamps did little to dispel the dark.

There were few vehicles of any kind on the streets. It was suppertime for most families, bedtime for small children. A derby-hatted young man wheeled across the intersection on a jouncing bicycle as Jette approached the courthouse square at McKinley Street. Several restaurants were still open, their brightly illuminated windows providing additional light along the way. Pedestrians looked up in surprise to see a woman—Jette Allenby, at that—driving alone.

Jette had slowed Blue at the edge of town in compliance with the five-mile-an-hour speed limit. Rankled at the necessity of slackening her speed, she consoled herself that it would cool down the horse before they stopped. At the corner of Alameda she turned left, passed Union, and halted in front of the Swift Hotel at the corner of Hoffman. Before she could alight from the buggy the hotel porter jumped from the porch, took the reins from her hands and helped her down.

"Thank you kindly, Miss." The old man accepted the ten cent tip, pocketing it as he tied the mare to the hitching rail that ran the length of the hotel. Without waiting for him to assist her up the wooden steps which led to the glass-fronted entrance, Jette lifted her skirt and hurried into the lobby.

A white-haired war pensioner, permanent resident of the Swift Hotel, looked up from the checker game under one of the porch lights. He batted at a large moth that fluttered down from the round, frosted electric globe overhead. "Ain't that Elias Allenby's girl?"

"Sure looks like her." A younger man, in an ill-fitting linen suit that had once been white, let his eyes inventory the girl's physical assets as she passed them and entered the lobby.

"Think so?" A short, red-gallused man, his shirt collar so tight it seemed to be choking the fat of his neck, turned to stare after her. "You sure that's who she is?" he whispered.

"Ain't sure, but it looks like her all right." The old man tilted his straight-backed chair to see into the lobby. "By damn, I wonder what she's up to." He scooted his chair into a better position in order to watch proceedings.

"It's her." Another young man, seated a few steps away on one of the benches, walked over to the players. "I've seen her in the store plenty of times." The lanky clerk from Raizes Department Store hoped it would add something to his reputation as a man of the world to claim acquaintanceship with the beauteous Jette Allenby. "Even waited on her myself."

"Did you now?" The old man chuckled and poked a bony forefinger into the clerk's lean ribs. "You sell her some of that fancy underwear you got? She let you help her try it on maybe?"

The fat man laughed until he wheezed. "I'd like to try something on her, and it ain't no fancy underwear!" He began to cough and sat back, running a finger about his collar.

"Reckon it wouldn't be healthy to do much talking like that around town if old Elias was alive." The pensioner stopped grinning as he said the rancher's name. "Leastways, I wouldn't want him catching me saying nothing like that." He looked somber and reached into his hip pocket, withdrawing a flat bottle and passing it to the asthmatic. "Here, take a nip of this. That'll set you up good."

"Thanks, John." The fat man swigged the whiskey, handed it back saying, "Much obliged." He wiped his mouth with the back of his hand and said, "Why, look there, she's leaving already. Now just what you suppose she wanted?"

"Appears to me you're acting almighty like some curious old woman, Homer," the old man laughed. "Why don't you just go ask her?"

"Not me!" the fat man said with shuddering emphasis. "I got enough troubles of my own."

"What do you mean?" The young clerk sat down beside the checker opponents and leaned forward as if to make their conversation conspiratorial. He sensed he would have a bit of fascinating gossip to pass around at Raizes next day. "How come you to say that?" he asked again.

"Why, that Allenby girl's pure trouble, son." The man unfastened his collar to breathe easier and took a small paper packet of Cubeb cigarettes from his pocket, offered them around, and being refused, lighted one for himself. The boy waited for him to explain what he'd meant. "You know a man—name of Asa Beemer?"

The boy shook his head and the man went on, "That's just one reason she's trouble. And then some says that new doctor—the one as took over Doc Hill's practice—well, some says he's a mind to marry that girl. And she's set on marrying a man named Nate Trasker—him that's living here at the hotel.'' The beefy little man inhaled the herbal smoke and held it for long moments, then exhaled slowly through his nose. The boy waited for him to continue. ''Now if anybody was to really want trouble, he couldn't look farther and find no better than Asa Beemer. He's from New Mexico.''

''What's that got to do with anything?'' the clerk asked.

''Pretty rough territory. Pretty rough times, too.'' The old pensioner nodded as if he understood perfectly.

''Asa Beemer's wrangled and bossed around the Territory and here in San Genaro—for Elias Allenby. He ain't no man to set back and say, 'Thank you kindly' when some city fella comes along and takes his woman right out from under him. No sir!''

''Who's this Beemer?'' The younger man moved closer and pulled up a chair to sit beside them.

''You're new in town yourself, ain't you?''

''Yeah. Come last spring.'' He looked puzzled.

''Beemer's foreman and manager on the Allenby ranch. He was old Elias' right arm a good many years now,'' the pensioner said. ''Hey, look at there . . .''

''She's leaving . . .''

They watched as Jette hurried from the desk in the lobby. The elderly porter trailed behind her, then darted in front and helped her back into the trap and handed her the reins. He eased Blue backwards, holding her headstall until the buggy was maneuvered back into the street. He saluted smartly as the girl flicked the mare and drove off.

''Hey, Silas!'' Cubeb in hand, Homer Baumgarner motioned the porter to the checkers table. ''What'd she want? Where's she going in such an all fired hurry?''

''You ain't gonna believe this!'' The porter's laugh

was a dry cackle as he came up the steps. "She's going out Hurley Road!"

"She's never!"

"Yup, she is." He cackled again as he added, "Out to Harriet Selby's place."

The men on the porch sat in shocked silence and watched the yellow-wheeled buggy speed east and turn north when it reached Hurley Road. John Perks, the pensioner, took out his bottle and gulped down another stiff shot. "You're right, Homer. There's gonna be trouble," he said. "Did you see the look on her face when she come out?"

"I did, John. I did for a fact."

"If she's going to Harriet's, there's gonna be trouble."

* * * *

Hurley Road was a mean part of town, with railroad tracks running almost parallel, then slanting away, giving place to commercial stables, blacksmith shops, carriage and cabinet makers, and finally, between Fresno and Lopez Streets—Harriet Selby's place. Like its owner, it stood baroque and full-blown on its full city block of land. Carefully tended gardens surrounded it on all sides, their rotation of bloom providing lush decoration for dining room, gaming rooms, and parlors as well as the numerous bedrooms upstairs. It was painted a soft blue-gray with trim in sparkling white. Wide, shallow steps led up to the tile-floored porch that curved about the corner of the mansion to provide a view of the gardens. Fluted white wooden columns held the porch roof and rose in grandeur to form a second story balcony on the side away from the street. Dainty filigree railing, more reminiscent of Louisiana planations than California ranch country, was entwined with scarlet-flowered trumpet vines and rambler roses.

284

Had the business of the owner and the occupation of the inhabitants been otherwise, the mansion would have been considered the prize of San Genaro.

By night Hurley Road hid its ugliness. Lamplight pricked the dark here and there, and the newly installed electric lights at the railway station brightened its immediate vicinity. Jette urged the gray mare toward the brilliance that marked the notorious house of pleasure, resolution grim on her lovely face.

"Mr. Trasker? No, Miss, he's not in right now," the desk clerk at the hotel had said. "He left about half an hour ago. Mr. Marley stopped by and picked him up in his carriage." What he omitted from the information was that Lavinia Baldwin had accompanied the men.

"Have you any idea where I might find them?" Jette asked.

Jette had not needed to say it was important. The clerk could see that for himself. He was relieved when he could say, "Just as they were leaving I overheard them tell our porter that they were playing cards this evening."

"Where would that be?" Jette persisted.

He suddenly wondered if he should be repeating what he had heard. The virtue of silence in his line of work was wise, if not absolutely necessary. "I'm sure I'm not betraying any confidence," he decided aloud. "They were quite open about it, so I suppose it's all right to tell you." He leaned across the register and confided, "There's always a big poker game this time of month." Then he said in a lowered tone, "Politics, you know. County men have a little get-together, then have a friendly game somewhere." He imparted the intelligence with the relish of an inveterate gossip.

"Where?" She saw he was hesitant to reveal the game's location. "Really, I must know." There was something in her voice that warned him; something in the way her lower lids crept up a fraction of an inch over her black eyes—a momentary narrowing. He would tell her. He wanted no trouble at the hotel.

"I don't know how to put it delicately to a young lady like yourself." He tried to laugh, but succeeded in only an inarticulate, strangled whinny. At the flash of irritation in those penetrating dark eyes that pinioned him for answer, he continued, "They hold their game up at Harriet Selby's . . . ah . . . home." He winced, but added, "Up on Hurley Road, you know." His smile was sickly as he tried to amend his utterance. "But of course you'd not know, would you? Dear me . . . it's north seven blocks from here."

"I know where it is." The line of her mouth tightened, the soft, full, red lips pulled back against her teeth. "Thank you very much." She started to leave, but turned back to him and said, "You needn't worry about telling me where they are. I shan't say how I found out." At the man's look of relief she could almost smile. "Thank you. Good evening."

"Good evening, Miss." The paunchy desk clerk jerked a carefully folded handkerchief from his breast pocket and mopped his forehead and the back of his neck. He had committed a transgression for which he might have to pay. As he watched the girl whirl and stride through the lobby, then drive off in the light trap, he resolved that he'd much rather have to answer to Nate Trasker and Abe Marley then Elias Allenby's auburn-haired daughter.

Jette was surprised at her own state of calm. She should be seething. Her fury and hurt should be shaking her into weeping hysterics. Instead she felt a determination, sustained as much by hope as by anger, to ferret out the truth no matter what the consequences. It was as though she was being driven by a force beyond herself—a force like that which had driven her to defy her father, to confront him even in his drunken rages. She would face Nate Trasker the same way . . . now, tonight.

A tinkling, choppy two-step was being hammered out on the upright piano in the side parlor as Jette pulled up before Harriet Selby's mansion. Faceted cobalt-blue and wisteria-lavender glass, its beveled edges precisely leaded into a graceful fleurs-de-lys design, prevented anyone seeing through the ornate front door into the foyer. Jette could discern movement on the other side of the door, however, as she handed the reins to the elderly Negro who materialized from the dark at one side of the front steps. He handed her down from the buggy and watched in amazement as she made for the porch.

"You don't want to go in there, Miss," he said as he saw who she was. He shook his head and edged in front of her. "You're a nice young lady, you run along home. This ain't no fit place for the likes of you." His face in the blue and lavender light shining through the closed door looked like polished ebony, his eyes sad and reproving.

"But I must go in." She sidestepped the old man and strode across the porch to the door. She turned and said, "I must—and I shall."

"Your daddy wouldn't like it none if you was to go inside."

"My father's dead." Jette was amazed at how easily she could say it.

"I know, Miss. I'm sorry he's gone." The old man's voice left no doubt as to his sincerity.

Jette considered the man with curiosity. "I knew Father came here now and then, but why should you be sorry?" she asked gently.

"He was good to me." It was a simple answer, from a simple man. Elias had not needed to be kind to anyone, certainly not to old Emmanuel Hazlitt. That he had been, and that he was remembered with respect and affection by Harriet Selby's footman brought a sudden pang of remorse. "Please, Miss, don't you go in there.

You want to see somebody, you let me ask them to step out here on the porch.''

"There's a poker game here tonight. I want to see someone who's here to play—Nate Trasker.'' She did not want the man to get into trouble, yet she remained adamant in her intent.

"I'll go see if he's come yet. You just set down and make yourself comfortable and I'll be right back.'' Emmanuel Hazlitt seemed relieved as Jette perched on the edge of one of the wicker settees that decorated the darkened porch. "That's right, Miss.'' For a brief moment the door stood open as he went inside.

Harsh blue-white light from the crystal chandelier's hissing mantle-lamp glaringly illuminated eddies of tobacco smoke that issued from windows to the right of the door. Over the refrain and melody of a piano-roll waltz from the side parlor came soprano giggles and ribald, baritone laughter. Blinds of the parlors were pulled down only to the middle of the panes, with lamplight shining through the open lower half. There was no breeze and the flounced lace curtains hung motionless in the stifling heat.

A white tomcat, its fur combed to fluffy perfection, sat on the window sill, half-way between the light and dark. Jette watched as the cat lifted first one paw, then the other in its lazy, nocturnal ablutions. A thin red collar from which depended a tiny silver harness-bell encircled the animal's neck. The cat gave the bell a few desultory licks with its rough pink tongue and jumped from the sill into a soft-cushioned chair on the porch outside.

How like that cat I am, Jette thought. *But if I jump* . . . Jette wondered if ever there could be a safe place to which she might jump, a place of comfort and security.

At the sound of heavy steps on the petunia-edged walk leading up to the porch she abandoned the cat and turned to see who Harriet Selby's customer might be. Even in the dark she could distinguish the man's hulking outlines. He was taller than her father had been, his shoulders wider, with an aggressive squareness. An arrogant sway in his determined walk suggested he was drunk. Slack jaw and vacant, unfocused stare testified that he had already patronized a few of San Genaro's saloons before getting the urge to visit Hurley Road. His hand reached for the doorbell. He succeeded only in jamming his knuckles into the woodwork three inches from the mark.

"Goddam!" he swore aloud and tried again. Again he missed. For a moment he stood, dogged in his resolve to announce his presence. He doubled up his fist, held it before his eyes and prepared to hammer on the door. Jette turned her head from him, a kindness to save the man embarrassment.

"Well, now, what've we got out here . . . and all alone?" He let his fist fall and craned his neck, a move that disturbed his precarious balance. He stumbled, his feet refusing to accompany him across the porch. With the weight of his heavy trunk slamming his knees into the tiled flooring, he bellowed in pain and frustration, but he crawled on all fours toward the girl.

"Hey, I ain't seen you here before, have I?" He grinned ear to ear as he focused on her. The hand he rested on the arm of her chair was broad and thick-fingered. He transferred the hand to her knee. "Must be a new girl, huh?"

"No, I am not," Jette stammered and slid out of the chair.

"Been here all the time? Where's Harriet been keeping you?" He was good looking in a rough way, with curly dark hair that fell in ringlets from a wide, square forehead. The fact that Harriet's girls usually fought over his attentions had assured him of his welcome . . . until tonight. "I asked you a question,

289

honey," he said, sounding like a disappointed child. "Ain't you gonna even answer me?" The pout was ludicrous on a man of his size.

With one mighty effort he tried to heave himself erect, bracing himself on the chair as he did so. The chair overturned between them. He looked down at the obstruction, then up at her, a slow smile creeping across his stubble-shadowed face.

"Come on now, don't play hard to get with me," he pleaded. He guffawed at the idea of one of Harriet's girls being coy or maidenly. "It ain't like I'm taking something that ain't already been took!"

Jette looked wildly about her. There was no exit from the end of the porch on which she had trapped herself except over the railing and down six feet into the shrubbery. As she backed away from the man, he followed, pushing the chair aside with one hand and lurching to maintain his unsteady footing. The white tomcat scurried from under their feet, dashing along the side of the house and into the street beyond. The man watched stupidly as the animal made its escape.

"I hope you ain't planning to run me no footraces like that cat, honey," he laughed. "I just plain ain't in no shape to try to catch you." He passed a hand over his face as if to wipe away the fogginess that insisted on obscuring his view of the girl.

Jette edged away from him, but found herself cornered. He was patient with her. He'd let her get used to him first.

"Now if you don't be real nice to me, I'm gonna have to go in and tell Harriet on you." There was a subtle change in his voice, just enough to make the girl realize he was no longer joking. "Come on now, honey, what's your name?"

"I am not one of Harriet's girls!" Jette almost shouted. But he heard only dimly. His mind was made up—he wanted the slim, titian-haired girl in the ridiculously proper suit and school-marm hat. Even as he looked at her in the dim light that came from one of the parlor windows he could feel a cruel, urgent need in his loins. As Jette interpreted the grin on his face she tried to dart past him. She repeated in a hoarse whisper, "I am not one of Harriet's girls!"

" 'Course you're not—you're the Sunday-school teacher that's moved into the parsonage next to the Baptist church." He caught her with one huge arm and pulled her to him. "I could tell that right off . . . why, you're just visiting this here cat-house to comfort them downfallen women inside." He looked down at her as she struggled to free herself, her movements only serving to increase his desire.

"Leave me alone!" she choked out as he clasped her against his body.

"Harriet ain't never had none like you before . . ." Beneath his wide hands Jette was powerless. "And I sure as hell ain't never had none like you before neither." His chuckle was deep in his throat, with less humor and more threat.

Jette's boot heel slammed into the arch of his foot. He flinched with surprise and pain. For an instant he relinquished his grip on her. She wrestled him off balance and got as far as the front door before he grabbed her and pushed her into the long, cushioned settee positioned in front of the game room windows.

"Let me go!" she shrieked. But he was on her, the smile on his rough face erased by rage. His arms held her as in a vise, his heavy body pressed the very breath from her. She gasped and clutched at his face as he bent over her, but her driving gloves—so primly correct—prevented her from digging into his face.

"By god, I'll take you right here," he growled into her ear, his breath hot in her face. With one arm he held her, with the other he tore at her clothing.

Emmanuel Hazlitt threw open the front door and

peered into the half-light of the porch. "Mr. Wade! Stop it!" The elderly Negro grasped the man's collar and twisted it in his fist, momentarily strangling him quiescent. Stunned, struggling for breath, Jubal Wade turned from Jette, his glazed eyes fixing on Hazlitt. There was no warning move—just a sudden lunge and thrust with his entire body, sending the old man backwards across the porch, bouncing him against the half-open door.

Jette slid from the settee, attempted to gain her feet. Her only thought was to flee—forgotten was the reason for her visit to Harriet Selby's. Crouching beside the open window she tried to push herself erect against the wall. Her legs would not hold her weight; she was trembling uncontrollably. She did not see Jubal Wade as he turned back to her.

The blind of the game-room shot up, the pane banged upward and anxious faces peered from the lamplight out into the dimness of the porch. Jette was unaware of all save her need to escape. Wade squared himself, planting his legs wide apart, belligerence in every line of his powerful body.

Slowly, deliberately, he moved toward her. From his massive shoulders his arms hung like stopped pendulums. He glanced back at the fallen Hazlitt as if surprised to see him sprawled on the tiled floor. To Jette, all was swirling darkness, like smoke that curled from the game-room. She clung to the window frame, easing herself upright, inch by inch.

"Wade!"

Jette recognized the voice, but could not remember to whom it belonged. She groped for the arm of the settee. Her hair, freed from its hat and loosened from its tortoiseshell pins, fell across her face like an auburn veil.

"Wade! Stop it!" the man's voice repeated. Jette could see that he was as tall as her assailant, but his head was held arrogantly; his shout was a command.

Jubal Wade wheeled and swung wildly, his enormous arms flailing like sledge hammers with no target. Coordination between whiskey-fogged brain and fist was impossible. His opponent dodged gracefully to one side and in the same move landed a felling blow to Wade's mid-section. He doubled over, but returned to the attack like a stunned bull in a slaughter chute turning on its executioner. It was as useless. He slumped and fell, collapsing into a heap on the tiles.

"Darling, are you all right?" Nate Trasker lifted Jette in his arms. "What in the name of God are you doing here?"

A woman's voice said, "Stand back . . . let him take her inside." There was a shuffling and pushing as the crowd shifted aside. "Emmanuel, are you hurt?" the voice asked with a note of anxious concern.

"No, ma'am, Miss Harriet. I'm all right." The old man staggered to his feet and shook his head as he looked at the unconscious brawler. "He never done nothing like that before. What you want to do with him?" He rubbed his elbow and shoulder as he peered down at Wade.

"Take him into the back bedroom downstairs," Harriet Selby directed Hazlitt and another of her male employees. "And be sure he's locked in. Bring me the key."

"He come to, he'll knock the door down," Hazlitt ventured.

"I can buy another door." She dismissed them and followed Trasker into the hallway. "Nate, bring her into my sitting room." She edged around him and led the way toward the rear of the house. "Here . . . I'll open the door for you."

Harriet Selby's apartment on the first floor was both spacious and beautiful. The sitting room was tastefully furnished with large-scale red mahogany and exquisite

Persian rugs in shades of rose, maroon, cream and cerulean blue. Meissenware vases depicting cherubs and garlands echoed the delicate rug colors in porcelain and gold. Overhead hung a cut-crystal chandelier which scattered soft light from three ormolu oil lamps. Lush ferns and potted palms added touches of living green not at odds with the scheme, but enhancing the maroon velvet upholstery and rose satin drapes and cornices. It was a woman's room, opulent and serene, intended for conversation, not seduction.

Nate Trasker followed Harriet into the room and gently lowered Jette onto the velvet sofa before a white marble fireplace. He took her hands in his and pulled her fingertips to his lips.

"Darling, are you all right?" he repeated. The flutter of her eyelids told him she was barely conscious, trying to return from the darkness that threatened to engulf her. He held her pale face in both his hands and caressed her cheeks. Her black eyes, moisture sparkling in the long lashes, sought his. For a moment she returned his anguished gaze, then clung to him, giving way to raking sobs.

"I was such a fool! How can you ever forgive me?" she whispered.

"I can forgive you anything, Jette. You know that." He held her tenderly, clasping her to his breast.

Harriet Selby stood looking askance at the couple, her arms akimbo, her head tilted back in a blatant appraisal of the girl. "I don't want to interrupt a touching moment, but I think you owe me an explanation, young lady." There was icy demand in her tone.

Jette looked to Nate, who only nodded his head in agreement. "I came to see Nate," she replied. She tried to sit up, but Nate placed a restraining hand on her and she fell back into the rose satin pillows.

"May I ask how you knew he'd be here?" Harriet

challenged.

"I was told he'd be here." Jette realized she had blundered in response to the woman's attack. "It doesn't matter how I found out," she said defensively.

"No, I suppose not," Harriet said with a shallow laugh. "But young ladies of your station in life don't go calling on their gentleman friends in places like this." She gestured to include the entire establishment. Blood-red garnets and brilliant-cut diamonds on her hands and wrists flashed beneath the chandelier. "I ask you again . . . why?"

"Harriet, I'm not at all sure it's up to you to demand an explanation." Nate Trasker smiled as he said it, but there was cold, honed steel in his light eyes. Harriet Selby, however, was adamant. This was her business, her home, and the girl a dangerous intruder.

"I don't give one good damn what you think, Nate," Harriet countered. "This girl—who should certainly know better—has caused trouble for me just by coming here. I don't like trouble, and I won't countenance it. Not from her, not from anybody." She walked to the center table and removed a long, thin, black, Russian cigarette from an enamel and cloisonné box, lighted it with a match from above the fireplace, then flung her challenge to Nate. "I won't have trouble from anybody. Not even you, Nate." Her face, a mask of well-controlled emotions, gave no indication of her anger.

"That's unfair, Harriet," Nate said. "Jette meant you no harm I'm sure."

"I'm not overly concerned about what's fair and what isn't." Harriet pointed to the room across the hallway. "Jubal Wade may have done something despicable, but I want to know why. And mind you, I say 'may.' My business prospers only at the sufferance of the sheriff, the Board of Supervisors, and the fathers of the town who don't want their own daughters raped right out on the streets in broad daylight. I want some

295

answers handy when I'm asked about what's happened tonight." She sat down across from them in the fireside chair of cream velvet, carefully arranging the rustling silver and blue silk of her flounced and ruffled gown.

"You have no right . . ." Nate began.

"On the contrary, I have every right!" Harriet retorted.

"Please . . ." Jette interceded. "Please don't quarrel about it." She pushed herself up by one elbow and turned to Harriet. "She's right," she said to Nate. "She does have a right to know." Jette faced the woman. "I had to see Nate tonight. I was told about the game that's held here . . . and I came. That man . . . he thought . . ." She groped for the words. "That man thought I was one of your girls." Jette stifled an urge to sob by pressing her hand to her mouth. It had been her own foolishness that had brought her to such a pass and she alone was responsible. "I tried to tell him, but he didn't believe me . . ."

Harriet leaned back in her chair and expelled a long, fragrant stream of smoke from her scarlet lips. She squinted as some of the smoke drifted back into her eyes. "I see. And since he didn't believe you, he tried to get friendly."

"That's right." Jette did not miss the arched eyebrow that asked more than the words. "But he didn't . . . hurt me." She could not bear to face Nate's questioning glance. "Nothing . . . nothing happened," she declared quietly.

"Well, that's a comfort!" Harriet's expression was fervent. Across the hallway a door slammed shut and the sound of a key turning in the lock told them Jubal Wade was temporarily out of the way. The woman was visibly relieved. "Did you tell your driver to wait outside?" she asked.

"I drove myself," Jette replied. "Your man took care of my mare and trap."

Harriet Selby's laughter was not what was termed ladylike, but full and honest. "Well, Nate, it seems you've picked yourself a girl with a mind of her own. And probably a temper to match, unless I'm very much mistaken." She dusted the cigarette ash into a cut-glass saucer and crossed the room to a tiered mahogany table laden with decanters and delicate glassware. "Miss Allenby, I'd never have thought a girl like you'd do such a thing," she chuckled as she poured cognac into three globed glasses.

"Why not?" Jette asked.

"Because none of the young ladies around here—at least none of those I've seen or heard about—would take off in a trap and drive alone in the dark to see a man at a cat-house." She was still laughing as she handed the drinks to Jette and Nate. "Cheers," she saluted them as she swallowed the mellow liquor.

"My business with Nate was private," Jette explained. "I saw no reason to bring anyone else into it—not even a driver."

"You really are like your father." Harriet circled the sofa and looked closely at the girl, an amused smile on her handsome face. "You don't look much like him, but you sure as hell think like him."

Jette looked quizzically at the woman as she resumed her seat. "I knew your father pretty well," Harriet said. "He wasn't much with the ladies, but he liked to try his luck at the tables now and then. He was good, too." She said it with admiration and looked away quickly as if remembering had brought pain. "See here, if I leave you two to sort this out between yourselves will you promise me to keep it quiet and dignified? If you reach the point where you're going to get physical—in any way—" She arched her brow and stared at Trasker. ". . . let it be somewhere else. You can go out the back way whenever Miss Allenby is sufficiently recovered." It was a direct request for them to leave.

"I'll take Jette home as soon as she's up to it," Nate reassured the madam.

"Shall I tell Abe and the other gentlemen you'll be back?"

"No," he replied slowly. "But would you ask Abe to step in here in a few minutes?"

"Certainly," Harriet agreed. "If you'll excuse me, I have my business to run." She gathered her stiff silk skirts of blue and silver and whispered from the room.

Nate smoothed the auburn hair back from Jette's forehead and kissed the tip of her nose as he smiled down at her. It was as though he were indulging a wandering child who had just been found. "Now do you want to tell me what was so urgent?"

"I feel so foolish." Jette turned her head from him. She could not meet his open, steady gaze, so filled was she with chagrin at her own behavior.

"But, darling, it had to be something terribly important."

"It was . . . but it isn't now." She thought about the tan envelope on the seat of the buggy outside. "I'm glad I didn't bring it with me when I came up to the house. If someone had opened it . . . if something had happened to me . . ." Her black eyes clouded with anxiety at the thought.

"You aren't making one bit of sense yet, sweetheart," he shook his head in mock sorrow and coaxed her to look at him. "Bring what into the house?"

Jette pushed herself to a sitting position. "The envelope . . ." she attempted to explain.

"Yes, the envelope . . ." He was teasing her, smiling at her as he held her close. He smelled of expensive bergamot lotion and the carnation in his lapel was fresh and clove-scented. "What about the envelope?"

"Daisy Howard . . . you remember . . . Mrs. Millege's cousin from Cincinnati?" Nate nodded he did

298

remember the woman, then Jette went on. "She thought she recognized you from somewhere before. Mrs. Millege said she must be wrong, so Mrs. Howard said she'd look up some stories that had been printed in Cincinnati papers a few years ago about some young man who had swindled an older woman out of a lot of money . . ." It all spilled out in one confusing sentence. There was no indication that Trasker comprehended its meaning, no change in his facial expression save for a slight narrowing of his eyes.

"And you thought she was right?"

"She sent Ziphia Millege some clippings . . ."

"And was she right? Am I this wicked villain?" He was still mocking her, the suppressed smile on her face pulling at the corners of his thin lips. He tilted her head toward him with one finger under her chin. He made her feel childish, ridiculous. "Is that what brought you here?"

She nodded and hung her head, unable to continue. Trasker pulled her to him, his hands slipping under the disarrayed suit jacket. Gently, softly, he cupped her breasts and could feel the quick response of her aroused passion, the faster beating of her heart beneath his fingers. Her dark-lashed eyelids closed and she was aware only of the desire he created within her. His mouth covered her parted lips, his tongue exploring the warm sweetness of her mouth.

"Marry me, Jette. Tonight. Right now."

"Oh, Nate, I love you so . . ."

"Then marry me, darling," he murmured in her ear as she clung to him.

"Yes . . ." The need for him became unendurable. She sighed, whispering the one word he most wanted to hear, "Yes . . . yes . . ."

299

Chapter 13

Jette touched the square-cut aquamarines at her throat. They were icy cold against her skin, and the fog-laden air that crept from the bay and in through the open window was damp and frigid. She shivered and held out her arms to Nate.

"Does San Francisco make goose-bumps on everybody, or just on deliriously happy brides?" She welcomed his arms about her and held her head up for his kisses.

"I hate to disillusion you, sweetheart, but I'm afraid it does that to most visitors. It takes quite a time to get accustomed to the raw climate here." He spun her around and inspected her evening toilette. "Do you have a wrap to cover your shoulders?"

"Mother gave me her sable cape. Fortunately that sort of thing never goes out of style." She rummaged in the wardrobe that occupied one side of the small dressing room. "Ah, here it is." She draped the rich brown fur about her shoulders and turned for his approval. So beautifully did the electric-blue décolleté gown and shimmering blue gems compliment the perfection of her bare shoulders and burnished russet hair that her husband could only stare. She was exquisite.

"I'm not at all sure I should allow San Francisco to see you like this." He bent and kissed the hollow of her neck. "On the other hand, I want the entire world to see my wife—and envy me."

"Oh, darling. . . ." She returned his kisses, then turned abruptly from him. "If we continue like this, we shan't have any dinner. Abe and Lavinia said they'd wait for us downstairs and we're late already."

She led the way to the door, pulling him by the hand behind her. He closed the door, tested it to see that it was locked, then pocketed the key. An older couple, resplendent in formal evening dress, passed them in the hallway, their glances lingering on the lovely young woman. The man averted his eyes, but not before his wife had jabbed him cruelly in the ribs. They nodded in greeting and murmured, "Good morning," as they awaited the elevator.

As the polished brass doors opened in the Keniston Hotel lobby there was an audible and observable pause. Heads turned and whispers exchanged. Handsome and wealthy people were not uncommon in the Keniston—indeed, the hotel prided itself on its select clientele. There was, however, something far out of the ordinary about the couple leaving the elevator that caused a ripple of speculation and excitement.

Impeccably attired in high-collared white linen shirt, ruby studs, white silk cummerbund, and imported black English broadcloth full dress suit, the tall man inclined his fair head to listen to his companion. His lips parted in a smile that triggered shallow dimples in his tanned face, an effect at once unexpected and charming. His quiet laughter, like his voice, was deep and vibrant. But it was the spectacularly beautiful young woman on his arm that riveted everyone's attention. She moved with the unconscious grace of a lithe animal, no mincing timidity in her step, but sure, joyous exuberance. In the light that was refracted from myriad electric globes by pendant prisms, her hair shone like spun copper, her black eyes and full, red mouth the despair of the women who watched in envy.

"You, my love, are creating a sensation," Nate whispered to his bride. The hush of the lobby was not lost on him. He patted her gloved hand on his arm and guided her to the luxurious lounge area at one side of the lobby. "You are conquering the city!" he declared.

301

"I wasn't aware that I was at war with the city." She glanced around, the smile on her face brightening as she spied Abe Marley and Lavinia Baldwin across the room.

"You two certainly made a royal entry just now." Abe Marley rose to greet them. He turned to Lavinia and asked, "Do you still want to go out to dinner with these people?"

"This is their honeymoon—they are the ones to be noticed and made a fuss over." When Lavinia smiled, she approached beauty herself. She was gowned in heliotrope-colored henrietta cloth overlaid with black silk Spanish guipure lace. The only sign of her continued mourning was an ebony and black lace fan she carried. Her hair, unlike Jette's simple coiffure, was ratted and supplemented with straw-blond fall and switches, a wing of heliotrope feathers tucked into the crown and curling around one jeweled ear.

Lavinia appraised Jette's gown and wrap. She nodded and smiled up at Nate, saying, "She's lovely. I think you did very well for yourself—certainly better than you deserve."

"I second that motion," Marley grinned.

"Oh, Abe, please don't sound so much like a chairman!" Lavinia chided the politician, but he seemed to enjoy it. "Nate, if either Montague or Cameron ever sees Jette, you're going to have to fight them off with a stick." She thought a moment and added, "It's possible, too, they'll dangle a vice-presidency before your nose, but you'd better warn Jette that they're predatory where pretty women are concerned." Marley gathered Lavinia's voluminous cream satin cape and draped it about her shoulders, his hands remaining on her arms in a manner conveying intimacy.

The woman turned to Jette and said, "You do look ravishing, dear." She encircled the girl's waist and preceded the men from the lounge. "Let's get these men

302

to a restaurant before they can start talking business again."

"Where to?" Marley asked. "Tony's down by the wharf? The Whaler? Maybe Maxime's?" He took Lavinia's arm and headed out the main entrance as the uniformed doorman attended them. "The manager here at the hotel recommends a new place that's supposed to be unusual—La Marmite, over on Market."

"If we may vote, I say La Marmite," Lavinia said. "They have musicians who stroll around the tables and play requests," she explained to Jette. She sighed as Marley handed her up into a carriage at the curb. "Hiram and I wanted to come to San Francisco, but he wasn't able to make the trip."

"Sounds like a good place to begin the evening," Nate said. Marley nodded, and Nate instructed the cabbie, "La Marmite Cafe, over on Market Street," then settled into the seat beside Jette.

"Yes, sir!" The driver touched his cap and in a moment they were off at a fast clip, heading for the main thoroughfare.

"I've always thought music with dinner is so nice," Lavinia said. "Makes dining out an event, not just a meal." She sighed again and added, "And I so want this to be a special evening—for all of us."

"Vinnie, you're an incurable romantic," Trasker said.

"I suppose I am," she replied with a langourous, sideways look at Marley. He was an imposing man, past fifty, but retaining an indefinable attraction. Perhaps it was in his high-cheekboned face with its deep-set eyes, or perhaps in the shrewdness of his steady gaze that seemed to see even that which those whom he encountered might prefer to keep hidden. He was at ease in his full dress, as he was in every situation. At ease—and pleased. He tucked Lavinia's arm in his, his hand covering hers. They had registered in different rooms, on different floors, for the sake of propriety, but Jette had the feeling one of the rooms would not be put to much use during their stay. She did not judge them. They were Nate's friends and business associates. Jette accepted their behavior as their own affair, no concern of hers. And, too, she reminded herself, her own behavior had not been above reproach.

As the hired carriage clattered down the roughly paved street toward Market, Jette could only wonder what life with Nate would be like. Surely there would be other occasions such as this. He had sworn there would be many. Not that the aura of their honeymoon could ever be recaptured, but his business affairs, he had said, would bring him to San Francisco frequently. There would be trips to Chicago, perhaps Portland and Seattle, wherever cities were growing. She could contemplate their journeys with pleasurable anticipation.

"I'll want you to go with me as much as you can, darling," he had told her in Harriet Selby's sitting room. "I don't want to be apart from you any more than absolutely necessary. We'll have a grand time of it. I want to show you off wherever I go." He had been excited as a schoolboy as Abe Marley had tapped discreetly at the door before entering the sitting room.

"Abe, can you get a marriage ceremony performed tonight?" Nate had asked.

"Right now . . . tonight?" Abe Marley was astonished by the sudden request.

"Yes, right now! Tonight!" Nate had stood up and pulled a chair closer to the sofa and indicated Marley should sit next to Jette. "She's agreed to marry me right away, and I'm not going to let her off this time."

"You've already got the license, haven't you?"

"We have."

"And a ring?"

"Oh, yes, it's a beautiful ring," Jette had replied.

"And Killigrew's in the game-room trying to outbluff Harvey Cutsworth with a pair of fives." Marley clasped Trasker's hand in congratulations. "I think it can be arranged," he had said. "I hardly think, however, that Harriet's house is quite the place to hold the formalities." He asked Jette, "How does the Judge's chambers sound?" Then, *sotto voce*, he added, "Much more respectable, wouldn't you say?"

"That would be perfect!" Jette, still unsteady on her feet, arose, ready to go that instant. "I'd like that. But will Judge Killigrew agree?"

Nate Trasker had laughed at her question. "Love, whatever Abe Marley wants, he gets." He hugged her and winked at Marley. "Isn't that right, Abe?"

"Damned right," Marley replied. "All settled?"

"All settled," Jette said, her eyes aglow with happiness.

"Good. In the judge's chambers . . ." He looked at Harriet's ormolu and porcelain clock over the mantel. ". . . in one hour. How's that?"

"Fine, Abe. We'll be there," Nate had said. Jette had combed her hair in Harriet's dressing room, smoothed her suit as best she could, and left with Trasker by the mansion's rear entrance. Nate had taken the little blue roan and light trap and had driven them to the Swift Hotel. From his suite of rooms they picked up the license and the wedding band; from the hotel's porch they picked up Homer Baumgarner and John Perks as their witnesses.

A light limning one of the windows on the south side of the county courthouse showed them they were expected. Within minutes they were man and wife.

It had been past eight o'clock the next morning when the trap had pulled up in front of the Allenby ranch house. Verdie, her sleepless night showing in her pinched face, followed the two dogs as they rushed out the front door and met the buggy. She could not entirely hide her shock as she saw who had driven Jette home. Alone in Jette's room as she packed for the trip to San Francisco, Verdie had assumed an air of relief.

"Did you show him the clippings from the newspaper?" she had asked Jette.

"Yes, and the picture." Jette folded the fragile lace and cambric nightshifts and placed them in the middle drawer of the steamer trunk.

"What did he say?" Verdie did not wish to coax the story from her daughter, but she wanted to know what had happened to bring about the girl's radical change of heart.

"That it's ridiculous, of course." Jette slid the drawer shut and opened the lower one. "He said that we could make a trip down to Cincinatti from Chicago when we go there from San Francisco. We can go to see this woman, meet her, and she can assure me—face to face—that Nate is not the same man."

"That certainly sounds forthright enough," Verdie had said. Nate Trasker probably was telling them the truth. No man would risk making such an offer it were apt to result in his exposure. Still, a nagging doubt refused to leave. "And what did he say about Lavinia Baldwin? And why all the subterfuge about Farrier Development and Montague-Cameron Trust?"

"Farrier is only an operating branch of the Trust. Once the Trust is known to be interested in a project, land prices shoot up and prevent their obtaining advantageous options or purchases. Farrier Development goes in first and buys the land or buildings; the Trust does the financing."

"Is it legal?" Verdie could not believe it was as simple as it sounded. Ignorant of corporate law, she had no way to know whether or not such an arrangement were legitimate, but she recalled Russel Carr in Los Angeles saying it was at best unethical. "Aren't they bound by certain laws?"

"Nate says it is perfectly within the laws of all states."

"I see. Yes . . ." But Verdie doubted. "And what about Lavinia?"

"She was a representative of Farrier Development. She and Nate investigate the territories where there is greatest growth potential. They were both sent out here to size up this area as an investment possibility. They had to be circumspect about it—after all, it's difficult to buy up land in some counties because the railroads were given the land by the government and they can control the prices and the use made of the property." Jette seemed satisfied with her knowledge.

"But Lavinia . . ." Verdie began.

"Lavinia turned over everything to Nate when she married Hiram Baldwin. Then when her husband died so suddenly, she found she was forced to ask for her position with Montague-Cameron back. She had to earn a living."

"Whatever for? Hiram Baldwin had a considerable estate." Verdie was puzzled that his widow was left in straits.

"It seems Mr. Baldwin didn't manage his estate very well. When she'd paid up all his outstanding debts, there was nothing but the land left. And as she told me, you can't eat land." Jette went to the walnut wardrobe, removed the electric-blue dinner gown and spread it carefully on the bed.

"You spoke with Lavinia?" Verdie was aghast at the unconventional marriage ceremony, which was sure to cause a furor of scandal, but that Jette should be involved with the notorious Lavinia Baldwin was almost more than she could bear. "Where did you meet her?" she demanded to know.

"At Harriet Selby's."

For the time it took the girl to fold tissue paper under and around the gown, then place it in the lower drawer of the trunk, her mother uttered not a word. Finally Verdie said, "I'm not going to ask you what in the name of God you were doing at such a place, nor even what Lavinia or Nate were doing there. I don't believe I want to hear about it." She turned to her daughter and watched despairingly as the last garments were packed and the trunk shut and locked. "At this point I can only wish you happiness, Jette."

An unaccustomed note of reserve had altered Verdie's attitude and speech, as if by Jette's impulsive step a breach had formed between them. She looked wistfully at the small, flat, moired silk case which she had removed from the office safe downstairs.

"These are yours now, Jette. They were your grandmother's favorites. I suppose she loved them more than everything else she owned." Verdie flipped open the lid and inspected the flawless blue beryls. "She never forgave me for marrying Elias. That's why she left them to you."

"Thank you, Mother." Jette did not reach for the case, but allowed her mother to hand it to her. She bent to kiss Verdie's cheek. "They'll be my favorites, too." The two women stood looking at one another, pain and doubt in Verdie's eyes, joy and elation in Jette's. Before Verdie could say or do something to shadow the occasion with her own misgivings, she hugged Jette and fled from the room.

"I'll go see to some breakfast. You'll want to be off as soon as you've eaten. You don't want to miss your train."

As Verdie descended the outside staircase to the back patio, she caught a glimpse in the distance of the pall of dust rising from the shipping yards and spur track to the south and east. Asa Beemer would be supervising the loading of a herd of choice pureblooded cows from the north pasture. The shipment, the largest ever from San Genaro County, was headed for Rancho La Gabriela, near San Diego, not for slaughter, but for herd-building—exactly as Elias Allenby had intended.

She would break the news to Asa this evening after dinner. Jette was now beyond his reach—exactly as she had intended.

* * * *

"San Francisco is a marvelous place for a honeymoon," Lavinia said. "I quite envy you two." She did not turn to glance at Marley. It would have been too pointed, and although she was not a subtle woman, Lavinia Baldwin knew how best to play her men. She let Marley turn to look at her.

"What is that place?" Jette asked excitedly as the carriage hurtled past a brilliantly illuminated marquee and lobby crowded with well-dressed people.

"The Palais Theater," Nate said. "Would you like to go?"

"I would indeed!" Jette answered with enthusiasm as she briefly read the posters. "Julia Marlowe as 'Barbara Frietche.' Do you know I've never been to the theater? My father seemed to think anything connected with the theater was wicked. He wouldn't allow Mother and me to go."

"You've never seen a stage play?" Lavinia asked incredulously.

"Oh, we went to the high school programs in San Genaro," Jette replied. "But that hardly counts as theater."

"I suppose old Elias felt our local thespians less apt to lead you astray than professionals." Abe Marley laughed as he went on, "And yet to think of it . . . Elias attended Harriet Selby's functions with no such qualms." He smiled at Jette and added, "You'll forgive me, my dear, but I do find that somewhat incongruous, don't you?"

"Put that way, yes, I do," Jette said. "It seems that so many men live by double standards."

"Don't speak ill of the departed," Lavinia interrupted.

"I'm not speaking ill of Elias, Vinnie, only pointing out a bit of truth concerning the frailties and foibles of men," Marley said.

"And of women. . . .?"

"Oh, no, you don't! You can't trap me there," Marley laughed. "Ah . . . here we are, ladies, and not a minute too soon." They peered from the carriage windows through the fog as they pulled up before the cafe.

"As you say, Abe, not a minute too soon!" Nate said. "I've the distinct feeling we men might be bested by these two if we aren't careful."

They alighted from the vehicle, Jette and Lavinia dashing to the shelter of the overhead canopy. Heavy fog swirled down the street where dimly outlined figures threaded in and out of lighted doorways. Sounds, muffled by the mist, echoed errily along the wide street as if they had no point of origin. Jette tugged the short sable wrap tightly about her neck and shoulders.

"I do so loathe the weather here," Lavinia said petulantly.

"You've been here often?" Jette asked. Lavinia cast her a curious glance, as if she had been taken off guard.

"Not often, no. But I've been here on company business a few times," she replied a bit too quickly. She caught Marley's arm and hurried into the blaze of light in the foyer, leaving Nate to escort Jette after he had settled with the driver.

The waiter, his Gallic appreciation of feminine beauty causing him to attend the four-person party at the window table a bit more solicitously than usual, had served cherries flambé and was pouring fragrant, rich black coffee into dainty demitasse cups when Jette first noticed the short, heavy-set stranger across the room. He was staring, his thick neck hunched down into the expensive, beaver collared overcoat he had refused to relinquish at the hat-check stand. Untouched on the table before him was an order of fresh trout amandine and delicate petitpois. By his bulk alone he evidenced a love for eating, but the neglected food betrayed his uneasy mind. Without seeming to return his stare Jette observed him, wondering why he should be so fascinated by their foursome. Were her aquamarines so valuable that they had attracted his attention?

"Darling, there's a man over there . . . no, don't look around yet . . . who's been watching us for almost half an hour," Jette whispered to Nate. "Ever since he came in, he's kept his eye on us. I hope I'm not just being melodramatic, but I can't help wondering why."

Lavinia shifted a bit in her chair, intrigued to see who it might be. "You've probably garnered an admirer, Jette. San Francisco appreciates beautiful women, you know." She twisted about, prepared to return the man's stare. Instead, she almost dropped the tiny cup in her hand, her mouth forming an unvoiced exclamation. She shot a quick glance at Trasker, whose face only betrayed his surprise by a reflexive tightening of the jaws and one quick movement of his hand as he placed his spoonful of brandied cherries back untasted in his dish.

"Do you know him?" Jette asked.

"No, I'm afraid not," Trasker replied and dipped into his cherries again. "But if he bothers you, we can leave and be just in time for the last performance at the Lido Varieties."

She surreptitiously watched the stranger, then said, "Yes, let's do that." She touched the linen napkin to her lips and tried to ignore the man. There was no need to fear anyone, for after all, she had Nate beside her and Abe Marley across from her. Still a shiver coursed through her.

"Cold, sweetheart?" Nate asked.

"Yes, I am," she said. "You're right, Lavinia. The weather here leaves much to be desired." But it was not the drizzle and fog that had chilled her and filled her with sudden apprehension.

When they had left, she could feel the man staring after them. As they caught a carriage and headed for the theater district she had a last glimpse of him. He flung a bill to the waiter and rushed out the door, hailing a cab that careened dangerously in its attempt to catch up, then slackened its pace and trailed just out of sight in the fog.

* * * *

"A honeymoon's intended for bride and groom, not for bride, groom, and business associates," Abe Marley announced. "One nightcap and we'll leave you two to your own devices."

"Ah, and such lovely devices," Lavinia sighed and snuggled closer to Marley, but her eyes were on Trasker. She still appeared upset by their encounter at the Cafe La Marmite. The man had not overtaken them, nor did they see him again, but it was obvious that his appearance had made an impression on her. Throughout the olio sketches and routines at the Lido she laughed and applauded, but constantly she searched the audience from their box as if expecting the man to be there.

After the theater they entered the elegant bar at the Keniston, selecting one of the private booths which lined the wall on one side. Marley ushered Lavinia into the plush bench and signaled a waiter.

"Now do you two want to tell Jette and me who that chap was at La Marmite?" Marley slid into the seat and leaned back, one arm extended across the table top. He was smooth, his tone of voice giving no hint of anger, nor did his facial expression alter in the least. A smile lingered about his wide mouth; the tanned flesh about his light brown eyes still was creased into laugh lines.

Nate Trasker and Lavinia Baldwin exchanged questioning looks. "I don't know what you mean, Abe." Lavinia's hands were busy with her hair, her bodice, the corsage of violets and white roses at her breast.

"Perhaps it is your business alone," Marley pressed. "But I can make it my business with one call at the nearest police station." He hesitated just long enough, then added, "That is, if I must."

Trasker removed a cigarette case from his coat and offered it around, with both Lavinia and Marley accepting. Marley struck a match and held it for Lavinia, then for himself. The courteous gesture somewhat put the woman at ease, but she waited for Trasker to make the decision.

"I think we can keep the police out of it," Nate said. "He's Clarence Pomeroy, of our Chicago offices. He's never to contact us directly. What he's doing here in San Francisco I don't know. Wherever he goes, land speculators follow. Big time speculators. If he's just seen talking to us, as much as saying a polite 'hello,' there goes our careful planning. They can move in overnight and ruin everything we've worked to get put into shape. They've done it before . . . they'll do it again."

"Clarence Pomeroy . . . that's the man who set up your offices in Los Angeles, isn't it?" Jette asked, now thoroughly alarmed.

"That's right." Nate drew slowly on his cigarette and exhaled slowly as if to gather his thoughts. "Something big must be up. Maybe they've got wind of what we're planning in San Genaro."

"They? They who?" Abe Marley was interested.

"I've got a hell of a lot of money riding on your project in the County and I don't want to find myself having to fence shadows. Who are we talking about?" He was not asking. The slight smile remained, but his eyes were cold, almost hostile as he demanded an answer.

"I won't know that until I talk with Pomeroy, will I?" Trasker had no intention of sparring with Marley in a public place. He said nothing as the waiter deposited their drinks before them, accepted a bill for the check and a coin for tip. As soon as he was out of earshot, Trasker continued, "He'll get in touch with me, one way or the other, but he won't do it right out in the open. We've managed to keep Farrier Development separated from Montague-Cameron and we aren't going to show our hand unless we're forced."

"I don't understand, Nate. You both sound so ominous, as though there might be danger." Jette in turn demanded an answer. "I have a right to know what's going on. Is there some sort of danger?"

Trasker was visibly worried. The smooth brow furrowed and lines about his mouth and blond moustache etched deeper into his handsome face. He was a while replying. "Not physical danger. I take it that's what you mean."

"I do," she said.

"Then no, there's no physical danger." Nate's smile was perfect, the dimples darting into his face, relieving the hardness that had gathered there. "See here, Marley, let's not spoil a wonderful evening by conjuring up apparitions that may never materialize."

It was past midnight when they left Lavinia and Abe in the lobby. Tomorrow they were to continue on to Chicago to attend to a few matters of business, while Jette and Nate stayed in the bay city for a few days before rejoining them. Their hurried good-nights did not make Jette less uneasy. It seemed there was too much haste in their leaving, even for newly wedded

314

people who wished to be alone.

Try as she might, Jette could not shake off the fear that clutched at her from every dark corner. As she prepared for bed she tried to recall every word that had passed among Nate, Abe, and Lavinia during the evening. The fact that Marley and Lavinia had accompanied them to San Francisco at all was reason enough to cause her to wonder about their relationships. Marley was not in the least secretive before Jette as to his involvement in the San Genaro project, nor did he attempt to downplay his role or his own personal investment in the scheme. But what part did Lavinia really play?

Nate had cautioned Jette that whatever she might hear being discussed was not to be repeated. She was not offended by his dictum, although it piqued her curiosity to know more of the details and why their need for silence. "They" and "others" might try to move against Farrier Development and Montague-Cameron. The man from the cafe had not been a welcome addition to their honeymoon celebration. But like Marley and Lavinia, he would probably be gone next day and she could forget about him and the anxiety he brought to them.

Something was not right, though. There was no use in evading the issue. Evading it did not make it go away. She had heard her father tell of the days in Wyoming and Kansas and Montana when settlers who wanted to farm the land were massacred by ranchers who wanted the land free for grazing. He had seen at first hand the atrocities committed by both sides in the quarrel. That he had taken part in retributive actions was well known in San Genaro, and many feared his anger. Surely Elias must have known worry. Tonight she had seen Nate worried. She had seen his resolution, the set of his jaws, the momentary dilation of his eyes as he—unlike Elias Allenby—mastered his anger. She was not sure, however, that she cared more for his dispassionate, controlled demeanor any more than her father's irate wrath. With Elias, one knew instantly how one stood. But how could anyone know with Nate?

"I'll take your jewel case down to the safe now," he said. "Did you want to leave anything out for morning?" He picked up the moired silk case from the dressing table and waited for her reply. "Darling . . . what's the matter?"

"I'm afraid, Nate." She shuddered and covered her face with her hands. Dinner at the fashionable La Marmite; gay, laugh-filled vaudeville at the Lido; and pleasant nightcap of grenadine frappé in the crystal and silver Keniston bar—what should have been a memorable and perfect evening had been metamorphosed by the elusive and myserious Clarence Pomeroy into a frightening encounter that left her tormented with misgivings. Nate sat down on the narrow bench beside her, peering at her image in the mirror of the dressing table.

"Pomeroy?" He said the one name as if it were anathema. She could only nod her head. "Damn the man," Nate said under his breath. "Why the devil did he have to show up now of all times?" He put one arm around her shoulders and laid his head against hers, his lips brushing the rim of her ear. "Don't give him another thought, my love. We have four days to enjoy just being together. I'm sorry about Abe and Vinnie, but it couldn't be helped." He was apologetic, but she could sense the tension in his embrace and see it still clouding his face.

"I liked being with them. There's nothing to be sorry about on their account." She resolved to not make his problem greater by adding her own concern to his. "Besides, we are alone now, and as you say, we have four whole days . . ."

". . . and nights . . ." He stood up abruptly and

slapped the moired case in his hands. "I'll hurry with this and be right back." He grinned at her in the mirror and bent to kiss the nape of her neck. "Mrs. Trasker . . ."

"Yes?" She could not resist laughing at him.

"I just wanted to say it out loud."

"It sounds lovely." Their eyes met in the mirror for an instant before he dashed for the door of their suite. "Hurry!" she called after him.

From the bureau of the bedroom she removed the fragile hand-embroidered night shift of soft white cotton and lace. The previous night, hectic with the hasty ceremony and improvised celebration in the Swift Hotel's restaurant and bar, had not been one upon which she might look with romantic affection. Their first night together as man and wife should have been full of moonlight and flowers, tender words and soft caresses. Instead, after her escapade with a drunken Jubal Wade at Harriet's, there had been raucous toasts in the hotel's bar and a midnight supper that lasted until past one o'clock. She had almost collapsed from sheer exhaustion. Nate had carried her, half asleep, to the accompaniment of hoots and ribald advice, up to his suite of rooms where she had slept until he awakened her at five.

This night, their first in San Francisco, would really be their first night as man and wife. As Jette combed her long hair before the mirror, she forgot all else but her determination to make tonight memorable for them both. She ran hot water in the marble-framed tub and bathed quickly, wretchedly certain each minute that Nate would return and find her unready. Stepping from the luxurious tub she shivered even though the bathroom's steam radiator was hissing. She hurried to don the nightgown which she had not dared show her mother. It was modest only in cut, with a deep yoke, smocked and embroidered bodice, and softly shirred

317

skirt that clung, revealing rather than hiding her young body. A blue satin ribbon was tunneled through lace from the neck, crossing and separating her high, round breasts, and tied on one side. The saleswoman from whom she had bought the trousseau had been scandalized by the new wraparound style—a sinful Parisian innovation, surely the ultimate symbol of decadent sensuality.

Jette touched the cut-glass stopper from a bottle of Amaryllis du Japon to her temples, the hollow of her neck, her breasts, her hips and thighs. Using the lamb's wool puff she dusted her body with scented powder, then wrapped the nightshift about her and tied the ribbon below her left breast.

Down the hallway outside their suite the elevator hummed to a halt. She sped to the door and listened expectantly, but the arrival continued down the hall. She returned to the dressing table, unfastened her hair and bound it with a blue brocade ribbon. She studied the effect in the mirror, turning first to one side then the other. Satisfied, she crossed the room and laid out Nate's silk nightshirt and cashmere robe, her hands arranging each garment as though it were sensate to her loving touch. The bed had been opened by the hotel maid while they had been out, its hemstitched linen turned back over a fluffy eiderdown quilt of pale yellow satin.

Although weariness had no place in her plans, as she waited, wandering about the spacious suite too restless even to look at the newspaper Nate had tossed atop the bureau, she began to feel the accumulated results of two days of frantic excitement.

Just for a minute, she promised herself as she curled up on the chaise. *Just until I hear his step in the hallway*. The bed was too pristinely beautiful to disturb before Nate could share it with her. The room grew chilly, but she did not know it—she slept.

Somewhere a door closed and a key scraped in a lock. Jette sat up suddenly. The lights were still on. Nothing had changed. Except the clock. Twenty minutes to four! *That's not possible*, she told herself. She slid her toes into the blue velvet slippers that had dropped from her feet. She inspected the onyx and gilt clock on the mantel. The hands pointed to twenty to four. She rushed into the dressing room. Nate was not there. Nor in the bathroom. Dismayed, she rushed about the suite. The closet! No, that would be ridiculous. But she looked.

Shaking more from panic than from the cold, she pulled on her silk dressing gown. Quickly she inspected Nate's belongings. Nothing was missing. His suitcases were in the closet, his trunk in the corner of the room. Her hand was trembling as she picked up the telephone.

"Is . . . is . . . the bar still open? she asked as the operator came on. "No? Then is the restaurant?" She sat down on the awkward, channel-backed side chair by the telephone table. "Is there a place nearby where someone might go . . ." Fear gripped her as she considered other possibilities. "Is the manager available? Yes, the night manager if he was on duty shortly after midnight."

At half-past four a quiet tap told Jette the night manager was at the door. She rushed to the summons, threw open the door, hoping to see Nate with the man.

"Mrs. Trasker, what may I do for you?" The man, mindful of his, the hotel's, and his female guest's reputations, had brought the night housekeeper with him. She stood deferentially aside as they entered the suite and closed the door.

"This is Mrs. Burton," he said quickly. "I'm sure she can be a great comfort to you right now. I'm Mr. Algood, the night manager." Jette could only nod her head to ackowledge the introductions. Her teeth were chattering and the pupils of her eyes wide with fear.

Algood led Jette to a gold plush sofa near the radiator and seated her. "There we are. That's better," he pronounced to put her a bit at ease. "From what you told me on the telephone I gather your husband hasn't returned?"

Numb from dread, Jette only shook her head.

"Please try to help me put this together, Mrs. Trasker." His voice was firm, but coaxing. He wanted no hysterics and certainly no excess noise at such an hour. "You say he came downstairs with your jewel case to put into the safe?"

With an effort to control her growing alarm she replied, "Yes, that's correct. It was shortly after midnight."

"Please don't be offended if I must ask you some pertinent questions. I'm not prying, you understand." He pulled up a side chair for Mrs. Burton then seated himself beside Jette.

"I understand," Jette said. Her hands were clenched together, her elbows tight to her sides as though she were pulling herself into a compact, defensible knot of muscle and nerve. "I'll tell you anything you need to know."

"Good. Now—and do be honest with me—did you and your husband have angry words?" He smiled as he said it, but a slight twitch of one side of his face revealed his nervousness in the situation.

"Oh no! Nothing like that!"

"There was no quarrel, nothing to make him want to go somewhere for a few hours to collect himself before he returned to you?" The Keniston had witnessed lovers' quarrels before.

"No! I swear to you, it was not like that at all. We were just married yesterday . . ."

The manager cast a knowing glance at the housekeeper who glowered back at him. She did not approve of the way the man was handling the problem.

320

"Did he have pressing money problems that might cause him a great deal of worry?" He was thinking as much about the hotel bill for the bridal suite as he was of the missing guest.

"No. There were definitely no money problems."

"Can you think of any reason at all that he might . . . well, just want to go away by himself for a while? Do you have friends here in the city? Perhaps he met someone?"

"He has no friends here other than those here at the hotel."

He raised his eyebrows and sat back to look at Jette. "Have you called them to see if he is with them?" he asked logically.

"No. I'm sure he wouldn't be with them. You see, he was just going to take my jewelry down to the safe . . ." She began to see she had made a mistake in not calling Marley and Lavinia right away.

"Shall we give them a call, just to be sure?" He had already picked up the telephone. "Who are these friends?"

"Mrs. Baldwin and Mr. Marley, from San Genaro."

"I want to speak to a Mr. Marley . . . yes, here in the hotel." In a few minutes he had ascertained that Nate Trasker had not contacted Abe Marley since they had parted in the hotel bar earlier. Mrs. Baldwin did not answer in her room, but shortly called Jette's room and spoke with Algood. No, she had not seen Trasker since having a nightcap with him and his wife in the bar.

"Perhaps someone else . . ." He stopped when he saw the stricken look on Jette's pale face. "You've thought of something?"

"We were with friends at the La Marmite for dinner and all through dinner a strange man . . . a member of the firm for whom my husband works . . ."

"Yes?" The man tried to keep exasperation from his tone.

"This man didn't want to join us, but all through dinner he kept watching us . . ." She stopped, realizing that she had perhaps been extremely foolish in her fears.

"Ah, there, you see!" He spread his hands to indicate the solution of the problem was, after all, simple. "He didn't wish to intrude in your celebration. That's undoubtedly it." He smiled broadly and patted her clenched fists. "They've probably gone off to discuss business matters and just lost track of the time."

"On his honeymoon?" Mrs. Burton was skeptical. A frown from Algood silenced her.

"You may be right, of course," Jette said reluctantly. She thought a moment, then asked, "Did my husband deposit my jewel case in the safe downstairs? You were on duty then, were you not?"

"Yes, I was." Algood's composure was completely shaken by the direct question. He glanced uneasily at the housekeeper, but found no reassurance in her steady gaze. Finally he admitted, "No, Mrs. Trasker. He did not."

"Let me order some hot tea for the poor girl," Mrs. Burton said. Her sympathy aroused by the beautiful young bride's plight, she took over for the consternated Algood. She went into the bedroom and brought out a woolen blanket from the foot of the bed to wrap around Jette. She picked up the telephone and said, "This is Mrs. Burton. Give me Room Service." The housekeeper, unused to such emergencies, could only think of creature comforts to aid the stricken girl. She ordered black Ceylon tea, breast of turkey sandwiches, violet and lemon marguerites. She touched Jette's shoulder and stood beside her, almost daring Algood to upset her further.

"Are you certain Mr. Trasker had no one in San Francisco whom he might . . ." Algood stopped as he caught sight of Mrs. Burton's scowl. He was hesitant to press Jette too hard, but he was beginning to be worried himself. A missing guest was not the sort of thing to flatter a hotel's image; a missing guest plus missing jewels was something the Keniston management would not tolerate.

"If you can assure us that your husband had no reason to disappear like this . . ." Mrs. Burton was convinced the matter was beyond the night manager's competence. She waited for Jette to answer.

"He had none, please believe me," Jette said.

"Then perhaps we should call the police," the woman suggested.

Algood was appalled. "I don't feel that's indicated quite yet," he said indignantly. He could imagine police traipsing into the ornate lobby and loitering about, asking questions of the guests. Still, the young woman was visibly upset—and her husband was missing. "I'm sure by morning you'll hear from him and find out all your worries were for nothing." To the older woman he said, "Why don't you stay here with Mrs. Trasker for a while? I'll let you know the minute we find out anything downstairs."

"That won't be necessary . . ." Jette started to say.

"No trouble at all, Mrs. Trasker," the housekeeper said. "No one should be alone at a time like this."

Puzzled and by now thoroughly alarmed, Mr. Algood opened the door as a waiter trundled a tea cart into the room and left it in charge of Mrs. Burton. That the hotel did, indeed, have a problem, Algood was convinced; that he should inform the police he was also convinced—but extremely reluctant. If Mrs. Trasker, who was certainly the most beautiful bride they had ever accommodated at the Kenston, was telling the truth, her husband should not be missing. Any man who abandoned a woman of her loveliness on their honeymoon was either sadistic or most unfortunate. If the former, the Keniston was in no way to blame; if the latter, and should it become public knowledge, the hotel's innocence would be sullied. Especially with missing jewels. Mentally he was preparing a report to the management.

"Tell me, Mrs. Trasker, how valuable are your jewels? You must understand it is a question not only I, but the police, must ask." Algood could see no way of avoiding that part of the dilemma. "And are they insured?"

"Yes, they're insured along with other pieces from my grandmother's estate. As to their current value—I have no idea. You see, I inherited them only yesterday . . ." Her face suddenly drained of color as the meaning of his question became apparent. "You think that someone . . . because of the jewels . . . or that he . . ." She could not finish.

"At this point I don't think anything specific, my dear," he consoled her. "But we must consider everything."

Down the hall the elevator stopped, its door opened, closed, and footfalls sounded dully in the passageway. Jette ran to the door and flung it open.

"Jette!" Lavinia Baldwin threw her arms about the girl and led her back into the room. "What's happened?" She sat Jette down and took her hands in her own, noticing how cold they were. "You poor thing, what's wrong?" Jette could not speak, her breath catching in her throat as she looked helplessly from Lavinia to Abe Marley.

Marley, his hair still rumpled, robe hanging unevenly about his ankles, took one look at Algood and Mrs. Burton and surmised the trouble. "He's still gone and no word?" They nodded silently. He strode to the telephone, jiggled the receiver-hook impatiently for the switchboard operator.

Without another word to anyone in the room he barked into the mouthpiece, "Give me the police!"

Chapter 14

"You can see the necessity for, shall we say, discretion in letting this become public knowledge." Abe Marley bent closer to the man across the table. The bar was noisy with rough-clad workingmen who seemed to delight in baiting and joshing the dozen policemen who were partaking of the largesse displayed along the massive polished mahogany counter. Situated across the street from the station house, Sharkey's bar catered to a democratic assemblage. In deference to Inspector Hankins, Marley and the officer had been ushered into a semi-private booth at the far end of the room. Business, by the nature of the place, could be transacted aloud amid the hubbub and still remain confidential.

Hankins studied the man opposite him. They were of a kind, with identical self-assurance and tenacity. Even their clothing in its conservative, almost old-fashioned cut was similar, as was their closely cropped graying hair and wide, thin moustaches. Marley was a man whom the inspector could both respect and understand. He decided he would not guard his remarks.

"You say 'discretion.' Am I to take it that you have more than casual interest in the situation?" Hankins asked.

"You may, indeed, take it that way," Marley answered. "I have a great deal of money in the venture." He waited just long enough to add emphasis to what followed. "Booth Killigrew has invested in the enterprise, too. Heavily invested."

Hankins' eyebrows twitched a trifle at mention of Killigrew's name, but not so much that it betrayed his own suddenly aroused interest. "Is that Judge Killigrew . . . the one Sacramento's talking of putting up for governor next election?"

"The same." Abe Marley stirred sugar into the cup of black coffee the waiter had deposited on the table along with a trayful of sliced roast beef, onions, white and yellow cheeses, hard boiled eggs, bread and butter, and fat, green, sour pickles. A condiment tantalus containing horseradish, mustard, chutney, catsup, and vinegar perched precariously at the edge of the table. Hankins, always a prudent man, pushed the tantalus to the center of the table. Not only prudent—but practical. He paused to consider the unpleasant possibilities inherent in his position in the case.

"All right," he finally agreed. "We'll keep it tight. No need to let it get to the papers and be blown out of all proportion. No telling what sort of wild speculation those boys might indulge in." He need not add that they would make a field day of it should they learn of Marley's and Killigrew's connection. It would be the sort of story that appeared for a few days on page one, slanted to pique curiosity and give rise to vicious gossip, then dropped when no longer newsworthy, with no explanation or apology should anyone be unfairly maligned. "Mind you, I'm not guaranteeing anything if things get out of hand or if this whole affair turns out bigger than we expected."

Hankins took a slice of bread, slathered it with butter, heaped on beef and cheese, daubed it copiously with mustard before capping it with onions. There was no way he could bite directly into the outsize sandwich, so he began devouring it from the corners, tilting it, evening it with bites from top, bottom, and sides. Marley concluded the inspector would tackle any problem presented him in just such a fashion—methodically, sensibly, nibbling away at it.

"I'd be less than honest with you if I didn't add my own thoughts to what you already know about Trasker's disappearance," Marley offered.

"I thought you'd get to that sooner or later,"

Inspector Hankins said around a mouthful of beef and cheese. "You should really eat something, Marley. It's one thing for that pretty little girl not to eat, but for you . . ." He shook his head. While he waited for Marley to continue, he began to build another enormous sandwich. He handed it over to the politician and ordered him, "Go on, eat it. Best roast beef in the city. Sharkey picks out his own meat. Gets down to the packing house every morning, four-thirty sharp. And that white cheese comes from down by Monterey. Old-line Spanish family out in the Carmel River Valley makes it. That's something you can't get back East." He repeated the layering of beef and cheese for himself.

Abe Marley had not eaten breakfast—food was far from his mind. Finding Nate Trasker was paramount, but Marley now found he was hungry despite his concern. The waiter refilled his coffee cup and replenished the bread and butter. Hankins could afford to wait for Marley to explain himself. Hankins did not trust the testimony of hungry men any more than he did overly ambitious and cautious men.

"I think Trasker was in some kind of hot water." Marley measured sugar into a teaspoon and stirred it into his cup. "I saw his face when he discovered who was watching us at the La Marmite last night. That man, Clarence Pomeroy, wasn't someone Trasker wanted to see. At least not last night . . ."

"Or perhaps on his honeymoon?" the inspector opined.

"Perhaps." Marley tasted the coffee, then attacked the beef and cheese again.

"But you don't think that was all of it?" Hankins again waited.

"No, I don't," Marley replied. "A few days ago I noticed a chance in the man. Seemed edgy, nervous. Not like a man of his sort. Something was up and I asked him about it, but he said it was nothing out of the

327

ordinary."

"Woman trouble maybe?"

"Jette Allenby's a handful, all right. Enough like her father to be hard to handle, but I feel there was more to it than that."

"You think this Pomeroy's appearance last night ties in with Trasker's taking off?"

"Bound to," Marley said. "You could have it the wrong way there, Inspector. Trasker may not have taken off—he could have *been* taken off. And that's exactly what worries me."

"From what you told me of the man, I'd say he was more than capable of taking care of himself. Not the sort of chap I'd choose to pick a fight with."

"But he had Jette's jewelry and he wasn't armed. Anything could have happened."

"The Keniston isn't the sort of place where hoodlums are apt to be skulking in the hallways or behind the potted palms."

"But it is possible?" Marley asked.

"Oh, of course, anything's possible if you put it that way. Are you certain you know nothing more about this Pomeroy that would give us a thread to start with?"

"Just what I've told you," Marley answered, barely able to keep annoyance from his voice. "Did you find out from the Chicago police where he's supposed to be staying here in San Francisco?"

"Afraid not," the inspector said. "We drew a blank there. Chicago says there's no one at either office—Farrier or Montague-Cameron—which is damned strange, if you ask me. And neither place has a telephone. Neighboring offices were of no help, except that they say there is no regular office staff. People just come and go, no routine, no schedule. Mail goes into slots in the doors. No janitorial services, so nobody sees the inside of the offices. Seems to be a very secretive operation." Hankins watched Marley for signs of

328

surprise, but found none. If the information was news to him, he covered his shock well.

"Did you have Chicago check with business licenses? Tax rolls, that sort of thing?"

"Oh yes. That's pretty routine—just to see that everything is in order." Hankins forked into a piece of cherry pie. "And it does seem to be in order as far as that goes. I'd like to check further into their capitalization, things of that sort, but I have nothing to go on and it takes a court order."

For once Marley's guard was dropped. "You're suspicious of the business?" he asked. He, himself, had begun to entertain doubts. Now to know that the policeman also was suspicious—merely because of Trasker's disappearance—raised alarms he could not ignore.

"Just a hunch. At this point, all I'm really concerned with is a missing bridegroom," Inspector Hankins said.

"And the bride's missing jewelry," Marley reminded him.

"That, too. Yes, of course." Hankins seemed preoccupied for a few minutes. "You say this Trasker is from Chicago?"

"The business is located in Chicago, but he's originally from someplace in New Hampshire. Manchester, New Hampshire, to be exact." Abe Marley looked closely at the inspector and was not reassured by what he saw. "Now see, here, Hankins, if you know something more about this than I do, I think it's your obligation to tell me." He was once again the politician using leverage to obtain what he wanted. "Booth Killigrew can't afford to be tied in to anything—or anybody—that causes an officer of the law to look like you do right now." Marley was alarmed, but still attempted to keep it obscured.

"It's just that your description of Trasker fits pretty closely that of a confidence-man who used to work the

East Coast," Hankins replied. "Worked with different accomplices, male and female. We got fliers out here off and on for several years, then they stopped. Seems they either quit that tack—maybe split up and went to something else—or went straight."

Inspector Hankins ate in silence for a while, letting Marley turn that information over in his mind before he went on, "When we find your friend I'd sure as hell like to have a woman from Ohio take a good look at him."

"You sound pretty well convinced already." Marley was growing angry, but could not afford to let it surface. Nor could he admit that beneath it all, he was beginning to believe that he and Judge Killigrew had been used as cat's-paws in Nate Trasker's ambitious plans. "You haven't even heard the rest of my thoughts on the situation."

"I wouldn't say I'm already convinced," Hankins retorted. "At this point I'm obliged—by law—to presume your friend is just who he says he is, and is a legitimate businessman who just happens to have disappeared. But on my own part, I don't like business arrangements that can't stand scrutiny by light of day." One eyebrow crept up a fraction of an inch as Hankins observed Marley. He was experienced enough to recognize even Marley's well-controlled reactions. "As to listening to your opinion, please continue."

"Sorry. I guess I sounded like a petulant gossip-monger shooed away from the back fence." Marley chuckled, glad that he could still laugh at himself.

"You did at that," the inspector agreed. "But I'd like to know what else you have in mind."

"Nate has a lot of his own money tied up in this San Genaro development plan and he's just bought a ranch, so it didn't seem unusual for him to need cash in an emergency," Marley began. "I thought nothing of it when he asked me a few days ago to take a note for five thousand dollars . . ."

330

"A note with the ranch as security? Or a part of his interest in the business?"

"The ranch."

"And what reason did he give for needing cash?"

"That he had a few personal obligations that needed tidying up." Marley realized the story was overly simplistic. "I didn't pry into exactly what the obligations were. I figured that was Trasker's affair. He gave me the note and surety, and that was sufficient reason for me. After all, for all practical purposes we are the equivalent of partners in this venture."

"And you trusted him, still trust him, I suppose?"

"I do." Marley said it and wondered if he really meant it or if he were trying to rationalize his position. "From what little Trasker said, I inferred he had been suddenly pressed . . ."

"By anyone in particular?"

"No one that I know of directly." Marley was chagrined that it was the truth.

"But you suspect somebody?" Hankins guessed Marley was holding back in his admission. "Do we get back to women troubles?"

Abe Marley sighed, suddenly feeling self-doubts which had no place in his usual routine. "Yes, I'm afraid so. I think Trasker wanted to ease a certain little lady out of his life before he got into trouble with Jette Allenby."

Hankins nodded sagaciously. He recalled the rather flamboyant blonde beauty of Lavinia Baldwin and the fact that Marley and Mrs. Baldwin were traveling together. "If that is so, then it can't have much bearing on this Clarence Pomeroy, can it?" He appeared to puzzle over his own supposition as he drained the last coffee from his cup. "On the other hand," he mused, "there may very well be a connection. It's odd that these things occurred within a week or ten days, isn't it?"

"When we find Trasker we'll know, won't we?"

Marley could not resist answering him in his own way, with a question.

"You gave him the money."

"Naturally."

The inspector had to admire a man who was at once affluent enough and generous enough to aid friends in financial matters. He even caught himself wondering if Marley could use an extra man in San Genaro County—or if Judge Killigrew might need an ex-policeman in Sacramento. His attention, however, quickly returned to his current investigation. "You gave him cash?"

"I did." Marley sensed the inspector's next question. "There was no reason not to. The note was good. And Trasker's title to La Coruna is legal and in order."

"Did you give him a draft . . . a check . . . or cash?" . . .

"Cash!" Marley repeated with a touch of heat.

For a long time Hankins said nothing further, seeming to mull the facts over again. "And now there's a wife in the picture," he said at last.

"The note to me was transacted before the marriage, so has precedence," Marley said.

"But that would make it more difficult to exercise, wouldn't it?"

"If it came to that pass, yes. But the wife is wealthy in her own right so I'm sure that would pose no problem. And she's going to be a lot more wealthy after her mother's death. She'll come into the Allenby ranch since she's the only heir."

"I see," Hankins mumbled over a forkful of tart cherries. "So you gave Trasker the cash, he was grateful in the extreme, but continued visibly upset and agitated." He looked to Marley for confirmation. "Then his wife—as you've told me—on her marriage inherits both a trust fund and jewelry of considerable value."

332

"I see what you're getting at," Marley did see, and the implication disturbed him.

"Have you any idea what the gems would be worth?"

"None at all."

"Well, I do. At least within shooting range. And if they are flawless, as the girl told me, they'd buy several ranches and leave a good deal of pocket money left over." Hankins slid his pie plate to one side and took a cigar case from the breast pocket of his coat. "A mighty temptation to a man in need of cash."

"I can't believe that of Trasker."

"Can you believe it of the lady in question? Or from what you know of this Clarence Pomeroy?"

"No, sir, I cannot!" Marley was defensive for the first time. His personal judgment had been called into question. Since his success in San Genaro County politics was dependent upon just that talent, he felt in the inspector's remarks the sting of criticism. "I refuse to believe that of any of them."

"That wouldn't alter the facts." Hankins passed the case to Marley, who accepted one of the short Brunswick Perfectos. "I've got men out right now, covering every known or suspected receiver and fence. We telegraphed Los Angeles, Portland, Salt Lake. Too early to hear from them, but we'll hear soon if the aquamarines show up for sale. The pearls, topaz brooch, things like that, could be gotten rid of easier, but not those aquamarines."

"Then you think . . ."

"What I think doesn't matter a damn, Marley. Only when I *know* will it begin to matter." Both men busied themselves with the masculine ritual of clipping the end off the cigar, perforating it, testing the draw. Then Marley held a light for them both. They smoked, with no words between them for a time.

Finally Marley said, "You could be right, of course. I disagree, but you could be right. Trasker's wife has too much money in her own name, now that she's married, for him to feel the necessity of committing a criminal act when he could get funds from her.''

"Would she give them to him?''

"I'm sure she would. That girl loves him so much she'd go to hell for him if he asked.''

"But you've told me she's got an uncommonly good head for business,'' Inspector Hankins reminded him. "Wouldn't she want to know what he needed it for? Even if she's deeply in love with the man she'd be apt to demand an explanation of some sort.''

"True. But she'd give it to him,'' Marley averred. "I'd stake my life on it.''

"Marley, you're a mighty reckless man with your life.'' Hankins smiled through the cloud of pungent smoke that hovered about their booth. "If there's one thing I've learned in my line of work, it's that you can't ever be sure what another person may or may not do in a given situation. There's nothing as treacherous as human nature. Emotions and resultant actions are totally unpredictable.'' He motioned the waiter, held his hand out for the bill. He did not protest, however, when Abe Marley insisted on paying.

They emerged into gray daylight only a shade brighter than the interior of Sharkey's saloon. The street was congested with midday traffic and the sidewalk was crowded. Pedestrians hurried along, intent on seeking shelter from a cold wind that made trying to manage an umbrella in the slight drizzle a frustrating experience. Although wan luminescence overhead indicated the sun was trying to burn through the overcast, it was losing the battle as brisk gusts pushed fog over the sand hills and obliterated street after street. Inspector Hankins pulled up his coat collar as they crossed to the station house.

"I'll go see if Chicago's come up with any additional information,'' Hankins said as he led the way. "They said they'd telegraph us immediately. And I sent a wire to that woman in Cincinatti. I think she'll be interested enough to send a reply."

Inside the station house all available electric lights were on. They did little to dispel the gloom. The walls, painted a dingy, pratical gray, only augumented the dismal effect. As the inspector opened the door to his office, a uniformed man rushed to intercept him.

"Sir, I think you'll want to see this right away." The man handed him a telegraph message and waited as his superior read it through. "Any reply, sir?"

"Later. Thank you, Franklin. That will be all for now." Hankins waved Marley to a chair and closed the door. Seeing that the inspector did not remove his coat, Marley sat down on the edge of the seat, one hand on each knee, ready to follow the inspector's lead. "You should see this," the officer said quietly and tossed the scrap of paper to his visitor.

Abe Marley abruptly sat back into the chair as he read and re-read the telegram.

"Now how far off base do you think I am?" Hankins asked. He shifted the cigar in his mouth, spilling ashes down the front of his coat. He flicked at them impatiently and began pacing the narrow room.

"This isn't conclusive of anything," Marley said. "It only proves that the woman was angry and curious enough to follow up on a bit of unfounded gossip. It certainly doesn't mean Trasker's the same man." Marley was groping for a rational and safe explanation. He was a realist, however, and reluctantly admitted, "It would bear checking out at least. I think we should see this woman as soon as possible."

"We?" Hankins shot him a peculiar look. Remembering Marley's connection to Judge Booth Killigrew, he resigned himself—not too reluctantly—to the politician's accompanying him on his next interview. "Come along," he invited Marley and shoved the

335

telegram into his pocket.

* * * *

The desk clerk rotated the hotel register to allow Inspector Hankins to glance down the list of guests. "There's been no one register by the name of Mrs. Palma Owens. We received a telegram over a week ago for reservation, along with a money order for us to hold the room in case she was late getting here."

"She never arrived? Is that it?" Hankins frowned as he asked.

"Yes, inspector, she never got here. Since she'd already paid in advance we've kept the room available, even moved her luggage up there." The clerk was nervous and seemed to take it as a personal affront that the woman had not put in her scheduled appearance.

"Why didn't you notify the police of this fact?" Hankins asked.

"Why? Whatever for?" The clerk was aghast at the idea. "It's done frequently, sir. People miss a train. They take ill at the last minute and forget to cancel. Things like that."

"You say her luggage came on ahead of her?" Marley asked.

The clerk stared insolently at Marley as though trying to decide if he should reply to him. Marley was not, after all, an officer. It was to the inspector that he said, "Mrs. Owens had made arrangements to stay with us for a month. She was going to make a trip down to the Los Angeles area for a few days, but intended to keep the room here, as it were, for her *pied-á-terre*. The lady has stayed with us many times over the years, so we saw nothing unusual in complying with her request."

"You admit it's unusual for a guest to be overdue this long?"

"Well, put that way, yes, I suppose so."

"I do put it that way," Hankins challenged the clerk. "It doesn't happen all that often, does it?"

"No. Fortunately it does not." The man cast apprehensive glances around the lobby, hoping none of their other guests would overhear the interrogation. Since there was no way he could avoid answering the policeman's questions, he could only pray it would soon come to an end. The afternoon matinee performance at the Tivoli Theater in the next block would soon be out and many guests would be returning to the hotel.

"This Mrs. Palma Owens—she's a woman of substance?"

"Oh my, yes. I'd say very substantial." The clerk smiled as he recalled the gratuities the woman dispensed with lavish regularity.

"Do you have any information about her . . . perhaps the names of someone to contact in case of emergency?" It was only a long shot, but one worth trying.

"As a matter of fact, we do. We keep extensive files on our regular guests . . . what their food preferences are, if they like certain flowers better than others . . . which color schemes they prefer . . . things of that nature. A gesture of our concern and efficiency, you understand," he explained as though he were trying to convince both men of the hotel's superiority over more humble establishments. "Are you certain it's necessary for me to . . ." He had anticipated the policeman's request to see their files.

Hankins was in no mood to equivocate. "I assure you it will be most embarrassing for the hotel if you don't," he said.

With the information supplied by the hotel, Inspector Hankins dispatched messages to two close relatives of the missing Palma Owens in Cincinnati. As he and Marley waited in the station house for a reply to his inquiries, the telephone on his desk gave two sharp

337

rings. Hankins lifted the receiver and spoke into the mouthpiece. "Hankins speaking . . . yes, of course I'm in . . ." He waited for the man at the police switchboard to plug in the incoming call. "Yes, this is Inspector Hankins." He covered the mouthpiece with his hand and said to Marley, "If you'd like a drink, there's a bottle in the cabinet over there, bottom drawer."

"Thanks. I'll take you up on that," Marley said. "This damned weather gets into a man's guts." Marley drew out the indicated drawer and extracted a bottle. He glanced about for something into which he might pour the whiskey.

"You'll find a glass in the lavatory," the inspector said and jerked his head toward the closed door next to the window. As Marley searched for the glass, then poured himself an inch of bourbon, he heard an exclamation of surprise.

"You say he was brought there this morning . . . at seven o'clock . . . I'll have a few words with your staff about their reporting procedures when I get there." He waved to Marley and signaled to him to put on his hat and coat. "Yes, I understand that, Sister." Exasperation was evident as he seemed to wait through a lengthy explanation. "You say he's in stable condition? Will he be able to talk if I come right over? Fine . . . yes, thank you, Sister. Yes, I'll be right there." He slammed the receiver onto the hook and jumped up, grabbing his coat and hat as he hastened from the office.

"Trasker?"

"Right. At Saint Vincent's Hospital. It's down in the Barbary Coast area," Hankins flung over his shoulder.

Marley downed the whiskey before following. "He's alive?" he asked as he shut the door behind them.

"He is," Hankins confirmed. "He's been pretty well worked over by somebody who knew his business and

338

he doesn't make much sense yet . . . but he's alive."

They were already out of the station house before the first telegraphic reply came from Cincinnati.

Chapter 15

Jette leaned forward in the carriage seat, hands clenched about the small tapestry handbag in her lap. Awakened from a fitful nap by the inspector's telephone message, Jette had not bothered to dress for the weather, but had thrown on the sable cape and ran bare-headed and kid-slippered into the mist to the waiting police vehicle. A clanging emergency bell scattered buggies, automobiles, and pedestrians from their path as they sped toward Saint Vincent's Hospital.

"We should have told Lavinia," Jette said to Abe Marley.

"I don't think that's quite in order yet," Hankins put in. He chose to ignore the questioning look Jette gave him.

"She'll hear all about it in due time," Marley said.

"I know you're only concerned about your husband at this point," Hankins told the girl. "But I think you ought to know that there was no trace of your jewelry." He added as if to make it more final, "No sign of the case, either."

"It's only Nate I care about, Inspector." Jette bit her lower lip to keep from giving way to the emotional turmoil that swept over her. Nate was injured—how badly? Was he conscious? What had happened and who had assaulted him . . . and why? "If only I hadn't sent him down to put my things in the hotel's safe . . ."

"I know exactly what you're thinking, Mrs. Trasker,

but it isn't so." Hankins braced himself as the horses took a corner too fast for the passengers' comfort. "It isn't your fault."

"But I sent him . . ." Her chin trembled and tears spilled down her cheeks. Abe Marley, sitting beside her, did not see, but Hankins removed the fastidiously folded handkerchief from his suit coat's breast pocket and handed it to her.

"You're in no way to blame for what happened," Hankins said.

"You mustn't think such a thing," Marley cajoled her. "And you won't want Nate to see you with your eyes all red, do you?" He knew he was patronizing the girl and regretted it. Never at a loss for words until now, he scarcely thought how best to console her. He was too worried himself, not only for Jette and Nate Trasker, but for the entire development scheme and his own involvement. If Hankins was convinced that somehow the elusive Pomeroy, Lavinia Baldwin, the attack on Nate and theft of the jewelry all were connected with Farrier's extensive plans for San Genaro, then it could only mean that both his and Judge Killigrew's positions were possibly subject to opprobrium.

Added to the list of coincidental happenings—already enough to cause him to wince when he considered the implications—would be the missing woman from Cincinnati, Mrs. Palma Owens. Marley could not admit even to himself that Hankins was right in his supposition that it all tied together in some fantastically complicated plot. And to think of the voluptuous Lavinia Baldwin being a factor in the plot gave him pain. Not that he would seriously think of marrying the woman—his own freedom was too precious for that sort of alliance—but in her arms and bed he found solace and comfort as lagniappe along with the myriad ways of her passion. The prospect of parting with Lavinia was fully as hurtful as that of any probable loss in the development project.

Marley could find no words to allay Jette's fears. He put an arm about her shoulders and let her lay her head against him. "Don't worry now, Jette. Don't worry," he repeated, as much for his own benefit as for hers. "We'll be at the hospital soon and you'll see everything's going to be all right." As the police carriage rattled into the roughly-paved gambling and brothel district he could only pray it would be so.

Saint Vincent's Hospital was built flush with the sidewalk, its stone and brick rising three stories above the tumult of the tawdry street. It was hope and hospice for the human flotsam that beached itself in the alleys and doorways along the infamous Barbary Coast. A white marble cross over the door was guard enough for the entryway and no bars prevented access to the premises. A white-robed sister looked up from behind a counter badly in need of fresh paint.

"May I help you?" she asked as Jette rushed through the wide, double-hinged front door. As the door swung open she caught a glimpse of the police vehicle and its uniformed driver pulled up outside. "You must be Mrs. Trasker," she said with a quick, reassuring smile. "Your husband has been asking for you." She rose from the desk and came around into the foyer.

"Please . . . take me to him," Jette pleaded. The sister took her by the arm and patted her hand as she walked her down the corridor to the right. "Is he all right?" Jette asked.

"He'll be fine in a few days." To Hankins and Marley the sister said in a hushed tone, "Follow me, gentlemen, but I will ask you to be as quiet as possible. You may wait outside the ward, if you will. We're very crowded and have only wards so we ask visitors to go in one at a time. I'm certain you understand." She was hardly five feet tall and her robes diminished her apparent height further. Her brisk, determined step and assertive manner left no doubt as to her capabilities; her gentle greeting by first name—to many who seldom heard their names pronounced—as she passed ambulatory patients in the hall demonstrated her sensitivity and compassion for San Francisco's derelicts. She halted before an open doorway with a faded and peeling '107' stenciled above the lintel.

"I'll take you in, Mrs. Trasker," the diminutive nurse said to Jette. "Gentlemen, if you'll wait here . . . ." The smell of iodoform and carbolic and chloroform hung as thick in the empty corridor as the mist outside the hospital.

"Thank you, Sister," Hankins said and stood, hat in hand, across from the doorway. As the women entered the ward he sniffed at the medicinal hospital smells and wrinkled his nose. "Let's stand down there by the open window," he suggested to Marley. The two men wandered down the corridor and leaned against the window sill. Cold salt air crept through the six-inch slit, freshening at least that portion of the hallway. "I'll give them a few minutes and we'll go in and hear what Trasker's got to say." He did not relish the task ahead, not for the sake of Trasker, but for the lovely young wife.

Sister Teresa led Jette through the congested ward. Three bare electric light globes dangled from the high, tinned metal ceiling on unadorned black wires, their quidistant glows insufficient to illuminate more than the space directly below. Narrow beds, some with rails bolted in place about them, lined the white plastered walls. Several beds were enclosed with muslin curtains. From one issued the sibilant gasps of advanced pneumonia, but only Sister Teresa recognized its import.

It was toward the cubicle beneath a series of small, inset clerestory windows at the far end of the ward that the sister guided Jette. Elderly men, too old to care about life anymore, turned to watch the tiny robed nurse and lovely auburn-haired young woman as they passed. Even though distress and fear spoke eloquently from her anguished face, they envied the man in whose arms she would soon be. Some, remembering another face, a form, a voice, turned away and closed their eyes.

The attending nurse stepped aside as they neared. "Is Mr. Trasker awake?" Sister Teresa asked quietly.

"Yes, and he's very insistent that he leave as soon as possible." She smiled as she realized that her supervisor had brought the young woman. "Is this his wife?" she asked.

"Yes, this is Mrs. Trasker. Is he ready for visitors?"

"He's presentable," she replied and parted the curtains for Jette to enter, then pulled them shut for privacy. Both nurses bustled down the line of cots to where a wizened, mumbling old man was attempting to crawl out over the restraining rails.

As Jette entered the flimsy room, she hesitated, pressing her knuckles against her lips as she saw Nate. An extra sheet which covered his body had been securely tucked under the thin mattress, and a coarse gray woolen blanket was folded across the foot of the bed. He lay on his left side, facing away from her, but even at a few yards she could see the livid bruises. At the slight whispering of her silks he opened his eyes and turned his head.

"Darling?" He pushed himself over and sat up. "Darling!" Jette was in his arms, feeling the roughness of the hospital shirt, the rasping of his whisker-stubbled face against hers, his kisses hard and wild upon her mouth. He buried his face in the hollow of her neck and rocked her in his arms as she clung to him.

"Oh my darling . . . I was so frightened . . . so afraid . . ." Jette wept against his shoulder. "When you didn't come back. . . ."

"My poor girl!" His long fingers tangled in her hair

343

and pulled her head to his breast where she could hear the pounding of his heart. There was no longer the scent of bergamot about him, but disinfectant and castile soap. "I'd never cause you worry or hurt. Forgive me, dearest."

"There's nothing to forgive—I'm only glad you're alive." She pulled away from him just far enough to look in his face. His strangely-pale blue eyes held none of their customary luster, nor did he seem to be the dashing, dapper bridgegroom of the previous day. His face was swollen, purple discolorations evincing the ferocity of the attack to which he had been subjected.

"Why?" Jette asked the one word as she gently touched his bruised forehead. "Was it the jewelry?"

"Partly," he said and sighed. "They're gone. I tried to fight them off . . ."

"You shouldn't have! You should have let them take the jewelry," Jette chided him. "You are all that's important to me—not the jewelry. You should have given them whatever they wanted and not tried to do anything." She looked into his eyes, an expression of fear betraying her sudden terror as she said, "They could have killed you!"

"Shh . . . shh . . . It's all right," he soothed her and held her to him until she stopped shaking. "I'll be fine. Good as new in a few days the doctor tells me."

When she had regained her composure, she asked, "Who were they? Can you give the police a description?"

For a moment Nate did not reply. He searched her face, then turned away, toward the white muslin curtains which surrounded his bed.

"You do know who it was, don't you?" She was shocked to see that it was so. She had not considered the possibility until now. "Who was it?" she demanded.

"Jubal Wade," he replied, pronouncing the man's name as though it were distasteful on his tongue.

"Oh dear God!" She lurched away from him, her hands covering her face. "It's my fault. It's all my fault!"

"No, darling, it isn't your fault at all. Jubal Wade's a ruffian—always has been. He's been in and out of trouble with the law for years according to what Harriet Selby told me."

"But he was angry with me . . ."

"And I gave him good reason to be angry with me," he reminded Jette.

"None of this would have happened if I hadn't gone to Harriet's." She slid off the bed and stood with her back to him, unable to face him as she accused herself. "If I'd just trusted you . . . if I hadn't gone to Harriet's when Mrs. Millege showed me those newspaper clippings . . ."

Jette could not see the frown that flitted across his bruised face. "Come back, sit down, Jette," Nate coaxed her and patted the mattress beside him. "I won't say it had nothing to do with you. Obviously it did. All I can tell you is that in no way is it your fault. Wade wanted his revenge . . . and he got it. Along with your jewelry."

"But you said, 'they.' He had someone else with him?"

"Yes, some other man." Nate looked up in surprise as Jette parted the curtains. "Jette?" he said in bewilderment.

"I'm going to bring the inspector in. He and Abe are waiting in the hallway outside."

"And Lavinia . . . Mrs. Baldwin?"

"No. Just the three of us came. They didn't want to waste time telling her anything. They just wanted to get me here," she replied, "and they want to talk to you. I'll only be a moment."

Marley and Hankins followed Jette to the end of the ward and entered the partitioned section. Without waiting for introductions, Inspector Hankins identified himself to Nate, and took out a small black leather notebook and gold mechanical pencil with which to jot down facts as Nate related his story.

"Your wife tells me you recognized your assailant," Hankins said. He looked about for a place to put his hat, but finding none, put it back on his head. "Is that true?"

"It is," Trasker replied. "I had an altercation with him night before last, in San Genaro."

"Name?" The gold pencil poised above a small square of paper.

"Jubal Wade!" Jette said before Nate could reply.

"Jubal Wade!" Abe Marley exploded the name. "That rotten bastard! Oh, I do beg your pardon, Jette." He was somewhat chagrined at his lapse in discretion. He moved closer to Trasker and stood beside the girl. "What the devil was he doing here?"

"He'd evidently learned that Jette and I were married and where we were planning to stay in San Francisco. It wouldn't have been difficult to do—we made no secret of our plans. He simply came after us. Thank God he got to me and not to Jette." Nate took his wife's hand and squeezed it. "You see, Inspector, Wade had entertained a few ideas about my wife. He'd been drunk and making a nuisance of himself. I found it necessary to settle him down."

"You fought with him?"

"I did."

"Where did you run into him last night?"

"I'd rung for the elevator—I was taking my wife's jewelry down to the hotel's safe—and they came from the adjacent hallway. They must have been waiting there for me, expecting me to do just what I did."

" 'They?' " Hankins glanced up in surprise.

"Wade and another man."

"You recognized the other man?"

346

"No, I'd never seen him before, and I don't think he was a close friend of Wade's either."

"What makes you say that?" Hankins was interested.

"Wade was being careful not to call the man by name. Very carefully avoided it. But there was something in their conversation . . . It wasn't as if they were well acquainted and I felt there was some sort of disagreement between them."

"It could not have been your business associate, Clarence Pomeroy then?" Hankins made the name an implication all by itself. If he had expected a startled reaction, he was disappointed. Trasker merely shook his head and smiled.

"I follow you there, but you're on the wrong trail, Inspector." It was painful for Nate to laugh and the occasion did not merit hilarity. Instead he smiled as broadly as his bruises would allow, and said, "It definitely was not Pomeroy. Clarence Pomeroy has no need to play highwayman—robbing tourists to make a living. He's a man of considerable substance."

The phrase caught Hankins' attention. It was the exact statement made only a short time ago by the hotel clerk about the missing Cincinnati woman, Mrs. Palma Owens. *People of substance,* Hankins thought, *should not be involved in criminal affairs, nor should they appear on missing persons reports.*

"But you did definitely recognize Jubal Wade?" Hankins asked.

"Inspector, one can hardly mistake Jubal Wade after fighting with him even once." He held his hand for them to see. It was lightly bandaged across the knuckles and palm. "I did that last night on his jaw—before he sent me down."

"Can you describe the other man? For the record," Hankins emphasized the seriousness of the situation. He noted Wade's description, then the one of the second assailant, rechecking frequently to be sure he had it exactly right. "Sister Teresa told me earlier that you were a bit incoherent when you were brought in to the hospital. She says you weren't making any sense at all. Couldn't tell what had happened. Can you manage that now?"

"Wade said he had a few matters to discuss with me and said I had a choice of coming along with them peaceably, or having his friend shoot me where I stood." At Jette's quick gasp of fear Trasker said, "I'm sorry, darling, but that's the way it was and I can't be accurate by using euphemisms."

"It's all right, Nate," she said and kissed him. "It's just the thought that I might have lost you . . ."

Hankins cleared his throat and shifted a bit on his feet. "This other man, then, was armed?" he asked.

"He was—a pocket revolver, very short barrel, probably a 32 caliber Colt by the look of it; double action, self-cocking shell ejector. Pretty flashy sort, nickel-plated, more the sort for displaying rather than using. Had it been blued and his hands a bit steadier, perhaps I'd have thought a little longer about trying to take them on." He touched Jette's arm and caressed her cheek with his bandaged hand. "It was foolish of me. I realize that now."

"But what did Wade want?" Marley was impatient to hear the rest.

"He was half drunk and spoiling to get even. We went down to the ground floor and since there were people in the lobby—the theater up the street had just let out and a lot of the hotel guests were returning—they skirted that area and went out through the employee entrance at the side of the building. You're familiar with the place?" Trasker asked Hankins.

"Yes," the inspector replied. "It opens on a side alley that cuts through street-to-street."

"I didn't much like the looks of it, but with a revolver in my ribs I didn't have a great deal of latitude. I'd

348

hoped they wouldn't discover the jewel case. I thought I could let Wade have his go at me; maybe I'd be lucky enough to deck him instead. But it was useless. They demanded the case. It was as though they'd expected me to have it on me."

"And you gave it to them?"

"To Wade, yes, I had little chance, had I?" Trasker answered with the question. "At first I thought Wade just wanted to give me a good thrashing."

"Had any of your party seen this Wade earlier in the evening? None of you had knowledge of his being here in San Francisco?"

"No, absolutely not!" Abe Marley said angrily. "I'm sure if any of us had seen the man we'd have been put on our guards and this would never have happened."

"It is just possible, however, that he had seen you. He could have seen Mrs. Trasker wearing the jewels and decided to have his revenge and some profit, too. That would certainly account for his lying in wait for you at the hotel. It would have been only a matter of timing—if it hadn't been tonight, it would have been another." Hankins accepted that part of Nate's recitation without reservation. "Please go on, Mr. Trasker."

"There's very little more to it. I'm afraid I indulged in some foolish bravado. I refused to leave the alleyway. The evening shift of hotel employees was leaving and I felt it would be safer to take my drubbing there where there might be witnesses than to leave with them. You must admit, inspector, your city has some unsavory sections, most of which are poorly lighted and even more poorly patroled."

Inspector Hankins nodded agreement. "Quite true, Trasker. Unfortunate, but true." He waved his hand for Nate to finish.

"I knew if they got me away from the hotel area it would be an even more dangerous situation. I didn't think Wade would kill me, but the other man was an unknown factor. So I refused to go. I knew they couldn't shoot me there without being heard or seen and they'd have to flee down that alley one way or another and expose themselves to risk. I tried to start a fight with Wade, dared him, insulted him . . ." Nate halted a moment. "I won't repeat in front of my wife what I said, gentlemen, but if Wade had really intended to kill me he would have done it then."

"But he didn't . . . and he didn't fight you right then and there?" Marley seemed puzzled. "That doesn't sound like Wade. No sir! He's a born brawler. Fights for the sake of the exercise it gives him."

"I knew that I was in deep trouble when he didn't rise to my bait. There had to be more to it than the simple act of getting even with me and robbing me of Jette's jewelry. As a group came out of the employee's entrance into the alley, I took my chance and lunged for the gun. I succeeded in knocking him against the wall, but he clung to the revolver. Wade came at me—since I'd forced the issue—and the next thing I remember is waking up at the bottom of a stairwell with four or five—and here, my love," he said to Jette, "I'll use euphemisms—four or five ladies hovering about, pulling their petticoats tight against their legs so they wouldn't bloody them on me. I can only presume these good ladies notified the sisters here at the hospital and had me transported from their establishment. There's no way I can tell you more. Quite simply, I don't remember."

Hankins gazed at Trasker, his face giving no hint as to how he had taken the recitation. "You remember nothing of how you came to be down in this section of the city? It's a long way from the Keniston Hotel to the Barbary Coast."

"No, Inspector. I hate to disappoint you, but I recall nothing."

After considering for a moment Hankins asked, "Do you remember what passed between this Jubal Wade and his friend in conversation? Was anything said that might give us something to go on? Names? Places? Were they to meet someone afterwards?"

"Inspector, if I could tell you anything significant, I'd be only too happy to do so. Wade—and perhaps the other man, too—left their gentle marks on me and stole my wife's jewelry. It's my turn now to think about revenge."

"You'd be well advised to leave that to us," Hankins warned him. "In the meantime, you're free to leave the hospital whenever the doctor feels you're able. Will you be returning to the Keniston?"

"Of course he will," Abe Marley replied. "I'll make arrangements to get him out of here as soon as possible."

"Inspector Hankins, I don't understand." Jette turned to the policeman. "You just now said Nate was free to leave the hospital. Does that mean he isn't free to do whatever he wants?" There was more than a hint of resentment in her question and her black eyes flashed behind their dark lashes. "Are you saying we can't leave San Francisco?"

"We'd prefer he stay in the city until we get a line on what happened. He's the only one who can help us get to the bottom of it," Hankins explained. "Mr. Trasker wouldn't be much help to us a few thousand miles away, now would he? I'm not insensitive to your circumstances, believe me, Mrs. Trasker. I realize your visit to San Francisco was intended to be your honeymoon trip and I'm sorry it's turned out so badly for you both." His manner turned brusk as he continued, "But it is essential your husband remain for a few days until we can sort this out. It's only fair to warn you both that there exists the possibility, too, of some danger until we can find this Jubal Wade."

* * * *

"Such things just do not hapen at the Keniston, Mr. Trasker." The agitated night manager nervously plucked at a speck of lint on his serge sleeve, caught himself and made a smile with his thin lips. Muscles on the right side of his face refused to behave and twitched miserably. The incident had occurred during the time he was on duty and while he could not be held liable personally, he had taken it as a blemish on his and the hotel's records. "The management of the Keniston feels that the balance of your stay with us is certainly not of your own choosing and they therefore offer you their hospitality free of charge."

"That's very kind of them," Nate said. "Please convey our thanks to the management and assure them we feel they were in no way responsible." Nate pulled the yellow satin quilt up under his arms and relaxed into the plump down pillows at his back.

"Thank you. Yes, thank you both," Mr. Algood beamed his relief. "I'll run along then." He turned to leave, a bit too abruptly he felt, so retraced his steps and added, "Now if there is anything at all you need or would like, just let us know. Room Service has been instructed to pay special attention to your requests." He backed from the luxurious bedroom, perspiration on his forehead catching the light from overhead electric lights in the ceiling fixture.

"I'll show you out, Mr. Algood," Jette said and hurried to open the door for the fidgeting manager. "And please tell Mrs. Burton how much I appreciate her helping us."

"Yes, indeed. Our pleasure entirely," he said in a whisper and glanced cautiously up and down the corridor to make sure no hotel guests were within eavesdropping distance. "Remember, anything at all you require . . ." He could not quite muster another smile, but his moustache moved spasmodically as though he was trying.

"That's considerate of you. Thank you so much. Good night." Jette closed the door and sighed, grateful for the man's generosity and concern, but even more for the calm and silence of the suite when he was gone. She was not tired so much from physical exhaustion as from emotional depletion. The strain of the past few days had begun to show in her drawn face and the lavender shadows about her eyes.

"Comfortable?" she asked and pushed the small wheeled serving table close to the bed.

"Aside from a few aches and pains, I'm very comfortable," Nate replied. "Now sit down with me and let's do justice to Algood's dinner." He saw she hesitated to sit down in the upholstered easy chair the manager had drawn up for her near the bed. "I don't know about you, my sweet, but I'm ravenous. That's a sure sign the patient's recovering."

"Do you think you should take something for the pain?"

"No, I'll be fine." He caught her hand and brought it to his lips. "It dulls the senses as well as the pain. I don't want to miss a thing tonight. We have some catching up to do, Mrs. Trasker."

"But you're supposed to rest," Jette protested with an embarrassed laugh. "What you have in mind isn't exactly what the doctor had in mind."

"On the contrary, it would be exactly what he'd have in mind if he'd just been married to the most beautiful woman in the state of California—and cheated of sharing her bed two nights in a row." He leaned across the bed and lifted the cover of the soup tureen. "I must confess, though, I'm desperately hungry. The best that I can say about he food at Saint John's is that it's nourishing."

"Let me serve you, darling," Jette said and ladled

delicate clam bisque into thin porcelain soup dishes. Algood had personally presented their dinner and had shooed the waiter from the suite before him. A glass-lined invalid tray, complete with cut-glass bud vase and blush rose, had been provided upon which Jette arranged the meal, taking hers nearby.

It had been past seven o'clock when the ambulance had pulled to a stop under the crimson canopy in front of the Keniston. Once Nate had changed into his own silk nightshirt and velvet robe and had been made comfortable, he was hungry. Still too shaken by her ordeal to have an appetite, Jette delighted in attending to her husband's needs. Watercress and blanched lettuce salad with chives, browned parsley-potato balls, halibut a la flamande, fragile meringues with strawberries and whipped cream, strong black coffee kept hot over an alcohol burner . . . the menu, kept simple in deference to Nate's role as convalescent, was perfection.

Jette poured coffee in tiny cups, handed the fragrant, steaming demitasse to Nate before resuming her seat beside the bed. They had spoken little as they ate, Jette watching, anticipating his every need.

"You've not done justice to the hotel's generosity," Nate said as he observed her dishes on the serving table.

"Would you like to finish mine?"

"No, thank you, dearest. Mr. Algood's portions are more than adequate." He stretched widely and lay against the ornately carved headboard and pillows at his back. "Complete, solid, wonderful comfort," he sighed. "I'm afraid I'm a sybarite at heart. I should never be exposed to such luxury and service." His face, still showing ravages of his attack, was nevertheless handsome to the point of beauty as he closed his eyes and smiled in contentment.

"Oh, Nate, how can you take what's happened so calmly?" Jette's eyebrows puckered with anxiety as he turned his head and the bruises were emphasized by the

354

slanting light from the electric lamp on the nightstand.

"Are you angry with me?" he asked in surprise.

"No, of course not, darling." She was hurt that he should even ask such a question. Then as she considered what he had asked, she said, "Yes! I am angry!" She reached across the satin quilt and touched his arm. "Not with you, though. You must believe that." She looked away from his scrutiny. Perhaps she imagined a sudden coldness in his eyes. "I'm just angry that Jubal Wade could do this to you . . ."

"To us, Jette. To us," Nate corrected her. "He not only ruined our honeymoon—my hurts will heal—but he's robbed you of your grandmother's bequest. What bothers me more than anything else is that I was the instrument used in robbing you."

"Darling!" Jette's demitasse cup rattled in the saucer. She abandoned it and came to sit on the bed beside Nate. She held his face in her two hands, the weight of her body almost tipping the invalid tray on his lap. "I don't care about the jewelry. Believe that. If I had lost you I'd have died. I couldn't face life without you . . . not now . . ." She bent her head and kissed his mouth, feeling his teeth hard against her lips. "My darling . . . Oh Nate, if I'd lost you . . ."

* * * *

In the sitting room of their suite the onyx and gilt clock softly chimed the quarter-hour. Jette turned her head to glance at the window across the room. A faint lessening of the dark about the lower sill showed where it was. Heavy gold drapes effectively eliminated what little illumination from the street lamps and the hotel's exterior lighting penetrated the fog. Only Nate's deep, steady breathing broke the utter silence. Even carriages and cabs had ceased passing in the street below, and the cable-cars had long since made their last trips. It was

355

impossible to guess what time it was. She did not know whether she had been asleep for hours or minutes.

Carefully she moved to the edge of the bed, listening to be certain she had not awakened Nate, then slid from beneath the quilt and felt her way into her slippers. Recalling where she had tossed her nightshift and dressing gown, she moved silently across the darkened room. She shivered as the wet air from the window blew across her naked body. Softly she padded to the window and pulled aside the drape. Fog hung like a dense curtain beyond the glass. Against the fuzzy, indistinct nebulae surrounding the street lights the mist was visible as it sifted down like fine rain. Nothing about San Francisco could be more different from San Genaro than the fog which either enveloped the city or lingered, ever-visible and threatening, off the coast in a white, rolling wall. To Jette it seemed her life, her marriage to Nate, were engulfed in fog, menacing and sinister—like the descending dark world the poet envisioned.

She would not admit the suspicions that persisted, like the fog, just beyond consciousness. Resolutely she dropped the heavy velvet and reached for her Parisian nightshift.

"Jette?" Nate's whisper startled her.

"Yes, darling."

"What are you doing?" His voice was languid with sleep.

"Putting on my gown." She shook her garment and attempted to find the armholes and ribbon ties.

"I'll turn on the light for you."

"No need," she said, but he pulled the brass chain and the ecru-shaded lamp glowed dully from the nightstand. "Thank you, dear. I'm sorry I wakened you." She pulled the gauzy gown on and fastened the ribbons beneath her breast.

"Can't you sleep?"

"I woke up just now." Jette stifled a yawn with the

back of her hand. "May I get you anything?"

He threw back the sheet and quilt and walked toward her. She gazed at his nakedness unashamedly, her eyes glorying in the hard, muscular perfection of his body. The bedside lamp limned his slender waist and flat belly in amber light. Hair as fine and glistening as spun gold shimmered on his arms and legs, and as he moved nearer, on his bare chest and crotch. He moved with easy, animal grace, his long, thin feet silent on the Turkestan rug.

She held out her arms to him, eager for him to push away the encroaching fog and doubt. As he took her in his arms and bent his head to kiss her she could see the angry welts and bruises that marred the pale smoothness of his skin. So filled was she with tenderness that everything save his warmth, his body against hers, his breath in her ear, his mouth seeking hers . . . all else was effaced by the loving passion he gently aroused. His hands pressed along her back, slid down to almost encircle her waist and caressed in silken strokes the firm, rounded buttocks and thighs beneath the veil of gown, then sought upward, fondling the high, girlish breasts. She writhed in response, her hands flat upon the hardness of his chest, her fingertips triggering urgent desire in his loins as she traced the soft aureola about his nipples. He pulled the ribbon ties and opened her nightshift, undraped it from about her shoulders and let it slip to the floor about her feet.

Sweeping her into his arms, Nate carried Jette to the bed, lowering her into the spot still warm from his body. Again she held out her arms, entreating him silently, demanding he satisfy the hunger within her. In the soft light he stood looking down upon her, waiting, not to tease, but to coax her into an agony of need. Slowly he lay beside her, touching, kneading her flesh with his fingers, creating an anxiety that only he could relieve. She arched into his embrace, her ready body trembling as he entered to make them one. She groaned as she felt the sharp, penetrating thrusts and unconsciously moved in passionate response. Deliberately, gently, he brought her to ecstasy, only then giving himself to the quick oblivion of release.

Jette lay exhausted and fulfilled. Nate's rhythmic breathing made her smile into the dark. He slept like a small child, sprawled across the bed, one arm across her body, his head on her breast. As the slight wind disturbed the curtains and drapes at the window she pulled the quilt up over them and listened to the silence that only their own breathing disturbed.

She loved, and was loved in return. Being woman to Nate's man gave her purpose and contentment —something denied her before knowing him. Steadfastly she refused to think of the future, the possibility that Jubal Wade would continue to seek his revenge. There were other possibilities, too, all of which she pushed from her thoughts. Now, each minute, being with her husband, lying in his embrace and loving him with all her being . . . this was the only thing that mattered.

Chapter 16

The telephone in Abe Marley's suite at the Keniston Hotel had quit ringing by the time he rolled out of bed and stumbled, half asleep, into the sitting room.

"Damn!" he swore under his breath. He twisted the handle on the steam-radiator and waited until the vent hissed. He tied his robe about him and pulled the shawl collar up around his neck.

"What is it, Abe?" Lavinia called from the bedroom. The insistent jangle of the telephone had not completely

358

awakened her, but as she realized Marley was no longer beside her she grew alarmed. "Abe?"

Marley rubbed his eyes and looked at the clock above the mantel. "My God, what an hour to be calling people," he mumbled in disgust.

"What did you say, Abe?" Lavinia came into the sitting room, her hastily donned dressing gown only partially closed in front. With her blond hair falling almost to her waist, she appeared younger than her years until she came to stand near the open window. In the cruel gray morning light tiny lines, unseen by artifical illumination, betrayed her thirty-four years. The lush complexion of evening turned sallow and colorless by dawn. "What was it?" She asked the question as though she expected the worst.

"How the hell do I know?" Marley replied in irritation. He slammed the window shut and fastened the drapes back. "They didn't wait long enough for me to answer." He groped for the telphone and waited for the switchboard operator to cut in. "Hello . . . yes, this is Mr. Marley in 417. You rang my room just now. I wonder if you could tell me . . ." He shifted his weight, slouching against the wall as he listened to the operator. "Yes, I see. Would you try to get him back and put through his call immediately? I'll wait right here for it."

"Abe, lover . . . tell me what's wrong!" Lavinia rushed to his side, the wrapper falling away to reveal the voluptuous body underneath.

"Inspector Hankins called," he replied wearily. His nights with Lavinia invariably left him lethargic until after breakfast. He sat down heavily in the diminutive telephone chair and yawned. "Give me a shot of that brandy, Vinnie."

"Before breakfast?"

"Please, Vinnie, no lectures or comments." There was more than irritation in his voice. She selected the decanter with the appropriate sterling silver chain and

359

label and poured an inch of brandy in a water glass, handing it to him as she came to sit opposite him.

"Did the operator say what he wanted?" she asked. Marley shook his head and drained the glass while Lavinia watched with increasing apprehension. Even as they had made love during the night she had attempted to glean from him some hint as to what he and the inspector knew or suspected. That he was close-mouthed under such circumstances had only served to spur her on to greater display of ardor. Even that, however, had been ineffectual. He had said nothing.

"More?" She took the glass from his hand.

"No more. Thanks." He rubbed his eyes and ran his fingers through his hair, pushing it back pompadour style. "Must be important for him to be up and about at this hour." He stretched his legs and leaned back in the chair. "Go on back to bed, Vinnie."

"I should go back to my own room," she said and pulled the flimsy dressing gown about herself.

"You think we're covering up our tracks well enough by your shuttling back and forth from one room to another?" He resisted the urge to laugh. This morning he did not feel like laughing. Nor did he feel like lingering abed with Lavinia. "Do as you like. I'm going to ring for some breakfast now that I'm up. You might as well stay here and join me. I'm sure nobody in San Francisco would be too shocked at finding a beautiful lady in a gentleman's quarters."

"Abe, you're so good to me," she said. By morning light she could see the lines of worry that furrowed his forehead and the dark circles about his eyes that told of his fretful night. "I'll go make myself presentable. Perhaps a dressed lady won't be quite so shocking." She bent to kiss him before she headed for the bedroom.

"What shall I order for you?" he asked. "Same as usual?"

"That'll be fine. Ask them to make the bacon crisp."

Her voice trailed away as she closed the bathroom door. There was no use in pushing Marley for information. If he intended to tell her anything, he would do so in his own time; if not, she would only succeed in annoying him. She tested the water in the tub, threw up the porcelain lever that activated the circular shower overhead. A luxurious perfumed bath would be preferable, but she sensed the need to hurry. A call from the police so early could only presage a crisis.

At the first ring of the telephone, Marley seized the instrument and barked into the mouthpiece, "Marley speaking . . . yes, put him on . . . yes, Inspector, this is Marley." He listened, his face in no way mirroring his reactions to the policeman's message. "Yes, of course, Inspector. I won't say I'll be happy to perform such a service, but I'll certainly do it . . . In an hour and a half? That will be fine. I'll wait for you in the lobby."

For some minutes he stood by the fourth-floor window, looking out on the awakening city. It was still foggy, but even as he watched the mist was retreating and the east brightening across the bay. The day promised to be fair and clear.

Inspector Hankins pulled the sheet back to reveal the pallid face. No fleck of blood at nose or mouth gave evidence of the violence done by the bullet. The dark curly hair, so unruly in life, was more so in death, falling in tight ringlets.

"Is this Jubal Wade?" Hankins asked.

"It is." Abe Marley walked closer, his foot almost touching the prostrate body. "Yes, that's Wade all right."

"Do you know the other man?"

Marley took a careful look, peering at the second man sprawled on the barren wood floor. "No," he replied.

"Ever see him before?"

"Never." Marley turned away from the sordid sight. "I have no idea who he is . . . was. Not one of Wade's friends from down our way. I know most of his associates in San Genaro. This man wasn't one of them." He walked over to the open door and breathed deeply of the freshet of air that swept up the narrow stairs from the lobby. He steadied himself by a hand on the railing.

"Sorry, old man," Hankins whispered out of the hearing of the other policeman in the room. "Necessary procedure. I'll get you out of here right away."

"It's all right," Marley said and passed a handkerchief across his moist forehead.

"It had to be done." The inspector clasped Marley's arm briefly, then returned to the dingy room.

Marley was glad he had eaten a solid breakfast before accompanying Hankins to the ramshackle hotel on MacPhail Street. On an empty stomach, his trip would have proved onerous. The nameless old hotel, a survivor of earthquakes and fires for several decades, was a sailor's and dock worker's abode whose itinerant guests paid in advance, day by day, asked no questions nor answered them. Too near the wharves and water to ever get dry inside, the building retained the sour smell of dampness, its peeling wallpaper decorated with spots of mildew.

"When did it happen?" Marley asked when he had recovered.

"Near as we can tell at this stage, twenty-four to thirty-six hours ago. They'd paid for a week in advance so nobody went into the room," Hankins said. "One shot for each man. Close range. Both sitting down, judging by the angles of penetration. May have been somebody they knew and trusted. Powder burns on the clothing. Wade got it in the back, as if he'd been caught by surprise. The other one probably started to jump up and turned. Caught it high up in the left chest with the bullet exiting in the small of the back."

362

"Someone must have heard the shots," Marley ventured.

"But no one wants to admit it. That's the way it is down here." Hankins sounded irritated. "Damned near a point of honor with these people." He made it clear that the denizens of the area were distinct from those of more respectable neighborhoods of San Francisco. "We're not apt to get any help from them."

"Inspector, this door was picked open. No force used on it, but it was picked." A young detective in plain clothes announced his finding. "Wasn't done by an expert, either. Clumsy job."

"That doesn't surprise me," Hankins said. "But it isn't as it seems at first glance," he added cryptically. He examined the gin bottle, the two glasses, and the contents of the victims' pockets. The miscellaneous items had been spread out upon the table. The younger man stood respectfully aside as the inspector continued, "This is expensive imported gin. Not the sort common brawlers like these would buy. Doesn't fit at all."

"They were flush with money," Marley reminded him. "They'd taken whatever Trasker had on him."

"And so they stop along the way to their hideout down here and buy the best gin available for their celebration." He mused on that possibility, but shook his head. "No. That just doesn't fit for men like our friends here. I don't know their tastes, but I'd hazard a week's pay it wouldn't be gin. A decent bourbon or rye maybe . . ." He turned to Marley and motioned him to start down the stairs. "I think we've seen about all there is here."

To the rest of his men Hankins said, "Carry on as I've instructed you. I'll be checking back in at the station the rest of the day. Leave any messages for me there if anything turns up." After accepting their murmur of compliance, he descended the litter-strewn stairs and joined Marley on the street below.

"No trace of the jewelry?" Marley asked, relieved to be outside once more.

"None whatsoever. Nothing of value at all. It's my opinion—for what it's worth at this juncture—that someone wants us to either believe that robbery was the motive for the murders or that the room was entered and burglarized after the men were already dead." He smiled at Marley's look of surprise. "There are ways a real criminal does things, my friend, and this was not done their way."

"Perhaps you'd better explain. I'm no expert on such matters, fortunately." Marley climbed into the waiting cab. "If theft was the motive, and if it was done by anyone who knew his business, it would appear differently?"

"It would, indeed. This would not have been overlooked." Hankins settled himself into the seat and called up to the driver, "To the Keniston Hotel," then handed to Marley a thin, gold and silver cigarette case.

Marley whistled appreciatively. "This must have cost a pretty penny." He turned it about, admiring the engraving. "Tiffany, no less." As he tripped the catch and opened the case to examine the interior, he looked up at the policeman in amazement. "I see what you mean."

"Our elusive Clarence Pomeroy." The inspector offered Marley a perfecto, held a light for him, and they smoked in silence for several blocks. "We'll go tell Mrs. Trasker the news. She should be enormously relieved that Wade's out of the way."

"And Nate?"

"It should be interesting to see how he takes the news," Hankins said. "Wade and his friend are one matter." He continued as he tapped a finger on the cigarette case, "This is quite another matter."

Inspector Hankins was not a man to reveal the cards he held in his hand. He was not yet sure he held a winning hand. "You say Pomeroy hasn't contacted you?" he asked Nate. "Wouldn't that be unusual, even considering the circumstances of your business negotiations?"

"It is most unusual," Trasker replied. He remained in his velvet robe and slippers and was lying on the elongated chaise in the sitting room. "Needless to say, I'm beginning to worry about him. We must be circumspect, it's true, but to fail to get in touch with me . . . well, I don't understand it. It isn't like him at all."

"We've had no luck in finding out from your Chicago office where Pomeroy is staying in the city," Hankins said. "It seems no staff is on duty at either Farrier Development or Montague-Cameron. Is that unusual?" Hankins left no doubt that he thought it most irregular.

"Not in the least," Nate countered. "Almost all of our business is conducted in person. There's no need for an extensive staff. They have personal secretaries who attend to any correspondence and any trivia that may come up, and of course the firms' attorneys, but they don't necessarily remain in the offices."

"I'd be grateful if you'd tell Mr. Pomeroy—in case he does get in touch with you—that I'd like him to step around to the station and have a word with me." Hankins rose to leave.

"I'd be glad to, Inspector." Nate got up from the chaise and escorted the man to the door of the suite.

"If you'll excuse me, Mrs. Trasker, I'll be on my way. Sorry to have intruded on you again in this fashion, but I was sure you'd want to be kept informed."

"Yes, Inspector, I'm glad you let us know." Jette still could not believe that such a thing could occur, certainly not in her own life. "I was hoping they'd be caught, but that's a dreadful thing to happen to them. I'd never

365

have wished them such a fate.''

"Well, rest easy on that count. They probably bragged to the wrong sort of people. Or maybe they tried to dispose of some of the jewelry and were followed to their room.'' Hankins sounded confident as he added, "We'll get to the bottom of it, I'm sure. Good afternoon, Mrs. Trasker . . . Mrs. Baldwin.'' He faced Marley and said, "Thanks again for your help.''

When Inspector Hankins was gone, Nate turned to Jette and said, "You really shouldn't have upbraided the man the way you did, darling. He's only doing his job.''

"But he had no right to be so inquisitive about your business affairs! They have nothing to do with what happened either to Jubal Wade or you!'' As she stood in the sunlight streaming through the window her hair blazed with bright copper highlights, her cheeks still flushed from the quick anger she felt at the policeman's questions.

"My sweet, he is an officer of the law and as such has every right in the world to ask any questions he feels pertain to a case. If we get miffed, that's our fault, not his.'' Nate sat down on the gold damask chaise and lighted a cigarette. Bruises, now turned purple-blue, mottled his face, but the swelling had disappeared. He seemed perfectly content.

"Perhaps so, Nate, but I still intend for us to return home tomorrow.'' Jette turned to Marley and asked, "He can't stop us, can he? After all, it isn't as if we had committed any crimes, is it?''

"I'm afraid he can stop you—all of us—if he wants to, Jette.'' Marley perched uncomfortably on a stiff side-chair before the fireplace, his brown felt fedora in his hand. "Why don't you wait another day, just to mollify him, and let me talk to him for you. Then decide what you want to do.''

"But our trip has been disastrous!'' Jette began

pacing the length of the sitting room. "I just want us to go home and try to forget all this!"

"What Abe says sounds reasonable, love," Nate said. "I'm damned if I see why we shouldn't go where and when we wish—it is our honeymoon and we had planned to enjoy ourselves—but with all that's happened . . ."

"All right, if that's what you advise," Jette said with a hestitancy that told of her lack of conviction. "We'll stay."

"That's exactly what I'd advise," Marley said.

"Why should they? Why should we?" Lavinia, who had remained out of the discussion, strode to confront Marley. She had changed into a tight-fitting pale blue afternoon suit and ponderous picture-hat of black maline with pink roses beneath the brim. "Just tell me one good reason we all shouldn't leave!"

"I'll give you several, Vinnie, any one of which spells one hell of a lot of trouble: Nate was robbed; Nate was beaten up and could have been killed; Jubal Wade was killed; his friend—whoever he was—was killed; they were either robbed or their room burglarized after they were killed; Jette's jewelry is still missing . . ." He looked askance at Lavinia and concentrated on Nate as he added, ". . . and it seems this Clarence Pomeroy may be missing, too."

"That's ridiculous!" Lavinia retorted. "You know why he can't contact any of us right out in the open."

"I know the reason you've given me and the police . . ." Marley's shot hit its mark. Lavinia turned abruptly to confront him. Her sudden scowl divulged more than she intended.

"Mr. Pomeroy may have gone on down to Los Angeles. Maybe he prefers to get in touch with us down there," Lavinia theorized. "Our land acquisition is too critical to jeopardize right now. It's possible someone's sniffed out our plans. If so, he'd be cautious in the extreme." She avoided watching Trasker, but her eyes flicked his way several times as though she were awaiting some indication from him as to what she should say. Jette came to sit beside her on the divan.

"All the more reason for us to go home," Jette said.

"No! We'll do as Abe suggests." Nate's thin mouth was set into a straight line of determination. "I want no trouble from the inspector." His tone implied he wanted no trouble from her either. He was about to say something more when a sharp knock sounded at the door of the suite. "Who the devil?" he muttered and sprang to answer the summons. He threw open the door, startling the blue-uniformed and aproned maid who stood outside, her arms laden with clean linens. A utility cart with buckets, soap, fresh sheets and towels, brooms and mops, had been pushed against the wall to the left of the door.

"Is it convenient for me to take care of your rooms now?" she asked. She was young, scarcely more than a girl, her hair neatly tucked beneath a ruffled dust-cap. At the sight of Abe Marley and Lavinia she backed away. "Maybe I should come back later?"

"No, no," Jette said and came to her side. "Please come right in. It's all right." Nate closed the door behind the girl and returned to the chaise as Jette led her into the bedroom. "I have some clothes that need pressing and some hand laundry that needs doing. Can you take care of it for me?" Jette asked.

"Yes, ma'am. I'd be glad to." The girl began stripping the bed as Jette laid out the clothing on the back of a chair.

Abe Marley's frown deepened as he listened to their chatter. He moved closer to Nate and Lavinia, standing before the fireplace as if he were reluctant to sit beside either one of them. "You two listen to me . . ." He glanced at the bedroom doorway to make certain that both Jette and the hotel maid were out of earshot.

"Something Hankins didn't tell you was that he found a fancy cigarette case under Jubal Wade's body. I don't know why he didn't tell you, but the fact that he didn't makes me think of some questions of my own." His voice dropped an octave to a growl. "The case he found belonged to Clarence Pomeroy." He waited for the fact to register and be reflected in their faces. "I see that sets you both thinking. Good!"

"Then it would seem the inspector has one more problem, wouldn't it?" Nate relaxed back into the depths of the cushions with his long legs comfortably stretched the length of the chaise. He drew deeply on the cigarette, exhaling smoke in a thin stream.

"Is that all you've got to say about it?" Marley was angry, his face no longer the jovial politician's, but a man caught up in an embarrassing and dangerous episode. "If the implications don't come to mind . . ."

"Several implications occur to me, Abe." Nate crossed one ankle over the other and waved Marley to a chair opposite him. "As long as you're not going anywhere right now, sit down." The movement and action infuriated Marley, but he sat down, still holding his hat in his hands.

"By God, I'd sure as hell want to know what happened if I were you!" Marley kept his voice down. "You didn't bat an eye!"

"I do wonder—what do you expect me to do? The Chicago offices know where I am. All Pomeroy has to do is wire them and find out. I don't know how a cigarette case belonging to him came to be with Jubal Wade. A dozen possibilities occur to me, some of them not very attractive, but I can't be responsible for Clarence Pomeroy. If he's gotten into trouble, I'm sorry and I'll do all I can to help. Further than that . . ." Nate dusted ash from his cigarette into the glass and mahogany stand beside him. "You can hardly expect me to become exercised before I know what's happened, can you?"

"Abe's right, Nate. Pomeroy should have been in touch with you before now, even if just by telegram." Lavinia was uneasy. Abe Marley's backing and his personal interest in contracting for and obtaining options on land in San Genaro County were too important to risk losing. "Send a wire to the Los Angeles office just in case he should go there."

"Fine. Would you mind doing it for me?" Nate asked, his smile including them both. "And this afternoon perhaps we should go see the inspector and determine—if we can—just why Jubal Wade and his friend came into possession of Pomeroy's cigarette case. Would that put your mind more at ease, Abe?"

Through narrowed eyes Marley looked from one to the other. He had committed himself and his own money to Farrier Development and therefore to Nate Trasker. Regret it as he might, he was in, and short of financial ruin and possible disgrace, he could see no way out. "That would certainly demonstrate your concern at least." He rose to go and turned to say, "Just in case the worst has happened, you'd better have some damned good answers handy for Booth Killigrew. He's going to have a lot more questions than Inspector Hankins." He settled his hat on his head, touched the brim on both sides and pulled on his kidskin gloves. "Remember one thing: Killigrew's going to be the next governor of this state and at the first breath of scandal or any even faintly unsavory deals he'll throw you both to the wolves and get out of it unscathed. He can do it—and he will. I can promise you that much." He didn't wait for either of them to show him to the door. Instead, he left abruptly and slammed it behind him.

Unseen by Nate and Lavinia, Jette had been standing in the door to the bedroom, uncertain as to whether she should intrude in what seemed to be business matters. When Nate became aware of her presence he snapped, "You might as well come in and hear it all. There's no need of you sneaking around and eavesdropping.''

"Nate! How can you say such a thing to her?"
Lavinia reached for a cigarette from the box on the
smoking stand. "She is your wife, for God's sakes. I
should think you'd have no secrets from her. This does
affect her, too, you know." She motioned to Jette to sit
beside her.

"I think you owe me an apology, Nate," Jette said,
not caring if the maid overheard or not. "I could hardly
help hearing what was said. No one was whispering. If it
was supposed to be confidential why didn't you close
the door?" Anger flared in her black eyes as she stood
at the foot of the chaise. Nate sensed an ugly crisis in the
making and jumped up, catching her in his arms.

"Forgive me, darling! I didn't mean that." He held
her close, burying his head in the hollow of her neck.
"It was a rotten thing for me to say. It's just that so
much has happened . . . I'm half crazy with worry!"
He felt her quick response and kissed her. "Say you forgive me, Jette."

It was a minute before she replied. How could she
remain angry with her husband when he was so
troubled? Surely his problems were now hers also. If her
forgiveness was important to him, then he must have it.

"Of course I'll forgive you, Nate," she said. "It's all
so dreadful. I understand," she soothed him and
caressed his face until the lines of worry disappeared.

Lavinia Baldwin watched for a moment, then picked
up her handbag preparatory to leaving. "If you two will
excuse me, I'll go send that wire to Los Angeles and try
to get Abe calmed down. I don't know what Inspector
Hankins told him, but he's fired up enough to do something foolish. He could quite easily upset the apple cart
if we don't watch him."

"Thanks, Vinnie. And wire Chicago and ask what the
hell's going on." Nate released Jette and took Lavinia
to the door. "After all this, I think Jette may be right.

371

We should all go home to San Genaro before we get into more trouble. We should leave the San Francisco police to handle matters as best they can by themselves."

"Perhaps you're right. I'll talk to Abe." Lavinia glanced at herself in the mirror by the door, straightened the collar of her suit. "Ta-ta for now. Bye, Jette. Don't you worry too much."

Lavinia hurried down the corridor. Somehow she had to convince Abe Marley to return to San Genaro. If they waited, who might be next to meet with violence? She could only wonder if in San Genaro they would find safety.

Chapter 17

The way the buggy careened down the lane toward the ranch house at La Coruna spelled urgency. From such a distance Jette could not discern what sort of vehicle it was or who was in it. Dust roiled in its wake to be swept away by the hot, dry wind. It could not be Nate returning home from Los Angeles. His business—a consultation with hydraulic engineers—could not possibly be finished so early. He had said to expect him back in a few more days. For an instant Jette felt the clutch of panic. Had something happened to her mother? *But, no, that could not be*, she reminded herself. She had seen Verdie only yesterday and she was fine.

By the time she had hurried to the other end of the house and had put water to boil on the kerosene stove in the summer kitchen, the carriage had pulled into the courtyard. As Jette glanced from the kitchen window and saw the two men alighting, she could hardly believe her eyes. Hadn't the episode in San Francisco been enough? Did they have to bring it down to La Coruna?

"Afternoon, Jette." Abe Marley tied the team to the hitching rail and took off his wide-brimmed hat as Jette came from the adobe. Before she could greet either man, Marley asked, "Is Nate here?"

"No, he isn't," she answered with asperity.

"How are you, Mrs. Trasker?" The other man doffed his black derby and stood waiting in the hot sun. His face was impassive, with no hint as to his mission at the remote ranch. As Jette saw the expression on Marley's face she frowned.

"I'm very well, thank you, Inspector." She was too upset by their unannounced appearance to think about inviting them into the coolness of the veranda overhang. "I hardly expected to welcome you to La Coruna," she said. "May I ask what brings you here?"

"You may, indeed," he replied. "I'm here to see your husband." He had not smiled as he greeted her, nor did he smile when he answered her question. "Where is he, Mrs. Trasker?"

"In Los Angeles, on business," Jette said.

"May we come in?" Marley asked and stepped into the shade of the terracotta-tiled porch. He sensed her animosity and hoped it would not prove an obstacle. "We must talk with you, too, Jette."

"Very well. Please come in." Jette led them to the parlor which was several doors down the long open corridor. Inside, the adobe had remained cool, its thick walls protecting the interior from excessive heat. She indicated they might sit in the small upholstered chairs arranged before the open window where the curtains fluttered in the sporadic gusts. "I think you'll find that spot a bit cooler," she said. "I've put on water to make tea, or perhaps you'd prefer lemonade. I have it already made."

"Lemonade would be fine," Hankins said. "I'm afraid I'm not accustomed to the extreme heat you get in these inland valleys. I seem to be much too warm

373

most of the time, and thirsty all of the time." He felt giving her something specific to do would break down her initial hostility and open the way for their conversation to be more productive.

"Please sit down, gentlemen," Jette insisted, remembering that the ranch was, after all, famous for its hospitality.

"Thank you," Abe said and heaved himself into the chair. The ride from town had been hot and jolting even though the county had only recently re-graded the highway north of town. "Lemonade would be fine for me, too, if it's no trouble."

"Tecla made some early this morning before she left," Jette replied. "Please feel free to take your coats off if you like." Both declined her suggestion and she continued, "Why men must suffer through the summer in woolen coats to be considered properly dressed is beyond me. Make yourselves comfortable and I'll be right back."

"Mrs. Scott isn't here?" Marley asked in surprise. He cast a peculiar glance at the San Francisco policeman, its meaning lost on the young woman. "You have no one with you?"

"Not today. There was a death in her family over in Las Lomas and she's gone to help out until after the funeral. If you'll excuse me, I'll only be a minute . . ." She picked up her skirts and hastened down the porch to the kitchen and turned the burner off beneath the water. She had been foolish to think any women friends—who might prefer tea—would come barreling out to La Coruna on such a day.

A large oak refrigerator sat in the coolest corner of the storeroom off the kitchen, and from its ice block she chipped enough ice to fill their glasses and cool the pitcher. From a shelf in the pantry she took the gaudily enameled cookie tin and arranged a plateful of molasses wafers, ginger snaps, and vanilla cremes. Her hands trembled as she placed the refreshments on a tray and carried it back to the parlor. As though she were trying to put off the inevitable unpleasantness of their visit, she prolonged the serving before seating herself across from them.

"I think you can guess why we're here, can't you?" Hankins asked without any preliminary remarks. He had immediately sensed her antagonism and defense reaction to his call.

"You've asked about my husband. I gather you're here to harrass him further about what happened in San Francisco." She sipped the tart drink and eyed him over the rim of the glass. He did not flinch at her accusation, nor did he avert his eyes from her resentful stare.

"My dear Mrs. Trasker, I do not intend to exchange mutually irritating words with you. You've suffered beyond endurance—Mr. Marley has told me of how you lost your father recently—and I've no wish to add to your troubles, but I have no choice." He accepted a wafer and made three bites of it, allowing Jette to consider what he had said. "He also tells me you're an exceptionally intelligent young woman, so I refuse to believe that you've never entertained suspicions about your husband's business affairs." Again he let her think about his meaning.

"Listen to him, Jette!" Marley warned. As he saw her stiffen in anger he said, "Listen very carefully to what he has to say." She started to say something in reply, but he held up his hand to silence her. "Believe me, girl, your life may depend on it."

Jette looked bewilderedly to Hankins for confirmation of Marley's alarming statement. He nodded slowly, his eyes riveting hers. "What he says is correct, Mrs. Trasker."

She could not reply. But neither could she admit to the doubts that had plagued her whenever she wondered about Nate's financial dealings.

"Mr. Marley tells me your mother lives on a ranch nearby. Do you think you could go stay with her until we get this all cleared up?" Hankins asked pointedly. "It may be important that you do." She only nodded, unable to utter words in answer.

"First of all, let me say I found out that somebody right here in San Genaro paid Jubal Wade to go up to San Francisco," Marley intervened. "He paid Harriet Selby for the damage he did to her place the night you and Nate were married. And he asked her to hold onto a few extra dollars for him until he got back. He never said where he was going. Hinted he was told to keep his mouth shut, as a matter of fact."

"Just what are you trying to say?" Jette demanded.

"Let me finish . . . Now it wasn't like Jubal Wade to traipse after you and Nate just to get even. Maybe he was a worthless sort, but he never was a fool. And from what I know of the man, he wasn't one to hold grudges. It didn't fit that he'd spend all that money and effort to come after either of you for spite. He liked to have a lot of fun with whatever money he earned. And, too, he was spending money hand over fist the morning after he'd had that set-to with you and Nate—money he ordinarily didn't have."

"What does that prove?" she asked.

"That someone here wanted him to show up in San Francisco that same night. Wanted that enough to pay him a lot of cash."

"And I suppose you think that someone was Nate?" Jette flared. "That's ridiculous! Why should he?"

"Wait . . . there's much more," Hankins said. "Very quietly a few days ago I had Hiram Baldwin's body exumed."

"Why would Lavinia do that?" Jette asked.

"She didn't," Marley replied. "We had Judge Killigrew issue the order."

"But why?" Jette was horrified.

"Mr. Baldwin had been slowly poisoned by arsenic," Marley said.

"I don't believe it!" She jumped up and paced nervously before the fireplace. "I won't believe it!"

"Nevertheless, it's true." The inspector unbuttoned his coat and mopped his face with his handkerchief. "Do you have any idea where Lavinia Baldwin is?"

She looked frantically at Marley. Surely they could not mean what they were implying.

"Tell him, Jette," Marley urged her. "If you know where she is . . ."

"She's in Chicago," she replied. "She went on to Chicago from San Francisco. She had business to atttend to at the Chicago offices. We saw her off on the train before we left for home."

Hankins shook his head slowly. "She didn't go to Chicago. She didn't go anywhere on that train. My guess is that she got right off after you left her."

"Has Nate said anything to you about her?" Marley asked.

"No, nothing!" Jette said in dismay. "Why would she do such a thing?"

"At this point we can only surmise her purposes. We want to find her and ask her about Mr. Baldwin," the policeman said.

"Are you going to arrest her?" Jette asked.

He did not reply immediately. Finally he said, "Yes, we are. We're charging her with the murder of her husband. You see, we've found the pharmacy in Los Angeles that sold her the arsenic. They remember her very well."

"But it might have been someone else . . ."

He shook his head. "No, Mrs. Trasker. Lavinia Baldwin is a very distinctive woman in appearance. It was she, all right." Hankins seemed saddened by the knowledge. "She inherited her husband's property and only recently sold title to your husband, not for what

377

it's actually worth, but a good deal less. Did you know that?''

"No! I did not!" Jette stopped pacing and abruptly sat down in the chair opposite them again. She was obviously shaken by the news.

Hankins helped himself to more lemonade and swirled the ice about in the glass. "Do you recall the newspaper clippings that one of your friends showed you? The ones telling of a woman in Cincinnati being bilked of a lot of money? Mr. Marley mentioned them to me," he explained. "Do you remember the case?"

"Yes, I remember very well. Nate and I were going to go see the woman after we left Chicago. As you know, we never got that far. We still plan to go see her—just to set such allegations to rest once and for all," Jette said. "But what has that to do with Lavinia—or Nate's buying her ranch?"

"The body of Mrs. Palma Owens was found a few days ago," Hankins said quietly. There was no way he could soften the blow. "Are you all right, Mrs. Trasker?" Jette's face had drained of color as she listened to his recitation of facts. He took her glass from her shaking hand and placed it on the tray. "I'd spare you this if I could, but you must understand the situation. Can I get you anything?" he asked.

"No, no. I'll be all right," she stammered. "Please go on."

"Mrs. Owens had been told by a Mrs. Daisy Howard, also from Cincinnati and with whom you're acquainted, that the man who had disappeared with the proceeds from the sale of some riverfront property of hers had turned up here in San Genaro under the name of Nate Trasker. She determined to come see this man for herself and took a compartment on the train. Her relatives in Ohio informed us she'd planned to come to San Frnacisco anyhow, to her customary hotel for an extended stay, and was to make a trip to Los Angeles

378

and San Genaro to confront this man. She'd reserved a suite of rooms in San Francisco, but never arrived. Nor did she contact relatives. The railroad notified the proper authorities and was working on her disappearance when we contacted them. We got to backtracking on her, and found she'd been on the train throughout Colorado and into Utah. Somewhere between there and San Francisco she disappeared from her compartment.''

Hankins paused a moment before continuing. ''Her body was discovered not far from Salt Lake City, in a ravine beside the roadbed. She'd been ready for bed, dressed in a nightgown and robe; her hair done up in kid-curlers. No one we've interviewed recalls seeing or hearing anything unusual. We can only guess that she was pushed out the window of her compartment.''

''She could have fallen,'' Jette interrupted.

He shook his head sadly, saying, ''Not likely, Mrs. Trasker. In fact, it would almost be impossible, even though she was a tiny woman.''

''She might have started for the dining car and fallen out in the vestibule . . . the windows might have been open and she was dizzy or something . . .'' Desperately Jette groped for a reason.

''It won't do, Mrs. Trasker! A woman of her wealth and fastidiousness would never allow herself to be seen in public with her hair in kid-curlers and attired as she was. From what her sisters and brother tell us, she'd never let anybody see her like that.'' He sighed and added, ''No, she didn't leave the train either by free will or by accident.''

''You forget one thing, Inspector,'' Jette said triumphantly. ''My husband was always here in San Genaro or in San Francisco for the past number of weeks. There is no way he could be responsible for her death.''

''But I'm not accusing him of Mrs. Owens' death.''

''Then what exactly are you accusing him of? First

you tell me about Jubal Wade's being hired to show up in San Francisco. Next you say Lavinia Baldwin killed her husband with arsenic. Now you say this woman —Mrs. Owens—may have been killed . . ." Jette's voice acquired a sharp overtone. "You want to know where Lavinia is . . . and where Nate is . . ."

She was becoming distraught. Hankins recognized the signs. He glanced about the room for the liquor cabinet. "Marley, could you get Mrs. Trasker a tot of whiskey?"

"I don't want whiskey!" Jette almost shouted. "I want to know what you're trying to tell me! I want to know what you're trying to do to my husband!" Abe Marley jumped up and opened the doors of several cabinets before finding the shelf of bottles and glasses. He poured a shot glass full and insisted Jette drink it down. He waited until she returned the glass empty, then sat close to her and held her hand in his.

"There's also the matter of Clarence Pomeroy," Hankins went on. "He's supposed to be a member of the same firm as your husband and Mrs. Baldwin." He paused for emphasis. "He's still missing."

"Now, Jette, I know what you're going to say," Marley put in quickly. "We should be able to get in touch with the Chicago offices and find out about Pomeroy." He patted her hand and made her look directly into his eyes. "The offices are just dummies, Jette. They were set up a few years ago and made to appear legitimate. Nominal taxes were paid, and papers all properly filed, but there's nothing behind them . . . nothing at all. Booth Killigrew got hold of a judge in Cook County and asked him to look into the set-up. It's fake, Jette, fake!"

"It can't be true, Abe!" she pleaded. "It's some sort of mistake on your part. It has to be!" She begged him to admit he could be wrong in his assumptions. "All you've told me can be coincidental . . . all of it!"

"Mrs. Trasker, I am not a believer in plural coincidences," Hankins replied. "Here we have far too many. They give the lie to themselves. Whenever there's a series of such incidents it has been my experience to find they are all somehow connected. Much like a string of islands whose tops are seen in mid-ocean . . . under the water they prove to all be strung together, parts of one gigantic mountain range. Just so, a string of seemingly disparate coincidences must be connected. In this case, I believe it is large scale fraud—which now includes robbery and murder."

"Do you see why we want you to go to your mother's for a while?" Marley asked. "Will you do that?"

"No!" Jette pulled her hand away and backed from them. "No! I won't believe it!"

"Where is Nate?" Marley asked. "If he's innocent, we'll be only too happy to help him establish the fact. I've got a lot of money at stake in his development project. I happen to believe in what he says he's trying to do here in the county. But as the inspector says, there are a lot of things that need clarification."

"I won't quibble, Mrs. Trasker," Hankins said. "Your husband has a lot to account for. Where is he?"

"I told you before—he's in Los Angeles."

"Where in Los Angeles?"

"At the Imperial," she said angrily. "He always stays at the Imperial Hotel."

Marley looked to Hankins, then back to Jette. "He's not there, Jette. The inspector asked the Los Angeles police to pick Nate up. He's not at the Imperial."

Twilight fell, a colorless pause in the cloudless day. The searing santana wind also paused to observe the transition between scorching day and cool night. Jette had not accompanied Inspector Hankins and Abe Marley out into the courtyard as they took their leave. If Marley had been insistent on her going to stay with

Verdie, Jette had been equally determined she would remain in her own home—in her and Nate's home. She still sat in the parlor, her hands in her lap, her eyes unfocused and unseeing. Seth Scott had come in from the barn at four-thirty, and finding her alone in the house suggested one of the wives of the hired hands should come stay with her. She had declined his offer. She wanted no company. She must think—alone, and clearly.

As the sun began to dip below the blue western hills, she determined what she would do. Perhaps her action would be wrong. Many of her moves had been very wrong. She had to ask herself the one important question and answer it honestly: Did she love Nate enough to believe in him despite all evidence presented by Hankins and Marley? And regardless of the coincidental happenings that seemed to indict Nate beyond all doubt, Jette found she could still answer, *Yes, I love him that much*.

She could hear Seth out behind the ranch house tossing feed to Tecla's chickens. She almost laughed as a laggard hen, jealous that she would miss her share of grain, flew down from the lower branches of a pepper tree across the courtyard and ran as fast as her yellow legs could go toward the rear of the adobe. The smile lingered on Jette's face, then faded slowly as she rocked monotonously in the heavy oak chair that faced the fireplace.

"Seth!" she called suddenly from the open window.

"Yes, ma'am?" He strolled across the poultry yard scattering cracked corn as he walked.

"Please harness up the trap for me," she said as he drew near the house. "And make sure the lamps are all right."

"The trap?" Seth Scott could only wonder what she might want with the buggy at that time of day.

"That's right. I'm going to town and catch the evening train to Los Angeles." She brightened as Scott glanced at her face in the waning light. The help must not know anything about Nate's troubles. Although Marley and Hankins vowed it would be kept confidential until something definite could be proved, such news always filtered out into the community soon enough. It would not, however, come from her. "I want to surprise Mr. Trasker." Realizing how peculiar it must seem to their foreman she added, "I've got to go to Los Angeles soon anyhow and pick out furniture for the spare bedroom so I may as well go tonight and be ready to start my shopping first thing in the morning."

"I'll be ready to drive you in about fifteen minutes," Seth said.

"That won't be necessary. I'll drive myself."

"Oh, no, ma'am, I can't let you do that. Mr. Trasker wouldn't forgive me if I let you go do something like that. Besides, it ain't too safe for a lady . . . that's a long way to town." He would brook no argument on the matter. "I'll bring the buggy around directly." Before she could protest, he started for the poultry house. "Think we can make it in time?" he asked. "I mean we'll have to hurry to get there by train time."

"I'll make it," she replied. "I *must* make it." Seth gave her an odd look before hurrying to leave the feed pan in the corn bin. He took off at a lope toward the barn, yelling to one of the hands to bring the bay team in from pasture.

She must get to Los Angeles and find Nate. She could only hope to do so before the police might. It was small comfort to know that nothing would appear in the newspapers until Nate's and Lavinia's stories could be heard. Of more solace was the knowledge that tangible proof, the sort a court requires as evidence of commission or complicity, was totally lacking. Circumstantial evidence was another matter. She would not let herself think of it. He had to be innocent!

It was late by the time she boarded the evening train

to the city. Light supper was still being served in the dining car and she made her way back to it, hoping to find a table to herself. Time . . . time to think, time to find Nate . . . time itself was precious now. She could not waste any of it in small talk with strangers. She hardly knew what the waiter placed before her. Eating mechanically, rather than with relish or from hunger, she turned events of the past few months over in her mind. Always she came back to the same overwhelming realization: she loved Nate. Loved him despite accusations and doubt.

Instead of resuming the seat in the passenger carriage allotted to her, she located an empty one in another car, gathered her skirts and slid into it. Alone, she could ponder her position and what she must do. Beyond the train windows the evening darkness was complete. The glass served as a mirror in which she could glimpse herself, but the image was repellent to her and she turned away.

The swaying of the train, the repetitive clack and rumble as it sped south, soon dulled the sharp edges of her fear. Weary and frightened, in spite of herself, she dozed.

"To the Imperial Hotel, please," she said to the sleepy cabbie as he heaved her portmanteau into the carriage. The streets, teeming by day, were all but deserted by night as they made their way from the station to the center of the hotel and business district. Jette marveled at how different Los Angeles appeared by night—more like the somnolent pueblo of its origins than the vital rail terminus and shipping center.

The hotel's lobby was still ablaze with electric lights, an extravagant display calculated to epitomize the management's confidence and reliance on modern innovations. The cabbie handed Jette out of the carriage, swung down her luggage and escorted her into the hotel. The doorman and bellboys were already occupied with other guests' requirements and the desk clerk cast a hurried, disapproving look at their arrival.

"Thank you," she said to the cabbie and paid him, handing him an extra tip for the lateness of the hour. He doffed his dusty hat and left her alone in the vast lobby. As she awaited her turn before the oak counter she tried to recall where Nate might have gone in the city. Since the police did not find him here at the Imperial, where could he be? Why had she thought she could locate him if they could not?

"Yes, miss?" The desk clerk cleared his throat and tapped impatiently with his pen to catch her attention. "You wish to register?" he asked when she looked up in surprise.

"Yes, please. I'm Mrs. Nate Trasker. I'd like to stay in my husband's room. I have some business to attend to in the city and thought I'd come down and meet him when he arrives tomorrow." She could not ignore the startled look he gave her. "That's room 539," she explained. "I don't believe my husband has returned to Los Angeles yet. He should be here tomorrow," she lied to provide the reason for Nate's absence. "He hasn't checked in yet, has he?"

"No, ma'am, not yet." The desk clerk appeared confused and glanced uneasily toward the office behind the counter. "If you'll excuse me, I'll just check to see if 539 is available." He handed her the steel-nibbed desk pen and turned the register for her to sign as he ducked into the office. A burly man in a dark, short-lapeled suit and bowler hat peered from the glass partition at Jette, then nodded his head and picked up the telephone on the desk beside him. The clerk returned to the counter, saying, "I'm sorry, Mrs. Trasker. Room 539 isn't available, but I can give you a room on either the fourth or sixth floor."

"But my husband rents 539 on a permanent basis. I don't understand," Jette said.

"It's . . . it's . . . being renovated," he replied a bit too evasively. "Cleaning, painting . . . that sort of thing. We have a lovely room on six. Bright all day and very quiet. Nice view from the windows." He was trying hard to sell the alternate room to her. She could only wonder why until she put it together with the man in the office who continued to watch her. "Room 623 is quite nice . . ."

"That would be fine." She was too anxious to waste time arguing about the location of her accommodations. "May I leave a message here at the desk just in case my husband should check in? I don't want to miss him."

"Certainly," he said and waited expectantly as if she intended to give him the message verbally. Reluctantly he handed her an envelope and note paper with the hotel's address and a line engraving of the building embossed in black. He waited as she dipped the pen, wrote a few lines, then sealed the envelope.

"I'd be most grateful if you'd see he gets this as soon as he comes in," she said as he jangled the small bell on the counter to summon a bellboy.

"Happy to oblige," the clerk said and smiled, but he cast an apprehensive glance back toward the office where the man in the bowler continued his surveillance, telephone in hand.

Room 623 was in the middle of the building, its windows giving a view of the low hills north of the city. Street lights twinkled in graduated rows up the slopes, disappeared at the crest and reappeared on the next hill top. A three-quarter moon, unseen from the room, hung low over the horizon to the east in a clear, cloudless sky. For a moment Jette gazed from the window after the bellboy threw it open.

When he had left she loosened her high-necked blouse, ran cold water into the lavatory and splashed her face and the back of her neck until she felt some of the fatigue diminish. She could not afford herself the luxury of even a few minutes' rest. If she were to find Nate, she must begin tonight.

Obviously the police, at Inspector Hankins' request, were waiting for Nate in case he returned to the Imperial. Had her coming upset some plan they had afoot? The more she thought of the clerk's reaction to her request for room 539 the more she was convinced it must be occupied by policemen. There was one way to find out for herself. She touched a powderpuff to her face, donned her suit jacket and cautiously peered from the door of her room. No one was in sight. The sixth floor was, as the clerk had promised, very quiet. Not a sound betrayed a presence in the corridor. She shut the door silently and tiptoed to the end of the hallway where she found the stairs and descended to street level, then made her way to the rear of the building.

"May I order some coffee and sandwiches to send upstairs?" She halted before the crimson velvet rope which closed off the dining room. A waiter in white coat and dark trousers hurried to the cash register desk and took an order form from a tablet.

"I'll be glad to take your order. Your room number?" he asked and wet the indelible lead pencil with his tongue leaving a purple spot on the tip.

"Oh, I'll pay you for it here. You can send it up in a few minutes to room 539, if you will." She forced her most ingratiating smile and withdrew several bills from her bag.

"Very well." He paused, waiting for her order.

"I think ham would be fine. With mustard and butter. Four sandwiches. And a pot of black coffee, enough for two." It would have been laughable had it not been in deadly earnest. She found it almost easy to form the smile on her lips as she paid the waiter, then retraced her steps to the stairway.

She prayed the corridor would be empty and that the police had not stationed anyone in the halls outside of room 539. As she approached the door, however, she neither heard nor observed the slightest thing to indicate she would be discovered. Familiar with Nate's room, she knew a communal bathroom for female guests was opposite and down the hall several yards. Since the door of 539 swung in such a manner that whoever opened it could be clearly seen from the bathroom, she entered and waited. Fortunately, no one was in the bathroom. Soon she heard the service elevator at the end of the corridor stop, its doors open, and a food cart clatter down toward her place of hiding. The waiter passed, then knocked at room 539.

"Room service," he said quietly, his face near to the shut door. She held her breath as she peered from a crack in the bathroom door. There seemed no reply from the room. The waiter knocked again, a trifle louder and more insistent than before. "Room service," he called out.

The door opened far enough so whoever was inside could see the waiter. Suddenly it was flung back and a man's voice swore in anger. He was big, with a heavy-featured face and the build of a man accustomed to something more physical than police work. He looked up and down the hallway and for a moment Jette's heart almost stopped as he spied the women's bathroom. In the poor light she could not see the color of his eyes or his complexion, but he had the look of one who might welcome personal combat. She shuddered as she realized that Nate could have walked right into the trap.

Surely he was innocent. Why, then, did police lie in wait for him? Did they really expect Nate to come to his room at the Imperial if he were guilty and trying to evade capture? Only if he were innocent would he return to his lodging. Inspector Hankins and Abe Marley said they were going to arrest Lavinia Baldwin. Surely they could not expect her to come to Nate's hotel room. Why would she? Jette had so many questions, so many doubts—and no answers.

Some movement, a slight shadow at the far end of the corridor, caught her eye. By its very furtiveness it called attention to itself. Because of their positions, neither the policeman nor the waiter could see the barely perceptible motion. Jette was not certain it was a man until he moved again, passing directly beneath the red exit sign at the fire escape door. The quick glimpse was enough.

It was the missing Clarence Pomeroy!

Chapter 18

Between the bright intersections of downtown Los Angeles were lonely stretches of abysmal darkness. At each corner hung street lamps suspended on wires that swung wildly in the santana wind, creating grotesque shadows on store fronts of brick and plaster. Standard lamps, their columns painted a verdigris-green, were more decorative than efficient. Few carriages and only a handful of automobiles were on the thoroughfare, and except for the immediate area around the late-night establishments, there were even fewer people to be seen.

As the cab rounded the corner of Broadway, Jette surveyed the empty street and was forced to reconsider the wisdom of her actions. Up ahead she could see lights from the Harmony Theater and a collection of carriages waiting for the end of the late performance.

"Your husband?" the cabbie had asked when she said she wanted to follow Clarence Pomeroy's hack. At her look of dismay he said, "Well, now never you mind, little lady, he won't get away from us."

"Don't get too close . . . I don't want him to know I'm following him . . ." Jette was breathless as the driver helped her into the seat. She had not liked his looks, but his horse and cab were new and well cared for and in her haste she had no time to select another.

Perhaps she should have informed the police at the hotel that Clarence Pomeroy, who was supposedly missing after an attack and robbery in San Francisco, was in fact under their very noses. By the time she would have convinced them, however, he would have slipped from their grasp. No, she must follow him herself, see where he was going and whom he would contact. Since he had departed the hotel by its fire escape, his behavior was suspect. Had he intended to meet Nate? She could only guess and guesses would solve nothing.

"He's getting out, ma'am," the driver said in a hushed voice. "Next block. Want me to pull up beside him?"

"No, no!" she replied and leaned far enough out to see where the cabbie pointed with his whip. "Stop just beyond those buggies waiting outside the theater," she ordered him. Already the audience was filing from the Harmony and making its way into the street. The first few cabs were pulling from the ranks by the time Jette passed the now darkened theater. "He won't notice us if we stop here," she reasoned aloud.

"Right you are." They halted at the end of the line of hacks and private carriages, maneuvering inconspicuously into position.

Jette kept her eye on the cab across the intersection. It had stopped before a second-rate hotel whose plate glass front windows stated in plain white letters, "Westmoreland Palace, Reasonable Rates by Day, Week, or Month, Finest in the West." Pomeroy stood with his back to the light and paid the driver. He looked surreptitiously up and down the street, then, satisfied, turned and entered the lobby.

From the alley beside the theater a few performers were straggling out onto the sidewalk and heading in the direction of the hotel. As if in answer to Jette's unvoiced question, the cab driver said, "The Westmoreland's a theatrical hotel, ma'am. Mostly folks from traveling shows and vaudeville stays there. Ain't much of a place, but it's handy for 'em." He spat into the gutter and shifted his quid from one side of his face to the other. "You planning on going up there alone?"

"Yes," Jette said and put her hand on the door handle. "I must!"

He jumped down, opened the carriage door for her, took her elbow as she alighted. Three young women still in exaggerated stage makeup left the alley and strolled toward the Westmoreland. Gusts of wind whipped dirt and debris into doorways and corners and sent the women's skirts flying. The driver watched appreciatively and held a hand to his own tall-crowned hat. "I'd be glad to go with you, if you'd like somebody along," he whispered.

"That's not necessary, but I do thank you." Jette wondered if she should be so quick in refusing his help. "You will wait for me, won't you?"

"I think maybe I ought to go in with you—just in case. Course, that's up to you, ma'am." He spat again, careful to aim with the wind. "I'll be here. You can count on me. You need a policeman, you just give me a holler, hear?"

Thus reassured, she joined the crowd leaving the theater. It was small comfort to know the man would be waiting a good half-block away. The thought of his summoning a policeman almost terrified her more than the chance she was taking in pursuing Pomeroy.

Despite its grandiose name, the Westmoreland Palace was far from palatial. The lobby was decorated with nondescript furniture past its prime, and threadbare rugs which were more hazard than comfort underfoot.

Yellow light from gas lamps did little to dispel the gloom of its antiquated, high-ceilinged interior, and the carbon from their sooty flames had left a distinct, grimy pattern above each fixture. Lobby and halls were resounding with raucous laughter and a desperate gaiety as the performers sought the haven of their dingy rooms. Badly framed theater bills were everywhere on the walls. In one corner of the small writing-room an elaborate cherrywood easel held a dramatically retouched photograph of Sarah Bernhardt, her waist nipped to a handspan. Jette accompanied the giggling girls, careful to attract as little attention as possible. As they entered the lobby she glanced around, and seeing no sign of Clarence Pomeroy, walked to the registration desk. Within a few minutes she continued on to the rear of the building along the main corridor, a room key in her hand.

"My luggage will have to catch up with me," she had told the elderly man at the desk. She felt she was becoming adept at lying when necessary, and excused it on the basis that it would help Nate. "I'll have to telegraph home for money to buy clothes if it doesn't get here," she laughed.

"Happens all the time," he smiled understandingly. "I'm sure one of the other girls will let you have a few things. We're all used to it." His grin was all but toothless in a face that had at one time been handsome; his voice was still rich and deep with the projection and enunciation of one accustomed to the stage. "I hope you find your room comfortable."

"Thank you, I'm sure I shall," she murmured and followed his pointing finger. "Down this way?" she asked. He nodded and watched her go, then looked at the name she had signed into the register.

"That's right, Miss Williams," he called after her. "Now to your left." She was beautiful, her voice well pitched and modulated, but she was not of the theater.

No matter, he thought as he watched her graceful walk, *the Westmoreland never asks for credentials if it's paid in advance*.

Written in the register were dozens of improbable names whose manufacture was deemed necessary because of the lack of romance and euphony in those bestowed at birth. There were some that Jette recognized as featured in advertisements for the area's theaters. Two others were of a very different sort. Printed anonymously in large, bold letters were names unlikely to be chosen for their attractiveness on marquee or playbill: Herbert Stemble and wife, Gertrude. The entry was dated three days before.

"Could you tell me where the Stembles are staying?" she had asked with a broad smile. "I'm so anxious to see them again. It's been simply ages since I saw either of them."

The elderly man consulted his records and said, "Let me see . . . yes, here we are . . . room 359."

"Are they in?" She could not see the key to 359 in its box behind the counter. He looked and put a hand into the receptacle to make certain.

"I'm sure they must be," he replied. "They just had a visitor go up a few minutes ago."

"Oh? Who was that?"

"Couldn't say, Miss Williams. He didn't give his name."

"Well, thank you anyhow." She was relieved that there was no telephone service in the hotel. She could not be announced and her visit's purpose defeated. With all the noise and confusion in the halls there was little chance that she would be unduly noticed as she made her way to the third floor. She pocketed her own room key and looked for the numbers on the doors as she worked her way to the rear of the building. None of the theatrical tenants seened to be billeted in that section of the hotel, a courtesy to the non-thespian guests. The hallway was deserted.

The room for which she looked was situated in the far corner of the building, adjoining a side hall which led to the fire exit. A light showed beneath the closed door and from the open transom overhead. As she drew near she heard the hushed tones of an angry conversation.

In sheer joy she stretched out her hand to knock. Suddenly as distinct words reached her ears she stopped in horror. Riveted before the door, she could only listen in disbelief and growing terror.

"Why the hell did you have to push her off the train where she'd be found?" There was no mistaking Nate's voice. "God damn it, man, you've ruined everything!"

"Calm down, both of you!" a woman cautioned them in a forced whisper.

"What the devil was I supposed to do?" The man's voice was high-pitched and nasal—new to Jette. She knew it must be Clarence Pomeroy.

"You were sitting there, all snug and neat, taking no risks . . ." the nasal voice complained.

"Risks! I'll remind you of one risk I sure as hell had to take because of you! Jubal Wade would have delighted in killing me outright."

"That wasn't the brightest plan I ever heard of . . ."

"It got us the jewelry and got rid of Clarence Pomeroy," the woman said. "If I hadn't promised Jubal the rest of his money afterward, he'd have killed Nate and caught a ship to Alaska."

"Just what the hell did you tell him to make him go after Nate like that?" A chair scraped on a portion of uncarpeted floor just inside the doorway. "You go to bed with him?"

"There wasn't time," the woman laughed quietly. "That would have been an experience," she sighed.

"Damn you, Vinnie! You don't care where you get it, do you?" Nate's voice was caustic.

"Yes, I care! But since you married your pretty little plaything I haven't had much attention from you, have I?"

Jette covered her face, unable to utter a sound or move. Why had she not seen their relationship before? Why had she blinded herself to such a possibility? The night she had seen Nate driving east along Las Lomas Road she knew the truth—then denied it to herself. She wanted the voices inside the room to stop. They didn't.

"If you just hadn't had to indulge that fat stomach of yours and go to the La Marmite . . ." Nate began.

"How the hell did I know you'd turn up there?"

"You were supposed to keep out of sight!"

"Vinnie and I . . ." the stranger began.

"Vinnie should have gone on to New York and booked our passage just like we'd planned. Instead you both come back here and endanger all we've worked for." Jette could hear Nate begin pacing, first on the carpeting, then on the bare wood. For a moment she feared he might open the door. She almost wished he would, and strike her dead where she stood. It would be less cruel. "You're both fools!" Nate exploded.

"I couldn't stand to be away from you so long, darling," Lavinia said with a mirthless laugh.

"She didn't trust you," the man's voice was harsh and threatening. "And neither did I, Nate!"

"But to go to the Imperial tonight! What did you expect to find there?"

"As I said before, I didn't trust you. Simple as that. I had to see if you'd kept out a little something extra for yourself."

"For God's sakes, you've got the jewels!" Nate growled.

"That's not enough! You've got all the capital we've raised on the two businesses. Do you honestly think Vinnie and I would ship ourselves off to Johannesburg with just those damned blue stones to fall back on?"

The man's nasal whine rose in accusatory rage. "Do you think we'd trust you to leave that fancy wife of yours and bring us our shares?"

"Shut up or you'll have us all in trouble!" Lavinia's high heels tapped to the door. It opened a crack just after Jette had whisked out of sight in the side hall.

Jette stood trembling in the drafty exit, unable to think coherently. The transom slammed shut and the voices continued but Jette could no longer make out the words. She groped her way to the exit door and opened it. Dry, hot wind blasted her in the face and tugged at her flat-brimmed hat. Teetering against the railing she smothered the gasping sobs that rose in her throat. Gathering her skirts tightly about her legs so she might more easily descend the iron steps, she worked her way silently down the rear wall of the hotel.

As she felt her way along the alley behind the Westmoreland, she remembered the key. She felt for it in her pocket. A chill of fear swept over her. The key was gone!

As she had stood aghast before that awful door something had slipped to the floor beside her, but she had not noticed it at the moment. Only now did she recall it, now that it was too late. Inevitably they would find the key. Inevitably they would ask the desk clerk to whom it belonged. He was sure to describe her accurately. They would know!

She had heard too much to remain safe should they find her. It would do no good to deny knowledge of their guilty admissions. The man Nate called Clarence Pomeroy had killed Palma Owens—had he killed Jubal Wade and his companion? Or had Nate killed them? She could only wonder if Nate would kill her, too.

She stumbled out of the alley and into the darkened street. True to his word, her cab driver awaited her return. As she ran toward him, he flicked the horse forward and halted near the corner. Setting the brake quickly, he jumped down and assisted her into the cab, slamming the door as soon as she was seated.

"Where to, lady?" He peered at her face and clucked his tongue. "Bad as that, eh? Say, I'm awful sorry, ma'am." He wagged his head in commiseration, hat in hand. "Where can I take you?"

"To the nearest police station, please." She choked the words out, despising herself for it, and yet helpless to do otherwise. She did not have to repeat the request although his expression changed subtly. Catching an errant mate with his mistress was one thing; informing the police was quite another. He hopped into his seat and urged the splendid hackney into a tight turn, then a fast trot down the echoing street.

The police station was of yellow brick with rococo white plaster ornaments more suitable for a department store or residential building. An illuminated white globe hanging over the front entrance shed barely sufficient light to enable Jette to see the brass-lipped stairs that led up to the first floor. She pushed through the double swinging doors and hesitated before entering.

"Yes, ma'am?" A uniformed officer spoke up from across the room. Gray-haired and florid of face, he sat at a paper-littered desk behind a high counter that partitioned the office proper from the entryway. "May I help you?" He rose and came to lean on the counter. Inside the station was stifling despite open windows at the far end of the room. "Ma'am . . . are you all right?" he asked Jette as she clung to the counter for support.

"I want to report some people . . ." She could not find the words she wanted. Several other officers glanced up as she attempted to express herself. It was not every night a woman as beautiful as this one came calling at their station. Their sly smiles were soon erased as they recognized her anxiety.

"You wish to report some people?" the desk sergeant

397

prompted her. "Just what did you want to report about them?" His demeanor left no doubt that he would much rather spend the balance of the night on something other than detail work. "Well, ma'am, just what was it?" he asked sharply.

"They killed someone," Jette stated, scarcely believing what she said. Immediately the other men gave her their full attention. Several in plain clothes moved closer.

"Won't you come in and be seated?" The older man opened a gate in the counter and ushered her into the office. He pulled up a chair and spread an official report form out on his desk. "Let's start at the beginning, shall we?" He selected a freshly sharpened pencil from the desk drawer. "First, your name?"

"Mrs. Nathaniel Edmond Trasker," she said so softly he had to ask her to repeat it. He carefully filled in the proper blank.

"Place of residence?"

"San Genaro. La Coruna Ranch, San Genaro." Why didn't he want her to tell him about the murders first? She gripped the edge of her chair as she sought to preserve a semblance of reasonableness and dignity.

"I see. Yes," he muttered and spelled out the information. "And who are these people?"

"My husband, a Mrs. Lavinia Baldwin, and a man known as Clarence Pomeroy." It was maddening, the slowness of the procedure as he printed out the names.

"And what exactly is it they did? Who are they supposed to have murdered?" His deliberateness infuriated her until she wanted to shriek the story into his stolid, complaisant face.

"There was no supposing!" she countered. "They killed a Mrs. Palma Owens, a woman from Cincinnati." It was surprising how calmly she could tell it now. "The man known as Pomeroy pushed her off a train in Utah and killed her."

He looked askance at her, his expression one of undisguised doubt. "What makes you think they did this?" he asked.

"I heard them talking about it."

"Did they tell you they did this?" He was no longer writing.

"No, I was standing outside their hotel room and heard it. The transom was open . . ." She could see he did not believe her. "I swear that's the truth!" she cried.

"And where was this?" He doggedly pursued the prescribed routine, his pencil poised above the lines and blanks on the paper.

"At the Westmoreland Palace Hotel." She wrung her hands in desperation. "You must go pick them up right now. They're planning to go to Johannesburg . . . they've got my jewelry . . ." She knew she was not making any sense to them. She looked from one to the other of the policemen listening nearby and seeing disbelief in their faces, she all but shouted, "They killed her! Don't you understand? They killed her . . . and they'll kill me!" Their only reaction was to glance uncomfortably away.

"What makes you think they'll try to kill you?"

"Because they'll find out I heard them. I dropped my key right in front of their door." How could she possibly explain in such a way that they would realize she was telling them the truth? She had begun to doubt her own sanity. After all, her mother was supposed to be insane!

"What key was that?"

"My room key . . ." He had put the pencil down. Jette fought the urge to scream and continued, "You see, I followed this Clarence Pomeroy. He was supposed to maybe be dead in San Francisco, but I saw him and I followed him to the Westmoreland. I had to pretend to rent a room there . . . the key was my room key . . ."

"And you found them in a room together?"

"Yes."

"All three?"

"Yes!" She felt suffocated in the confines of the station.

The officer taking her report sat back in his chair and tilted it on two legs, crossing his arms over his ample front. "I want you to answer me honestly, Mrs. Trasker," he said. "Is your husband having an affair with this woman?"

"Yes. Yes, he is! He has been all along, right from the time he met me." Too late she realized he had set a trap and she had fallen into it. "But that has nothing to do with the rest of what happened," she protested. "They did kill Mrs. Owens . . . and Jubal Wade, in San Francisco . . . and some friend of his . . ." *My God in heaven*, she thought, *they don't believe me*!

Frantically Jette thought of any way in which she might convince them she was telling the truth. "I'm not making up a story to get even with my husband," she said carefully. "If you want to verify the facts, I suggest you get in touch with an Inspector Hankins, who is with the San Francisco police. He's in San Genaro right now, staying with a Mr. Abraham Marley. They're both familiar with the circumstances."

The desk sergeant considered her challenge for a moment as he rocked in the unstable chair. "We could telegraph them. It will take a while. Where can we get in touch with you?"

"You must act now—they'll be gone and you'll never find them!"

"All right," he finally consented. "We'll give them a call." Quite obviously he did not intend to take any drastic steps until he had verified her fantastic accusations. He reached for the telephone that rested on an extendible holder at the edge of his desk.

"Hello, central? This is Sergeant McIlrath at Central Avenue Police Station. Can you put through a call to the city of San Genaro?" He waited while the operator checked to see if the town was a member of their exchange. "You can? Fine. I want to speak with an Inspector Hankins, who can be located at the residence of Mr. Abraham Marley." He covered the mouthpiece with his hand and asked Jette, "What's this Marley's address?"

"I don't know, but it's on McKinley Street, above Murdock's Pharmacy. He has a large apartment there."

The sergeant sat listening intently for a moment, then hung up the receiver. "I'm sorry, Mrs. Trasker, but the lines are down between here and San Genaro. Must be all this wind we're having. According to Central, they can be fixed in an hour or so—or a day or two." He sat back, lacing his fingers over his brass-buttoned uniform.

"There is another way you can check," she said and felt hopeful once more. "You have some men at the Imperial Hotel, waiting for my husband to show up at his room there. I think there's one in the lobby, at the registration desk, and I saw one in his room."

"You saw one of our men in your husband's room?" The tone implied he was now interested. "Did he identify himself as a policeman?"

"Well, no, I didn't speak to him. I hid in the ladies' room across the hall . . ." She collapsed back into her chair. "Can't you find out who those men are and ask them?"

McIlrath glanced coldly at the plainclothesmen. "You got anybody up there?" At their denial, he said, "Then we'll check Hope Street." They nodded agreement and he picked up the telephone again. After a few words with the station farther north in the city, he turned to Jette, saying, "They don't know anything about it, ma'am."

"But they must! Somebody must know about it. Inspector Hankins said . . ." But there was no use continuing. She could see it in their faces. They were puzzled, but unbelieving. If there was no one to corroborate her allegations, why should they believe one word she had said? "Oh please believe me," she pleaded. "Inspector Hankins was working with your police department. He had agreed to keep it as quiet as possible because Judge Killigrew had money in my husband's company. In consideration of his involvement they wanted it kept out of the newspapers. Can't you call someone else?"

At mention of Killigrew's name the men exchanged cautious glances. To avoid interfering with state politics was the safest course, especially when the state's probable next governor might be implicated. "I suggest you run along now and let us look into the matter," McIlrath said. "Where can we reach you?"

Suddenly to Jette the place seemed to dissolve into confused swirling mist. Overhead the lights appeared to dance an idiotic cadence and furniture tilt crazily. She slumped in her chair. The policeman sent his chair skidding on the waxed floor as he caught her before she could fall.

"I was afraid of that," boomed a voice from the foyer. The cab driver bolted up to the counter.

"Who the hell are you?" one of the policemen asked.

"She hired my cab over to the Imperial and had me follow some fella over to the Westmoreland . . . you know, over in the theater district." He twisted his hat in his hands as he watched the men try to bring the young woman out of her faint.

"This fellow she was following . . . was he her husband?" the sergeant asked.

"Yep, that's what she told me. Went into the Westmoreland and she had me stop across the street from the place while she went in and took a look."

Shaking his head as he stared down at her, he said, "Woman as pretty as her . . . a man'd have to be a damned fool to do her that way."

"Did she say anything about him murdering any-body?"

"Pshaw, no!" He shook his head again. "Ask me, she's caught him with some other woman at that there hotel and it was just too much for her."

As she became aware of her surroundings again, Jette turned from one to the other of the men about her. It was futile to try to convince them that what she had said was true. They did not believe her. They would not. Even if they did, even if they went to the hotel and spoke with Nate and Lavinia, they might not pick them up. She was a witness and the police calling on Nate would only confirm the fact. The thought struck her cold with terror. She was a witness!

"We'll look into it for you, ma'am!" the sergeant promised her before she left on the arm of the driver. "We'll look into it right away." She did not believe him any more than he believed her. It had all been useless. By the time they could talk with Inspector Hankins and Abe Marley she would be dead, perhaps shoved out another train window and found a week later in a culvert. She had the hysterical urge to laugh aloud when she realized that if she were found in such a way there would be no kid-curlers in her hair. She wanted to cry for Palma Owens, but found she could not even cry for herself.

"You want to go back to the Imperial, ma'am?" the cabbie asked as they neared the carriage. The wind whistled down the empty avenue and gave no relief from the heat. He grabbed at his hat.

"I suppose so," she replied wearily. She accepted his hand into the carriage and sat in numbed silence as they drove off. She lay back in the seat and closed her eyes as the cab bumped north along Central. Only now did she fully realize the dangerous position in which she had placed herself. If the police decided to go to the Westmoreland and speak with Nate, or if Nate discovered her key and put two and two together, she must not stay at the Imperial the rest of the night. Yet she was much too exhausted to take the mail-milk-and-meat train back to San Genaro at three o'clock.

All at once she sat bolt upright. "Driver!" she shouted. "Take me to the nearest public telephone," she ordered him. "Is there a place near here?"

"Yes, ma'am. The exchange is just a block up that way," he said and pointed left at the intersection. "They got public phones inside the building that's open all night."

"Hurry," she said anxiously. He flicked the smooth-gaited hackney and reined it to the left in a tight turn. A large square structure loomed ahead, in its center a small indented entrance area illuminated by an overhanging electric sign. Without waiting for him to help her from the cab, she raced through the revolving door and into the telephone exchange.

Although the hour was late, Russel Carr was gracious in his greeting. Breathlessly Jette related her plight. She could not be certain he believed her, but apparently he was interested enough to be concerned.

"I insist you come right out to my home," he said. "I won't hear of you returning to your hotel." He realized now was not the time to upbraid her for her foolish behavior. "Listen closely, Jette," he said. "Promise me you'll do exactly as I say."

"I promise," she whispered into the phone, at last feeling a modicum of safety.

"Can you trust your driver?"

"I think so. He doesn't believe me any more than the others, but he's at least helpful and sympathetic."

"Good. Have him bring you directly here. My address is 2311 Grandview. That's in the Westlake Park

404

district. Your driver will know where it is. Can you remember that?'' His voice was calm but conveyed an urgency that set her teeth to chattering.

"Say the address once more," she asked.

"2311 Grandview Avenue, 2311," he repeated. "All right?"

"Yes, I have it," she replied. "Thank you, Mr. Carr."

"Quite all right, my dear. Now do hurry. I'll be waiting for you. In the meantime, I shall make a few telephone calls of my own."

Jette replaced the receiver on its hook. She hated to leave the safety of the busy place. A battery of women operators sat behind long switchboards that resembled tangled jumbles of black rubber cord and plugs. The murmur of voices as they answered calls and made connections was comforting to her, but as she headed once more into the street, fear returned along with the darkness and the hot, whipping wind.

"Where to, ma'am?" the cabbied asked and yawned broadly.

"Westlake Park . . . 2311 Grandview," she said. Weary to the point of shaking, she crawled into the carriage and braced herself in one corner, hoping she might doze until they arrived. It proved useless. Soon they were traveling northwest along Wilshire Boulevard, duplicating Jette's trip with her mother to the park some weeks earlier. Palm fronds ripped from gray, heavy-trunked trees littered the streets and for several blocks they were forced to dodge debris without benefit of street lamps. An entire section of the city was without electricity where broken branches had snapped the fragile lines.

Russel Carr's home sat regally above the street behind a triumph of the stonemason's art. Retaining walls of pink stone surmounted by white cement capping enclosed smooth green lawns and closely-pruned flower-

405

ing shrubs. In design the edifice imitated an Italian villa, with fluted columns and high, multi-paned windows. A marble-floored porch extended the length of the front, with a low marble balustrade surrounding it on three sides. A semi-circular drive of glistening white concrete curved before the house to a flight of shallow steps that led up to the house. One end of the lower floor was ablaze with light as the hired cab drew up and stopped.

"This here's 2311, ma'am," the driver announced in hushed tones as he opened the carriage door. He was properly impressed with the magnificent mansion. Even as they alighted, Russel Carr came from the porticoed entry.

"I'm sorry to involve you . . ." she began.

"Nonsense. That's what friends are for, isn't it?'

"I haven't paid the driver yet," she said as he led her away.

"Then allow me." She started to protest, but he shook his head and continued, "No arguments. I insist as a friend of the family. If you'll excuse me a moment, I'll have a word with your man."

"Yes, sir?" The cabbie straightened up and squared his shoulders, giving his attention to the owner of the house.

"I want you to go back to the Imperial Hotel and get Mrs. Trasker's things. Ask the desk clerk when you go in. There should just be the portmanteau, shouldn't there, Jette?"

"Yes, just the one piece of luggage," she responded.

"Everything's arranged. They'll be expecting you. I want you to take it down to the railway station immediately. One of the maids will have it packed and ready for you. You're to check it at the depot under my name: Russel Carr." He waited for the man to acknowledge the name.

"Yes, sir. That's Russel Carr." He touched his hat in salute.

"Correct. On no condition are you to mention Mrs. Trasker's name to anyone. She's in grave danger and her life depends on your discretion and silence." He allowed the man to think it over before asking, "Is that perfectly understood?"

"Yes, sir, it is." His eyes went to Jette, who stood on the top step of the porch, her outline silhouetted against the light from the reception rooms and library behind her. "Yes, sir, Mr. Carr. Not a word to nobody."

Carr withdrew a fold of paper bills from his coat pocket and peeled off several, still holding them in thumb and finger as he proffered them to the driver. "And you agree to do exactly as I've said?"

"Indeed I will." In a lowered voice he added almost apologetically, "I had no idea it was so serious. Is it really like she said?" He was awed by his role in the drama.

"I'm afraid at ths point I don't know anything about it, but if she's said so, I believe her implicitly." Carr held out the bills to the man. "Will you do it?"

"I will. Count on me, sir," he agreed. "Not one word to nobody," he said.

"And remember, you have no idea where she went after she left the police station—just in case anyone should ask."

"Not even the police if they ask me?"

"That's another matter, of course. But be certain it is a policeman who's asking." Carr gave him the bills. The cabbie did not bother to look at their denomination. He knew it would be more than adequate for his night's employment and his continued silence.

As Russel Carr escorted Jette into the house he said, "Well, young lady, we must see to your safety, mustn't we?" He led her into the library where two chairs had been pulled up to a tea table laden with a light supper and a carafe of cold white wine. An elderly servant in bathrobe and slippers pulled out the chair as she seated herself. He was bleary-eyed as though he had been awakened from a sound sleep, and while he poured the delicate Rhine wine he suppressed a yawn.

"Will there be anything else, Mr. Carr?" he asked.

"No, thank you. Run along to bed." Carr was eager for the man to leave. What he must hear from Jette should remain between them and not become subject for gossip among the servants.

"Yes, sir. Thank you." The man glided silently from the room and only when he gained the polished marble floor of the hallway could Jette hear the pat, pat, pat of his slippers.

"I'm going to take you home to your mother's," Carr stated and passed her a plate of tiny, crustless sandwiches. "You can be looked after and precautions taken there for your welfare. Until this entire matter is resolved you will need all the protection you can get. I do hate to be so blunt about it, but it's the truth, and I feel that's what you want at this point." He spread a dab of wine-cheddar on a cracker and gave it to her. "You must eat, Jette. I insist you do."

She was astonished that she could swallow a morsel, but she found she was hungry. Perhaps it was the reassurance he gave her. In his home, beside him, she felt safe. Her mother had felt the same way in Carr's presence without knowing or even questioning why. Jette sipped the light wine and nibbled at the cracker. She relaxed into the comfortable reading chair, at last feeling less fearful.

Russel Carr rose and pulled shut the drapes despite the warmth of the room. Keeping his future stepdaughter safe was the most demanding job he had ever undertaken. He had warned her about the land promoters the first time he had encountered her and her mother. He had not known then that she would marry anyone connected with Montague-Cameron Trust—not that it would have done any good to try stopping her. If her husband was the murderer she alleged, Carr wondered if any place on earth would be secure from Nate's vengeance.

Chapter 19

Asa Beemer handed the Damascus-barreled Greener 12 gauge to Carr.

"Fine shotgun," Carr said as he broke it and checked it thoroughly before slipping the shells into place. "Nice heft to it," he added appreciatvely.

"This one's a Lefever automatic," Asa said about the one in his hands. "Almost as good as that one. Not as fancy, but it shoots fast." He had cleaned the weapons himself after taking them down from above the fireplace. A 12 shot, 44 caliber Winchester carbine, its wicked barrel a cold blue, had been reassembled on newspaper strewn before the fireplace. Ammunition and cleaning rags littered the hearth.

"Do you really think it's necessary to issue arms to the men?" Verdie Allenby walked around the guns spread out on the floor of the parlor. Primly she gathered her skirts and petticoats close as she perched on the edge of the sofa, careful to pull her feet back from the deadly guns. "I can't help feeling it would be better if no one had them."

"That may be, ma'am," Asa said. "But we can't take any chances. If Trasker doesn't get rounded up in Los Angeles, you can bet he'll come this way and he isn't going to come for any tea party." He rechecked a long-barreled Colt Peacemaker and loaded the cylinder with six 45 caliber cartridges. "Severo's a good, level headed kid. He isn't going to take pot shots at anything that wiggles. I've been hunting enough with him to know his style. Don't you worry, Mrs. Allenby."

"Worry!" She wrung her hands in her lap, the frown on her face deepening as she watched the men. "Oh, Asa, how can you say that? Right now I'm so frightened I hardly know what I'm doing from one minute to the next."

"You needn't worry, Verdie. We'll see that Jette is well protected." Russel Carr sat back on his heels and took her hands in his. "If you want me to, I'll stay on here until this is settled."

"We can't keep you away from your business, Russel," Verdie said. "That would hardly be right of us."

"My business can run itself very well without me for a while. Nothing disastrous has happened whenever I've been away traveling. You and Jette are going to be my family soon, God willing." He patted her pale cheek and chuckled. "If anyone should help out right now, it is I," he said. Asa Beemer looked up at both of them and grinned his approval. "I'm sure he agrees, don't you, Asa?"

"You'll be welcome, Mr. Carr. I hope we don't need you—or anybody else—but just in case . . ." He stopped as he saw the look of consternation on Verdie's face. "Is Miss Jette still asleep?" he asked quickly. He refused to alter his term of address when he referred to Jette, in spite of her marriage.

"She was a few minutes ago. I was hoping she'd take something to make her sleep right through till tomorrow, but she refused any medicine." Verdie rose and started for the dining room. "If you gentlemen will excuse me, I'll go see to dinner." Asa glanced at the woman as she disappeared into the other room. He could not suppress the smile that spread across his wide mouth. To be included with Russel Carr as a gentleman in Verdie's regard pleased him as little else could at the moment. He wiped his hands on a rag and fitted his own army-38 into its holster, then buckled it about his hips.

"She's a lovely woman, Beemer," Russel Carr said. "Was it so difficult when her husband was living?" He had no qualms about asking such questions of Asa. It was evident from the ranch manager's attitude toward her that he respected and liked Verdie. "Did she suffer a bad life with him?"

"Elias was a hard man." Asa gathered up the soiled paper and stuffed it into the fireplace, tamping it down beneath the kindling and small logs already laid. "Whatever went wrong between them was a long time ago. I guess old Elias never did forgive her. Foolish way to go through life, hating what happened and being too damned stubborn to make things right again." He fingered the butt of the revolver, slapped at it to see if the position was exact to his reach. Carr watched him with growing respect.

"Where did you see trouble, Beemer?" Carr asked.

"New Mexico mostly," Asa replied. "You can say I'm no stranger to it."

"Yes, I can see you aren't." Russel Carr extended his hand to Asa. "Glad you're with us, young man," he said. They clasped hands as if an unspoken agreement had been reached between them. At the sound of the rear parlor door opening they turned, surprised as Jette came into the room. She was dressed in a dark pink calico jumper with dainty sprigs of blue and yellow flowers in lines up and down the fabric. A fresh white lawn guimpe with high cotton lace neck was tucked into the jumper and a sash of blue silk matching the one in her hair completed her toilette. She had combed her auburn hair back and caught it about her head with the blue sash which fell to her waist. Freshly scrubbed, her face had the delicate sheen and tint of a child's, palest pink with lavender-blue shadows that hinted of her sorrow. She was barefoot and cared not a whit at the impropriety of her dereliction.

Without a word, she walked to the collection of guns. She stared at Asa, her intense black eyes divulging the shock she felt as she saw the holster and gun at his side. She covered her face with her hands and turned away.

"God in heaven! What have I started?" she moaned as though in physical pain. "What have I gotten us into?"

Asa Beemer stood before the fireplace, his lean arms hanging inert from shoulders that ached to draw her to him, hold her close and never let her go. With his feet wide apart in his customary easy slouch, the cartridge belt fastened about his hips, she was taken back to the first time she had seen him. Her father had been interviewing him for the lowly job of extra hand during the fall roundup. She had been only a girl. While Elias' Indian and Mexican vaqueros were unsurpassed horsemen and superb with the lariat, their treatment of expensive purebred stock was too violent and thus too costly. Elias had hired the silent youth, made him a permanent employee, and after years of patient coaching, had made him his second in command—and his prospective son-in-law. Hadn't Jette learned to despise him because Elias had decreed him her husband? She had repulsed him with vicious, slashing words. Why should he choose now to risk his life in her defense?

"If you'll pardon me, Miss Jette," Asa drawled, "I'll get on over to the store. I must see Severo and Benito." He longed to touch her, to say it would be all right. He could only pick up his sweat-stained hat from the mounted elk antlers at one side of the fireplace and go, leaving by the patio door.

Jette ran to the door and watched him as he hurried along the path beneath the oaks. She could see the lanterns in front of the ranch store, and passing in front of them shadows flitted back and forth as the hands gathered for their instructions. Asa Beemer—the man she had loathed—was making arrangements for her

412

protection.

Russel Carr carried the guns to the long table behind the sofa; he checked the safety on each one. There was no way he could hide his concern. The guns were there . . . Asa was going to speak to the men . . . the house dogs were kept close by at all times . . . dogs from the village were tethered near the main road. Jette was the only witness alive to testify against Nate. If he decided to leave the country as he had originally planned, all would be well. If, however, he decide to silence the one witness who could convict him . . . Jette shuddered and turned from the patio door. Carr wiped his hands on a piece of oily cloth and finished tidying up.

"I don't think your mother was pleased with our preparations," he said. "Is she fightened of guns?"

"What?" Jette realized he had been speaking to her. "Oh, I'm sorry."

"Woolgathering?" He followed her apprehensive glance to the store and workmen's village. Deftly, he drew her away from the open door and coaxed her to sit beside him on the sofa.

"What did you ask me?" She tried to concentrate on what Carr was saying.

"Your mother . . . is she afraid of guns?"

"Yes, she's terrified of them. Always has been since I can remember."

"But she tolerated them in the parlor?"

"She had no choice in that, Mr. Carr." Jette slumped into the sofa and stared at the empty gun rack over the mantel. "My father wanted them there. And there were more in his office."

"I see." Carr did see, and said no more. "Aren't you pleased with your mother's progress? She tells me she needn't go back to her doctor in Los Angeles unless she wishes to do so. That's truly remarkable." He smiled as he sat beside her. "But your mother is a remarkable woman." He turned to face Jette before he said, "It's

413

customary for a man to seek permission of a woman's father or older brother when he asks for her hand in marriage." Jette looked up in total surprise. "In my case I must ask you, mustn't I?" The tanned and handsome face wrinkled just enough into good humored laugh lines to make his suggestion less stuffy and formal.

"I don't quite understand," she said. A slow smile tried to form about the corners of her mouth. For the first time in many hours she felt it was appropriate. "Perhaps you should explain," she teased him.

"You know very well that your mother has become dear to me, Jette." His demeanor changed to solemnity. "When she feels she is well enough, I want her to marry me. She's not been happy for a long time—I think I can make her happy. When my wife died I thought I couldn't go on living. Somehow I put my life back together and after almost six years of being alone I realize that what I most need is to share it with someone I care for," he said tenderly.

"You're aware that Mother hasn't been well." Jette could anticipate the gossip sure to rise should Verdie remarry.

"I do know that—and please forgive me if I overstep the limit of good taste—I'm aware that she was brutalized by your father. I hope I may have the privilege of changing all that." His very earnestness was touching.

Jette allowed her smile to broaden. She had known that her mother and Russel Carr had been seeing one another, but had not imagined it had gone so far. For the moment she forgot the guns which lay on the table behind her head. "Are you seeking my permission to marry her?"

"I am," he said with no flicker of amusement. "Do I have it?"

"Of course you do! I couldn't be more pleased."

"Thank you, my dear. That does make things much

easier." He settled back and warmed to their conversation. "I feel we could be very happy together. She shouldn't be isolated on this ranch. She spoke of having Mr. Beemer take over here, leaving us free to live in the city." He saw that he had struck the proper chord. "You agree, don't you?"

"I'm sure of it. She's always hated it out here, so far away from gaiety and friendship. Father . . ." Jette felt a pang of guilt as she mentioned her father. "Father was . . . well, difficult. She's not been happy for a very long time."

"Verdie, I've been speaking to your daughter about us," Carr said and stood up as she came into the parlor from the dining room. She looked anxiously at Jette, as though she expected a storm of protest. Jette flew to her mother and hugged her, their laughter girlish, their faces pink with sudden exhilaration.

"I'm so happy for you both," Jette said. With her finger she traced a tear that tickled down Verdie's cheek. "No more of that, darling. That's all behind you now."

"She's right, you know." Russel Carr took Verdie in his arms. "There'll be no more of that." He bent to kiss her cheek. Jette watched, amazed at the change wrought in her mother by his gentle embrace. Never could she recall Elias kissing Verdie. Not once in her life could she remember her father holding Verdie in his arms or demonstrating his affection for her. With a rush of the old anger she found she hated him still. Verdie's face glowed with her infatuation, her hazel eyes sparkling as she led Carr into the dining room. She was more beautiful than Jette had ever known.

"Come along to dinner," Verdie said. "We'll have a little celebration, won't we? There's some imported French champagne in the root cellar. I'll have Elvira get it for us. We can cool it in that ridiculous silver urn." She prattled gaily as they took their seats at the dining table. "Where's Asa?" she asked. "You've not had words with him, have you, Jette?"

"No, Mother . . ."

"Asa had to attend to something at the store," Carr was swift to interrupt. A quick glance at Jette warned her not to tell her mother why Asa had gone. "He'll be back after a bit. He said we should go ahead and eat, not to wait on him."

It was enough that the guns were to be distributed and guards set. He did not want Verdie to know that both he and Asa thought it necessary to patrol the grounds themselves.

* * * *

Elvira refilled the water goblets and placed the pitcher on the sideboard. As she brought the small cordial tray to the table, she almost stumbled over Pecky, who whined and jumped up directly in her path. The spaniel put his paws up on the low window sill, his nose wriggling as he sniffed the hot air blowing through the screen. What he smelled did not please him.

"I'm sorry, Mrs. Allenby," Elvira apologized. "Pecky got in my way."

"Quite all right, child," Verdie said. "He has no business being in the dining room anyway."

"Mr. Beemer wants him to stay inside," the girl explained.

"I know," Verdie said sadly. The fact that the dogs were needed close to the house—indeed, inside it—was in itself a worry to her. She poured a thimbleful of green creme de menthe in Jette's liqueur glass. "Russel, perhaps you'd prefer a brandy?" she asked.

"The kummel will be fine," he replied. He spoke to Verdie, but he kept his eyes on the dog. As she passed him the fragile, thistle-shaped glass he asked, "Where's Buff?"

"In the office at the other side of the house," Jette

416

said, her brows drawing together in concern as she turned around and patted the black and white dog. "Pecky, you hear Asa coming back?" She scratched his pate and jaws. With her fingers she could feel the low pitched growl deep within his throat.

Suddenly she pushed back her chair, pulled aside the curtains and peered out the window. She sniffed the air, then bent quickly to fasten the shoes she had hastily donned before sitting down to dinner.

"What in the world are you doing, Jette?" Verdie asked.

"Smoke!" Jette whirled about and ran for the patio door in the next room. "I smell smoke!"

"Jette, don't go out there!" Russel Carr called after her, but she was already slamming the door behind her. Without waiting to excuse himself, he raced through the parlor and out into the patio. Against the lantern light from the ranch store he could see her skirts flying as she sped toward the men. What filled him with horror was the bright flickering orange glow that outlined the store and horse barn and the grove of oaks beyond the main house. Even as he ran he could hear the shouts. From the workmen's village an alarm bell shattered the calm of the evening with its clangor.

Benito Galvan was handing out shovels from the racks at the store while Severo Mireles pulled heavy duck-canvas hay stack tarpaulins from the storage loft.

"Get that canvas out there!" Asa yelled to several youths. "Take along plenty of rope." He tossed them heavy-bladed sheath knives and small hand axes. "Tell 'em to start dragging across the fire as it comes, but not where it's got any wind behind it. Understand?" The entire complement of hands had been trained repeatedly in how to fight brush and grass fires—the inevitable accompaniment to the dry months of California.

The ranch store was the center of commotion, but farther out in the pastures and feed lots lanterns were bobbing and weaving in frantic activity. Horses, catching the primordial warning of danger on the night air, stamped and whinnied their fright as saddles were thrust upon them and girths hurriedly cinched beneath their bellies.

"Get those water wagons hitched up and wet down the fence line," Asa directed Severo. "I want that herd moved out quick. Benito, do you have someone you can send over to take care of those heifers?"

"Yes, sir. They've already gone out to the east lot." The old man shooed a small crowd of anxious women and frightened children away from the store. "You want the women to pack up their valuables?"

"It'll give them something to do. Yes, tell them just in case . . ." Asa jumped from the elevated porch and started for the horse barn when he saw Jette. In the light from the lantern that hung on the porch he could see the fear in her black eyes. "You have no business out here," he said. "Get back to the house." He made no reference to her safety.

"Should we pack, too?" she asked, breathless from running. "Is it that bad?"

"There's no way to know yet. You might make sure all your records and ledgers are in the safe. Throw something into a valise." He no longer slouched, but was drawn up to his full height, a head taller than Russel Carr, every inch taut with tension in the emergency. "I haven't time to waste talking. Go back to the house and stay there. If the fire gets away from us and heads this way, I'll send a rider up with word to get out." He knew the tiled roofs and adobe walls were fairly safe, but he would take no chances with lives. "I'll have Benito stay here with buggies and wagons. He knows exactly what to do."

"Can I help in any way?" Carr asked.

"You ride good?"

"I was twelve years in the cavalry."

418

"Then you ride good," Asa said. "We can use another rider to drag the grass."

"I can do it."

"Only on condition Jette goes back to the house," Asa said. "We can't worry about you and the fire, too," he said to Jette.

"Then I'll go," she assented.

"Carr, you come with me. I'll cut you out a good horse," Asa said. It mattered nothing to him that Carr was in a fine suit and patent-toed slippers. At the moment, time and the fire were all that mattered. "You can go out with Severo to the south pasture."

"Certainly," Carr agreed. "Explain to your mother for me, Jette," he called back over his shoulder.

"Asa!" Jette shouted over the din. He had turned on his heels and had walked rapidly eastward along the path to the barns. Jette took a step toward him as he turned to look back at her. "Be careful!" she called to him.

There was a momentary hesitation in his step. "I'll do that," he said and took the slope on a run.

* * * *

Round-eyed with fear, Elvira Mireles tidied up the dining room and replaced the thistle-shaped liqueur glasses in the china buffet. The smell of smoke was penetrating the house even though they had closed all the windows and shut the doors. Socorro had joined the other women in the village, as much to be by Benito's side in the crisis as to help ready the families for possible evacuation. Elvira pulled aside the curtain and tried to see out the window. An angry red-orange glow still showed along a low ridge to the southeast. She crossed herself and leaned against the sill, her nose almost touching the pane. *Don't let the wind start up*, she prayed silently. So far, not a leaf stirred. If it remained windless, they had a chance to knock the flames down before they could do too much damage.

"Come, child, you stay in here with us," Verdie said as she saw the girl's distress. "We want us to be together, right where Benito can find us if it becomes necessary." She was amazed at her own calmness. She put an arm about the young Mexican girl and coaxed her into the parlor where Jette had assembled a few needed items for each of them in separate pieces of luggage. Documents and the ledgers and essential records had been locked into the office safe. Currency used for the ranch payroll and their jewelry had been dumped unceremoniously into a small leather satchel along with extra pairs of stockings and underdrawers. Pecky and Buff paced nervously from one to the other of the women, Pecky barking in irritation as the marmalade-colored tom cat that had the run of the house came to perch atop the pile of suitcases and valises.

"Did Socorro feed the cat?" Verdie asked the girl.

"Yes, ma'am . . . some of the fish left over from yesterday." Elvira sat forward in the easy chair at one side of the fireplace. She kept watching the door to the patio as though she were expecting the fire to burst through at any moment.

"Did you put Asa's dinner back for him?" Verdie hoped to distract the girl's attention. "Is it where he can find it if Socorro isn't back by the time he gets here?"

"Yes, ma'am," the girl repeated, but kept her eyes on the door. "I put it in the warming oven over the stove."

"That's fine, dear. I'm sure he'll be ravenous when he takes time to eat." Verdie opened her embroidery basket and selected a hank of lavender thread and unraveled a length. "Your eyes are sharper than mine, will you thread this for me, Elvira?" She held the needle and thread to the girl.

Buff came from his tour of the sitting room and stood before the window of the parlor that overlooked the

420

rear patio. Cocking his head to one side and pricking his ears erect he began a growl that ended in a loud bark. Pecky dashed into the dining room and pawed at the window, then raced into the parlor and scratched at the door, all the time barking furiously.

"The fire!" the little maid wailed and dropped the embroidery needle in her apron. "The fire's here!" With trembling fingers she searched for the needle and jabbed the thread at it.

"Nonsense, Elvira. We'll have plenty of warning before it gets this far." Verdie tightened the hoops on which a linen hand towel was stretched. "Run look out the door, but don't let the dogs out."

The girl rushed to the door and held Pecky's collar as she opened the door a crack. The smell of burning grass and brush hung thick in the air, but there was no sign of the blaze being nearer.

"Would you like to go down and see if Socorro and Benito need you?" Verdie knew the girl was terrified. Perhaps being with her own people would lessen her fear. "I don't believe we'll need you right away. Just promise me you'll hurry back here if . . ." She did not finish the sentence.

"I'll come right back if they don't need me," Elvira promised. "Thank you, Mrs. Allenby." Before her employer might change her mind, the girl hurried down the path to the village.

"Jette, come sit by me here in the light," Verdie said as she knotted the lavender floss and poked the needle through the blue-lined pattern on the linen. Jette picked up the orange cat and sat with him curled in her lap, his purring and the tick of the standing clock comforting sounds in the silence of the house. "Do you like Russel Carr?" Verdie asked.

"Very much. I told you that the first time I met him." Jette forced a quiet laugh. "You were angry with me for speaking to a strange man—remember?"

421

"How foolish we are sometimes." Verdie sewed a few stitches, completing an aster petal in the design, then put it aside. "I want to marry Russel. I think we could be happy, the two of us," she mused.

"He's a fine man, Mother." Jette wanted to ask her if she loved him, but did not. "I'm sure he's very fond of you," she said. "I'm glad you won't be alone."

"Yes, that is important—especially as we grow older." Her look became faraway as she added, "But then I've really been alone—except for you—for many years." She turned to her daughter, an expression of keenly felt pain shadowing her face. "Of course, I don't want to leave you here on the ranch all by yourself."

"I'll be just fine, Mother. I'll have work to do." Jette scratched the cat's chin until he drooled in contentment. "I have a great deal to learn about managing a ranch. No need to worry about me."

"My poor, poor child," Verdie all but wept. The huge mongrel ambled to her and nosed at her hand, knocking the embroidery to the floor. She patted the dog's broad head and moved her feet to enable him to hunch close to her. "Could I have stopped you, Jette? Should I have tried harder to keep you away from Nate?"

"It wasn't your fault. Please believe that. I fell in love with him. You couldn't have stopped that." Even as she spoke of Nate it seemed something remote, something that had happened to someone else whom she knew only slightly. And yet the ache in her heart would not go away. "You'll never know how grateful I am that nobody has said, 'I told you so.' "

"That would be a useless and cruel blow added to those you've already suffered."

"Mother, what happened between you and Father? And please don't put me off this time. Maybe my knowing that will help me put my own life in perspective. I think, too, you owe me an explanation of some sort."

Jette could not say why it had become so important to her to learn why her parents had lived for years in hatred and resentment. Yet she knew it was necessary for her to know and understand if she were to understand and endure her own misfortunes.

"Your father was a violently jealous man, Jette. I was much younger than he and if I so much as passed the time of day with a gentleman he imagined all sorts of things that weren't so." Verdie spoke slowly, her soft Virginia accent manifesting as she recounted unhappy memories.

"There was a young man your father hired as a fence-rider when we were having problems with some of the squatters over in the San Lucas foothills. They needed cattle and thought nothing of cutting the fences and rustling a few head. This boy had been born at Collyer Meeting, Virginia, not far from my home, but his family lost everything during the war and he had come West to find his fortune." Verdie looked away as tears welled in her eyes at the recollection.

"All he found out here was hard work, little money, and his own death," Verdie said.

"Father?"

Verdie nodded. "Yes, your father killed him, poor boy, and not a soul stood up to him for it. He didn't even call him out and give him a chance to defend himself." For a moment the old wildness appeared in her eyes, but she swallowed hard and called the fat little spaniel to come sit on her lap. The dog lumbered to her and sprang onto the sofa and onto her knees, his pink wet tongue licking at her hands. She hugged the animal to her until she could continue.

"He was so lonesome out here—just as I was. We knew a few of the same people and we would speak of them now and then when we'd meet. Then your father had to make a trip to Mexico. Your father never told me what he did on those trips he made, but I could guess.

423

Someone would always send us newspapers and there would be an account of a gunfight or a raid—something violent and with killings. He was a hired killer, Jette. Praise be, he was usually on the side of right, but that didn't lessen the guilt of it. I heard whispers here and there about his reputation. You can still hear them in San Genaro.

"While he was in Mexico I took ill with the fever. He'd hired some immigrant Irish people to oversee the Alisos section and they'd brought the fever with them. I was very sick and the doctor feared I might lose you—I was a few months along then. Ben heard about it and that I was all alone with only the Mexican help on the ranch so he'd ride over from the San Lucas cabin just to see how I was. He'd bring me wildflowers. He knew how homesick I was for flowers . . . ." For a few moments she could not go on, then resumed the story in a whisper.

"Your father came back unexpectedly, much earlier than he'd planned. He'd already told Ben never to come to the main house again, never to even dare speak to me. When he discovered Ben in my bedroom . . ."

"Oh, Mother," Jette said in sympathy. "Is this what you've hidden all these years?"

"He shot Ben right before my eyes!" Verdie's voice rose in a cry of anguish. "He killed that boy without mercy. We were both strangers in a vicious, wicked land and we fell in love. And he died for it!" The memory was too much for her and she wept, loud, raking sobs that shook her in their violence. Jette jumped up, letting Rusty, the cat, land on his feet before the chair. She put her arms about Verdie and rocked her gently, feeling the anger and torment that her mother had been forced to live with for over twenty years. She could not comfort her because she could not erase the horrible injustice by Elias Allenby. The comfort would have to come from loving and being loved again.

424

When the woman stopped and asked Jette to fetch her a handkerchief, Jette knew the gnawing purgatory that had warped her mother's life had at last ended. A lifetime of misery! And only because she had dared to love another man instead of the killer Elias had become. As Jette rummaged in her mother's bureau in the back parlor the rage she had felt for her father slowly slipped from her. He had imprisoned himself in his own dungeon. *Perhaps*, she thought, *we all imprison ourselves*.

* * * *

"Benito says to tell you they're stopping the fire at the fence line. Asa said if they can hold it there, it will die out. It makes its own wind, but there isn't any real wind so by midnight they'll pretty well know." Little Elvira was flitting about the adobe as though she had never been concerned about the brush fire. "If the wind rises from the west like it usually does toward midnight, that's good. It makes the fire go backward on itself and helps put it out." Her prattle was simple, gleaned from snatches of conversation as the men returned to the ranch store with news of the battle.

"That's fine, dear. I'm glad to hear it," Verdie said. She was on the green leaves of the linen towel now, her needle darting in and out rapidly as though she must meet a deadline in its completion. "Did you see Mr. Carr anywhere?"

"No, ma'am." Elvira adjusted the wick of the lamp on the center table as it began to gutter. "Socorro says she'll want all the bread we can spare. Maybe I should go set some dough. By morning she'll need a lot more. I'm to cut the loaves and put meat in the oven—all it will hold. Asa says they'll have to feed the men where they are."

"Haven't they got the cook wagons?" Verdie asked.

"Yes, but it would take too long to get them fitted up

and anything cooked. Asa hopes it will be over before we need them." The cook wagons, rusting in the equipment barn, had not been in use for some time and were not kept provisioned.

"Perhaps we'd all better see to it," Verdie said and tossed her needlework in the basket. "Come along, we'll see what's in the cooler." Pecky leaped from the sofa and yawned.

Jette watched her mother in amazement as she assumed her rightful role as mistress of the house. Verdie seemed eager to take her place in the emergency beside the rest of the ranch workers. As they hurried to the kitchen she rolled up the sleeves of her light cotton gown. There was a spring in her step, a vitality in her voice that had never been there before. Jette whistled to the two dogs. Only the cat responded.

"Come on, you two," she coaxed. Buff and Pecky refused to leave their post by the patio door. After being scolded for whining and barking they had remained silent, but continued their vigil with an occasional yap of supplication. "Oh, don't make such a fuss! You don't need to go wee-wee," she chided them. Reluctantly they followed her into the kitchen and sat at the screen door, pacing from dining room window to door and back.

"I'm surprised no one from the Larsen Ranch has come over to see what's going on," Verdie said as she took one of Socorro's aprons from a peg behind the door. "They're on high enough ground—surely someone over there can see the flames."

"Mr. Beemer sent the Rodriguez boys over there and over to . . ." Elvira stopped abruptly. She looked apprehensively at Jette.

"Yes?" Verdie urged the girl to continue.

". . . to La Coruna . . . to tell Aunt Tecla and Uncle Seth," Elvira said. "Mr. Beemer wants them to send as many men as they can to stop the fire here. He says they've got to help us if they don't want it to spread to them."

Jette realized all too well the fear cattlemen know at the dreaded words, grass fire. Soon, she knew, hands from both ranches would come barreling down the drive and out to the command center at the ranch store. Odd that she had not thought of La Coruna's being endangered also. Nate should be here to help. Nate . . . She flung open the cooler door, banging it against its jamb, and forced herself to give her attention to their immediate problems. "We have plenty of butter in here for house use, but . . ."

"Check the ice locker, dear," Verdie directed her. She began to pull bushel baskets of potatoes and onions from the pantry floor and dragged them into the kitchen.

Jette unlatched the meat compartment of the ice locker which was built into the north end of the house in such a fashion that the sun never reached its walls. "There's a whole crock of butter in here," she said as she tugged the heavy stoneware container nearer the door. "And plenty of meat." She pulled at the geared chain that propelled hanging meat on an oval track above the blocks of ice. She shoved several slabs past and called to Verdie, "Standing ribs, a ham, side of veal . . . .here's the crown roast of pork you had Benito save for you when they butchered two weeks ago. There's side meat and bacon . . ."

"Good. We shan't have to go out to the smoke house," Verdie said. "We can send one of the men out to the root cellar later if we need to." She left unvoiced the thought that chilled her to the marrow—that she must not allow Jette to venture outside or to be left alone for even a few minutes. With both Russel Carr and Asa Beemer away from the house and all available men needed to subdue the fire, none were left to provide protection. There had been no discussion of priorities—

the fire must be stopped. Many lives and livelihoods depended upon it. Jette's safety had suddenly become secondary to the greater danger. "How much wood do we have for the range?" she asked.

"Roque finished the stack by the oven outside," Elvira replied. "And he filled the kindling box this morning." She realized what Verdie was thinking. "I filled the kerosene stove myself just tonight," she added.

"That should see us through till morning," Verdie decided. "Elvira, build a good fire for the big oven in the range. We need it hot right away. Don't forget to set the draft. Jette, lift down the ham and start trimming it. You'll find cheesecloth and string to tie it in the drawer under the flour bin. If we put it on to boil now, it will be ready by breakfast."

It was as though Verdie had never relied upon Socorro Galvan for the past two decades. Knowledge long unused returned in a flood as she directed the girls. Soon the bread, with an extra handful of sugar to hasten the leavening, was set for first rising. Kettles of stewing meat littered the surface of the enormous wood stove, while a blue-enameled coffee pot was placed to boil over one of the burners on the oil stove. Bread baking, done in the primitive but efficient outdoor oven, would have to be done much later. Verdie could only hope that one of the men would return to the house and start the slow fire in order for the oven to be brought up to temperature by the time they needed it. She could not be certain the other ranchers would send enough provisions along with their crews. When the need arose, the food must be ready. She did not let herself think of the possibility that they could not halt the flames.

The two dogs curled up on the kitchen floor beneath the table and chairs at one side. Rusty, the marmalade cat, patroled the area, his tail twitching disapproval of the dogs' invasion of his territory in the kitchen normally forbidden them. Pecky and Buff lay sprawled, noses to paws, as they waited for scraps and tidbits to be tossed to them, but they remained jittery.

The stench of brush smoke competed with that of roasting beef and pork. Even the laundry stoves in the wash house had been laden with tubs of stew. Now and then Verdie wiped her face with the borrowed apron and stood at the screen door, her glance wandering to the store and barns, and to the lurid glow to the southeast. As if she were trying to obliterate all thought of anything save the cooking chores at hand, Jette pared and cut vegetables into laundry tubs. It was not her first experience with brush fires. Five years before, the east pasture had blazed following a lightning strike. The same frantic activity had ensued, with Elias Allenby in charge of the frenzied attempt at control.

With the back of her hand Jette brushed back the auburn lock that stubbornly refused to stay tucked into her bound hair. Her hands were white with pastry dough. "That's all the pans we have, Mother." She pinched the edges of the pie crust together and sliced the residue of dough from the rim of the pan.

"Make the rest into turnovers," Verdie said wearily. The heat of the kitchen was unbearable although the windows and door were wide open. She could not chance throwing open the doors in the rest of the house to create a draft. If only she knew how to use the weapons that lay on the table in the parlor! The women might protect themselves . . . but from what? For a few exhausted moments her old confusion returned and she sat down on one of the oak chairs at the table. "Elvira, chip some ice for us and I'll make some lemonade." She looked about the kitchen, for a brief instant wondering what it was she needed. "Lemons . . . lemons . . ."

Elvira glanced up in surprise. "Yes, ma'am. I'll run get some." The trees were only a few rods from the north end of the adobe. She touched a match to the utility lantern and hurried to the grove, glad of the chance to cool off in the breezeless night air. Gathering an apronful, she started for the house when a slight movement along the fence to the north sent her racing to the kitchen. Jette heard her sandals on the patio and threw the door open quickly.

"What is it?" Verdie gasped in fright as she saw the girl's terrified face.

"Along the fence . . . something!" Elvira spilled the lemons into the sink and let Jette extinguish the lantern. The sight of Verdie's perturbation warned her to be careful in her reply. "It scared me . . . a jack rabbit or maybe one of the dogs from the village . . . it scared me . . ." she explained. "It's eyes were like red hot coals!"

Jette stifled a nervous laugh. "You probably frightened it more than it frightened you. It's probably trying to get as far from the fire as it can." She set the lantern by the door and wiped the bail handle clean of dough. "No telling what will get flushed out of the brush along the creeks down there. Remember when that young bear holed up along the south branch?"

Verdie made a sound of acknowledgment and nodded her head, but her thoughts were not of the pitiful creatures fleeing the flames. It was not the animals she feared.

Chapter 20

"Mrs. Allenby . . ." Elvira had stopped sifting flour from the one-hundred-pound bin of the cabinet. "Mrs. Allenby . . ." She pointed with one floured hand and stared at the dogs who had scrambled from beneath the table. "Look at them!"

Jette turned to watch the dogs, both of which were crouched in an attack position, the mongrel's broad head lowered, lip curled above huge canines. A ridge of coarse tan hair had risen along his spine, while Pecky snarled, his nose rubbing the screen as he tried to escape from the kitchen. This was not just their reaction to the excitement and scent of smoke. It was beyond that—something was out there in the dark. Something had aroused their animosity.

The three women watched in growing alarm. It was as though both animals were trying to convey to the women their knowledge of a presence only they could detect. Buff left off his gutteral warning growls and now barked furiously. Pecky pawed at the door in a frenzy. For a moment Jette was afraid the mongrel would try to leap through the screen.

Without a word Jette pumped water over her hands in the tin sink and washed them clean of pastry dough, then took the kerosene lantern from the floor. Bending to light the canvas wick, she snapped shut the isinglass window and placed the lantern on the chair by the door, then rushed into the parlor and returned with the Greener 12 gauge shotgun.

"Jette! You mustn't go out there. You can't!" Verdie's voice had the fine edge of hysteria. She threw herself in front of the screen door. "I won't let you go!"

"Someone has to. It could be a badger or bob cat or God only knows what. It's probably one of those wild dogs from La Coruna," Jette said with a matter-of-factness that surprised even herself. "Asa thought he'd killed them off. He may have missed one." She checked the safety trip on the heavy weapon and dropped a handful of extra shells into her apron pocket.

"Please, Jette . . ." Verdie begged.

"Mother, that shipment of calves for La Maravilla is in the lot this side of the barn. We can stand to lose some chickens to a coyote or a badger, but we don't want to have one of those prize calves dragged down."

"Let Elvira go get one of the men," Verdie pleaded. Elvira's dark eyes went round with fear as she peered into the blackness outside. She did not relish going out with the only thing visible the glow of the fire and a few lanterns in the vicinity of the store. "She can bring one of the men here," Verdie said.

"We haven't one man to spare." The truth of Jette's statement made Verdie pause in her protest. Until reinforcements from neighboring ranches came, what she said was only too literally true. "Asa needs every man jack of them on the fire lines," she reminded her mother and made herself laugh in spite of misgivings. "What sort of ranch woman am I if I can't see to a stray coyote or calf-killing feral dog?"

"Wait until one of the men comes back," her mother wailed. "You don't know what's out there!" All three women knew she did not refer to coyotes or feral dogs.

"Let's not let our imaginations carry us away, Mother," Jette said, summoning her reserve of equanimity. "You and Elvira stay right here. If Benito or the Rodriguez boys come to the house, tell them I've gone up toward the barn."

No matter how she protested, Verdie's statements would not have the ring of reason, but of pure emotionalism. Nor could she stop Jette. If the calves were threatened, there was no time to wait for the menfolk to take action. "Take the dogs," she finally said.

Jette considered for a moment, then agreed. "If it will make you feel better . . . but I'll take them only on the condition that you bring the guns in here and keep the revolver handy. Will you do that?"

Verdie bit her lip, her face evincing her reluctance. "All right," she said. Jette did not wait to see her ultimatum carried out. Elvira threw open the door and held it for Jette to pass into the patio. With one lunge

432

the mongrel dashed ahead, leaving the waddling spaniel to accompany Jette.

The darkness was intensified by the dense spread of oak branches overhead. The small pool of flickering light from her lantern only emphasized her isolation and danger. Shrugging off her qualms, she whistled the dogs to her side, the mongrel racing back and forth in impatience.

Far to the east she could see pinpoints of light that showed where one of the heavy water wagons was drawing a load from the well in the pasture. She tried to see into the dark beyond the feeble light she carried, but it was useless. The night was moonless and clear, the stars dimmed to faintness by a high, thin veil of haze. As she neared the fence she heard Buff growl. The spaniel slowed and waited behind the larger dog. The mongrel lowered its head and began weaving back and forth, nose to the ground as he endeavored to pick up the scent. Pecky clung to Jette's side, barely a step ahead of her.

A rustle in the dry weeds under the blue gum hedge triggered both animals into a furor. With one leap the mastiff-faced mongrel cleared the fence, leaving Pecky to squirm beneath the wire through a shallow depression in the dirt close to the gate.

There was no way Jette could keep pace with the dogs. If she heard them begin baying as they did when treeing raccoons or opossums, she would follow the sound. It was more important, however, to see to the herd of purebred Angus calves in the lot. Quickly she ran down the path to the pasture gate, set the lantern on the rutted roadway and unfastened the lock with one hand, all the time keeping the shotgun at the ready. Although it was awkward, she refused to abandon the gun for any reason. She thrust the gate shut behind her and seized the bail handle of the lantern, surprised at her steadiness.

433

"Pecky! Buff!" she called out and tried to listen for any noise to indicate their whereabouts. Walking carefully along the edge of the barnyard she made her way to the side lot where the shipment of stock destined for Rancho La Maravilla had been confined. There seemed no undue disturbance within the herd. Other than the fright caused by the smell of smoke and the initial flurry of excitement, the fat black calves appeared untroubled as they clustered about water troughs and salt blocks. "Pecky . . . Buff . . ." She strained to hear an answering howl or bark. Only the restive noises of the cattle and distant barking of dogs in the village disturbed the quiet barnyard. The windmill stood silent and idle. Not even a whisper of breeze ruffled the blade-shaped leaves of the blue gum hedge.

Growing tired from the weight of the lantern and gun, her arms felt leaden, yet she had no choice but to continue. Had the creature she'd heard in the weeds been either bobcat or coyote it would be most unusual for it to hunt so near an inhabited area. Of course from what stockmen told her, feral dogs were much more cunning and posed a far greater threat, especially where calves were concerned. She hitched the walnut gunstock up under her arm and rested the lantern on the rim of a water trough. She would make a circuit of the lot, keeping to the fence line, and patrol up to the main cattle barn. It was unlikely the animal would bother the larger stock. There was the possibility it might double back and pick off a goose or duck, perhaps try for the poultry house, but the La Maravilla calves were what concerned her most. They had been contracted for, paid for. She was responsible for their delivery. As soon as some of the men came back, she could yield up the Greener and return to her cooking chores. But until then . . .

Carefully picking each step as she went, Jette worked her way toward the main barn, pausing now and then to

434

listen. Through the eucalyptus she could see the lamp-light in the house. Over in the workmen's village there seemed to be much scurrying between the cottages and heavy wagons which were lined up, ready to pull out at an instant's notice. From such a distance she could not see the buggies, but she knew the Rockaway and phaeton were in the driveway, with the little mare, Blue, harnessed to the trap. With any luck, and if the wind did not rise, they would not need the vehicles.

As she viewed the village and main house from the slight knoll upon which the barn was built, she began to realize the burdensome responsibility her father must have felt in such circumstances. Beyond the highway, farther to the west, lay the other Allenby village of Alisos, with its band of expatriate Irish, its pastures extending from the city limits of San Genaro north to the Larsen ranch, and encompassing the Las Lomas foothills and countless acres of untamed mountain land. To the north lay La Coruna. Eastward beyond the flaming grass pasture, Allenby holdings ran well into the San Lucas Range. All the people—men and their families, wives and children—all had been in Elias' care. Right now in this emergency they all had need of his great strength. For the first time since his death, Jette wanted to weep for him and for the long, ugly years he and Verdie had let slip by in festering jealousy and hatred.

Remembering Elias, remembering the way he had died, she also recalled Asa Beemer's accusation of Nate. Had Nate arranged her father's death—just as he had arranged for Palma Owens to be pushed off the moving train? She did not want to believe such a thing. And yet, Elias had died.

Rounding the high-railed bull pen she was startled by the sound of furtive movement near the barn. No one should be at the barn—all the men and youths had been pressed into service either on the fire lines or out in the pasture herding stock onto safer ground. Feeling foolish at her fright, she convinced herself it was nothing. Certainly it could not be a wild animal—not that close to a building. All the same, she tripped the safety on the Greener and fingered the heavy shells in her apron pocket.

Holding the lantern before her, she made her way past the pen, up to the barn's main entry. The huge sliding doors were standing partially open and from inside came the quiet sounds of ruminating cattle. The shotgun's cold steel was slight comfort when she considered that any shot from it could maim or destroy the very cattle she was trying to protect.

Her hands grew moist with a fear that suddenly intensified as she wandered down the long aisles between stalls. Cows, their sleek black bellies swelled with calf, chewed regurgitated cud and turned to watch her with liquid, brown eyes. They seemed unperturbed. Still, she wished the dogs had not deserted her.

"Stop where you are, Jette." The voice came from behind her. "No! Don't move. Just set the lantern on the keg there and put the gun on that bale of straw." Jette could hear the ominous click of a revolver being cocked. "I'm past playing games, Jette. Do as I say!"

It was hot in the barn, but her teeth began to chatter and perspiration beaded her face. "Would you shoot me, Nate?"

"I'll do whatever I must." He waited a moment and when she did not obey he said, "I'd advise you to do exactly as I say if you've any regard for your mother and Elvira." Trasker's voice was low, hardly more than a whisper. "Put the gun down, Jette."

Trembling until she almost dropped the lantern, Jette laid the shotgun on the bale, then placed the light on the top of an oak keg used as a stool by the barn boys. "What do you intend to do?" she asked, trying to keep her voice from breaking. She desperately wanted to shout, but no one was near enough to hear. Nor could she risk calling his bluff. If he shot her, it was one thing, but she could not endanger Verdie and Elvira—two more killings would not increase his punishment. "What do you want? Why did you come back?"

"For the payroll." He strode from hiding and roughly turned her around with one hand; with the other he brandished a small revolver before her face. "You see, my love, I am not playing games." He was disheveled, his clothing dusty, with dry bits of grass clinging to trouser legs and the skirt of his coat.

"But the payroll . . ." she started to protest.

". . . is in the safe," he said. "And you're going to get it for me."

"It isn't mine to get! It belongs to the hands."

"You're going to get it for me."

"I won't!"

"You will, Jette." He brought the gun barrel so close to her breast it brushed the white apron. "I need it."

"You can't get away with it, Nate. The men . . ."

". . . have their hands full with the fire." He picked up the 12 gauge and tucked it under his arm, pocketing his own revolver. He bent to retrieve the lantern and motioned for her to move before him to the door. "I made sure they'd have plenty to occupy them elsewhere."

"You! You set the fire?" She whirled to face him, her black eyes flashing in the dim light. "How could you do such a thing?"

"As I said, I do what I must. Just keep going, Jette," he ordered her, swinging the shotgun up. "And remember, one wrong move, one sound, and I promise you won't like what this shotgun will do to your mother and that little girl at the house." The viciousness of his threat was emphasized when he gave the lantern's key a twist and extinguished the flame. "We don't want to call attention to my little visit," he said as he set the

437

lantern aside. "But I think we can find our way back down to the house, can't we?"

In the darkness Jette stumbled down the path which led west from the barnyard. She listened intently, hardly daring to draw a breath. In the distance Buff and Pecky barked in furious pursuit of the interloper. There was no question in her mind that Nate would shoot both animals if they returned and gave the alarm.

"Open the gate," Nate said. "And do it slowly." She glanced fearfully at the ranch store beyond the trees. Suppose someone from the village saw them, came to meet them? She unlocked the heavy gate and swung it back, waiting for Nate to walk ahead a few steps, then shut it behind them. Down at the house she could see lamplight shining from the ground-floor windows. Figures passed back and forth in the kitchen, flitting in and out of the light as Verdie and Elvira continued their food preparation. She had no way to warn them, and if she did—what could they do?

"Where's Benito?" Trasker asked in a whisper.

"Over at the store and village."

"Where are the buggies?"

"In the barn, of course."

"Don't lie to me!" He jabbed the barrel savagely into her back. "I was over there. There isn't a horse or a carriage in the place. Where are they?"

"In the drive and lined up along the lane."

"Harnessed? All ready to go?" He sounded hopeful.

"Yes," she replied. "They're to evacuate the families if it comes to that." One escape seemed to present itself. "Any minute now men from Jake Larsen's place will be here." She knew the information rattled him by the way he cursed under his breath. He had not counted on a confrontation.

"Where are the riding horses?"

"You should know—you're responsible! They're all out in the south pasture."

438

He swore softly and asked, "Does Benito have riding horses at the store?"

"I don't know. Why don't you go see for yourself?" Jette could not help goading him. "If you're worried about leaving, why not go right now—before Jake Larsen's men get here or before somebody discovers what you're up to?"

"Because you're going with me, darling." His voice was cold steel, cold and deadly as the Greener 12 gauge he pointed at her back.

"Why? Why should I go with you?" She raised her voice in rage. "Do you think I don't know what you intend doing?"

"I have no idea what you may be thinking," he replied as he prodded her forward. "The reason you're going with me is that you have no choice in the matter." They had reached the edge of the kitchen garden. Once more she listened. Surely the dogs' barking was closer now, much nearer.

"Why did you come back for the payroll? It's hardly big enough to do you any good." If she were going to die, she wanted answers to her questions. "It certainly isn't enough to risk your life for." She slowed her steps, delaying their arrival at the house. Then it dawned on her. "Ah! I know! Lavinia and Clarence Pomeroy didn't trust you—I heard them both say so." She could not resist the wild laugh that startled her husband into lagging behind a few steps. "They took everything, didn't they?"

Nate did not reply, but she kept on. "Did Lavinia find out the police exhumed Hiram Baldwin's body and are going to arrest her for his murder?" Again she knew he was caught off guard. She turned and saw the shock on his face. "You didn't know that? I'd guess she must have found out somehow and decided not to wait around for you. Did she and that man abscond with everything?" she demanded. "Is that what happened?"

"Yes, damn you! Yes, that's exactly what happened."

"So you come running back to your wife to save you!" In a movement so swift she had no time to react, he struck her in the face with his free hand.

"No more talk!" His command was a low-pitched growl. He grabbed her arm and twisted it behind her back, forcing her to her knees. "I'm going to tell you this just once, so listen carefully. You're going into the house and get the payroll. Give any excuses you want to your mother and Elvira. Just get it and bring it to me." He could see the women through the open kitchen window. "I'm going to keep this gun leveled at them. I can't miss at this range. A shotgun does terrible things, Jette," he said ominously. "It can shred an arm or tear off a head or cut a man in half." He wrenched her arm until she whimpered with the pain. "Remember that when you go inside. If you do anything—anything at all—to prevent my leaving safely, I'll come back and use it." In the faint lamplight from the window she could see his handsome, high-foreheaded face. He wore no hat and his blond hair fell at odd angles as though he had not bothered to comb it. She knew it meant only one thing: his getaway had been so quick and unplanned he had had no time to take even the commonest necessities.

"Not a word to them about my being here," he said. "Do you understand?" This was not the gentle lover she had fallen in love with and married, but a killer who had spoken of his brutal experiences in the South African campaign against the Boers with no trace of feeling or emotion. "Understand?" he asked again. She nodded her head, unable to speak.

He pulled her from the path and pushed her ahead of him. She could hear Elvira's busy chatter and her mother's reply as they basted the roasts in the oven. She wanted to enter the house by the patio door, going

440

directly into the parlor where the luggage was stacked for quick evacuation, but remembered Verdie had locked all the doors. She must go through the kitchen and there would be questions. There was no other way.

"Go!" Trasker shoved her across the patio, the shotgun pointed toward the open window of the kitchen. Terrified lest she fail, Jette opened the screen door and entered.

"Did you find whatever it was that set the dogs off?" Verdie asked as she came in. The kitchen was hot and redolent of baking pies and roast beef. On the work table the bread had risen in smooth lumps, pushing up the damp towels covering the pans. "What was it? A bobcat?"

"I have no idea what it was," Jette replied and avoided looking at either Elvira or her mother. "The dogs kept on going. I heard them way out in the orchard somewhere." She continued on into the dining room. "Whatever it was, it didn't go up by the barn."

"Were the calves all right?" Verdie called in to her.

"Yes, they're fine. They don't even seem to be upset from the smoke and commotion," she answered as she hurried to the stack of suitcases and hand baggage. Moving aside a small portmanteau she seized the leather satchel with the money and jewelry. It would be better to go out the parlor door, she decided, rather than risk their seeing her with the satchel and wondering what she was doing with it. She crossed the room and twisted the key in the lock.

"Jette! What are you doing?" Verdie had followed her into the room and stared at her in disbelief. "Answer me!"

"I can't explain, Mother. Please don't ask questions," Jette pleaded. She opened the door, but Verdie flew to her side and slammed it shut.

"I demand you tell me what you're doing with that money, Jette. You seem to forget that this ranch is mine

441

to run, not yours." She backed against the door, her hazel eyes blazing with aroused anger. "You have no right to that money. I shan't allow you to take it out of this house."

"Mother, I must! I can't explain, but please for God's sake trust me . . . let me go!" Jette heard the hushed tread of Nate's boots on the flagstones. The shotgun, she knew, was pointed directly at them. It mattered little that the window was closed. Glass could afford them no protection against the 12 gauge's blast. "This is something I must do." Jette reached for the door knob, but her mother remained adamant.

"Young lady, I don't know what you're up to, but that satchel is not leaving this house." Although she was small and far from strong, Verdie was determined. "Put it back and we'll say no more about it." Jette heard the crunch of Nate's boots much nearer the house. He was too close—he could not miss.

With suddenness born of her desperation Jette thrust her mother aside, catching her off balance just enough to send her sprawling sideways to the floor. Verdie's shriek of anger and pain went unheeded. In an instant Jette was out of the house, running as fast as she could past the wash house, past the garden. Behind her she could hear Nate. He kept to the grass to cushion the sound of his tread, but he was not far behind. She did not stop to look back until she had almost reached the gate to the barnyard. Breathless, she stopped and glanced over her shoulder. At least she had lured Nate away from the house.

"What the hell do you think you're doing?" he snarled as he caught her arm in a bruising grip. She dropped the satchel at his feet and struggled to break his grasp.

"There's your precious money!" she spat with fury. "Take it and go!" He bent to pick it up with one hand, the Greener still clutched in the other.

"Open it," he said, and held it out to her. Slipping the catch open, she spread the satchel wide and let him plunge his hand into its contents. His fingers groped about until he realized what the loose trinkets were. He held up a small choker of canary diamonds and seed pearls. "I thank you very much, my dear." He brought the piece to his face in order to see it closely. "So far my luck is running exceptionally good."

"It can't last for long," Jette said as she closed and snapped the lock on the bag. "Here come Jake Larsen's men."

Down the main drive toward the highway she could see faint yellow specks of light heralding the approach of hands from the nearest ranch. Even as they peered into the dark they could hear the jangle of harness bells and hoofbeats as the crew thundered toward them.

"If you meant to use one of the buggies to get away it seems your escape route is blocked," Jette observed.

"By no means," he contradicted her. "You're going to see if Benito has a horse saddled up for us. I'm going to be right where I can watch you both. Remember there are a lot of women and children milling around over there who would get hurt if you try to warn him. One false move . . ." He did not need to finish his threat.

"I understand," Jette said with resignation and started along the path through the oak grove. They walked in silence toward the ranch store where Benito Galvan was directing the women in loading up the wagons.

"Call the old man over here. Stand in the light where I can see you."

Jette went on past the trees and waited beneath the lamp hung on the porch. From the corner of her eye she could see the barrel of the gun as Nate aimed from cover of one of the gnarled oaks. "Benito!" she called out.

"Yes, Miss Jette?" The old man saw her and came to meet her before the store porch. "What may I do for you?'' His brown face was eloquent in revealing his anxiety and exhaustion. *He's too old*, Jette thought, *for such rigorous work—or to be placed in such danger*.

"Have you a horse saddled? One I may use?" she asked.

His eyebrows went up as he noticed her dress and apron. She was not garbed for riding, not even for side-saddle. "For you?" he asked. "You want a horse?"

"Yes, please. I want to ride out to see how things are going." He did not believe her. She could see that, but he shrugged his shoulders and trudged along the path around to the side of the store. "They aren't the best ones, Miss Jette," he explained. "I don't like to see you try any of these." He shook his head as he waited for her to follow. She did not dare move from the light. "All right, I'll bring one around for you," the old man agreed. He knew there was no way he could prevent her going if her mind was made up.

"Which one is this?" she asked as he brought a rangy quarter horse up to her by the porch steps.

"Pima . . . Pima, they call him." He held the gelding, waited for her to mount, then handed her the reins. "Keep him checked. He likes to run when he gets his head." The saddle, made for the width and splay of a man, did not fit her small hips and forced her into an uncomfortable position. He shortened the stirrups to her feet and reluctantly let her go.

As soon as she was out of the small pool of light by the store front she turned the horse into the grove where Nate stood waiting. With a few deft loops of the rope that hung from the saddle he improvised a sling for the shotgun. Once it was secured he took his revolver from his pocket and held it on Jette.

"Get behind the saddle," he ordered her. When she hesitated he held the revolver close so she might see it in the dim light and said, "I swear I'll kill them, Jette." He turned his head and listened as the horsemen and vehicles came nearer. "If that's what you want, I'll oblige you." He reached for the Greener in its rope sling.

Quickly she slipped her feet from the stirrups and slid backwards to sit on the horse's loins. The animal lurched nervously, side-stepping and dipping his head. Nate recognized the antics as those of a newly broken mount, but he had no time to select a better one. He calmed the gelding and led him in tight circles until he quieted down. In one swift leap he threw himself into the saddle and made for the open gate that led to the stables and equipment barn and pasture beyond.

Over her shoulder Jette could see Jake Larsen's men dismounting before the store and hear their excited shouts as the wagons pulled to a stop. Nate did not gallop the horse, but let it amble at its own speed until well past the buildings. Jette tried to cling to the high cantle with her hands and gripped the horse's flanks with her legs rather than clasp Nate about the waist.

She could smell the expensive bergamot lotion he used, and memories of lying in his arms, the beauty of his muscular, golden body next to hers, came flooding unbidden into her consciousness. They had ridden almost a mile before she was aware that she was crying.

Slapping Pima with an end of the rope, Nate spurred the horse faster. The sudden transition caused Jette to bounce and slide, her skirts and petticoats working up and leaving her stockinged legs exposed. Gasping with fright she grabbed Nate about the waist and clung tightly as the horse assumed a long easy stride and struck out almost due east. Although the stirrup straps did not fit his long legs, Nate posted with the horse's movements, his own body in perfect rhythm with the animal's. Jette felt his rib cage swell with each breath he took while her own came in tortured bursts.

Frantically she tried to devise an escape, but she knew him too well to test his vow to return and settle accounts with her by taking vengeance on Verdie and Elvira. She did not doubt for an instant that he would make good his threat.

To the south she could see an orange-red flickering line that seemed to advance in rapid spurts, then die out, only to rekindle a few yards ahead. Outlined against the glow she could see movement that showed where the crews were attempting to hold the flames.

Nate was not heading toward the fire. On the contrary, he guided Pima due east, at an angle to it. Ahead of them the San Lucas hills loomed black against the sky. There was no road in that direction—only the rail line.

The railway was a doubtful hindrance to the fire, although it was unlikely its ties or trestles would burn with the scarcity of fuel along its track. To their left as they rode were the rolling, oak-studded north pastures and open range beyond. Asa Beemer had wisely ordered shifting of herds across several barren and dry creeks which would provide natural barriers to spread of the conflagration. Should it become necessary, the stock could be driven up into the hills for safety, but Angus with their short legs did not travel well or fast. Saving the stock was both difficult and paramount. Buildings could be replaced, but the stock was needed to survive at all.

Jette was now past weeping. A numbness had gradually suffused her body and mind, erasing all physical pain and leaving only a void of feeling. Her arms encircled a man—only a man. He was not the lover and husband of her heart. She could not believe that Nate, the man whom she had so adored, could be capable of such heinous acts. The fire served one purpose only—to make good his escape. It had not mattered to him that he might destroy the entire community should the fire get away and wind change. And how ironic it was that Asa, whom she had loathed, must be the one to save them all.

She could not tell how long they had been riding, but as they skirted a slight rise and followed the rock-strewn bank of a dry stream she could make out vague rectangular shapes on the flat section ahead. It had to be the railway siding with a collection of cars shunted off the main line. The rails, which ran north and south through the Allenby land, had paid dearly for right-of-way. Unlike the San Joaquin Valley, the land had not been held by the government, but by old-line Mexican grants. The railroad was forced to bargain with men like Elias Allenby. By agreeing to Elias' demand that they connect the siding to his spur line, they had given him an advantage no other rancher in San Genaro Valley possessed—his own point of shipping.

Nate pulled the gelding to a walk at the edge of the graded right-of-way and eased him alongside one of the boxcars. Without a word he reined Pima in, dismounted and unfastened the rope sling. He took the shotgun in his arms before tossing the satchel into the car.

"The door's open beside you," he told her as he held the horse steady. "There's a hand rail to use. Get in." When she made no move he said quietly, "I could shoot you right here, Jette, if that's what you'd like. The way sounds echo against those hills over there, if I fired a shot every man in the north pasture would hear it. They'd come swarming along here to see what was going on. I can't get far in either direction along these tracks or east over the mountains. That would leave one route open—back toward the house."

"My God! You've come this far, you wouldn't . . ."

"Oh, but I would." There was no mistaking his intent. "I have little to lose at this point. I'll leave the choice to you."

Inside, the boxcar was pitch black. Not even a chink of light broke the awful dark. Slowly she eased forward into the saddle, felt for the hand rail on the car, and pulled herself in. The horse danced skittishly and before

447

Nate could control him, he bolted, reins dragging as he scrambled back up the slope and headed across the pasture toward home.

Nate stood swearing as he listened to the diminishing hoofbeats. From a distance came the whoops of the vaqueros as they coaxed the herds together and began their flight. Nothing could be heard from the south, but the fire brightened the landscape like a livid scar. Crickets silenced by their arrival began their spasmodic rasping once more.

Within the car, Jette was invisible. Although he knew his threat of reprisal would prevent her from either trying to run or attempting an act of desperation while he held a weapon in his hand, he fully expected her to take advantage of any opportunity should he become careless.

"Damn that horse!" he cursed as he paced beside the boxcar. "Where is he kept? In the barn?"

"Usually in the horse pasture. He's one of the new string Asa bought for us over at San Gallan." Jette was curious as to why Nate should ask about Pima. "We always keep a few that double as riding or harness animals." She did not expect a reply, but asked, "Why?"

"Because he'll probably go right back to the stables— or worse, back to join the rest of the horses down at the store or wherever they've put them to work." Revolver in hand, he placed the shotgun on the floor in the center of the open door. "Stand back and don't get any ideas about trying to grab that gun," he said and pulled himself up into the box car.

"And riderless, they'll wonder what happened to me," Jette finished his thought. She came to stand in the doorway where the air was cooler. "Yes, that might pose a problem for you, Nate," she gloated. Perhaps there was a chance for her after all.

He did not respond to her taunt, but struck a match

and pulled out his pocket watch. "I wouldn't build up any false hope, darling. We have only to wait until 12:07."

"What happens then?"

"The northbound freight is coupling these cars on and is bound for Salt Lake." He blew out the match and flipped it outside onto the gravel. "I obtained the information from a regular passenger on the line," he laughed.

"You mean a tramp." Jette stepped back into the darkness in order to watch him covertly. If only he would relax his vigilance for a moment! "And what are you planning to do with me, Nate?" she asked. "Am I to be pushed out over a river? Or maybe out over a steep canyon? Would that be better?"

"Shut up, Jette!" Some of the veneer of imperturbable calm had been penetrated. He turned and stared into the darkness following the sound of her voice. "Why the devil did you have to follow Cliff to that hotel? We would have been away clean and none of this would have had to happen!"

"Cliff?" She was pleased that he was disturbed.

"Clifford Percy—Lavinia's brother."

"I thought I'd followed Clarence Pomeroy," she said.

"One and the same." Nate sat down at the end of the open space, one knee up, the other leg hanging down over the edge of the car. His usual erect, military-like bearing had slumped round-backed against the door. Jette could tell he was weary although she could not see his face. Every line of his body, even his resonant voice, betrayed his fatigue. The shotgun rested across his lap, its barrel out the door. If only something . . . anything . . . would distract him!

She moved slowly nearer and sat down, not too close to him, her feet folded beneath her to one side. Her hair, loosened by their long ride, fell about her shoulders like a soft russet cape. She ran her fingers through it, freed the tangles and pushed it back from her face. Nate watched her, his eyes never leaving her as she tended her hair and straightened her skirt and petticoats. As she sat immobile he reached inside his coat and a slight metallic reflection told her it was his cigarette case he withdrew. He struck a match, held it to a cigarette and inhaled deeply, all the time observing her with watchful suspicion.

A waxing moon, within two days of full, had just ascended the summit of the San Lucas range. Its light was clear and white as it picked out in silhouette brush and rocks that dotted the gently slanting hills. Iron rails burnished to silver brightness by daily usage glistened in each direction. From a small motte of oaks a mockingbird roused from uneasy slumber and experimented with a few desultory notes. Except for a faint acrid smell of grass smoke, the night was serene in its placid beauty.

"In the time we have left, will you tell me why you did all this?" Her voice was low, with a throatiness more suggestive of the bedroom than a dusty shipping car on a deserted siding. "Surely you had some grand scheme." She turned to look at him in the moonlight. "Tell me, was I just part of the plan?"

"I see no reason not to tell you about it." He eyed her warily, took his revolver from his pocket and placed it by him along with the leather satchel. The implication was plain for her to read. She refused to give him satisfaction by reacting in any way to his gesture. "Yes," he admitted. "You were a major part of the plan. But my feelings were real enough." He breathed out through his nostrils a slow exhalation of more than tobacco smoke. "I fell in love with you, Jette. I hadn't planned that part of it." The mockingbird ran an arpeggio and fell silent. "I'm still in love with you," Nate said.

"Don't say that—not now, not after all you've done."

"But it remains true." The cigarette glowed ashy-bright in the shadows.

"How did I fit into your plans?"

"I thought that eventually we might gain control of most of this valley. Your father was right about the availability of water for irrigation. I saw the hydraulic engineer. I was going to get the Baldwin place from Lavinia. That together with your ranch and La Coruna . . ." Even now he was enthusiastic.

"But Lavinia and her brother wouldn't go along with it. Was that it?" Jette asked. "They didn't know about your own private plans, did they?" She had guessed the split among the conspirators had been late.

"There would have been plenty for them to go on to Johannesburg. They didn't need me," he said bitterly.

"You were going to double-cross them?"

"Call it what you will, Jette, they wouldn't have been the losers. They'd have had their big start in Africa and I'd have had mine right here in San Genaro Valley." He sighed as if putting an end to something. "All my life I've wanted my own empire—one such as your father had. I learned at an early age the difference between having money and not having it, and I promised myself one day I'd have more than enough." He tapped the ash out the car door and shifted to a more comfortable position.

"And I was to provide you with more than enough? Was that all I was to be?"

"Partly, yes."

"Did you plan on me in particular, or would just any girl with good prospects do?" The sarcasm in her voice was ugly.

He laughed quietly as he looked across at her. "Actually, I had considered making myself irresistible to the Larsen girls, but Abe Marley's description of you . . ."

"Did he describe Father's holdings, too?"

"Yes, he did. And when I met you . . ."

"Don't, Nate!" Her reaction was more of pain than anger. They sat in silence, listening to the crickets and mysterious rustlings in the brush along the rails.

After a while Nate recommenced, "When Cliff and I got into a spot of bother some years ago we shipped out to Africa for action against the Matabeles. We saw land out there ripe for plucking. A man could make a fortune in short order if he went about it right. We set ourselves a goal and a time limit." His voice grew even more bitter as he said, "But it's always what you don't plan that gives the trouble."

"This spot of bother—as you put it—was that your affair with Mrs. Owens? The woman in Cincinnati?" Jette led him back to his narrative.

"It was," he admitted readily. "She was a vain, silly old woman who should have known better. Insisted I was to marry her, for God's sakes! It wasn't as though I'd seduce an innocent girl." Jette said nothing, remembering the woman's fate.

"Through an attorney who dealt in British corporate law I learned we'd need a great deal more money than originally we'd counted on. To be permitted to do what we wanted, either a large capital account or a sizable bond was required. Non-citizens had to establish the fact that they're responsible before they're allowed to engage in certain businesses. We hardly came with the best recommendations, so we had to come up with more money. Always it comes down to money!" It angered him to recall his humiliation. "So Cliff and I managed to be invalided out of the Light Horse and began accumulating our necessary capital."

"By resorting to land swindles, confidence games?"

"We took from people as eager to fleece us as we were to fleece them," he defended hmself and his methods with a laugh.

"People like Palma Owens?" she baited him.

"Yes, by damn! Like Palma Owens!" he retorted

hotly. "And men like Booth Killigrew and Abe Marley
. . . men like your father . . . Do you think they got
where they did with Sunday school tactics and turning
the other cheek? The only earth the meek inherit in this
world is the few cubic yards they're buried under." Jette
knew she had needled him into anger when he went on,
"I'm not so different from the respectable manipulators
whom society adulates and lionizes. And when you
come right down to it, there is little difference in our
means and results. What I do may affect a few people;
what they do can affect millions."

She wanted to ask him if he'd killed Elias, but something in his manner warned her it was not the time to do
so. Later . . . if for her there would be a later . . .
Instead, she said, "So you came out West with your
land development scheme, took the investors' money,
married an heiress . . ." She wanted to shriek at him,
but kept her voice low and steady. "Tell me, Nate,
where are my aquamarines?"

"Cliff and Lavinia have them. They have everything."
He passed a hand across his face as though trying to
erase the dismal fact. Jette thought she might have a
reasonable chance to make a break. He caught her
glance and took the revolver in his hand. "I'll catch up
with them," he growled and brandished the weapon.
Jette shuddered at the cold avowal and its meaning.

A stealthy, secret crackle in the brush brought him up
short. He raised his head like an alarmed buck, holding
his breath to listen. Cosseting his revolver he quietly
cocked the hammer and rose to stand just inside the
door. Impatiently he motioned for her to get back into
the shadowed interior. The noise was nearer. Dry grass
broke and weed stalks snapped directly behind the boxcar.

Trasker could not see Jette where she stood. Softly,
cautiously, she moved across the floor, keeping to the
dark, until she was standing behind him. She was sure

he could hear the pounding of her heart and the gasp of her stifled breathing. Satchel and shotgun lay in the opening, the gun's heavy barrels dull in the moonlight, its stock only inches from Nate's boots. Scarcely audible, a displaced pebble rattled in the roadbed, this time in front of the car and to the right. Jette could see the revolver in his fist outlined against the backdrop of silvery sky.

Before he was aware of her presence she lunged, throwing her entire weight against him in one swift, reckless movement. Caught unguarded, he grabbed for the side of the boxcar, but so great was her momentum that he twisted outward and fell without a cry. Quickly she seized the shotgun and stood in the open door, her finger on the trigger. She fumbled with the safety, made sure it was off, and brought the barrel down, aiming at the fallen man.

Starting in fear, she stared as a tawny dog-like creature fled in terror, crashing through the brush across the right-of-way and melting into the hills. The coyote had given her a chance to make her escape.

Nate had fallen hard. The revolver was not in his hand, nor could she see it nearby. He made no move, nor uttered a sound. The shotgun was too heavy for her to hold in one hand as she attempted to climb down from the car. She could waste no time deliberating. Placing the weapon on the floor, she caught the handrail and vaulted to the ground. As she did so, Nate clutched at her skirts, pulling her half-way around, but she swept the shotgun into her arms and without taking aim, pulled the trigger.

Jette fell, the force of the blast sending her reeling backward against the boxcar. She was not sure whether the reverberating echoes were a trick of her paralyzed mind or merely the amphitheater of hills repeating the explosion over and over. Nate lay sprawled along the track, one arm flung across his chest, his face pallid in

the moonlight. Gingerly she bent to pick up the shotgun
and stepped near him. He was breathing, his chest rising
and falling with his shallow efforts. Using the gun barrel
she pushed aside his coat. There were no telltale darken-
ings of his brocade vest or white shirt. Apparently the
shot had gone wild and he had been only stunned by
concussion. Slowly she brought the barrel within a foot
of his head, her finger closing on the trigger.

He lay motionless, lips parted, jaw slack, his blond
mustache and fair hair glistening in the mellowing light.
"No!" she screamed. It was as though her father, ruthless and decisive, were prodding her to pull the trigger
and end her ordeal. "No! I can't!" she wailed into the
unhearing dark. Pointing the gun into the air she
removed the temptation by pulling the trigger. The
recoil jerked her, the pain in her shoulder bringing back
renewed awareness of her plight. Since she had cast
away the extra shells from her apron pocket as Nate
forced her down the lane to the house, the shotgun was
now useless. She did not see the revolver anywhere, but
had no time to make a search. If she could not find it,
neither could Nate when he came to. She grabbed the
satchel and ran.

Two blasts. She had signaled, but who would hear?
The horse, Pima, had not had time yet to return to the
ranch. When Nate regained consciousness he would
come after her again. If she tried to get across the
pastures she might be overtaken by the fire. Perhaps if
she ran, she could reach the Allenby spur. The first lot
of blooded heifers and proven cows was awaiting shipment north to La Maravilla. By now they would be
loaded into cars on the spur, with Maximilian of
Dundee allotted his own special quarters separate from
the females. Even with the grass fire raging, the cattle
would claim first attention at the spur, with some of the
crew on hand.

Jette ran south, keeping to the graveled edge of the

right-of-way, her thin-soled shoes doing little to protect her feet from the bruising stones. She gathered her skirts high, uncaring for modesty, thinking only of fleeing from Nate's vindictiveness. She had spared his life when she could have slain him, but she cherished no illusions that he would be grateful enough to let her remain a witness and threat to him.

Pain stabbed at her lungs. Her head was becoming giddy and sweat poured from her, yet her mouth and tongue were dry, her breath choking in her throat. From down the line she could see a flicker of brilliant light. She paused for a moment and listened. Judging by the train's whistle, it was cresting the rise south of San Genaro and would be at the station within a few minutes. Perhaps twenty minutes at San Genaro for transfer of freight, then another twenty minutes—perhaps less—to the loading dock on the spur. Why had she not listened to Asa when he was telling her about the freight train's schedule?

Stumbling, falling, only to rise and continue, on and on she ran. Twice she'd heard the train's whistle, but it meant nothing to her. And twice she thought she heard Nate pursuing closely behind her, only to find it was the peculiar acoustics of the valley manufacturing echoes of her own footsteps.

In the moonlight she could make out a dark depression ahead upon which the rails seemed to float. Manzanita Creek! Just beyond and to the right would be the spur. Far over in the pasture toward the fence line she could see the wavering orange rim of the fire, while here and there clumps of brush glowed in the blackened grass like isolated bonfires. Smoke billowed in roiling white banks, pushed by its own wind into fantastic moon-brightened clouds.

The trestle stretched across Manzanita Creek on a complex maze of creosoted timbers, with the roadbed dropping away to leave beams, ties, and rails as if suspended by air. Through gaps underfoot Jette could see the boulder-strewn abyss. She picked her way across, tie by tie, deliberately not focusing her eyes on what yawned below.

It was when she had reached the other side that she glanced back along the rails. Through the cut where the tracks sliced a hill rather than climbing it, she could see something moving. Still too far away for her to be certain as to what it might be, the possibility that it was Nate posed a greater threat than the exhaustion that was overcoming her. Breast heaving, gasping for each breath, she longed to throw herself into the drainage ditch and rest if only until she could ease the pain in her lungs. Clutching the pink calico skirt in her hand she headed for the angular shapes that loomed in the dark farther down the spur. She could hear no sounds of the men, nor could she spy any lanterns. Surely Asa would not leave the cattle unattended—not on the very night they were to be shipped. But the men would not be armed. What could they do against Nate, especially if he had found the revolver? By now the leather satchel felt made of lead. Her shoulder socket and wrist ached from the burden. At last she reached the first of the string of cattle cars standing on the tracks.

"Hello!" she called out, using her precious breath until she half fainted. When she recovered she called again, "Hello! Is anyone here?" She kept one hand on the rough wooden siding of the car, bracing herself to keep going.

"Hello!" she cried out as she looked around the corral and loading chutes. "Please . . . anybody . . . help me!"

Only the anxious lowing of the cattle answered.

Chapter 21

At the top of the loading chute Jette stood and listened. The heifers in the car beside her seemed restless, stamping and lowing their discontent at being confined in the narrow cattle transport cars. Furious that the stock had been left unattended, she was even more terrified that there was no one about. She was beginning to tremble violently. She could expect no help from anyone; if she were to survive, she must use her own wits.

Heels pounding as she ran down the steep ramp, she continued along the line of cars, stopping at each until she reached the one next to last. It was not a regular cattle car, but a closed boxcar adapted to special use by stockmen who shipped from the area on the railroad. Doors on both sides of the car stood open, with thick wooden gates secured in place across the opening. Jette tossed the satchel into the car and used the handrail to pull herself up. For an instant when she reached the floor level she was afraid she would collapse from exhaustion. Painfully she eased herself into the car, climbing over the stout gate and into the dark interior. Crawling along the side she dragged the satchel with her until she reached a spot in total blackness. She pulled her knees up and sat braced against the wall of the car, bundled into as small a space as possible. Her eyes grew accustomed to the dark. Nearby she could make out a bale of straw. Laboriously she pulled the bale at a right angle to the wall and curled up behind it.

By degrees the stabbing pains subsided and she began to breathe more easily. From the direction of town the train whistle sounded once more. It seemed no closer than before. It had been delayed in San Genaro. She could not expect help from the train crews either.

A hollow tread on the loading chute confirmed her

fears. Then another, this time nearer the more solid bottom of the ramp. Footsteps! Her heart was beating so fast she felt it a miracle she did not die right then. The hushed steps receded. Nate was going to search the cars one by one until he found where she had taken refuge. He had been able to see at a glance from on top of the ramp that there was nowhere in the pens and corrals for her to hide. She huddled behind the straw bale, waiting for the inevitable.

When Nate reached the car in which Jette was concealed he gave no warning he was there. A match suddenly flared in the doorway. From behind the bale she could see his face contorted with rage. Across it was written one thing—murder. The match spluttered and died in an instant. He could not have seen into the car. She heard him swear aloud, then silence.

He lighted no more matches. She could hear his feet in the gravel as he took a few steps her way. Had the side of the car not separated them, she could have touched him.

Did she imagine another sound? Horses? She would not delude herself that it was so. Instead, she listened intently for Nate's next move. He would not go away. Eventually he had to come into that freight car. She was too exhausted to run any more; she had no more strength.

Then he walked back to the door. His foot was on the metal round of the ladder and his fist slipped on the handrail. Something metallic hit the rail as he made a grab for it. The gun! He'd found the revolver!

Jette cringed in her hiding place, pulling her skirts tightly about her. Nate was not yet sure what was in the car. Moonlight slanted into the car, but he stepped out of the light and into the dark. He said nothing—not even her name. And yet he knew she was there . . . hiding . . . fearing for her life.

Nate unfastened the gate across from her and

propped it against the side of the car, then heaved the door shut. Undoubtedly he had reached the conclusion that the cattle would be shipped out tonight—otherwise they would not have been left loaded and waiting on the spur. Jete realized he was going to stay in the car, let the freight engine pick up the cars just as they would those at the siding farther down the line, then take his time finding her. Somewhere before La Maravilla he would take care of her, probably in the same way as with Palma Owens.

Jette felt the leather satchel beside her feet. He would find it, too. All he had to do was wait. When the cattle cars were shunted off onto the La Maravilla siding he would simply jump aboard the train and continue on to Utah.

She watched in horror as he removed the other gate, jumped down to the ground, his feet sliding in the loose gravel. He was loosening a hasp, then the door slammed shut. She could not get out without his hearing her. It was as though he were daring her to try to escape.

Jette had little time to wonder why he'd gone out. She heard the sound of a match scraped on the side of the car and a sliver of yellow light through the door opening told her he'd found a lantern. There had been one match left in the silver container he carried in his breast pocket. He had counted on that one match doing more than burn out quickly and leave him again in the dark.

As he thrust back the door a thunder of hoofbeats erupted from the road leading to the spur. There were no shouts, no voices, but a shot rang out as one of the horses neared. Nate had wasted one precious bullet.

"Where is she?" a man's voice yelled. He was close, and was answered by another bullet. The hoofbeats ceased as the men dismounted and sought cover behind the chutes and corrals. Another gun, of a larger caliber, exploded from nearby.

"What have you done with her?" The man was

within a few feet of her. As she jumped up and started for the door Nate swung into the car and tossed the lantern outside. It crashed with a flash of flaming kerosene.

"Get some sand on that fire!" Asa Beemer ordered someone. "I'm going in after him!"

"He's got a gun, Asa! He'll kill you!" one of the men replied in a hoarse whisper.

"That's train's going to be here any minute now, and once these cars are coupled on, we've lost him."

"Thatcher's gone down the line to the switch to stop 'em!"

"Yes, but that's not enough. We have no authority to hold that train and they can't wait here very long. They have to make it up to the El Pao siding in time to let the express go by. We can't expect them to stay on the line forever—they have too many cars and nowhere to put them short of El Pao."

Jette shivered as she listened. At least Nate had not yet seen her.

"Be careful, Asa," someone advised from behind the ramp. Another shot rang out, the report deafening within the car. Jette could hear the crunch of gravel beside the car as Asa Beemer crept along toward the open door. From Nate's vantage point he had a clear view of Asa. He raised his arm, the gun reflecting the lantern's flames just long enough for Jette to leap out of hiding and slash wildly at Nate's hand. He flung her from him and she fell headlong to the ground outside.

For the merest second Nate Trasker hesitated between his targets . . . Asa or Jette. In that instant Asa's gun roared. Nate whirled about and disappeared into the shadows. Asa ran to Jette, stooping by her side. A shot slammed into the dust only inches from her head. Asa stepped in front of her and faced the open door of the boxcar, making of himself an irresistible target. He flinched sideways as a bullet ripped into the soft flesh

461

between arm and chest. He fanned his gun, firing in quick succession at the spot where the flash of Nate's gun had been. He crumpled to the rails as another shot came from inside the car.

It began as a low rumbling bellow and rose to a high, trumpeting roar of fury. A strange stomping and rattle of an iron nose ring against the pen came too late as a warning. Wounded by Asa's bullets, Nate had delayed too long. With one mighty rush Maximilian of Dundee was upon him. Trasker's scream was stopped by the charge, its impact tossing him against the side of the car. Maximilian drew back and charged the limp form on the floor, lifting it over his head and slamming it down, worrying it beneath his lethal hoofs.

Rain made spasmodic pattering noises in the tin downspout at the corner of the upstairs veranda, much like the playful sounds of kittens chasing moths on a drum. Somewhere—a very long way off—a door caught by the breeze slammed shut. A soft, greenish light filtered under the lowered window pane, the air disturbing the curtains smelling sweetly of wet earth and clean-washed foliage. Buggy wheels crunched down the white graveled driveway and came to a stop in front of the adobe ranch house. Hushed voices murmured greetings and the front door shut, enclosing the voices within the parlor downstairs. Someone was shushing the dogs' barking.

Jette lay gazing at the ceiling, listening to the comforting, everyday sounds of living. Was that Severo Mireles whistling out in the front patio? He'd said he wanted to see where the rain trough was leaking but had to wait for the rainy season to find it.

The rainy season . . . Only to a Californian could the term bring such a thrill of assurance and anticipation. True, when the rivers overflowed after too many days of blessings, one wished the rains to cease. But next year it would be the same—they would endure the summer's heat and drought and sigh for the cool, gray days to come again.

A bevy of waxwings fluttered about the pyracantha shrubs, oblivious of the shower as they twittered and feasted on the bright orange berries. The birds had returned, as they had each year since Jette could remember. There was continuity, rhythm, expectation and promise. She liked that thought—expectation and promise.

The puffy eiderdown coverlet was new. She felt the blue satin piping and traced the embroidered quilting with her fingers. Verdie was buying beautiful things once more, and indeed, Verdie was beautiful and happy once more. Jette smiled at the ceiling as she thought of her mother and Russel Carr.

"Are you awake, dear?" Verdie opened the door and stood waiting outside in the hallway. "Doctor Hunter's here to see you."

"Yes, I'm awake." Jette turned her head to see her visitor. Her muscles were sore and stiff, but miraculously she was alive. "Was that his carriage just now?" she asked.

"No, he's been here for a while and had lunch with Russel and me. That was Abe Marley bringing Inspector Hankins out from town." Verdie pulled up a chair for Hunter and placed it beside the bed. "They'd like to see you, but if you don't feel up to it I'll tell them . . ."

"No, no," Jette interrupted. "I want to see them. I must!" She tried to sit up, but fell back as her head spun.

Hunter eased her back onto the pillow. "First, let's see how you're doing this evening," he admonished her.

"Evening?" Jetted asked in bewilderment. "What? Have I lost a whole day?" Verdie looked anxiously at the doctor and allowed him to answer.

"I'm afraid you've lost several days, Jette. You took a nasty spill. That crack on the side of your head when you fell . . ." He took her pulse and looked closely at her eyes, then moved her head forward, back, and sideways. "Now look directly at me, Jette. Follow my finger as I move it. There, yes, that's fine." He breathed on his stethoscope and warmed it in his hand. "If you'll just open your shift a bit, we'll take a listen." He applied the instrument to her breast and nodded. "Fine. Good girl. Right as rain in no time."

Verdie sighed, her thin shoulders relaxed. "If you two will excuse me, I'll see to our other guests." She left the door ajar behind her, but the wind shut it and Hunter did not bother to open it again.

"Asa?" Jette found she could say his name easily.

"He'll be fine. For a man who had soldiered in Africa, Nate Trasker was a poor shot." He looked away from her and shook his head. "I'm sorry, Jette. I shouldn't have . . ."

"It's all right, Miles." She touched his hand and made him look at her. "I'm sorry if I've hurt you. I never meant to. Please believe that."

"I do," he said. "You fell in love with him. Now that he's gone . . ."

She shook her head and sighed. "No, Miles. I'm fond of you, it's true. I want us to be close friends, always. But I know now we can't be anything more than that. I must be completely honest with you. I never want any misunderstanding between us." Her auburn hair spilled over the white pillow, giving her the look of a pale child. "That's all I can offer you."

He took her hand to his lips and nodded, but the smile on his face was forced. "All right, Jette. Then that's what I accept. But if ever . . ."

"No, Miles. I know for certain now."

For a few moments he said nothing, as if gathering his thoughts. "I must confess something that may change your opinion of me.''

"I doubt it,'' she said. "But go on . . .''

"I feel responsible, at least in part, for your father's death.''

"In the name of heaven, why?'' She was startled by his admission.

"I'd known Nate Trasker in Cincinnati,'' he said. Jette stared at him in disbelief. "He'd read in the newspaper about my accident and came to see me. He made me a straight business proposition: He'd finance my move to California, buy me a medical practice, and I was to repay at a regular ten percent. For a young doctor just beginning—and one in my condition—it was too good an opportunity to miss, so . . . I took it.'' He balled his fist and slapped it into his palm. "After I'd established myself we saw each other now and then. I admit I had to wonder why our relationship was supposed to remain confidential, and only after Mr. Allenby died did I realize its implications. You must believe me, though, when I say I had no thought of its sinister possibilities.'' His very earnestness caused her to look closely into his tortured face. "Inadvertently I made a reference to your father's condition. Later I realized that he'd been pumping me of information, subtly, of course, and I'd not been enough on guard.''

"Father's condition?'' Jette pushed herself up by her elbows and sat looking at him in wonder. "I don't understand. What condition?''

"He never wanted anybody to know of it. Doctor Hill had discovered your father had a heart problem and when I took over for him, Mr. Allenby made it plain that I was to respect his wishes to keep it confidential, too. As a matter of fact, when I suggested his family should be made aware of his condition he threatened to have me run out of town if I so much as intimated to anyone that he was not a well man.''

"Father had heart trouble?''

465

"He'd had it for some years. Didn't want sympathy. Didn't want anybody to know about it, not even you and your mother." In the fading light Hunter's face was troubled, his eyes mirroring the guilt he felt.

"I fail to see how this could have been responsible for Father's death, Miles," Jette consoled him. "He was trapped in that enclosure with Old Max . . ."

"I think your husband planned it that way, Jette!"

She closed her eyes and turned away from him. "Seth Scott and Severo Mireles both tried to tell me that's what happened. And so did Asa." She pounded the quilt with her fists. "But I didn't listen—I wouldn't listen!"

"Trasker knew that the slightest thing might cause a fatal attack. And I'm fairly sure he tried to provoke you and your mother into confrontations with Mr. Allenby."

"Hoping we'd cause it?" She was appalled at the knowledge. "God in heaven, how cold-blooded he was! And the worst of it is, I fell right into his plans, helping him . . . ." Jette wanted to cry with the remorse she felt, but found she could not. "You're in no way to blame, Miles. If blame is to be given, it should go to me, not you."

"I'm so sorry, Jette." Hunter held his head in his hands. "So much of this could have been prevented had I . . ."

"It's all right, Miles. It's all right," she comforted him. "Sooner or later it would have happened anyway. Perhaps we did hasten it, but we could never have prevented it. Father courted trouble . . ." Rain pattered against the window pane on the north side of the room. "The wind must be shifting," she said and watched the curtains' slow stirring. Hunter did not respond. "I'm glad you told me about him. It explains so much . . ."

Hunter appeared puzzled. "How's that?"

"Now I know why Asa behaved as he did."

"Yes, he probably knew," Hunter agreed.

Footsteps sounded on the veranda, turned into the open hallway, and halted outside her bedroom door. A light tap announced Marley and Hankins.

"Come in," Jette called aloud. She pulled the coverlet up under her arms and squirmed to a more elevated position.

"Mrs. Trasker," Hankins said and held out his hand, clasping hers gently. "I'm happy to see such an improvement in your patient, Doctor." The inspector was dressed in natty tweeds and a jaunty, feather-trimmed shooting hat.

"Jette, my dear," Marley said from the doorway. "Your mother said you were feeling better so we thought . . ."

"Please Abe, do come in. It's drafty in the open hall." Jette waved him inside the room and indicated a chair beside the blazing fireplace. "Mother said you wanted to see me. I suppose it's about . . . my husband?" She said it firmly, not equivocating.

"If you're up to it?" Hankins said doubtfully and looked to Hunter for permission. The doctor nodded and Hankins took the chair beside the bed as Hunter rose and stood aside. "I thought you'd like to know we took Mrs. Baldwin and her brother into custody yesterday. They'd gone down to San Diego and were booked to take a ship to Panama today. Just found them in the nick, so to say." He waited for her to say something, but when she remained silent he went on, "I'm dreadfully sorry about your husband. Please believe that." He turned from her black eyes so suddenly filled with pain, and had to look out the small bit of open window.

"If it's any comfort at this point," Hankins continued, "they tell us he planned to stay here with you. It was when Palma Owens decided to come out here and see for herself if he was the man she knew as Page Bascombe . . ." At her gasp of recognition he asked,

"Is something the matter?"

Jette had recalled the initials inside Nate's hat band. The silver marker had been inscribed "P.B." *Page Bascombe!* The marker had probably been a gift from Mrs. Owens to Nate. "No," she replied. She could not bear to explain why her suspicions had not been sufficiently aroused. "No, please go on, Inspector."

"We've looked into your legal status," Abe Marley spoke up. "La Coruna is yours, fee simple. Nate had paid for it in cash. There may be a matter of paying off some of the investors' money if they bring suit against you, but Booth Killigrew says . . ."

"They'll be paid back if I have to lose everything," Jette said. "Mr. Sandberg, the building manager where Nate had his offices, put everything he has into Montague-Cameron." She remembered the man's uneasy confidence in the company. "I'll go see the judge and find out what to do."

"You may not be responsible . . ."

"Legally perhaps not." Jette looked hard at Marley. The politician nodded. He was glad she was not an opponent, not with that conscience and determination.

"Booth says Nate's plan was sound. It was good. All it needs now is the right push. He thinks he can see that we get all the funding we need to complete it," Marley said. "That way we all come out winners. There's plenty of water underground and with concrete channels it can be transported without too much loss . . ." He was beginning to be enthusiastic. "I'm sorry, Jette. Forgive me."

"It's all right, Abe. I understand," she replied. "You believed in it all along, didn't you?"

"Not only did, but still do," he said.

"Then we'll do it. Somehow we'll manage," she vowed.

"We'll have to hold your jewelry for a while," Hankins interrupted. "Lavinia Baldwin had pawned the

468

pearls and some of the smaller pieces for passage money. That's how the police nailed them in San Diego. I hope you'll be patient with us." He was almost apologetic.

"That's the least of my concerns right now, Inspector," Jette said. "I'll welcome them back, of course, but there are more important things that come first."

"I'm afraid we'll have to ask you to come to San Francisco at their arraignment," Hankins said. "I know it's an imposition after all you've been put through, but it's necessary."

"I understand," she assured him. "Just let me know and I'll be there."

"Judge Killigrew would like to bring his wife out to see you when you feel up to having company," Marley said. "You made quite a conquest there. He wanted to know what had happened, but I thought it best he hear your side of it from you, if you don't mind. You'll be business partners if we can keep the project afloat."

"I'd like that very much," Jette said. "Perhaps in a few days . . ."

"Good. You send word in to them any time. Mrs. Killigrew sends her regards to your mother, too." Marley was doing more than delivering felicitations. What he was really saying was that Jette and Verdie were no longer exiled from San Genaro society. It was also possible they would be welcomed soon at Sacramento. Although the knowledge was small recompense, it made the reality of her nightmare more bearable. There was an end to it at last. Expectation and promise . . .

Chapter 22

Elvira Mireles tiptoed from the room and carried the tray out to the wicker table on the veranda before returning to pull the drapes and lower the wick in the lamp. The fire had burned low, with only a glowing bed of red coals remaining to take the slight chill from the night air. Quietly she adjusted the damper and shut the door behind her.

Her brother, Severo, had promised to bring Faustino Reyna to meet her this evening after her duties following dinner were finished. Tino was a handsome boy and held a job of consequence with Abe Marley in purchasing for the County. Elvira had sighed over him at Sunday mass and secretly envied girls in town who had opportunities to flirt and talk with him. A dozen times since Severo had told her Tino was coming he had found it necessary to assure her she had as good a chance as the city girls with young Reyna. If she hurried she could be finished with the dishes and change into her best red skirt and black bugle-beaded Eton jacket before he arrived. She fairly flew down the outside staircase and crossed the patio, going into the kitchen by the rear door.

Jette smiled as she heard the screen door slam and Socorro's staccato scolding. While Elvira had been in the bedroom Jette had feigned sleep. Unsure as to why she preferred not to be disturbed right now, she lay back on her pillow, eyes shut, luxuriating in the feeling of concern and love that surrounded her. Never before had she been so conscious of the ties among family, friends, and community. The fire had galvanized the ranchers into an enormous cooperative effort, but there was more to it than that. Her own personal tragedy and Asa Beemer's heroism had elicited more than sympathy. It had been in Anna Larsen's face as she took Jette's hand

and tried in her halting broken English to express her sorrow. It had been in Margaret's and Lucy's faces, and in their father's. The words spoken had little real meaning, but the emotion behind them was eloquent.

Russel Carr had agreed to stay on at the ranch as long as he could be of use, and seemed genuinely glad to shoulder some of the responsibilities. He had a knack of handling people, Verdie reported to her with pride and admiration. He had been as much at ease directing the men at the fire line as he had been in his own fashionable offices in downtown Los Angeles. With the combined crews they had halted the fire at the fence line—just as Asa Beemer had planned.

"When that little gelding came back with the reins dragging . . ." Carr had said, "Asa was a stricken man. His duty was at the fire line, but the thought that something had happened to you . . . ." Carr had shaken one white tablet from the small paper envelope and handed it to her with a glass of water.

"Then Pima didn't go back to the barn?" Jette had asked before swallowing the medication.

"No, he headed straight for the rest of the San Gallan horses. And mighty lucky for you he did." He had taken the water glass from her and replaced it on the small table by the window. "Your mother ran down to see Benito. She realized something wasn't quite right."

"I'm so sorry I had to push her . . ."

"She understands it was for her own sake you did it," Carr eased her mind. "Benito sent a boy out on a pony to tell us. We knew it had to be Trasker—that was the only possible answer. What had happened was the very thing we'd been trying to prevent in the first place. Asa figured he'd be heading for the railroad." Carr had warmed his hands before the fireplace and continued, "I've never seen a man so frightened in my life. I've commanded troops against Comanches and Arapahoes, but I'd never seen such an expression before." He had

471

turned and sat down on the bed beside her and shook his head as he remembered. "He must love you very much, Jette."

Doctor Hunter had instructed her to rest a few days. He had also insisted Asa Beemer would have to rest a few weeks and be careful for another month or so. Asa was weak from loss of blood and would bear vicious scars where Nate's bullets had found their mark. But he would live. Somehow right now that was the most important thing in the world to her. Ownership of the vast La Coruna, business partnership with the man who was sure to become governor of the state, return of the heirloom aquamarines . . . She counted her blessings, but only one really mattered—Asa would live.

Downstairs she heard Jake Larsen's laughter and the women's voices raised in coaxing. For a moment there was silence, then began the delicate introduction of a Schumann duet as Russel Carr and Verdie sat together at the piano. The rendition was imperfect and the old cherrywood spinet was not in perfect tune, but the music was gently joyous. Outside, rain provided a soft counterpoint to the wistful melody.

Although Doctor Hunter had returned to San Genaro, Abe Marley and Inspector Hankins had decided to stay over for the night. Verdie had imparted the news breathlessly as she accompanied Elvira upstairs with Jette's tea tray. She had been as delighted having guests on the ranch as a deprived child finding a full Christmas stocking.

Even though the old adobe's yard-thick walls effectively muffled noise, the music and laughter were audible through the open windows. From his room on the east side of the house Asa Beemer was sure to hear their gaiety. He was alone in his bed, the fresh bandages stark white against the dark skin of his chest and arm. Jette physically cringed as she recalled how he had deliberately drawn Nate's fire away from her.

472

Disjointed, episodic, only half-remembered, it filled her with horror. Quick, thunderous explosions of shots . . . acrid smell of powder mingled with grass smoke . . . . And Asa had just stood there!

A knot of aromatic resin in the eucalyptus wood snapped and sent a tiny shower of sparks flying up the chimney. She watched the blue flicker of flame as the resin burned itself out. Slowly she threw back the coverlet and slid from the bed, surprised at how light-headed she still was. She grew cold as she stood before the fireplace, holding her hands out to the fading warmth.

As she opened the bedroom door a gust of wind showered her with cool rain, wetting the skirt of her nightshift and her bare feet. The tiled floor was cold, the air crisp and sweet, a mingling of earthy, fertile things. In the middle of the hallway she could hear nothing but the wind in the trees and gurgle of water in the eaves trough around the veranda. She turned to the right, into the side hall, and hesitated before the first door on the left. Only the faintest sliver of light showed beneath the door. She opened the door and entered the half-dark room. An oil lamp with clear glass chimney had been turned down till only a thin rim of orange flame hovered above the canvas wick. Both windows in the corner of the room were opened from the bottom, and air coming in was aromatic with eucalyptus smoke. Occupying the far end of the room was a grotesquely monstrous walnut bed, its carved acanthus leaf head-board only inches from the low ceiling. In it lay Asa Beemer.

Jette listened for the piano and Jake Larsen's boisterous laughter, but only a tiny ticking from the alarm clock on the bedside table could be heard over the soughing of wind and rain. As she stood at the foot of the bed and looked at Asa she was struck by the utter loneliness of this section of the adobe. Its isolation was due not only to its position on the second floor, but to its outlook across the rear patio and oak grove beyond. There was about it a feeling of being separate and apart from the rest of the house. Even the fire crackling in the grate did little to dispel the effect. Yet Asa Beemer had lived uncomplaining in this room since coming to the ranch.

"You don't have to be quiet," Asa said. "I'm not asleep."

Dim lamplight behind her outlined her young body through the thin nightshift as she waited for an indication to come closer. Asa could not see the features of her face, although he could feel her intense black eyes meeting his own.

"How are you, Asa?" Her voice was husky, as if unused for too long a time.

"Doing fine," he replied. "And you?"

"I'll survive, but only because of you." Usually she had no trouble being articulate. This time was different. "I had to come and thank you. You were foolish . . . I didn't deserve your help . . ." Her hands fluttered in desperation as she sought to apologize.

"I didn't figure I had time to ask your leave." Jette could not tell if he were teasing her or not.

"Mr. Carr told me what happened at the siding. I'm glad you weren't hurt any worse than you were."

"I think we both might owe Old Max a 'thank you.' "

"Mother says he arrived at La Maravilla in good shape." She felt as awkward as a school-girl and realized how ridiculous she must seem. "She says Judge Killigrew's going to ask the telephone exchange to run a line out to the ranches along the highway."

"You mean so we can talk back and forth to see how Old Max is doing?" He was teasing her.

"Please don't make fun of me, Asa," she begged.

"I know it's cost you a lot, just to come in here and

474

talk to me," he said more seriously. "And I do thank you for making the attempt."

"Oh, it's useless!" She turned to go, her chin defiantly uptilted, a sign he recognized all too well. Beneath the sheet and light blanket that covered him his long legs moved as he rolled a bit to one side. A sharp intake of breath betrayed the quick pain that coursed through his shoulder.

"You mustn't try to get up!" Jette hurried to him and placed a restraining hand on his shoulder. As soon as she felt the rough weave of the cotton bandage she winced as if experiencing his pain. "Asa . . . I'm so sorry . . . ." Words were there, but refused her summons. She drew her hand away and turned from him, whispering, "Can you ever forgive me?"

"Can you forgive yourself?" There was no teasing or sarcasm in his question this time.

"I was so stupid . . . so blind . . ."

She stood with her back to him, head hanging in dejection. Asa could see her slender waist and thighs beneath the lace-trimmed gown. He longed to hold her to him, to feel that exquisite flesh yield to him. But he determined that she first must want him. He repeated his question, asking simply, "Can you forgive yourself?"

She shook her head, tumbling the unfettered auburn hair across her forehead. "No," she answered so softly he scarcely heard the reply. "No, I don't think I can ever forgive myself." Asa caught and understood the pleading in her denial.

"Then I guess I'll have to do it for both of us," he said.

"How can you after the way I've treated you?"

"Because you want me to." There was no way he could lessen her hurt as she looked down at the swathing on his chest and arm. "You do want me to, don't you? Isn't that why you came in here?"

"Yes, more than anything in this world, but that's hardly reason enough . . ."

"It's reason enough for me." She was so near he could smell the delicate rose and lavender scent left in her shift by the sachet she used. Still he made no move to touch her. He laughed as he leaned over the bed and saw her feet. "You'll catch your death, running around barefooted like that."

At his low chuckle she whirled on him, anger flushing her face. His arms were outstretched to her and he caught her as she flung herself into his embrace. She was sobbing, remorse and humiliation giving way as she fell into the comforting warmth of his welcome. He did not force his lips upon her mouth, but let her come to him— eager, willing, wanting the masculine hardness of his kisses, wanting the physical reassurance of his mouth on hers, his arms enfolding her.

"Everything's going to be just fine now. You mustn't cry anymore," he crooned softly until she was quiet. "I don't know much about pleasing a woman," he said as she buried her face in the pillow beside him. "I don't mean just in bed. I mean in the little things that mean a lot to you women—the things that don't mean much by themselves, but all put together make the difference between just living and really being happy." He pushed himself away just far enough to look down into her eyes where moisture clung sparkling in the dark lashes. "Are you willing to help me learn?"

She nodded and moved closer, resting her head on his uninjured shoulder. "I don't know how you can even speak decently to me . . ." His fingertips stopped her protest as he touched the softness of her lips. When a quiet laugh shook his chest under her head she raised up and tried to read his face.

"Girl, I love you," he said. There it was, plainspoken and honest. A humorous, lop-sided smile widened his mouth and the yellow lamplight was reflected in his dark eyes. She looked deeply into those eyes, almost afraid of what she might find revealed there. But, no, it was true—in spite of everything she had ever done and said, he did love her.

Suddenly wanting him and unashamed to express her love and need, she bent to kiss him, her mouth upon his, coaxing Asa to her own passion. She rose from his bed and unbuttoned the lace yoke of the gown and lifted it over her head, letting the shift fall to the floor about her feet. As Asa watched the graceful disrobing and saw her beautiful nakedness his own need manifested and a wildness surged through his very being. Still he waited, lying motionless under the light covers. That was the way it must be—she must come to him.

Without a word she pulled back the sheet and blanket and gazed at his lean, angular body. He wore no night-shirt, but lay naked save for the bandages. It was apparent that he wanted her, but she was puzzled that he made no attempt to take her. If he had wanted her badly enough before to try to force her, then why did he not respond now? His wounds, though serious, were not so grave to endanger him should he make love to her.

She sat on the edge of the bed and slowly pulled her legs up, turned to him, her long hair spilling across his chest. Caressing his face with her slim fingers she could feel the muscles of his jaw tighten and his body quiver at her touch. She understood, and loved him for his re-straint. This time was to be different.

Gently she took his hand and guided it to her breast at the same moment her mouth covered his, her tongue probing its hidden recesses. His hand, hard and steely in its strength, cupped about the velvet roundness, seeking the now erect nipple, then slid to the arc of her hips, pulling her closer, till the warmth of her body against his was like an unbearable searing pain. She made love to him, teaching him what pleased her, delighting him with her own eagerness and response. When she realized

477

she was near release, she slid beneath his lithe body, entreating him to bring her to ecstacy. Moaning as he entered, she stiffened and arched into his embrace, all else abandoned in the swift, delicious oblivion he gave.

* * * *

The lamp on the center table had gone out and only a few eucalyptus coals glowed in the fireplace. Asa's deep, regular breathing told Jette that he slept soundly. There was no need to awaken him. She crawled from bed, retrieved her nightshift and slipped it on before leaving. A cold wind whistled through the open hallway and fine rain spattered her bare feet as she returned to her own room.

In the rear parlor downstais, the clock had just chimed two. Long ago their houseguests had retired for the night in quarters facing east and south on the veranda. She was relieved that she did not have to pass their rooms clad as she was and at such an hour. Although Anna and Jake Larsen's presence would counteract any undue criticism of Verdie's entertaining so soon after the tragedy, Jette was certain they could not understand her tryst.

Verdie had found a new life. Jette knew beyond doubting that it was possible. For her it would be difficult, but now she had Asa. If, in spite of all, he could still love her, she knew he would not waver. Together they would be strong. Together they could build their lives in happiness and fulfillment. No longer did she harbor illusions that her life would be free of trouble, but when it came, they could meet it and endure.

Other than the storm, not a sound disturbed the total quiet. She closed the door behind her and arranged kindling and one small split of oak in the grate. Water in the wash basin was cold, but she placed the bowl on the hearth before the fire and bathed, then from the drawer took a blue flannel nightgown. As she combed her hair and tied it back with a ribbon she noticed the tea tray. Thin slices of buttered rusk were covered by a linen napkin beside the square chocolate pot. Verdie would know where she had been. Somehow she knew her mother would understand.

Outside, the wind was rising again. No matter—she was warm and content. As she had lain in Asa's arms a newfound peace had stolen over her. Memory of the past could not be wiped out, but wisdom gained at such cost would guide her and make easier the future.

After spreading the extra quilt from the foot of the bed over the coverlet, Jette snuggled into the pillow. Sleep came quickly.

She did not know when the storm abated and the east grew bright over the San Lucas hills. By seven-thirty roof tiles and graveled roadway steamed in the early sunshine. Buff, the mongrel, raced out of the kitchen and into the orchard to find the tawny half-dog, half-coyote bitch that awaited him in the brush along the fence. From the direction of town came the echoing rumble and hoot of the northbound 8:15 train to San Francisco. In the kitchen Socorro's voice rose to shrillness as she chided Severo for slamming the screendoor as he delivered the household's butter and cream fresh from churn and separator.

Jette turned her head and listened. Languidly she stretched and lay motionless, listening to the day beginning. Tempted to close her eyes again and sleep, she remembered last night's joy. There were things to do—accounts to settle, plans to be made for her mother and Russel Carr, for La Coruna, for herself and Asa.

Throwing back the coverlet, she ran barefoot to the window, pulled back the dark drapes and rolled up the shade. A slight breeze fluttered the curtains, bringing with it the sweet scent of earth and foilage after rain. Westward across the valley the Las Lomas mountains scintillated in pure, brilliant light.

It was a fine morning—in a newly bright and glorious world.